MILOŠ URBAN

Miloš Urban (b. 1967) grew up in Bohemia, lived for a time in London and now resides in Prague where he makes his living writing and translating literature – having translated authors such as Isaac Bashevis Singer and Julian Barnes from English into Czech – as well as working as an editor in a publishing house. Dubbed the 'dark knight of Czech literature', Urban is a writer of power and imagination whose acclaimed Gothic mysteries (ten novels – including *The Seven Churches*, the international bestseller published in English by Peter Owen – and one collection of short stories to date) are set primarily against the backdrop of the city of Prague.

'LORD MORD

By the same author and published by Peter Owen

The Seven Churches

MILOŠ URBAN

Translated from the Czech by
Gerald Turner

PETER OWEN PUBLISHERS
London and Chicago

PETER OWEN PUBLISHERS
81 Ridge Road, London N8 9NP

Peter Owen books are distributed in the USA and Canada by
Independent Publishers Group/Trafalgar Square,
814 North Franklin Street, Chicago, IL 60610, USA

Translated from the Czech *Lord Mord*
First English translation published in Great Britain 2013
by Peter Owen Publishers

ISBN 978-0-7206-1496-1

A catalogue record for this book is available from the British Library.

Typeset by Octavo Smith Ltd in Constantia 9.5/13.5

Printed and bound in the UK by
CPI Group (UK) Ltd, Croydon, CR0 4YY

Supported using public funding by Arts Council England

The translation of this book was supported by the
Ministry of Culture of the Czech Republic

The characters in this story are fictitious.
The Prague depicted here is fictitious.
Even the history is fictitious.

But Lord, the great cities are lost and rotting.
Escaping the flames is the greatest need,
and there is no comfort for the people
as their short time passes.

– 'Cities', Rainer Maria Rilke

Prologue I

Just lately speeches and outrage have been directed at one particular target: the Royal City of Prague.

Its good reputation is now scarcely more than a dream, and in terms of its representation Prague is regarded as one of the most backward of cities, the least endowed with intelligence.

Nay, worse still, its bad example has turned Prague into a sort of infectious plague, a stinking hotbed of all possible bad taste and licensed barbarity whose epidemic stench is beginning to engulf the most beautiful old cities of the kingdom.

Even foreigners no longer conceal their views, and people with a loving and sympathetic attachment to our nation are abandoning, maybe for good, this city of ours that once aroused such affection, because they are unable to look without anguish upon this suicidal venture and refuse to do so any longer. 'For goodness' sake, what's happening to you? Who is the cause? It's bound to be those Germans of yours again!' The pen writhes, convulsed with shame, when obliged to explain to those abroad that it is not the Germans but our own people, the worst possible of enemies! Because – and the Germans have an incontestable right to this testimonial – so long as the Germans were in charge of our community such brutalities were not committed. And Prague, that glorious, royal, historic, hundred-spired, golden

Prague, 'where there is not a stone that was not sanctified by the blood of our forebears' – but also not a stone at which the city council has not dared to aim its improvement axe – that Prague is still unaware of the barbarity of its achievement and continues to lay waste and vandalize, and no week – nay, no day – goes by without one being afraid to open one's newspaper lest he read there yet again that some 'genius', with the agreement of the entire council, has come up with some new proposal and is threatening to place its explosive charge in those places which after so much protest and grumbling were considered inviolable: the bridge tower, the Jewish cemetery, the synagogue, the smashing through of a wide street from the Old Town Square to the Vltava, the demolition of houses on the north side of the Old Town Square, the boring of a tunnel through the Vyšehrad Rock!

– Vilém Mrštík: *Bestia triumphans* (1897; edited excerpt)

Prologue II

I was awoken by a banging on the door of my apartment. I glanced around the bedroom – I was at home fortunately – and the second blessing was the light of day. Thank God. I called out, 'Enter', and scarcely recognized my own voice. I tried to clear my throat and started to shake with coughing. By some miracle I stopped it. It catches one unawares first thing in the morning, then drives one mad during the day, and by the evening it forces one to reappraise a thing a two. There was a mustiness in the air, but to let some fresh air in through the window could be even worse, as the lungs are a delicate part of the body. Someone entered the apartment – the concierge, to judge by the footsteps. He knocked on the bedroom door and opened it slightly. At first he did not look in, in case I had company. I did not. So he came in, apologizing for taking the liberty . . . I asked him what he wanted. He jerked his head, looked sideways and shrugged. Aha, I had a visitor, and he was probably standing outside. I motioned to him to let the person in. He disappeared but not before he had briskly handed me a glass of water. Bright fellow. A pity he had gone, because someone else came in. Two black spectres without heads or eyes, without visible bodies. They sailed into the room, an identical pair, and they came and stood by the bed. The concierge closed the door behind him, and I remained alone with those ghosts.

It struck me first of all that they were the dark souls of people

15

unknown. They were dressed in mourning, both of them with black veils over their faces. One had a large black hat on its head; the other's was slightly smaller. The one with the big hat carried a bunch of black roses; in fact, they were deep red. The other had a bright-red bouquet tied up with a black band. My head ached, the cold water cooled my throat, my bronchial tubes quivered with a repressed cough and my mind marvelled at the strangeness of death. But I did not know whose death it was.

A hat moved, and the head beneath it stirred, and I caught sight of a lock of blonde hair. The veil rippled; breath passed through it but no voice. A hand in a black glove pointed at the chair next to the bed. A tall top hat stood on the seat, and over the chair back hung trousers with a satin stripe, freshly pressed. The concierge had brought them yesterday, and I had managed not to touch them in the night. *Touché.* One of the women put down her bouquet on the coverlet, went over to the chest of drawers, opened one and chose a white shirt, a pair of white drawers, long black stockings and garters and placed them all on the bed. Then I remembered what it was all about. And that the death had already occurred – before any others. This was the outcome.

I requested my visitors to turn away, which they did without a word. I relieved myself in the chamber pot. I put on my undergarments and trousers, squinted at the mirror, rinsed my face in the porcelain washbasin, cleansed my teeth with powder, passed my hand over my cheeks – it would do – and splashed some cologne on myself from a flacon. They brought me a waistcoat and a morning coat from the wardrobe. The one in the scarf buttoned me up, and I reminded her that a morning coat is worn open. I parted my hair and combed my moustache in front of the mirror, arranged a handkerchief in my pocket, inserted the gold-framed monocle in my right eye and placed the brushed top hat on my head. I looked for my watch, but it was not in any of the pockets.

'I shouldn't think we'll have time for breakfast,' I said for appearance's sake in order to break the silence.

'I knew you'd oversleep,' said the one.

'That you'd deliberately oversleep,' the other added, 'so you wouldn't have to go.'

Then they each took one of my forearms and led me out of the apartment and the house. I was grateful to them for leaving the veils over their faces throughout the walk to the cemetery chapel, and no one could see who was accompanying me through the Old Town. There were some who might recognize my companions.

The ceremony was brief; the priest was well aware whose corpse was to be interred that day and who had come to say goodbye. And he was a good priest; he applied almost the same standard to everyone.

The girls who sold themselves in Jewry were of various faiths. As far as I could recall, Rosina Weinerová never spoke about God nor about Reconciliation or Providence. I was glad we were able to bury her in the cemetery and not outside its walls. A modest grave by the wall. I broke off a bud from the black bouquet and one from the red and tossed them both on the coffin.

There was no meal, and we went home our separate ways. Prague was abuzz. Children ran down the street, driving some plaything before them. It was impossible to tell what exactly as it was too fast.

I dropped into Karpeles's café. The clock on the wall was like the one at the station. I read the Czech and German newspapers until twelve, drinking one cup of coffee after another. At noon Karpeles brought me an open sandwich with Italian-style potato salad and Prague ham, which he described as 'Viennese', together with a jug of beer from the tap-room next door.

I asked him to bring me some schnapps, seeing as I was in mourning. He placed the bottle in front of me on condition that he would not have to join me.

17

I

Bestia Triumphans

Two Girls

I stood among the trees in Letná Park on an early evening walk above Prague. There was still enough light, and I was not alone. A few paces from me a photographer was unpacking his things. He set up a low three-legged stand and fixed a wooden box to it. He fiddled around with it and screwed something on to it. It looked like the handle of a barrel-organ. Then he said something. It was not to me but to himself. He looked at his pocket watch, leant over the apparatus and started to turn the handle. I put my monocle in my eye and gazed, like him, over the edge of the escarpment.

The river was calm. Four wide rafts floated along with the current, and passing them on the other side, in the direction of the Rudolf Bridge, was a long, low, brightly painted paddle-steamer, red in the bows, brown amidships and pale pink astern. Fishermen's rowing-boats shared the surface of the river with ducks, gulls and swans, with nets and fishing-lines spread out in all directions, with hunched anglers puffing on pipes and one young fellow in a dark cap standing urinating into the Vltava, caring nothing about the punts ferrying passengers and loads ceaselessly from one bank to the other, because it is a long way from everywhere to the towers and cables of the Franz-Josef Bridge.

On this side of the river a car of the water-propelled funicular was scaling the escarpment in the direction of the mansion, while the other descended, and because I could not see the road beneath the hill from where I was standing it seemed as if the funicular would shortly land on the surface of the river and mingle unobtrusively with the paddle-steamers.

I glanced to the right. From my vantage point it was further to the Rudolf Bridge than to the great bridge. A new one was still in the planning stage, and the plans were not at all mean-spirited. The architects' vision was to penetrate the Jewish Town like an arrow from a bow, but it was to be no Cupid's dart, as we were soon to discover. The ferry was inadequate for the needs of a metropolis, the punts go back and forth from one bank to the other like the pendulum of a clock, not stopping when the lamps are lit but continuing until midnight chimes from Prague's towers and spires.

I looked down at the lagoon and the mills, and behind them to the right I could see the whole of Josefov, East Jewry and West Jewry, just beyond it the tower of the Town Hall, the steep roof of the Old-New Synagogue and the lower-pitched gables of the High Synagogue. I could see even further, even beyond the boundary of the ghetto, in which the Jewish houses flocked around the Church of the Holy Spirit like hens around a cock. My gaze flitted with relish across the pointed roofs of the cottages and the massive roofs of the coal depots, potato factories and other buildings. I delighted in the little roofs of workshops and sheds, not to mention the thousands of chimneys, some of which were as big as cannons, others were 'kosher': with a lid in the style of a Jewish hat on top, in other words. There were chimneys that got narrower towards the top and swayed in the wind; they stuck out of the roofs or came straight out of walls, leaning on the houses as if on their last legs and they had been borne for donkey's years already by the cracked walls of the brickworks, joinery workshops, tanneries and breweries. Behind the chimneys the roofs, towers and spires of the Old Town churches protruded like splashes of colour on a painter's canvas. Still further away I could just make out the mass of the New Town with its giant boxes, apartment houses standing alone in sloping meadows, fields and vineyards, waiting until some other residential building of the modern day joined them in line.

I looked at the opposite bank through a flock of gulls. This nearer view was quite clear; the mist had spared Prague for once. White smoke billowed straight upwards from the funnels of the paddle-steamers, coiling high into the sky and off into the distance, somewhere above the meadows of Karlín and the military parade ground at Invalidovna. Above Poříčí, on the other hand, there hung an orangey-brown cloud, so near the ground that it obscured the view of the neighbourhood around St Peter's. Immediately beneath the cloud there stood opposite one another two mechanical excavators, the very ones that were recently unveiled to the blare of a brass band at the Provincial Jubilee Exhibition as a boon from on high for the Austro-Hungarian monarchy and especially for its industrial north governed by reason and healthy scepticism. On that occasion I had no notion of what those two monsters would be capable. They were similar but only in the sense of distant relatives. One of the machines demolished old houses; the other dug the foundations for new buildings. They were capable of working incredibly neatly and fast. Inventions in the field of construction were popular and welcomed everywhere. They moved hither and thither around the sleepy Bohemian landscape on their railway wagons, transforming it into an animated anthill. Then they returned to Prague and were bought by an association of firms engaged in urban improvement. And Prague willingly allowed those iron monsters to gnaw away at it, even permitting them to penetrate its old heart, as it looked forward to receiving a new organ, in the belief that only thus could it survive in the Europe of the twentieth century.

There were a few of us who saw things differently and saw different things, namely that the Jewish Town had never suffered so much and had never accepted its extinction with such calm and humility, totally reconciled and at one with the vision that the councillors and businessmen had painted for it.

I noticed that the man at my side was still turning his handle, but his box was no longer pointing at the city but at me.

I doffed my hat and bowed, and that sudden forward motion induced a fit of coughing.

It is impossible to predict these coughing fits. That one was embarrassing and insidious. I felt as if I was suffocating. I spluttered phlegm, trying to prevent myself from throwing up. Prague air has the ability to wander painfully around the alimentary tract and breathing passages. As always my handkerchief was near to hand and straight away at my mouth. I examined it carefully as my doctor had advised. The white satin displayed only a moist greyness and shreds of phlegm that I would not show anyone, although we who cough explosively and aggressively cannot help but to see it.

No sign of red, thank goodness. I crumpled up my handkerchief, returned the monocle to my right eye and turned to go. I raised my hat to a lady in a yellow-and-blue gown with a wasp waist and a Spanish-style skirt. But it was no lady. Everything was artificial, as I could see at first sight. The sensually cleft chin and the gaze through eyelashes; those heavy legs in ludicrously tiny shoes beneath the hem the skirt; the concealed bustle that caused her bottom to protrude abundantly. She was taken aback – perhaps she knew me slightly – and she mentioned my name to her companion with whom she was walking arm in arm. The latter was darker and younger – slim to the point of skinniness, a bit like a boy, were it not for the skirt and the comical little hat shaped like an Indian pagoda on her erect head, but I had never had occasion to amuse myself with them, let alone get involved. Letná was suffocating me. My bronchial tubes were rattling away like an old boiler, and the tallowy atmosphere dissipated my thinking. I nodded a second time and hurried through the park to the road to hail a cab, taking care not to let the stench of the horse assail my nostrils, and return to the part of the city where I felt at ease – just a few steps from those places where gigantic black demolition machines, driven by tiny little men, were in operation, emitting steam and the stench of oil with an ardour worthy of a Jules Verne novel.

I fled from Letná Park like a country bumpkin terrified by the metropolis, although I was born in Prague and had long been unable to contemplate life elsewhere. I had never had any fondness for the country. It was pleasant to take a trip there when the weather was fine, but come Saturday evening I would be ready to get back to town. Mama viewed it with displeasure: to her way of thinking a nobleman belongs to the land that the king bestowed on his ancestors, and my father was never entirely at home in town, even though he tended to regard his blue blood as more of burden and at best something superfluous or even anachronistic. But he left it up to me to decide where I wanted to live. I had been avoiding my parents latterly.

The cabman wanted to know where to put me down, and I shouted, 'Friedmann's!' I covered my mouth and nose with my handkerchief and listened to the rattle of the wheels on the old cobbles. The lamps were already being switched on, a much brighter light than the previous gas lamps that the councillors are currently installing in outlying parts of the city to replace the antediluvian oil lamps, whereas this light is modern, electric, clear and white, much better for illuminating the filth of the old streets and the new pavements. Those dog and hen turds, the pigeon and rat carcasses and all sorts of disgusting human waste – how clearly visible it all is now.

I reached into my pocket for my watch and remembered that I had been without it for two days already. Perhaps I had pawned it somewhere or even lost it. Or maybe someone had stolen it from me during the absinthe soirée before the funeral.

We drove through the gate into the Jewish Town, the first thoroughfare after crossing the river, straight into the most infamous corner of old Prague, where it was gloomy even during the day and where the red light of oil lamps shone in windows the whole time. Some of the houses were still surrounded by chains, recalling the time when the Jews were allowed out of their town only at certain hours. But there were fewer and fewer of the original inhabitants here now. It was decades since the Jews of Prague had been allowed to move out of the ghetto, and meanwhile a goyish riff-raff from every corner of the Czech lands had moved into the houses they vacated.

Not only men had come but also women, the poorest of whom discovered that rather than die from hunger even the ugliest of them could sell herself for a few handy pence. Wizened crones, hefty matrons and even skinny large-eyed children, boys and girls alike, all sold themselves on the Prague market in human bodies. Prague sighed, groaned and cursed, and the howls of copulating mammals was heard loudest from the lanes and backyards of the Jewish Town, and the City Hall was deaf to it.

We came to a halt beneath a green-and-white sign with an inscription in Czech and German: *Friedmann's Inn – For Your Pleasure and Satisfaction* in somewhat slapdash black lettering. The street stank. There was no light in the first-storey windows, but coloured lights burnt behind the large ground-floor window that consisted of little leaded panes of opaque glass. A traveller might mistakenly enter in expectation of a hearty supper, which he would certainly receive, but something else, too.

I tossed the cabman a coin and entered the establishment. Belisar, the old flunkey, was already there in the hallway, bowing and scraping, reaching out with his long arms for my hat and cloak. His Lordship this and His Lordship that, what brings His Lordship the Count to us this evening? Alas, we have no new merchandise . . . But he was silenced by a familiar voice from within the premises. The owner of the voice came out to greet me. She was still handsome, with a pleasant smile on her round face – plump would be more accurate – and gaudy yellow-tinted hair. She looked almost forty but was ten years younger, and her name was Otka, Otka Meyrinková. Her good manners once came from me, my bad manners from her.

I came towards her to embrace her, but she backed away as if I was about to hit her. A cough caused me to shake, and she now leapt back as if I had the plague. All traces of her smile had disappeared. Madame Friedmannová came over to see us. She had a new high coiffure with waved hair. She attempted a curtsy. She had little difficulty bending her legs, but it was not so easy for her to straighten up, and she winced. I kissed her hand and went on holding it. I grasped Otka's left hand, and I crossed their arms, which took the women aback. Then I kissed Otka's hand. The tongue can be a funny instrument. First I used it to polish Madame's enormous episcopal ring, then I inserted the point of it between Otka's fat middle and index fingers. They were like alabaster, naturally, with a scent of soap and eau-de-Cologne – washing dishes is not among her duties. The perfume started me coughing once more.

'Gracious, the Count has a chill. So why is he not in bed? His own, I mean.' The Madame snatched her hand from my grasp, snapped open her bone fan and held it as a shield in front of her face, but I had already calmed my bronchial tubes and caught sight of the stooped back of the flunkey bringing us imitation champagne on a silver salver which, to my amazement, he held high above his head. He deftly opened the bottle and poured out bubbly lemonade mixed with grape juice and alcohol.

'It's on account of the atmosphere, otherwise I'm as fit as a peasant.' I smiled at the Madame with such an array of white teeth that she lowered her fan. We clinked glasses.

'Well, stay with the Count, then,' said the Madame, turning to Otka. 'You won't be going upstairs anyway. And don't forget to keep a tally of what he drinks.' She displayed her yellow set of teeth, with one gap on the bottom right, and turned to go but said as an after-thought, 'One glass is quite enough for you, Otka. Bubbles only make you talkative.' Then, with her skirts raised, she waddled off to the room next door, which I believe was known as the 'green boudoir'. Two men had just entered it, headed by Belisar.

As I gazed after the group Otka emptied my glass. She gave a faint smile with maidenly lips, which in the light of the oil lamps did not betray their frequent usage at Friedmann's. And the dimples in her cheeks were still as charming as ever. We sat down in armchairs upholstered in blue satin. Ticking on the ledge above us was an alabaster clock with naked nymphs. Although it was going it always showed ten thirty, a time when one does not have to go home to one's wife yet. I refilled my glass with the sparkling wine. The bubbles cleared my head wonderfully. Suddenly my cough was gone and I wanted to forget about everything.

That was the last thing on Otka's mind. 'You're not cross any more, are you, Addie? About that funeral?'

'Why should I be?'

'About the fact that Zuzana and I came to fetch you. We thought you ought to go. Not that I'm trying to suggest you might have her on your conscience, heaven forbid, just that you ought to go.'

'I wouldn't have forgiven myself if I hadn't gone. You saved me feeling remorse. Thanks.'

'A pity you didn't feel remorse earlier.'

'But you did give me bit of a fright. Those black costumes and the veils. Like something beyond the grave . . .'

'They were borrowed – from a theatre. Zuzana has a client who sews costumes for it.'

'Zuzana goes with women now?'

'They're gentler than officers, aren't they?'

'I see. What about you? Do you take ladies to your room, too?'

'I don't. Not so far. Maybe the time will come.'

'Otka, an embarrassing thought has crossed my mind on a couple of occasions – what if here, say, or at Goldschmidt's, Dezort's or at Madame Golda's some respectable burgher were to encounter his wife because inadvertently they happened to be the next client of some girl's. "Goodness, my dear, what are you doing here . . . ?"'

I laughed, but she pulled a wry face. 'Addie, you always used to be the distinguished nobleman that I looked up to, but then you'd invariably crush me with some vile comment or other.'

'Sorry. But I really have turned over a new leaf. Don't you believe me?'

'No.'

'You look careworn.'

'Thanks. That really is the best thing to tell a woman. But look – I'm not sad any more.' The old smile again. The old one . . . 'They're going to knock us down, Addie.'

'It was to be expected. When is to be?'

'I don't know. Nobody knows much in advance. A stunted little fellow turned up at Dezort's, a dwarf of some kind, and right behind him was a great big bald geezer, three times the height of the midget. They brought some document or other that said the Dezorts had to be out by the end of the month. They pasted it to the gate and made clear that it was not to be removed.'

'So what happened?'

'The girls are packing up their stuff. We're the very next in line. They say the little fellow has already been. But there's nothing on the door, so I don't know.'

'Where will you go? Madame will find you somewhere else, won't she? The old campaigner . . .'

'There's talk of Žižkov, Karlín, those new districts. But I doubt the locals will want us there. It looks more like the very outskirts of the city, or a village outside Prague, such as Záběhlice – or, heaven preserve us, Bohnice. In all events it will be miles away. Those bumpkins will burn us at the stake, Addie, when they find out what we are.'

'It won't be as bad as all that. You'll always muddle through somehow. You can always find work doing laundry or cleaning.'

'Is that supposed to be my salvation? I wanted a position at your place . . .'

'You know very well it's promised to Gita. I couldn't refuse her that, Otka, and I wouldn't be able to provide for both of you.'

'Why should she, of all people, have a position with you, instead of me? You had me long before her. Aren't I as good?'

You're older. But I didn't tell her.

'I also had Rosina Weiner and Lojza Svátková before her, and so what? But I'm giving it up anyway.'

'So you ought.' She laughed. Her mouth was ugly now, her tongue painted with some purple disinfectant or other. 'You had all of us only for yourself. You paid us, and when you started to tire of us you sold us like some well-cared-for used goods.'

'Stop shouting. Someone will hear you.'

'Pour me another glass.'

'Only if you promise to be quiet.'

'All the same, the girls liked you, particularly Rosina.'

'I liked her, too.'

'You promised her you had a cosy little room for her, and she would wait in it just for you.'

'So what?'

'And that was supposed to be some kind of godsend? It was a *chambre séparée* at Goldschmidt's, not at some high-class Old Town café. And you moved me in there after her – when you'd lost interest in her.'

'She disappointed me. But we had an agreement, just as I had with you afterwards. I honour my agreements.'

She drained the glass as if it contained water and banged it down on the counter. Madame peeped into the room. I gave her a wink and waved my fingers at her, so the head of waved hair disappeared once more.

'And then I found a job for Lojza at Dezort's. You can't say I don't look after my girls. Did any of you have to work on the street?'

'Lojza is anyway, although goodness knows where exactly. Dezort is coming down at any moment.'

'Is that my business? It doesn't interest me.'

'It also didn't interest you when Rosina kicked the bucket. Except that old Goldschmidt had already kicked her out. What use is a girl with an illness? The whole of Josefov just for her, but no fixed address anywhere.'

'How did she die?'

'The plague – what do you think? They found her in a wooden shed just near to where they're building that high embankment. The lock wasn't broken. She was lying on some kind of shelf, one hand on her belly, the other on the ground, a pool of blood under her. She wasn't wearing any drawers, and it was obvious from just looking that she had been spreading her legs for someone. And he repaid her for it. Her head was weirdly twisted right to one side and there was a black line of dried blood on her neck. Someone had cut her throat, but he wasn't capable of slicing her head off – or he didn't manage to in time.'

'Dreadful. But how do you know all that?'

'Who do you think makes visits here?'

'You mean the gendarmes?'

'There you go. How about looking a bit sadder, Addie?'

'I paid for the funeral, didn't I?'

'I know. But you can't buy sympathy, can you?'

She disgusted me. 'You knew from the outset, Otka, that I'm no Samaritan. I want girls for myself alone and just for a limited time. No more than that. But I didn't come here to have a row.'

'All right, let's leave it. But why does Gita get more than we do? Why her and not one of us?'

'She doesn't have more. It's just that I'm not capable of turning her into . . .'

'Another whore?'

'Just getting rid of her, I mean. I don't want to hurt anyone any more.'

'Tiny pangs of conscience?'

'There might even have been something infinitesimal of that variety.' I did not explain to her how that cough gnaws away my lungs little by little every day.

'You're not planning to marry her, are you?'

'Move her in with me as a servant? Definitely.'

'Hey, Addie. Take me. Please take *me*.'

'For heaven's sake, Otka. What if someone were to see you at my place? You said yourself that the whole of Prague comes here.'

'And the country folk, too. Even your dear papa came to see me. The trouble is I wouldn't be able to tell His Lordship's dick from the rest.'

'Was that intended as an insult? I think I'll go home.'

'So why did you bother coming to see me then?' I was expecting to see some tears in her eyes, but they remained dark and dry. At least she didn't use tears as coercion.

'So that we could drink to Rosina's memory.'

'Well, may heaven be kind to her and hell merciful.'

'And I also wanted to ask about new merchandise. Do you know of any?'

'You have to buy me another bottle.'

I clicked my fingers at Belisar who did not need prompting. I lit up a small English pipe that I had filled at home. If I puff with care it does not provoke my cough.

Otka crossed one leg over the other and lit a Turkish cigarette. 'It is not merchandise as such,' she said, 'but it could be. It depends on you whether you manage to get hold of her – and whether she'll be of any interest to you. She's some young thing. A fellow brought her up from the country in a covered wagon, all the way from the highlands, apparently. It took them several days to reach here, where they seemingly have family. He's intending to find a place for her here with those relatives and then move on.'

The pipe was refusing to burn, so I put it away. 'What do you know about the girl?'

'They say she's pretty as a picture and that the madames will be fighting over her.'

'Her name?'

'The old cove with the hacking cough who brought her goes under the name of Karafiát. Apparently they burnt his house down at the place they came from. They didn't like Jews.'

'Well, well.'

'Some other women arrived with him, ugly old hags, but they're nothing to do with him, only the little girl he had under that awning. They say he makes her keep her face hidden behind a scarf, but the Madame saw her yesterday at the market. Here, Addie, mind you keep mum about all this. She doesn't want you to get anywhere near her. It would put the kibosh on it for her.'

'I'm no fool.'

'Madame made an offer for her, a decent sum apparently, and the old man took his stick to her.'

We laughed. 'Serves her right.'

'They say she has the looks of a Jewish princess. Long black hair and fantastic eyes that shine like brown gemstones. The whitest of teeth, apparently, and a straight nose – not a Jewish conk – and skin darker than mine or Gita's. She's not one of your whey-faced birds. The snag is she's so young.'

'What are Karafiát's plans for her then?'

'You'd buy her, wouldn't you? I expect he wants to find a place for her somewhere but not in an institution. I don't even know whether he found those Prague relatives. Nobody knows where he has been staying with her, not even the gendarmes. If you're clever, maybe you'll find her and charm her out of him somehow.'

I wanted to kiss her on the forehead, but she dodged. 'I'll come and see you again, Otka, and we'll drink some champagne together – the real stuff next time.'

She told me that I had a nasty glint in my eye. Then she got up, smoothed her dress and went off into the green salon.

I called Belisar, who already knew I wanted my hat and cloak. I tipped him and let him show me out.

The evening was damp when I left Friedmann's. Fog welled up between the glistening houses. A short way beyond the gate shone a streetlamp, and I set off in that direction along the deserted road. I had no problem walking. I stopped by the lamp and made out another light. This was the beginning of the demolition site. I walked on. There was the smell of a recent demolition. The fog was yellow with a tinge of orange – steam, smoke and brick dust. The pits and deep trenches waited for the construction of sewers and underground passages; only then would it be possible to fill in those graves. Modernity was to be ushered into Prague's Jewish Town for the first time in history – that is to say, hygiene and comfortable living. For the time being it looked as if a devastating artillery battle had taken place there during the day. Troops sleep at night.

I bet myself that I would not cough before I reached the next streetlamp. I lost the bet, my eyes streaming and my lungs at bursting point. I leant against the lamp-post and coughed noisily for a long time. It was something between choking and roaring. If a policeman had been passing he would have taken me for a drunk. I carefully examined my handkerchief in the dim light. Someone found my behaviour amusing; I heard a distinctly malicious chuckle behind me. It immediately stopped. Perhaps it was just the echo of my coughing.

I scrutinized the windows and doorframes of the adjacent houses and scanned with my eyes the piles of soil, pyramids of barrels, empty hen-houses and abandoned handcarts. Alongside the wall it was as dark as in a village. I sniffed the thick air. It stank of burnt coal, fish, horse dung and something that most of all resembled yeast. Across the low wide gateway to a scorched-smelling brewery with a cavorting row of arched windows a white rope had been stretched to indicate that a pit had been freshly dug in the darkness beyond. An ancient building had been torn out of the ground, roots and all. Beyond the rope, seemingly at the very edge of the pit, stood a man in a hat. It was impossible to see his face beneath the brim, but I was sure he was watching me. I could not even see his hands. His coat reached down to the ground, and the figure gave an impression of corpulence.

We gazed at each other for a long time, I in the light of the streetlamp, he in the shadow where no detail could be made out. Just when it looked as if the fellow had moved and was about to emerge from the darkness and present himself, in order to explain or perhaps apologize for his laughter – or demand my purse with menaces – he withdrew and disappeared beyond the gateway. At that very last moment in a flash of light that lit up his head and hat I caught sight of a monstrous face – or rather where there should have been a face I saw a reddish-brown rough surface that was somehow damp; an enormous birthmark, the sort known as a 'port-wine stain' that looks like a beef steak.

I had no wish to hang around any longer or to pursue him. I set off in the direction of the synagogues, leaving the river behind me with rapid strides, all the while looking back over my shoulder. I was cross with myself for being so reckless and putting trust in the modern era that permitted me to go out at night unarmed.

Madame Golda's tavern stood on the border between the respectable and the insalubrious parts of the ghetto. There was no need for me to ring the brass bell or bang on the doorkeeper's window. I had a key to the adjacent entrance, a covered wooden staircase leading up the side of the building to the first floor. The staircase ended right in front of the room that I had been paying rent for to Madame Golda, month after month for almost two years, as if the old crone was running a bona fide boarding-house.

I won't be paying for this much longer, I thought to myself, with a mixture of relief and regret as I knocked on the door with its little oval window of opaque yellow glass. I also had a key to that door, but I wanted to foster the illusion in Gita's mind that this was her home, not mine, I was visiting. That way she took greater enjoyment in my visits. And she knew how to display her gratitude as none before her.

I always gave her the opportunity of not opening the door. She had never availed of it.

She was sleeping now, of course, and it took a while before she came to unbolt the door. Then she pulled me inside the heated room.

In the corner glowed a stove whose red-hot hob and the sparks in the grid in front of the grate were the only light in the darkness. The room was in need of airing, but as I headed for the window Gita enfolded me in a crushingly possessive embrace that threw me into confusion. She took my hat and coat off and slipped her warm hands into my trousers. Held together like that we collapsed on to the double bed. The glimmer from the stove was reflected in her red hair and her white nightdress. She smelt of soap and the French perfume I had given her on the previous occasion.

I had no intention of turning my private whore into a public one, as I had with the previous girls. I would not be able to look myself in the mirror.

I kissed her, trying to taste a bit of feeling in it. It seemed to me that there possibly was some there, and the Gita truly gave me something more than her body and warmth.

My intention was to make her my housemaid and wait until some groom showed sufficient interest in her to marry her. She was beautiful enough.

While she massaged my neck and shoulders with her thumbs I thought about that Jewish princess. I was falling to sleep in bed still in my clothes. Half asleep, I allowed Gita to remove my boots.

II

The Speaker and the Crowd

A Letter from the Tyrol

Stay under the covers, walk around Prague with an Indian scarf across my face, wearing a long purple dressing-gown and with a warm eider-down around my body, with a bed on my shoulder suspended from special shoulder straps. Were I to go around the city like that I could manage to avoid coughing for the whole day.

That vision remained in the dream from which I had to emerge. I was awoken by the creak of the coffee mill. Gita was seated at the table in a green skirt. Above that she wore just a chemise, undone at her breasts. Her hair, which she had given a quick comb, fell forward over her face.

She had it all prepared, that beautiful image of herself. I turned away. Outside the sun was shining. It took me a few moments to get up. Gita was already frying eggs and bacon and cutting bread. She had been out first thing to get food and freshly roasted coffee from the new market before I woke up. The fire was burning anew in the stove.

She watched me take off my sweat-soiled clothes and in my naked state execute a few floor exercises that I had learnt from the Sokol gymnasts to loosen up my back and my neck.

'Get dressed or you'll start coughing again,' she said in a tone of voice not unlike my mother's, and then it started. I coughed my way from the bedroom to the closet, a former larder, where I had had a flushing pedestal pan out in a year earlier, the waste from which flowed through a special pipe down the outside wall and into the cesspit in the yard. (I had had the same apparatus installed in my apartment in the Old Town. Sometimes it became blocked and the pipes would freeze in winter.) I tried to pass water, but the cough tossed me from side to side, and I would never have been able to aim. So I urinated seated while listening to snatches of what Gita was saying in the other room: '. . . did I tell you? And when was Kubin here last? . . . I can't bear to look . . . funeral . . . those fantastic alcoholic drops! . . . you'll never even use them up –'

'The main thing is that you finished them up!' I yelled from the closet and pulled the chain with its porcelain handle. There was just enough water in the cistern, but when I turned the tap in the wash-basin just a few drops came out. 'And you haven't refilled the cistern again.' Water had to be carried up. The tubs stood on the staircase.

'I forgot, all right? I'll do it.'

I dressed quickly and went to breakfast. Gita gazed at me. I let her. For some unknown reason she looked as if she was pleased about something. So I said, 'It's come to my notice that they're hiding some Jewish princess or other in the Jewish quarter.'

Her good mood vanished. 'There's talk of some beauty.'

I sipped my coffee. 'They brought her up from the country, and they're lodged in some secret place. But the ghetto isn't safe. Rosina –'

'I know what happened to her.'

'Apart from that they are penniless. They are beggars, most likely.'

'But they say she's a child. I didn't hear anything about a princess, but I did hear she was extraordinarily pretty.'

'From the way you said that, anyone would think I was sending you to the gallows.'

'It's something like that. So am I to pack my things and go? I move down one floor and sleep with the first officer of the town garrison.' She slumped into a chair as if felled by an axe, a trifle theatrically.

'Have no fear. I've no wish for you to go down to Madame Golda or even to join Otka at Friedmann's, although I'd bet my rapier that they'd take you like a shot and would not hesitate to buy you from Madame Golda.'

'To Goldschmidt's then?'

'Not there either. You'll clean and cook for me. You know how to do that, don't you?'

'And anything else you need besides.'

'Nobody knows that better than I. Or at least I hope not.'

'I'm twenty-two, and I would sooner top myself than walk the pavement, believe me.'

'But I'm saying you can stay. As a housemaid.'

Her indignation and sudden despair were unfeigned. I had not been wrong about her. But I still found it hard to believe that this one was better than the other girls.

She had once had an affair with a waiter when they were working in a classy restaurant. After their relationship came to light she made plans to leave Prague and return home to some village near Pilsen where her father was the local carrier. She told me that he had lost three fingers from his right hand when on military service: he had shot them off when cleaning his rifle, and later his wife died in childbirth.

I once invited Gita to come to work for me, but it was at the cost of Otka, as it had once been for Rosina and Lojza, except that unlike Otka and Gita they were already selling themselves when I started to reserve them for myself alone.

But now that sort of life was beyond my means – besides which my health had deteriorated.

I searched for Gita's eyes behind those waves of ginger hair and found them, but her gaze was unbearable, and I looked away.

I got up from the table, donned my hat in front of the mirror, threw my cape over my arm and went out on to the staircase. At the front entrance downstairs I banged on the door, and it was opened by a drowsy manservant who mumbled that Madame was still asleep and in his view she would sleep until the afternoon. So I gave him the message that Madame Golda could let Gita's garret as of the next quarter.

The lanes were full of activity. I breathed in and then breathed out as slowly as I could. Nothing. No convulsion. My lungs were at peace. I felt like a walk. I set off along Josefov Street and then Pinkas Street in the direction of the river, and at the cemetery I turned right, going further into Josefov. There was no fear of anyone recognizing me or of anyone wanting to cause a scandal by claiming they had seen Count Arco emerge from a brothel on such-and-such an occasion. The salons of high society had no interest in me because I frequented them so rarely, and bourgeois and aristocratic surroundings bored me most of the time, although – lest I conceal myself solely behind a mask of inviolable disdain – I myself must have been boring company, both for the esteemed gentlemen and the charming ladies. Moreover, very few were likely to recognize me there in ill-famed Jewry, my universally pleasant face being invisible in a crowd. With his heart-warming candidness, my friend Solly once told me over a glass of absinthe that I looked more like a barber than a count.

I had taken that route a thousand times before, but from time to time it was still possible for me to lose my way in the ghetto. I intended to come out at the north-eastern end and catch a cab up to the New Town to do some fencing at the Sokol gymnasium. But I missed my turning from the outset, and when I found myself in dismal Bankside Street, where I counted seven beggars whose eyes lit up hopefully at the sight of me and who even raised themselves on to their unsteady legs, I decided to take a short cut into safer territory.

I went through the slatted gate in the corner of the cemetery and entered a courtyard. Held upright by piles of bricks was a row of hand carts filled with earthenware vessels that resembled ancient urns for the ashes of cremated corpses. Maybe they were simply flowerpots. Between the wall of a tall and ludicrously narrow building and the wall of a long building with low windows that had dropped down into the wooden sawdust-covered paving I caught sight of a narrow shoulder-width alleyway.

I guessed that it might be the street known as the Sheds. Once, when we were small boys, Manny and I gave our governess the slip and got lost among these backyards, animal pens and woodsheds. We enjoyed it immensely. In those days it never occurred to us that one of the locals might kidnap us and demand a reward. But in the end we were driven out by a gang of children who pelted us with mud and stones.

Over the years the yards and plots had disappeared. The inhabitants built weird little houses on them, which were close to each other because of the lack of space and which were never completed because more and more dwellings were added to them on the lower storeys as well as on the terraces and roofs. They became flimsier and more crooked as more and more people made their homes here. The ghetto had been abolished years before so that it might breathe freely as a separate quarter of the city. Instead it started to swell, and different races lived here side by side in harmonious poverty.

I entered the alleyway between mouldering walls, covered in soot and cobwebs, and looked beneath my feet in expectation of the worst kind of morass. A shallow gully ran down the middle of it, and I had to walk with legs apart like a mariner so as not to step into that muddy artery. Clucking hens leapt around in front of me as I disturbed their peaceful pecking of the muck in the gully.

Beyond the first house there was a low wall, which I remembered from the time when we were running from the clods of earth that flew past our heads. But whereas on that occasion I had not been able to see over the wall, this was no longer the case. I looked across a line of pantiles into a tiny neatly laid-out garden. In it stood three slender trees – the tallest a pear tree, then a mulberry with long branches and finally a stunted plum tree. They must have already been here in those days.

After some dozen or so more paces alongside the wall the alleyway ended in a gateway, beyond which there was light from an open door. I entered the gateway, and when I emerged at the other end I found myself in Rabbi Street at the corner of Josefov Street, where I had already been that morning. My head swam.

I decided to go in the opposite direction to the one I had taken earlier, lest I repeat my mistake, and then it struck me that everyone was going the same way I had that morning, as if drawn by something. Chimney sweeps and men in kaftans, women in headscarves and some with wigs, old market traders, young expectant mothers and those that no longer were, bearded tradesmen, house painters in soiled clothes and stooping myopic clerks. Grocers and shoemakers shut up shop and headed towards the river. It was a veritable exodus around the next corner. I searched among them for a familiar face that might explain it to me, but there was none to be found; the whores were asleep. And so I turned around and drifted with the crowd to the Old-New Synagogue and its surrounding wall and then beyond to the square around the public fountain where the people were congregating.

Nobody fetched water. Three gendarmes stood ten yards in front of the fountain and allowed no one to come closer – not that anyone was in a rush to do so. Behind them stood two glowering beadles in black hats and braided uniforms. Each of them held a staff in his hand. A tall man went over to them. He, too, was dressed in black like an undertaker, but it was not a uniform but a tailcoat and tight breeches. He shinned up on to the edge of the fountain and turned to the crowd. I knew him by sight. It was František Xaver Bürger, a powerful councillor and omnipresent figure at municipal ceremonies and official events. Adopting the expression of a tragedian, he cleared his throat, gripped his lapels and began to hold forth.

'A plague is sweeping Josefov!' The words swept over the heads of the onlookers like a rusty scythe.

There was silence for a moment as Bürger took a breath in order to continue, and an old man in an angler's hat said, 'Not true.'

Bürger was taken aback. His gaze sought out the bold individual, but he restrained his beadles, who were already making for him.

'As always I welcome all viewpoints – I enjoy a debate. It is not that I intend to lord it over you, ladies and gentlemen, but the arguments are all on my side. When I say "plague", what I mean above all is a catastrophe, my dear sir, although it is also a plague. There certainly is a catastrophe here, as I shall demonstrate right away,' Bürger said directly to the startled old man, and he did not take his eyes off him. Meanwhile he took some papers out of his breast pocket and unfolded them. The sun was reflected off the dazzling paper as if from a mirror and caused me to squint. All that could be seen was an unintelligible diagram. 'Plague? What is a plague if not this? It is all contained herein, the results of an investigation by the imperial commission for the development and hygiene of the royal city. Respectable Jews left long ago! There remain only riff-raff and the dregs of society. Down and outs and rats have made their homes in the derelict houses. Only ten per cent of the decent Jewish inhabitants have remained, and what is their reward? To be eaten by rats and ravaged by disease! That's the way it is.'

He started to cough, covering his mouth with his papers in lieu of a handkerchief. A few people wandered off, but others arrived, curious as to what was going on at the fountain.

Bürger finally fished out a handkerchief and wiped his mouth before continuing. 'Fornication, sin and disease are overflowing from here into Prague's other boroughs. What a disgrace this is for Prague! I am holding here a report by the municipal physician, the highly respected Dr Justus Preininger. Dr Preininger has calculated that the mortality rate in the former ghetto is three times higher than in the rest of Prague. And it is not simply because one section of the original population has refused to leave its homes, even though, according to the strict letter of the law they should have done so long ago. By no means. The highest death rates here are among young people. Which of you wants to see your small children die? Does anyone here? Just imagine: your children. A little coffin in a shallow grave.'

The crowd was silent. Somewhere in the middle of it a toddler whined.

Bürger's gaze settled on its mother, and he addressed the following words to her. 'Josefov is fatally overpopulated. It is impossible to breathe here freely. At any moment an epidemic of cholera could break out and transform this neighbourhood into a city of the dead. Just imagine. The ghosts of innocent children will walk these lanes, and each of those pale infants will knock on its own door and look with reproach into the eyes of all you irresponsible mothers and fathers – you, who remain here and behave as if no appalling threat hangs over the city. But that threat has many dragons' heads. Those threats are legion! Apart from cholera there is typhus and pneumonia and tuberculosis, not to mention gout, osteoporosis, dropsy, diphtheria, smallpox, gangrene and cancer of any organ you care to mention. You will not be spared. And in case that is not enough for some of you I have another treat in the form of madness, because this is the place that you will most likely fall prey to it – yes, you who visit houses of infamy that should have been torn down long ago and replaced by sanitary modern buildings after the manner of Vienna and Paris or other hygienic metropolises. Because the most pernicious danger for our dying Josefov is the disease called syphilis –'

At that moment he was interrupted by the voice of a woman. 'But what is that plague, young man, begging your pardon? Where is this plague that you're going on about?'

I had already seen the woman on several occasions at night at Madame Golda's. This time she was not so gaudily dressed but wore a white apron over a brown dress with frills at the sleeves. Quite pretty, with her hair hanging freely down her back and not many pimples on her chin. And a really large bosom.

Bürger looked down at her from the fountain like a judge at a murderer who had just confessed.

'The person who asks possibly knows something about it. Am I wrong, miss? Well, let me tell you something. The worst plague is prostitution in Prague – a hotbed of moral and physical degradation. And on my side I have arguments that will put paid to it for good and all. My arguments are in this scientific report drawn up by Dr

Preininger. What do your arguments amount to? Your charm? But what have pretty cheeks to tell us? Not much more than that you are not yet as diseased as you soon will be, because you are among the worst vermin of our old and glorious city.'

He could see he had done for her. They could all see it. She placed her hands over her loins as if he had stabbed her there, and she hunched her shoulders. I wanted to say some kind words to her, but they stuck in my throat, and I started to cough. Really loudly.

Bürger waited with a smile until I had stopped and straightened up again. I apologized, and he once more resumed his speech. 'You can see it. You can hear it. This neighbourhood is afflicted by the most dangerous maladies and riddled with the vilest snares for human health. I shall tell you something. There is a house not far from here, in Bankside Street, and in it, if you please, there live . . . how many? How many souls do you think live there, good people of Prague? Can anyone hazard a guess at how many poor wretches live in that little ramshackle one-storey house? Two hundred and sixty-eight souls, if you please, and that is outrageous in my opinion! Like some Transcarpathian village. Like in the remotest Balkan province of our empire. And just think, of those two hundred and sixty-eight souls forty-eight are children. Are our royal city of Prague and our beloved time-honoured Old Town to have these poor infants on their conscience? Are we to leave standing a house in which people are holed up in every available space like rats, from the cellar up to the attic? Or are we to blow such a hovel to smithereens with Nobel's dynamite and erect in its place a splendid building with dry apartments full of sweet-smelling air and sunbeams? With running water in the bathroom and kitchen, with a flushing water closet, with a cooking range or a gas stove and with electric lighting from the ceiling. The Electrical Companies of the Royal Capital City are at your service, after all. So help the City Hall and leave your old dwellings of your own accord. Move – only for the time being – into the alternative lodgings on the outskirts of the city. I am holding here an Act of Parliament – the Expropriation Act. So I ask you not to defy me but to run along before it's too late. In two or three years at the latest you'll be living in the home of your dreams.'

'If you can afford it,' interposed a voice in the crowd, and, surprisingly enough, it was my own. Bürger glanced at me, removed his hat, wiped the sweat from his forehead and gasped. The crowd waited to hear what he would say in response to my remark. But he seemed to be waiting, too. He smiled. Maybe he saw through me. Maybe he recognized a consumptive, now that he was confronted by one at last. And my innards were true to form. Red butterflies started to swirl around in my lungs, night moths started to flutter their wings in my bronchial tubes, and they all started to swarm upwards, so that I barked out a cough and bit at my sleeve, trying to pray to God-knows-who not to let me be overcome by a fit of coughing that I would be unable to rein in.

And it passed. But I could not stay there any longer. I raised the brim of my hat, met Bürger's gaze and then looked straight ahead. I walked through the empty semicircle between the beadles and the gendarmes, avoided the crowd and set off down Butcher's Street towards the slaughterhouse and from there in the direction of the Old Town Square. I did not look back.

I no longer felt like fencing at the Sokol gymnasium. I called in at the apothecary's at the House of the Moor and asked them to prepare me some new drops, paid an exorbitant price for them and poured a quarter of the bottle down my throat outside the pharmacy. It tasted like a herbal schnapps. Then I plodded home to my apartment in Long Street.

A letter was waiting for me there, left on the floor outside the concierge's door. I filled a pipe and lit it and broke the seal on the letter.

My first impression was of reading a transcribed telegram, but it was an ordinary letter.

Dear Karl Adam, my dearest of Friends!

Accept with this Dispatch my heartfelt Greetings from Harnack and please excuse my half-forgotten written Czech. I am never sure of myself with all those funny Accents of yours, so it's better that I leave them all out. I have to write to You that You'll never believe we're going to meet in the near Future? Yes, even though it's a Fact, and where else but in Prague of a Thousand Spires, that dear Place of my Childhood? I recall as You no doubt do also the Games we played together in Wintertrousers, when You came from the Countryside and how We two little Counts caught Fish in the Lagoon and threw them at each other. Well my long Stay in the ancient Homeland of my Family, in Cealium Germani as We call it, where my Parents returned with Me that time, as well as my Home Study of History, my Journey to Italy with Papa that eventually lasted two whole Years in Rome and then my unfinished Universitydegree, none of that allowed us to see each other for such a long time. But I would like to ask You, Karl Adam, my dearest Cousin, whether You could arrange for Me some Accommodation appropriate not only to my Standing but also to my less than satisfactory Financesituation. Quite simply a passable and not too expensive Inn in the Centre of the City, preferably as close as possible to You and our old Palace, even though I realize it was sold a long time ago and We will never get it back.

I can't wait for your Reply, Karl Adam! Well, what do You say? Isn't it high Time for us to spend a Night on the Tiles in Prague together? Papa and Mama would be very grateful to You. They have also sent the Request to your Parents. But I didn't want to go behind your Back and possibly disturb You at what might be an inconvenient Moment for You, for all I know. And I'm also looking forward to Stranov! . . . Look how the Ink has smudged here. I miss Stranov so much. Until I hear from You, I remain

Your faithful Friend.

Karl Emanuel Arco-Zinneberg, Harnack, Tyrol

I read the letter through once more, and I was not quite sure whether I was pleased or not. Karl Emanuel – never known in the family as anything but 'Manny', like his father – offered no reason for his planned visit to Prague. And yet it caused him tears, or at least he wanted me to have that impression – those tears that made the ink of the last lines run . . . I found it rather theatrical, but it was typical of Manny, of course. But if his parents had written to mine there had to be some serious reason.

When their shared palace in Prague was being sold years ago my father and my uncle had quarrelled, since when the families had not spoken with one another – apart from regular written greetings. My uncle Karl Manfred had insisted that a property like that could only be sold to the Emperor, the city or the Church. But my father, Karel Jindřich, had found a solvent buyer in the person of the Prague hotelier Antonín Hübschmann, who offered the best price. Money was needed to invest into the renovation and modernization of Stránov, our country seat that was going to rack and ruin. Even so, only a third of it was repaired; my parents could not afford to do more.

Mama was gradually transforming the castle into a 'Meierhof', with associated farms – or she was trying to. In her letters she urged me to give up loafing around in Prague and come back to take over the running of the estate. She had got into debt in order to buy some 'mechanical binders' and wanted me to come to see them. If I was not mistaken, her main concern was my health and my eternally festering lungs, which would be alleviated by country air and the stench of hay, woods, animals and slurry.

My father did not share her enthusiasm for the country. Recently he had scarcely spoken at all, least of all to me. Last Christmas he had told me I was a disappointment to him. But he hadn't explained in what sense. I understood him less and less. As far as I knew he spent every day seated in his study smoking his pipe and writing lots of letters. To whom, neither I nor Mama had any clue. I seldom made the trip to Stránov.

I sat down at my desk, unscrewed my pen, flushed it with water and dripped some ink into the reservoir. Then I got down to writing two letters. One was to my cousin, assuring him of a warm welcome in Prague. I addressed the second letter to my father, briefly informing him that I would take care of my cousin and that the two of us would shortly pay them a visit – but just a short one, I added at the end.

III

Solly

Recollections During a Fencing Bout

We salute each other wordlessly, hilt to lips. Then extend the arm to one side and assume the stance. We adopt the on-guard position, feet apart and knees flexible. Weight on the left, lightness in the right, the left arm loose, the hand clenched behind the back, the armed hand in front of the body, the blades pointing slightly upwards in the open position. Any other way of starting a bout would be pointless for us because Solly and I know each other too well. They watch us with respect, some of them with admiration, which is a mark of success among the Prague Sokols, because they all know that Solly is a Jew and that he could not give a fig for the national frustrations of the Czech population in the Austrian monarchy. Which goes for me, too. The swords touch and immediately leap aside is if burnt by the other.

So far few Jews had entered the main hall of the New Town Sokol gymnasium. Among the Sokol members here – brothers, as they call each other – there are many supporters of the Young Czech and Old Czech parties, although I have never ascertained the relative proportion. Both of them despise the Jews. As one of the nobility I am in better standing with the Old Czechs. The Young Czechs recognize pure Czech origins, which are quite hard to find in this country. I myself am treated by them with a cool respect, sometimes with suspicion. I have a sword and an épée, a coat of arms and origins that can be traced back to the seventeenth century, which they would simply regard as laughable. For them the bygone Battle of White Mountain is an affront that they strive to redress. In their eyes I am a symbol of the post-White Mountain epoch, a token of their ignominy. If I were rich, both sides would curry favour with me because I could assist their party. Since I am not, my origins are a source of merriment.

I was born in 1867, and I acknowledge all my forebears regardless. Their faults do not concern me. I have no children. My death will mean the historical end of an insignificant family line, and it has nothing to do with anything, apart from a few family ties and relations. But these ardent patriots have as much in common with the Habsburg court as we do. They sometimes tell me during combat at the gymnasium that now we have the twentieth century on the horizon the aristocracy does not matter – that the nobility and the Church have no influence at all on anything nowadays, as they are dead organs of society. And I tell them in reply that maybe the nobility no longer has its former influence or pride of place at the royal table, but it can do what it likes. Then I thrust.

Someone with a weapon under his coat cannot be chased out of the tavern, Solly declares, when patriots curse the Jews in his presence. And they are wary of him.

Now he is wielding a sword like the one I am holding, and the Sokols observe our jousting. Few of them risk striking the body with their sword. Cutting is too dangerous; they prefer épées with safety buttons and masks, as well as chest and limb guards. But for Solly and me fencing is no mere sport: an honourable and safe metaphor of combat. I once said in his presence that fencing is playing at the past. On that occasion he retorted that if he felt himself to be a Jew he would train for the future by fencing.

I feel fine today, no coughing or even barking any more. Perhaps those alcoholic drops gave me a fillip. We engage in body combat, and we leave striking the manchette to the Sokols, and anyway, apart from the fencing masters, they are not permitted to aim at the body.

A lunge at Solly, the standard opening, almost like in chess. He knows how to react. He parries it in front of his face as on a thousand previous occasions and mechanically deflects the blade. He takes two paces forward and feints a lunge. I parry from below, as if bowing to him, and I do not fail to award him a polite smile, to the delight of the onlookers. There is something narcissistic about fencing, as I have noted on many occasions, and all of a sudden I feel out of place without powdered wig, lace collar and cuffs, like a dancer who has forgotten to dress.

The swords click in a clock-like rhythm while the group of brother Sokols button themselves into their underwear. They have fine togs, plain and basic, almost hygienic. Dr Preininger is one of their members.

Turn the fist and thrust, then press and riposte, yield and riposte, then a thrust from below, direct parry and a thrust from above, lastly an unusual feint: a glissade upwards, yield, feint from below, direct parry and strike, again from above; the doctor would be no match for that, it never fails against amateurs.

It didn't impress Solly. In a lightning move he beat me crosswise and almost dislodged the sabre from my hand. His laughter filled the gymnasium.

We fence in white shirts and black knee breeches. I inherited my breeches from my father. Solly sewed his own in his shop in Celetná Street: Solomon Weiss, Drapery and Millinery. Ladies from all over Prague use his shop, as well as countrywomen who are in the know, not to mention worthy old maids and wives of respectable burgesses, who read his advertisements in German and Czech newspapers. Often they are miffed when a shop assistant deals with their orders. The proprietor of the establishment, an exemplary taxpayer, contributing to the Empire of his Imperial Highness Franz Josef I, saves his efforts for the most comely townswomen. He selects them at his ease in the concealment of the sample room at the back of the shop – ladies take their chosen fabrics there, and they are permitted, and even warmly encouraged, to drape all those cambrics, satins, velvets, chiffons, silks and poplins on their naked bodies.

My blade slides down his and connects with the hilt. I almost have him, our gentlemen Jew, with his hair like King Barleycorn. The like has not been seen. Where is the crooked proboscis or the nit-infested side locks that are a *sine qua non* of every issue of *The Darts* and other humorous publications? Where are the thick lips and the receding forehead that Czechs and Germans readily associate with Jews?

Solly has more or less the same build as I. Lightweight, in other words – built like a barber, he would say. But his blond hair is almost white; he has an even forehead, an upturned nose that you can see into, blue eyes and lips as thin as a hairpin. When he displays his teeth in a smile his Aryan face and small angular head sing a strident song of anarchist provocation of all European races. Solly is an original. Those who are better acquainted with him treat him warily. Apart from German and its Jewish version, the old language of the ghettoes, he speaks a Czech that is scarcely distinguishable from my own. His comment was that every language was a whore, because which of them was absolutely pure?

He raises the sword over his head, the hilt higher than the tip, aims at my forehead and cuts from above. I parry, riposte, we cross swords, we circle each other with three side-steps and exchange places, the sabres disengage, and we both cut horizontally from the right side. We are figures on double-headed cards; if we harm ourselves it is only ourselves we are harming. The weapons jangle and the blades slide down each other. They separate in a wide arc and ring again. We are sliding along each other's blades, but to my surprise the pressure of his arm slackens, the blade slides right to his neck, so I stop it. The scoundrel is counting on this: he has deliberately exposed himself, and I do not have enough time to return to the on-guard position. He sidesteps, and he has me; he strikes me across the ribs with the flat of the blade. Solly wins, and the Sokols applaud.

We take a break and go off to the side-room beyond the arcade. We draw some effervescent water and watch the brothers, inspired by our display, outdo each other with bold thrusts.

Solly is in a good mood. For a long time I have been the victor in our bouts. He sets his sabre spinning, and with a flick of his wrist he sends it flying straight up. The weapon embeds itself in the beam below the gallery. One of the men glances over and shakes his head. Oh dear, someone is defiling the sanctuary. But boyish pranks are so pleasurable. I spin my sword up to the ceiling, the point pierces the wood and the weapons hang there, trembling like pods in the wind. His falls first, and his hand catches it just above the floor. Then mine tumbles down, and I snatch it out of the ether as if nothing has happened. Solly swishes it twice in front of him, ready for a further bout. I go on-guard and am obliged to parry immediately. Blade rubs against blade, and the smell of sweat fills the room.

Solly is a discreet fellow. Whenever he speaks about the women who visit him for more than dress fabric he never divulges their names. But usually that is the limit of his discretion. What he does with them he describes in detail. Some of the women bring him gifts afterwards. They are women who have been his customers for many years. And there are others that he dispatches to a competitor before they have even had time to state their order at the counter. On one occasion he refused a beauty in my presence. She was a tall, big-bosomed lady with a clear oval face and beautifully manicured hands. When she had left the shop with a look of disappointment I asked him what he did not like about her. Instead of answering he pointed at his nose and was unwilling to speak about it further.

Two or three forward steps. Solly retreats. An attack to the head, the chest and the waist, then switch to counter-attack, cut from inside, riposte outside, and outside the face blade upwards, from below to the body turning the blade, cut to the outside and quickly withdraw. The problem is that I can scarcely catch my breath. I glance at a mirror. My face is lobster red. It is a sign that my lungs are not working properly, as Dr Kubin informed me. Solly is better off – a look of concentration on his pale features and no trace of breath-lessness. There are droplets of sweat like pearls around his nose and blond eyebrows.

Solly maintains that his father wasn't originally a Jew. An albino articled clerk in some law office fell in love with a beautiful black-eyed girl, and he didn't give a hoot that she lived outside the gates. He converted and was circumcised and had a Jewish wedding. He got the sack from his office, and his family had no further contact with him. With his Jewish wife he fathered a son, Solomon, and over the next nine years he became the most ardent worshipper of the Old Testament deity in the Austro-Hungarian monarchy. Then he started to rave about Zion and proclaim that the Jews belonged there and that it was their home. Jews had to learn to resist the goyish rabble. He forced Solly to carry a fish-gutting knife and taught him to fight with a stick. He knew why. When a pogrom happened it was one of the smaller ones. Some woman claimed a moneylender had cheated her, and the story got out. Five journeymen from the New Town stormed a street that had remained Jewish. They carried axe and shovel handles. They belaboured the backs of anyone they met before fleeing before the gendarmes. The night after that incident Solly's father disappeared. He left to fight for Zion and was never seen again.

Solly stands in front of the window, a dark silhouette brandishing a sword. Maybe he resembles his father. Years ago he met his fate in the shape of a woman, and on her account he threw away his previous life, his origins and his faith.

Jews inherit their Jewish identity from their mother. Solly had no doubts about his racial allegiance until the moment when a green-eyed girl entered the shop where he was working. It was odd that she came in alone, but she was not at all perturbed by the inappropriateness of her behaviour. She bought a blue hat, was accorded an enormous discount and permitted the young shop assistant to accompany her as far as Příkopy. She was eighteen; he was twenty-one. He invited her to an afternoon concert at Žofín, and she arrived in the company of her mother and grandmother.

Solly was caught slightly off guard. We fenced our way as far as the parallel bars, ducked under them and reached the gymnastic rings, which someone had left dangling. I manoeuvred him between them

53

and tapped him on the shoulder with my sword. It was unfair; the Sokols started to whistle. But they should have done that before when we abandoned our line. Fencing in a straight line is not to our liking.

He wanted to marry her. He would get his mother's consent as well as all the complications involved with changing religion. He did not avoid them, even though the parents of his intended would not open the door when he knocked on it bearing a bouquet of flowers. And so he pushed them through the gap under the door. They stamped on them and swept them out, but he stuffed them back again. Then he made his way around the house and caught sight of her through the kitchen window. There was lots of shouting, and she was sitting on a chair with her hands over her ears. She did not even glance out the window.

When he came back with flowers again the next day the maid told him that they had taken the young lady off to the country.

He bribed her with a gulden to divulge where they were hiding her. He hired an open carriage and horse along with an old rheumatic coachman. That was a mistake, as he told me later. If he had hired someone from the circus and paid him twice as much things might have turned out differently.

We chop the dust of the gymnasium into microscopic particles. The swords now jangle or, rather, clatter, somewhat wearily. Solly's eyes are red, and he looks abstracted. The swords in our hands feel heavier than flails, and our appetite for fencing has been washed away with our sweat. But we can't just end it there.

'Time passes more slowly in the country,' he told me on that occasion, 'but when something does happen no time is wasted. I arrived there from the middle of the village. The farm was on the outskirts. I went up to the door. It was a beautiful cottage. I banged on the door. The lace curtains on the other side of the window moved. A green-painted gate at the side of the house opened slightly. A dog ran out that didn't bark but snarled and bared his teeth, letting me know he would tear me to pieces. So I took a knife out of my pocket and showed it to him. He didn't want to get the message, in the same way that I didn't want to get his. He ran past me and went for the legs of the nag that had drawn me there. The old fellow walloped him with his whip, but by now four of the local yokels have started to mill around us, the blubbery birdbrain types, her cousins or something, and they had knotted sticks in their hands. Just a bit of village entertainment. I told them, I'll buy you beers and convert to your religion. How about that? They had no time for any such talk, and the smallest of them, scarcely fifteen, wanted to show off his prowess to his brothers, so he picked up his stick and went for me. I took it off him. He was no problem, and I gave him a good kicking, but then the others set about me. The coachman took to his heels and even chucked away his whip. I picked it up as a handy weapon, but I didn't get a chance to use it. They gave me a dreadful thumping. But that wasn't the worst of it. The worst was when she came out of the cottage and did nothing to stop them. She goggled at me like a silly sheep, with a scared look on her face as if she had no idea what was happening and that it was on account of her. They drove me into a slurry pit behind the farm, a sort of stinking pool in the bushes where the poultry were splashing around. That muck probably saved my life, otherwise those bumpkins would have done for me. It cost me dearly that blue hat I sold her, don't you think?'

But he wasn't the sort to take it lying down. He spent a week in Prague getting over the worst of it, and then he returned to the village. This time he borrowed a horse and saddle. He cut a thick stick from a hazel bush and sharpened one end to a point. He waited until evening – the poultry was still at the pond. He wanted a goose, but they were too big, so he caught a duck and wrung its neck. Then he impaled it with the pointed stick. When it was dark he poured paraffin on the duck, climbed on his horse and galloped to the farm. The dogs started to bark, but they were the other side of the gate and couldn't get at him, and he wasn't hanging around. He set light to the carcass, threw it over the wall and rode off.

Back in Prague he bought a newspaper every day. There was no report of a fire in the country, and the police didn't come for him. He was cured of his love for that girl. He stopped attending the synagogue and visiting brothels. He borrowed some money and opened his own shop specializing in ladies' fashion.

He lunges at me, upswing from left and right. It is not a prudent attack, more for effect, but so far it is fast enough to allow me to counter-attack. We push against each other, our sweat smelling of wine vinegar and metal. Solly has some kind of rage in him, and it even strikes me that he and I might have the same thing on our minds. Women have disappointed each of us differently, but one disappointment always resembles another.

I once told Gita about mine, one morning in bed when we did not feel like getting up. I was certainly not expecting it to enrage her. She went for me that time with her fists and nails. I had to hold her away from my body until she wore herself out.

Cut and flick and jab and parry protectively in front of the face, then watch the path of the sword tip and cut away; the height of the wrist is crucial: the hand hovers above the head like a bird of prey with a sharp beak; a cut from above that covers itself, overhand thwartwise and straight, and an attack to the body horizontally from the right, retreat one pace and then three paces forward. Ears ring from the clash of blades.

The story with Rosina that time was that she willingly did the non-commissioned officer's bidding, even though I was paying her and counting on her loyalty. Her best friend betrayed her to me. After that it was obvious that it was all over. Then came the last evening before I ditched her. I came to see her and did not even get undressed but bawled her out straight away. She begged me on her knees to forgive her; the lad lost an arm, she said, he was so good-looking, like a doll with its arm shot off, he used to visit me when I was working at Madame's, I wasn't with you yet, he was still just a kid and had both his arms; and then he came again wearing a uniform and one of the sleeves was empty.

If my disappointment hadn't been so sharp I might have even felt compassion, I told her.

'It was only once and only with my mouth, Addie. I had to do it for him, and I did it out of pity, and I'll never do it again.'

So I said, 'All right', and I rolled her over on to the bed and pressed her arms to the mattress with my knees. She thought it was going to be like the other times and was waiting to see what whims I had in store, but this time it was rather different. I had no desire to reconquer my territory, but I don't have any other explanation for my behaviour, the way I smashed her across the mouth and then her whole face, which she couldn't defend. Blood ran from her lips and nose, and tears streamed from her eyes. Then I got up off her, and while she was wiping her face I spat on her.

Dear me. A nobleman who lacks generosity and the ability to forgive is no aristocrat. Does generosity and forgiveness apply to barbers? I'm an odd kind of plebeian, like Solly, and sometimes people like that give me the creeps.

Shortly afterwards she became a queen of the pavement. I didn't give her a single crown, which I'm now ashamed of. After all, she didn't betray my love but my ludicrous pride and a monetary relationship that would come to an end anyway sooner or later. I have her on my conscience. And yet I have to admit I was relieved when she died. I didn't want to bump into her in Jewry and pretend that we didn't know each other.

I allowed my mind to stray from the contest, and I was now easy prey for Solly. At that moment of confusion I didn't see him but Rosina Weinerová. He launched a clumsy attack on me, and I swung at thin air like a beginner, as if I was confronted by a wraith and I wanted to cut it in half. Solly sidestepped and executed the simplest feint from the fencing textbook – he feigned a cut from inside. I parried directly (which was another mistake; I should have retreated). In a flash he retreated, shot his arm sideways and executed an exquisite remise. The flat of his blade struck the back of my neck and I saw stars.

Solly carried off the victor's laurels, and they even gave him three cheers. I didn't begrudge him them.

As soon as we left the gymnasium I started to suffocate. The air was a dirty colour and black barouches were jolting along the cobbles of Moat Street, and you had to keep carefully to the pavement in case one of them swept you off it. Solly thumped me on the back in an effort to make me cough, but it didn't help. Crouched over, I dashed to other side where there was less dust, and I leant against the wall of a house with a handkerchief at my mouth. Eventually the cough came. The sound of it was awful, but it was drowned out by the din of the street.

Solly put his arm around my shoulders and steered me to a tavern. The owner was afraid I might be infectious. They served me some marrowbone broth, and after a couple of spoonfuls the attack abated. I told Solly that if things continued like that we wouldn't be doing much fencing together.

Then some man got up from a corner table and came over to us. He had a full beard, wore a discreetly dark suit and held a bowler hat in his hand. Solly asked him if he wanted to join our table.

He shook his head and said, 'If you'll permit me, sir, I could hear that you have problems with breathing. I know of somebody who could help you.'

'You do?' I glanced at Solly, who looked just as surprised as I was.

'Ask after a doctor who has been spending the last few days in Prague,' the man continued. 'His name is Felix Hoffmann. He is a chemist, and he has a miracle remedy. Haven't you heard of him?'

'No. And where am I to find this doctor?'

'I don't know, sir.' He looked as if he was going to say something more, but he had second thoughts. He had a friendly manner, as if he truly only wanted to offer disinterested help, but there was something slightly untoward in his behaviour, a sort of nervousness or discomfiture.

I took a couple of coins out of my pocket and offered them to him. At first he refused them, but then reached out and took them. He nodded, and still holding his hat he left the tavern as if something had driven him away.

We found it amusing. 'Your guardian angel,' said Solly and took a drink from his beer glass. 'Except he looked like a secret policeman.'

He was right, there was something suspicious about the discomfited man. Nevertheless, I was determined to seek out that Dr Hoffmann. The risk of being taken for a ride was still preferable to waiting passively for the next time I would spit blood.

IV

The Loggia

News of the Miraculous Doctor

Scarcely a fortnight had passed since my visit to Otka Meyrinková at Friedmann's notorious hostelry when her place of residence and employment, where she so willingly worked, was closed down by a group of four actuaries and two gendarmes. They were headed by František Xaver Bürger, executive official in charge of the resettlement and urban improvement of old Josefov. It was achieved without protest. Otka then hauled a suitcase and a trunk with her clothes on a barrow to Madame Golda's, who took her in, well aware of her worth and reputation. That apart, it did not bode at all well, however, certainly not for Gita: it was only a question of time before the two of them would bump into each other in the yard and feathers would fly. And I had promised Gita I'd take her away. But we wouldn't all fit into the Long Street apartment, and, besides, I was expecting the arrival of my relative, the Count.

I put an advertisement in the Czech and German press and received three replies. I sallied out to reconnoitre.

An apartment was being offered in Rye Street in the New Town, an area to which I had never been attracted, even though it was near the gymnasium where I went to fence. It was so roomy and elegant that I could hardly believe my eyes. Third floor. Two rooms and a kitchen, lots of light, no communal balcony and so no postman peeping in the window. On the contrary, an elevated position above a lively street devoid of the hens one was always falling over in the Old Town, the Lesser Quarter and in Jewry. Here one could enjoy the warmth of bourgeois comfort and luxurious cleanliness for a price that was only slightly preposterous. I am not one to bargain, so that was the final price, but what's the point of haggling anyway? The apartment had a balcony, a cellar beneath the building and an attic beneath the roof for drying washing, which Gita would take care of gratis for me every week or the concierge would do it for a few ha'pence. Starching of shirts was included in the price. Moreover, it also had a bathroom with a boiler and a large bathtub – no washtub and cooking pots on the stove – and alongside that a separate water closet with a patent flushing mechanism and a cistern just below the ceiling with a crystal handle on the chain. The more water the better, all-inclusive comfort – hygiene is on the march and scoring victories throughout Europe. All things considered, it was appropriate there. Those enormous apartment houses were built on green vineyards when Prague was still in a hollow and on the hill over the river. There was no need for them to demolish old hovels here, as they had on the enormous Charles Square a little further down.

The accommodation was a trifle expensive for me, but I kept it in reserve.

The second apartment was not far from the lagoon in St Peter's Quarter, in a fine although slightly neglected old-fashioned building in sight of the industrial mills. The river was not visible either beyond them or below them, but the smell of it was quite strong, as was the smell of naphthalene as I climbed the staircase and entered the apartment through a double door. The landlord demanded three months' rent in advance. I complained about the dismal view from the window: a dirty street and the crookbacked roofs of the mills. He drew my attention to the fine coffered ceiling. I asked him for a chair, and when he brought it I climbed on to it and poked my penknife into one of the ceiling beams. Sawdust trickled on to me; the beam was full of woodworm and some fungus or other.

The third apartment was not an apartment but a cottage. It

stood right on the border of Josefov and the Old Town. It was as old as my pedigree, and it was known locally as the Loggia. Its two owners were in dispute with the municipality over plans to demolish it. They were both house painters, but alongside the stepladders stacked in their yard there were two easels with stretched canvases in frames. On one of them was an unfinished painting of a dark lane in the Jewish Town, lit up at one point with a burning torch, and on the other was an exact depiction of what one saw as he entered the closed courtyard of the Loggia.

What one saw was arches and above them a swelling wave in stone, as if one stood in front of a grotto – an artificial cave. It was amazing, and it came as such a total surprise that I actually shuddered.

The building certainly lived up to its name. The front of the house faced a curved street and a tiny square and did not differ greatly in shape or appearance from the average historic house in the Old Town, although it had considerably fewer windows and no decoration. On the other hand, the monumental inner gallery within the angular horseshoe of the building and courtyard was something quite unparalleled. It was not there to serve the house. The house was there in order to hold it within its embrace – like a man holding the woman he loves, it struck me. But the woman would have to be a giantess suffering from flatulence.

The gallery of the house was titanic and massive, but it was segmented, so it did not seem so heavy. It lined the wall at various levels, broken now vertically now horizontally. It was supported by angular pillars that only partly projected from the wall with a double cornice and gigantic capitals in the form of a scroll coiled forwards. Swallows' nests attached to their grooves were blackening. The rendering on the wall below was green from the damp. The arches beneath the gallery suggested drapery folds, something mysterious, as if it was concealing something. Above the arcades no single line was completely straight or right-angled, and the wall was both bulging and sunken in different places, but it certainly didn't cling to the ground or the sheer stucco walls. And yet it was cold, hard stone, which only gave the impression of being a shred from a travelling-magician's curtain.

I stood transfixed beneath those arches. I was so overwhelmed by that image of ugly beauty that my windpipe became constricted. I had not yet seen the interior of the building, but I knew already that this is where I wanted to live henceforth.

The house had only one upper storey. Above that came the reddish-brown slanting roof with dark dormer windows and once-white soot-covered chimneys topped by chimney pots and cowls like miniature wayside shrines to keep out the rain. A dove sat on each of them. The sun's rays played on the semi-circular roof tiles but no longer reached down as far as the yard. It was almost dusk. Beneath one of the arches a small goat stood on a bed of hay gazing at me calmly with yellow eyes.

I glanced at two men who were also present in the yard with me and the animal, but I had only just noticed them. They resembled each other. They watched and bided their time. Now that I had noticed them they smiled in the same way and raised their caps. I raised my hat and would have spoken to them but was prevented from doing so by an attack of coughing. Maybe it was the stench of the goat that spoilt my enchantment with that extraordinary place. The painters waited. One of them picked up a jug and poured some beer into a glass and brought it to me. At last we were able to introduce ourselves.

The brothers' surname was Urzidil, and they were christened Richard and Alois. They each had a bushy moustache, a well-worn jerkin, a paint-splashed apron and a veteran's cap. They looked the same age, a little over forty. They poured me another glass and brought out some chairs.

Richard, whose moustache merged into sideburns on his cheeks, took care of the conversation. Alois mostly stayed silent, glancing for a while at me and then again at his work on the easel, puffing from time to time at his porcelain pipe. Most of all they gave me the impression of two old bachelors. No woman showed herself there,

63

and there was no mention of any. Most likely contented old bachelors. But they had no cause for contentment, as it turned out.

Richard put me right – they were not intending to let the house but to sell it, and they had been trying to do so for some time already. But the municipality had forbidden it when they applied for permission. So they had offered it to the city, but the deal ran into problems at the outset. The council offered them a third of what they asked, and when they were unwilling to accept it they were threatened with confiscation. F.X. Bürger had personally issued the threat in his office. He had told them they must accept the municipality's conditions. It was in the interest of decontamination.

'I would confiscate him – in the interest of decontamination!' Alois stretched out his arms and mimed the violent throttling of Councillor Bürger. 'I know where the little fellow lives. I'll go and explain it to him, the bureaucratic runt.'

'And where does he live?' I wanted to know.

'In the Lesser Quarter,' said Richard. 'In a new house that was built by some savings bank or other. He lives on the upper floor, in a sort of vulture's nest. He needn't fear confiscation. Not that it's inaccessible, but he has some fellows guarding it. And apparently they're armed.'

Then we talked about the possibility of buying it. They admitted that they wanted a lot for the house. I pointed out that the building could not be exempted from the urban improvement plan, but they insisted that it did not fall within the urban improvement zone and even brought me the relevant document and drawing from the land register. That was why they were trying to sell it to someone who would pay a decent price for it and stand up for it against the municipality which anyway had no right to it.

It looked favourable. They asked from me two-thirds of what they had demanded from the municipality, and they had proof that the house was not to be demolished and would not be. After all even Bürger was no match for what was confirmed in writing.

I borrowed the documents relating to the house in order to get them verified. Everything tallied, so I sent a message to the Urzidil brothers that I was interested in the Loggia and within a month we would be able to shake hands on the deal. The only problem was that I did not have the wherewithal to buy that curious house.

One solution would be a loan. A bank was out of the question. Maybe a savings bank, but what surety could I offer?

Shortly afterwards I was sitting with Solly in a café explaining my situation to him. He told me – with a regret that I believed – that he could lend me something but not the entire sum by any means.

We were drinking absinthe. This by no means has such a good effect on me as it does on Solly. It inflames me and makes me cough, while also stimulating my urge to smoke a pipe. I had already smoked two pipes that evening, so that my tongue was numb and my throat felt like a furnace, which the alcohol only served to stoke up further. I asked the waiter for a carafe of water and downed it in one go without bothering to pour it out. Someone at a nearby table applauded me, and I got a fit of coughing. The waiter came up and asked obsequiously whether we were wanting to pay our bill. Solly slapped his gloves down on the table and knocked over his glass, but I pointed to him – he'll take care of it – and then staggered to the door, doubled up, with a handkerchief over my mouth. Outside, in front of the café, I looked to the world like a drunkard wanting to vomit but unable to, whereas I was, in fact, being shaken by compulsive choking. When Solly emerged with his scarf and top hat and his gloves in his hand he looked every inch the Beau Brummel. In contrast to me. He took me firmly under the arm and led me off to my digs. On the way he asked me, by the by, whether I had obtained the miraculous remedy yet.

I confessed that my pharmacist was an incompetent ne'er-do-well who knew not a thing about it.

'Or he pretends not to,' Solly commented. 'My doctor has already heard about the remedy. He says they are tablets. And that the Hoffmann fellow is a queer customer. Apparently he experimented in Germany with acid. He works for the Elbe Valley Works or used to. He is able to reduce a fever, possibly even one caused by malaria, and

65

he has something for asthma and maybe even tuberculosis. And I also heard, Addie, that he has a box of tablets always at hand. But it doesn't come cheap. And that's not all.'

We reached Long Street and thumped on the gate. The concierge shuffled up from the other side, opened the door and shone his candle in our faces. I pressed a half-crown into his palm, and he let us in without grumbling. He promised Solly to leave it ajar for when he wanted to leave.

'The snag is', Solly continued, after falling into an armchair, stretching out his legs and closing his eyes, 'that Chief Municipal Physician Preininger is intending to sue that Dr Hoffmann. The medicine doesn't have his stamp on it, you see, besides which the substance is exceptionally expensive. One would think it were gold. The Prague pharmacists are afraid that no one would buy it, and, of course, they've got the wind up about being prosecuted and losing their licences. That doctor has no easy task in Prague, if you get my meaning. Not in Prague or anywhere else. That's to your advantage. You're bound to squeeze a discount out of him.'

'Seeing that you're so well informed,' I retorted, 'tell me where I can find him.'

'That's precisely what I don't know,' Solly replied and fell asleep.

I didn't feel like sleeping. I went over to the window and looked out into the darkened street. A man in a dark broad-brimmed hat and a long travelling coat happened to be passing beneath the window. He hesitated, as if he sensed someone was watching him. He didn't look up but quickened his pace instead.

It struck me that it might be Dr Hoffmann. Maybe he is seeking me as desperately as I need him.

V

What Manny Brought

An Incident with Meat and a Pair of Boots

They were fine new engines. A dark blue locomotive with an Austrian eagle on its boiler sidled into Platform 1. It had travelled on its own straight from the factory to the station. A crowd of uniformed officials and actuaries swarmed around me, and I realized that I was at the wrong platform. I had wandered into an event I had nothing to do with. The engine let off steam, and when the steam cleared I caught sight of the executive official in charge of urban improvement. He was standing on some podium or other leaning over at the top hats of his subordinates, as if making sure that his men didn't stink and that they had clean collars. Alongside him stood a man with the look of a patrician. He held a gold watch and was comparing the time it showed with the time on the station clock. He was sixtyish. He put his watch away and said something. Bürger jumped down compliantly. The man removed his hat and held it theatrically in front of his body. It was effective, because the crowd fell silent. Then he began to speak. I couldn't hear what he was saying, so I took the opportunity to get a good look at him. The crown of his head was bald and surrounded by a wreath of white hair. His darting blue eyes beneath his round lined forehead held a vitriolic expression. Although he smiled, which is no easy feat when speaking to such a crowd, he stared ahead of him like a jolly executioner on a scaffold. I turned to a corporal from the municipal garrison and asked him who the man was. He gazed at me as if I were a country bumpkin and told me that it was Senior Alderman Leopold Meister, the Deputy Mayor of Prague.

'I thought so. And what's going to happen now?'

The answer was obvious, and he didn't bother to waste a second more on me. He watched with the others the performance that was taking place by the locomotive. Bürger handed a bottle of champagne to Meister on his podium. It hung from a cord, the other end of which, tied into a wide noose, had been tossed over the engine's chimney by a nimble minion. Meister counted to three, first in German, then in Czech, so to six, in fact, and then raised his arm and broke the bottle against the steam engine's shiny curved iron cladding. Dense smoke billowed from the chimney, and a shrill note came from the whistle. The officials applauded demonstratively, and Leopold Meister descended from his podium.

I looked around me. A dark-green locomotive had just drawn up at Platform 2. Apart from its colour, it was the other's twin, but it was dirty from its long journey. A station attendant announced through a megaphone that it was the train from Kolín and goodness knows where else. Platform 4 was blocked by a goods train, while Platform 3 remained empty, so I made my way there. I lit a pipe and added the smoke to the clouds of steam that condensed beneath the glazed roof above the platform.

Two minutes passed. Station clocks are supposed to keep precise time, and I still hadn't been able to find my watch. Indeed, I had already given up hope of ever seeing it again. Another train entered the station, drawn by an enormous black engine that looked like the father of the other two. The attendant announced that the Vindobona had arrived. He was shrouded in white steam, which then enveloped the people on the platform, including me. There was a screech of brakes, and the colossus, only heard not seen through the white clouds, came to a halt.

All that smoke started to suffocate me. I bent at the waist like a hinge, and my handkerchief ripped with the coughing. The world of motion and technology, the world of easy carriage of things and people from place to place had penetrated my ears and eyes as well as my nose and lungs, and I was taking huge gulps of what I didn't want. At that moment I regretted that I had ever considered making the journey to the devilish station.

When I finally straightened my back, the steam had almost dispersed and the engines had stopped their mighty blowing off, only the largest locomotive continuing to emit a thin wisp of vapour from its outlet, but the hiss was already drowned out by the racket on the platform. Amidst the ashen travellers and ruddy-faced porters, the sausage vendors and candyfloss sellers, the men in hardwearing trenchcoats and the ladies in green-and-blue travelling costumes that narrowed their waists and rounded their hips, amidst the round hatboxes, the elegant briefcases, the voluminous suitcases and the cabin trunks, amidst the Great Danes on leads and the miniature pinschers in arms, amidst the parrots in cages and the fishes in aquariums and amidst the armfuls of coloured flowers and the flowerpots with rubber plants and dwarf palms, there stood a giant with shoulders like a beam engine fanning his face with a low-crown hat. He was looking about him with the assurance of a man who has one or two relatives in every corner of the monarchy and is simply waiting for the relative in the crowd to notice him.

Since I last saw him he had grown by at least half a head. His chest and legs had also filled out; his waistcoat was bursting at the seams, and his trousers were threatening to split at any moment. His coat was slung over the arm that held with ease a brown suitcase of sturdy cowhide as if it weighed no more than an official briefcase. The other arm, with its muscles swelling out the arm of a grey linen shirt, went on fanning his face, which was youthfully joyful and full of expectation, with doe's eyes and smooth cheeks, flushed with excitement and health. In contrast with the hefty body, the face looked as if were made up.

Karl Emanuel Count Arco-Zinneberg, heretofore resident with his parents in a Tyrolean castle at Harnack, had arrived in Prague, and I had no idea why. I waved to him, but he didn't see me. A porter stopped by him and went to take the suitcase out of his hand, but when it was yielded up it slipped out of the attendant's grip, as if the quite ordinary-seeming luggage, which looked as if it contained clothes, two or three books and a few pairs of boots, actually bore a minor item of Austrian army artillery.

It looked as if he was absorbed by the ceremony on the adjacent platform, which had been interrupted by the arrival of the express from Vienna. Senior Alderman Meister had just raised a glass, and the other bureaucrats had followed suit. A toast was offered, but I couldn't catch a word of it across the tracks. Karl Emanuel looked on with a childish smile, and then his gaze scanned the top hats before jumping from one platform to the next and coming to rest on me. I adjusted the gold monocle in my eye socket and discreetly beckoned to him.

'Addie!' he roared above all the din, laughter and hissing, and, of course, as ill luck would have it, almost all the heads turned in our direction, including those of Bürger and Meister. The giant left the porter on the platform, jumped down on to the tracks and bobbed up on my side. Regretfully he didn't refrain from hugging me, intoxicating me with his minty breath while jabbering something to the effect that this was a fortunate meeting. Then he glanced at me and with the words 'Is it really you?' squeezed me by the shoulders. At that moment my monocle fell out, and like a nimble player of English football – the favourite pastime of the labourers and apprentices of the new districts – he caught it on the toe of his shoe. The glass rolled off, but it didn't break.

He bent down for it, and when he straightened up I had to tilt my head back. Manny looked delighted, and so I made an effort to give him a friendly smile. I was pleased, of course, but as I looked at him my feeling was more one of concern for some inexplicable reason. We shook hands, and I sensed that the interest of the titled gentlemen from the neighbouring platform had waned and they were once more celebrating the blue locomotive.

'Manny . . .' I feigned bonhomie and caught my breath. 'I'm glad to see you, too.' I kept my mixed feelings to myself.

I steered him to the exit. One porter trailed behind us with the suitcase and another with a cabin trunk as big as a wardrobe. When we had loaded up a cab and taken our seats – I without problem and Manny opposite me with his legs laboriously arranged – I announced to him that I intended to put him up at home.

'In your apartment? But I didn't want that of you! I told you so in the letter, didn't I? We'll both be uncomfortable.'

I explained to him that I would be offended if he stayed anywhere else but my place. So as not to embarrass him, I tactfully refrained from recalling his comment in the letter that he wasn't well off. It didn't take him very long to came to terms with my invitation.

'All right. But just for a few days. I expect it wouldn't pay you to have me put down roots there. Father told me to spend at least three months here, if you see what I mean.'

I threw him an understanding glance, but I was appalled. The man was still being pushed around by his parents, and he put up with it.

'Have you been up to something, Manny?' I asked reprovingly. 'And if you have why is your father sorting it out for you? You can certainly confide in me.'

My cousin blushed and looked even more dense. 'Please don't make me talk about it.'

'Why not?'

'I disgraced myself, don't you see? A major *faux pas*. But . . . officially I'm here for my health.'

I couldn't help laughing. 'In Prague?' I pointed out of the cab window at the havoc of urban improvement. 'This is the most poisonous of cities.'

Manny shrugged his shoulders and closed his eyes. That's one way of dealing with it. But I noticed that the tear sac of his right eye twitched. I expect he has had a hard time with his parents, poor fellow. Not that I'm a stranger to that myself.

I gave him the larger bedroom, which was where I usually spent my days and where I slept. I got the concierge to drag the bed into the smoking salon – in reality more of a dressing-room. Unfortunately I had not aired the room sufficiently, and as the concierge carried the bed over the threshold my nose and lungs were assailed by a dank smell of smoke. So I manfully cleared my throat and demonstrated to Manny, without need of explanation, that my health was going downhill.

The concierge left with an evasive expression on his face, as if he suspected me of having consumption or even whooping cough. When it finally started to ease Manny was standing in the doorway and extending his hand to me. In it he held something round and shiny, which my blurred vision, caused by tear-filled eyes, saw as something glisteningly membranous, full of tiny white eggs – or so it seemed to me.

'What is it?' I asked. Now I could see it better: it was a small flat bottle with rounded edges. I took it from his fingers. It had a threaded metal cap and fitted neatly into my palm. The two wider sides were smooth and flat, the narrow curved ones were ribbed. The simple light-blue label, without any maker's address, bore the single word: *Hydrochlorate*. Little white tablets rattled inside.

'Take one. It usually helps me with various things,' Manny said. 'I'll unpack, and then, if you don't mind, I shall go and have a wash after my journey.'

'The bathroom is at your disposal. I have told the concierge to heat the boiler.'

I unscrewed the cap and looked inside. Then I tapped one of the white tablets out into my hand and smelt it. There was no smell. I washed it down with water from the carafe.

I went over to the window, but on the way my knees became heavy and the window was suddenly further away than the house opposite. I lay down and listened to Manny unpacking his suitcase and making an inordinate racket in the process. But it didn't irritate me. My head was suddenly calm, likewise my bronchial tubes, and seemed as if my painful lungs had been miraculously replaced. Manny was whistling an aria from *The Magic Flute*. It was odd because it was a duet, and someone was singing to it. The aria started to sound as loud as an orchestra and opera chorus, and I conjectured that Manny had brought with him one of the latest musical boxes from Harnack. So we would have a jolly time. But where do those pictures come from? I wondered. When I closed my eyes I saw them more clearly, but the music was quieter. It was a beautiful performance, a perfect live tableau like at the Bohemian Jubilee Exhibition, except that this one moved. The black horse with the knight on its back, the music in the woods, the pure strings and full-blooded basses. The rider had a snake in each hand, the green-and-brown reptiles squirmed, but he held them behind their heads to stop them biting him. Then he threw both of them into the bushes, thereby driving out from her hiding a woman in a tattered garment. She had been bitten by those snakes, although they could scarcely have touched her. The knight dug his spurs in his horse's flanks and set off in pursuit of her. She escaped by jumping into a forest pool, swimming to the middle of it and looking around her. The man stood on the bank, holding his lance in his hand. He drew back his arm and hurled it at her. It struck her in the stomach below the water. She squirmed on it like a snake, and the water turned the colour of blood. The knight lay down in the bed of pine needles and started drinking the water from the little lake. Then the live tableau disappeared.

My eyes were open and my lungs calm, but my head ached slightly. Manny was sitting at the foot of the bed, shaven and in a change of clothes, grinning like a mischievous child.

'The urge to cough has gone, hasn't it?'

I nodded.

'And how about sleep? You wouldn't mind a bit more, I can tell.'

'Sorry. I'm being a rotten host today.'

'You were an hour and a half in limbo. But that's good.'

'It felt as if I was just dozing.'

'Promise me you'll take it sensibly – not more than one day, and that includes the night, too.'

'I promise.'

'Shall we sally forth?' Manny executed a few dance steps for my benefit – a bear's polka would be an apt description. 'It's beautiful out.'

I got up, and my head swam. My legs were so light that for a moment my feet couldn't even feel the floor. Outside the window it was drizzling.

Something made Manny laugh, and I took a proper look at him. His eyes had an odd sheen and were much darker than at first.

'You took a pill, too?' I asked.

He nodded. 'Just one a day. I've got it all under control.'

We looked like two wealthy upper-class toffs in our top hats and brushed tails, he carrying an ebony cane with a silver head in the shape of wings, I with a gold-rimmed monocle in my right eye. A clerk doffed his hat to us, and when we stopped at the corner for a glass of soda water and a tot of schnapps the tavern keeper asked us where we going.

'To a brothel,' Manny replied without hesitation.

We walked past the mills and the lagoon, where, at the age of eleven and possibly even when we were twelve, we used to play at river pirates and catch fish on the ice aprons. We used to escape here from our regular two-hour French lessons, and the French teacher did not report us because we didn't report on him that he used to have a tryst with a young woman instead of teaching us, for which he was paid.

We wandered among the riverside shacks and cottages of the former ghetto. The drizzle abated, and it brightened up. I glanced back to see if there was a rainbow over the river.

'Was this the place?' Manny asked, and I nodded. We were standing in front of a window that we had once broken one sunny day a long time ago. Someone, some youngster perhaps, had drawn a devil with horns on the door a few weeks earlier and scrawled under it the words *Achtung – hier lebt Kleinfleisch!* But the old man who lived behind it had refused to wash the picture off, and so it remained, and we used to walk by it, until I threw that stone to prove to my cousin that I wasn't scared of devils. I had no idea what

Kleinfleisch meant, but I found the odd combination of the words 'small' and 'meat' even more frightening than the horned creature drawn there.

That time I received a rare but all the more thorough thrashing from my father right on the spot, in front of the hovel. My mother protested to my father, and they had a row. Manny had been intrigued because he never even received a clip round the ear from his parents, and he couldn't understand why his uncle had been so angry.

It didn't end there. When the old man looked through the broken window and saw an expensively dressed gentleman punishing his son for his prank he didn't curse and demand compensation but, instead, dashed out with a bucket of water and a rag and wiped off the offending words. Surprisingly, this failed to appease my father. He pointed to the man and said, 'You see? That man is afraid. And we're all like that.'

I asked my mother the meaning of Kleinfleisch, and she replied, 'It's of no account.'

Then we watched my father go to the old man and offer him cash, but the latter gave him a respectful bow and then shut himself in his hovel. We couldn't understand it, I humiliated and tearful after my thrashing and Manny with a confused and goggle-eyed expression. My father left a handful of coins on the step, and my mother didn't speak to him for several days afterwards.

We were now standing in front of the hovel, which looked deserted. The window was glazed but was filthy with cobwebs in the corners.

The sun came out. 'They're demolishing this place,' I said and drew humid air into my lungs. I waited in case an attack of coughing would follow, but nothing happened. The pill was still working. We strode off down lanes taking us to the heart of Josefov and the notorious establishments that my cousin was evidently looking forward to. On the way we pointed out to each other places where rope-makers and basket-makers sat in front of their dwellings and where as boys we used to encounter tinkers, rag-and-bone men, travelling knife-grinders, or pretzel vendors with their wares strung on long sticks, and from afar we would hear the cries of street-sweepers shouting to the housewives to bring their ashes and rubbish out of their homes and tip them into their cart. Manny wondered what had happened to all those people, and I explained to him that trades and markets had now been gathered together into a single large market not far from St Martin's and that I would take him there if he liked. Street trading was a rarity nowadays. He replied that delicatessens and wholesalers 'all under one roof' were also the fashion in Vienna and that he detested such places because they were soulless – buying and selling was the only activity there, and no one lived on the premises.

In that manner we concurred in the course of our walk that when we were children the city was more abundant, more colourful and held out more surprises. We behaved like two thirty-year-old cry-babies who had lost something and were searching for it in vain.

But then Prague pulled a face at us as if to show that the exception proves the rule.

We stopped in front of a little shop, which was inside a house, although most of it was out on the street. The walls of the house and the passage into the yard were hung with lanterns, bells, saws, pails, sieves, mechanical gauges and scales, a picture frame, a large spoked wheel from a penny-farthing bicycle, a mortar and a clock showing either midday or midnight. Above the passage was a sign saying: *S. Roubíček, Dealer in Old Iron and Skates*. Beneath it a laundry copper was displayed on a stone plinth.

An old woman with her hair in a bun sat in a chair in front of the shop. She had a white shawl around her shoulders. She was reading the *Tagblatt*. At her side a bewhiskered and bespectacled man in a brown hat, black overcoat and down-at-heel shoes. He had his hands in his pockets and was sucking on a long pipe with a porcelain bowl and brass lid, the weight of which distorted his mouth and from which puffs of sweetish smoke rose at regular intervals like the ticking of a clock.

I stood transfixed, unable to move. The scene before me had no significance, but something around it or beyond it must have had. Someone crossed the street from the other side.

'Have you found something you want? Some weapon maybe?' Manny said from behind me. 'I have heard tell that danger sometimes lurks in brothels in the shape of that vile hydra known as syphilis. Better be armed.' He pointed with his stick at an enormous copper sieve.

The man in the front of the shop heard this and raised his pipe with the corner of his mouth. His spectacles glittered, and he rummaged in his coat pocket. The woman on the chair ignored us. She rustled her newspaper and put it down in disgust with a shake of her head. 'Nothing but the plague again.' Then she went to the back of the shop.

I reached for the newspaper and quickly looked for the news about crime in the capital. But there was only a statement by the chief of police about unexplained deaths in the recent period and the murder on the embankment of a certain woman with the initials R.W. There were no clues so far, but he appealed to the women of Prague not to go out unaccompanied by a man and not at all after dark, and should they, in spite of that, be obliged to go somewhere for a serious reason they should go out in pairs at the very least. I found that rather odd. If R.W. was supposed to be Rosina Weinerová, which it most likely was, then the police were linking her death with some other murders. I realized to my shame that I had no idea what was going on around me.

I looked up from the newspaper. The paving shone, and the air seemed unable to make up its mind whether the rain had freshened it or simply accentuated all the fumes from the houses and streets.

'Let's go, Addie,' I heard, as if from afar, and I really was about to leave when I finally understood what had previously caused me to stop in front of the shop.

Alongside the ironmonger's there were two more small shops, both with bricked-up vaulted door lintels. The further of the two had shop signs in Hebrew combined with Czech and German: *Smoked*

Wares, S. Berg Proprietor. Six skinned and gutted animals, their forelimbs removed and dark from smoking, hung from the door frame by their legs. Even through my monocle for distance viewing I was unable to make out what they were: they looked like martens or weasels or bats with their wings cut off. But it was a Jewish shop, kosher, in other words. The owner would not have been able to display or offer for sale any such monstrosities. Then it occurred to me that they were not entire animals at all but smoked ox tongues, like forearms of long brownish-violet meat, hung on hooks by their tips with the frayed blood-red roots at the bottom. They swayed in the breeze like the trophies of some Neolithic hunter.

'Are Jews allowed ox tongue?' I asked the man with the pipe.

He didn't reply. He froze, stopped puffing his pipe and silently observed me from behind his glasses in a watchful and possibly reproachful manner. Then he looked around to see if anyone else had heard it.

'Excellent idea,' Manny remarked, taking me by the elbow. 'I think it's time to eat, too.'

But I didn't let myself be led away. It was as if I had suddenly taken a liking to the spot. I turned my gaze to the smoked-meat shop again. Beneath the suspended tongues, which could have been but were not necessarily the corpses of forest creatures, stood a young man with an apron tied over his dark suit, lolling around as if he had just popped out for a snack and was loath to return to work. I expect he wasn't hungry, because although he was showing overt interest in Berg's smoked wares he was secretly observing a young girl who was passing by carrying a white bundle of laundry. She was slightly built, and she had an oriental-looking red shawl with green stripes and long purple tassels wound around her shoulders. Above her forehead a tuft of red hair peeked out from beneath her head covering. She was accompanied by a man with a lined face and a scrawny neck like a turkey. He carried a walking-stick and wore a black cap. Every so often he would stop and try to clear his throat, mostly with no result, as if his bronchial tubes were blocked. They approached the shop in the middle. *Maier Allerhand – Second-Hand Dealer – Trödler*, I read on the signboard. They were inspecting the goods. Second-hand clothes hung from the open shutters along with a jumble of footwear of every kind, clogs, work boots and slippers as well as jackboots and patent-leather shoes and even high-heeled shoes, some singly, others in pairs and even some that were different but which looked similar enough to be worn as a pair if need be.

The junk dealer's wife came out of the door wearing a red dress. She eyed the newcomers suspiciously. The man cleared his throat into his handkerchief, inspected it disappointedly, exchanged a few words with the girl and pointed at a pair of ladies' lace-up boots with a low heel, the nicest shoes in the shop. He hung his walking-stick on his forearm and fumbled in his purse as if searching for something that might once have been there but was there no longer. Then the stick fell from his arm. The girl, who seemed to be his granddaughter and couldn't have been more than sixteen years old, quickly leant down for it. When she straightened up my gaze met hers. The shawl slipped from her head, and the lane was lit up with her flaming red hair.

At that moment the youth in the apron, who was staring at her just as I was, except from the other side, whistled and smacked his lips. The old man glanced at him and raised the stick that the girl had handed to him. The boy chuckled. The man with the pipe and the second-hand dealer's wife waited to see what would happen. The youngster took a coin out of his pocket and placed it on the counter before reaching out to take one of those creatures – or tongues. Then he came over to the girl and dangled the meat in front of her face.

The old man brandished his stick and actually managed to hit his target. The youth winced and his hand went to his head, then he shoved the man. The girl dropped her laundry bundle, and I at last stirred my stumps and went over to give the loafer a thrashing. He went to run off but ran into Manny, who walked past him so that we had him between us. He whacked him with his stick on the same place as the old man, then dealt him few more whacks on his back.

The youth started to retreat in my direction, and I let him off lightly, just giving him a slap across the face.

I left the smoked meat on the cobbles but picked up the laundry and handed it to the girl. She was too young but was unaffectedly beautiful. In an odd kind of way she was not of a piece: her nose was small like a child's but sharper and slightly upturned. She had the lips of a grown woman and big brown eyes framed by long black eyelashes, but the arching eyebrows above were ginger.

'Thank you, sir.' No smile, no curtsy. She stood with her back straight and her head bowed.

'And you, too, sir,' the man said as he cleared his throat and bowed to Manny. He was deeply flushed and could hardly catch his breath, and a sound of wheezing came from his lips. Manny made light of it.

The junk dealer's wife arrived with that pair of the nicest shoes, and as if sensing a sale she declared stoutly that she didn't intend to bargain. The man replied that he didn't either and was about to move on.

'Are they intended for the young countess here?' I asked, and the question stopped him in his tracks. 'I'll buy them for her.'

'She isn't a countess. She's my ward, and we cannot accept such a gift, sir,' he said resentfully. 'This woman here wants a gulden and thirty kreutzer for them. What does she take me for?'

'But you can take it. Take it if the gentlemen is offering – they're brand new and they're real leather,' the dealer's wife told him persuasively, meanwhile thrusting the shoes into my hands. I handed them to the girl and paid the junk dealer's wife a gulden. 'Not a heller more.' She smiled and bit the coin, then tucked it away in the money bag. I expect it would be a long time before she did so well out of a sale again.

'I don't know how to thank you, gentlemen,' the old man said with a bow.

We shook hands. The girl said quietly, 'Let's go', and pulled him away by the sleeve. She didn't look at us again.

'Such a beautiful girl,' Manny observed, 'and her hair was really special, wasn't it? It hardly matched her face. It was red, like you sometimes see on . . . *cakes*.'

'You mean *tarts*.'

'Oh, yes, I'm always mixing those up.'

'It's probably safer to say "whores".'

Manny laughed. 'Well, are we going to find some?'

'After dinner.'

But the dinner was not to my taste. My cousin insisted on inviting me to smoked tongue. I couldn't get that girl's hair out of my head. It was just like Gita's, but it suited Gita's complexion and build, whereas it seemed out of place on that angelic being – almost like a wig. But what about those eyebrows?

That night Manny had two girl's at Madame Golda's, as he later boasted to me. I didn't even have one. I didn't even go there. I had no wish to encounter either Otka or Gita. I sat at home in my room smoking my pipe and musing about that old fellow and his ward, as well as the little bottle of pills from Manny.

When my cousin arrived and banged on the gate I went to open up for him and asked him about the medicine. But he was too drunk to reply – or at least he pretended to be.

He went straight to bed and I returned to my armchair with the little bottle in my hand. I examined it in the light of the oil lamp. Then I tipped the pills into my palm and resisted the temptation to swallow one.

I realized that I had to verify a couple of things. First, whether Manny's hydrochlorate, which had done me so much good, was the same miraculous preparation invented by Dr Hoffmann. Second, whether the red hair and the eyebrows of the girl for whom I had bought the boots were dyed. And, third, whether their owner wasn't by chance that Jewish princess, rumours of whose beauty have been circulating in Prague for several weeks already. I wouldn't have been surprised if she were.

VI

Unrest in Prague

An Invitation to the Country

When I was awoken before nine o'clock by shouting and the neighing of horses in the street I felt as if I had not slept a wink. In my head a steam crane with a demolition ball on the end of a chain was striking the left and right walls of my cranial cavity in turn.

Manny staggered through the door in a long nightshirt.

'Sweet wine. I'll never touch it again. Your wine's completely different from ours.' His words sounded reproachful, which I found unjust.

'It was fruit wine. You rarely find the real stuff since the vine plague.'

'Beer is the only thing that's worth one's while in Bohemia. That and girls.'

'They're better here?' I asked as I dressed, and I wondered what the row outside was about.

Manny looked out the window. 'At Harnack I had no opportunity to make an assessment. I mostly bedded our servants. But then they asked for more money, and it was necessary to change them.'

There was the sound of a gunshot from the street. I pushed Manny aside and looked down. Fortunately no one was lying there. Five or six men were running off at full speed. They seemed to be chasing someone who was already out of sight. They were mostly young, possibly students. As soon as they disappeared around the corner horses' hooves rattled on the cobbles and two mounted gendarmes with unsheathed sabres galloped after them. Then silence fell, but when I opened the window we could make out the sound of slogans being chanted in the distance, in addition to the usual sounds of the city.

We went out to Karpeles's café for breakfast. On the way I brought up the matter of the pills he had given me. I asked him where he had them from and who had manufactured them. I carefully observed his reaction, but there was nothing in his expression to suggest that he found my question insidious in any way. He had been sold the pills by some pharmacist in Harnack who had simply told him that they were a rare item and that he should take them for insomnia but never more than one a day. He had sold him only two packs, one of which I now had.

'I've not noticed you suffer from insomnia,' I remarked.

But he replied without hesitation, 'I'm cured now. Thanks to those pills, undoubtedly.'

We reached the Old Town Square. Men were milling about, excitedly discussing something. The café was almost deserted. Manny ordered strudel and coffee with cream, while I contented myself with a home-made roll with butter and jam. The proprietor served us himself, as he always did when I went there, and during our meal he stood to attention above us with a napkin over his arm.

I turned to him. 'Listen. What's that rumpus outside? Someone fired a shot outside our place this morning, and that doesn't look like a peaceful assembly in honour of the Emperor.' I pointed out of the café's front window at the square. The clusters of people were thickest in front of the Town Hall. Around the Marian Column there was a buzzing like around a hive. 'Join us for a coffee.'

Karpeles leant towards us and shuddered. 'It's quite simple. You should have read today's newspapers. They said there that there would be disorder on account of the language, if you get my drift. And it certainly does look like disorder now. It's all the fault of the journalists.'

Nonsense, I was going to say, but Manny asked, 'On account of which language?'

'Both of them, of course. Czech and German,' Karpeles explained, as if talking to a simpleton. 'Nowadays you can talk to the authorities not just in German but also in Czech, as you know. It was pushed through by the Czech representatives in the Imperial Diet. The Prime Minister went along with them, and they keep him in office – tit for tat. That's all very well, but in that case some of the imperial officials as well as some of the city bureaucrats are in a bloody mess, begging your pardon. Aren't they? I expect you can guess which ones.'

'Naturally. All the Czechs speak German . . .' I began, but when I saw how much Manny wanted to finish what I was going to say, I let him.

'Whereas no German speaks Czech,' my cousin nodded happily. 'I do, though.'

'Precisely,' Karpeles shrugged. 'Those bureaucrats should have their ears boxed. It's not true that none of them speaks Czech, but there aren't many who do, and they're the ones who'll move faster up the ladder now, if you see what I mean. At the expense of the rest. And this here', he said, pointing outside at the crowd, which was louder than ever, 'is the upshot of the reform. Officials in Prague creating a disturbance. Last time it was the labourers, today it's the pen-pushers.'

I stared sceptically at the large crowd of lads on the square. There could have been a hundred and fifty of them, maybe two hundred. 'A trifle young, don't you think? And look at their clothes. They certainly don't look like office workers to me.'

'The old hands wouldn't come to this. They've got families,' the café owner declared authoritatively. 'These youngsters are seriously nationally conscious Germans, and there are also quite a number of students among them. They could learn Czech, but they don't want to. It's demeaning for them, you see. They'd sooner get up to their shenanigans. They were brawling about it a while ago. Some of them only dress up as students – they'd hardly get into a fight in their official uniforms, would they? They're too fond of their braids and trouser stripes for that.'

'But someone must be organizing it,' Manny remarked. 'It's a great danger, Mr Karpeles.'

'I'm aware of that, My Lord, and that's why I'm just happy to be alive. As a Prague Jew I'm completely neutral in the matter. Look here. I can carry on my business in peace. I keep my opinions to myself, you understand, and I couldn't give a damn, begging your pardon, what language you choose to speak with the authorities. I can speak German, Czech, Yiddish and a few words in Hebrew, and that's quite enough for me.'

As if someone had overheard him and hastened to chastise him the front window of the café shattered and showered us with glass. It had been broken by a paving stone hurled from the square. The stone crashed on to the floor before the glass did and rolled along the floorboards right to our feet.

A brawl had broken out in the square. I shook the splinters of glass from my clothes, and Manny did likewise. Then we helped each other into our coats. Karpeles was shouting curses through the hole in the window and shaking with anger. Then he went behind the counter, picked up a bottle of spirits and took a long swig out of it.

'You don't have this in the Tyrol, do you?' I remarked to Manny when the crowd shifted in the direction of the Marian Column and we could finally leave the café. I rather regretted not having a staff like his. I wouldn't have said no to my sword at that moment.

Then at the other end of the square someone fired two shots, and people started to flee in all directions. Skirting the walls of the buildings we headed for calmer waters and acted as if we were uninvolved foreigners, justly outraged.

'Why do they involve the Jews?' Manny asked when we finally entered Celetná Street. But even that thoroughfare was beginning to fill alarmingly with new bands of irate men heading for the square. These ones were shouting in Czech, and some of them carried staves. Among them there were even some lads no more than twelve or thirteen years old who carried slingshots, and their pockets were stuffed with stones.

'Because they're the easiest target,' I said. 'We have to warn one of my friends. His shop is just a short step from here.'

Mounted gendarmes observed from a distance as the phalanx of singing Czechs wearing soft caps, most likely labourers from one of the ironworks in Vysočany, streamed from the Powder Tower into the narrow lane so that soon there was almost no room to move.

'I have a feeling', Manny sighed, 'that it's time we called on your friend.'

We worked our way quickly through the crowd and were soon standing outside Solly's shop, in sight of the Powder Tower. The blinds were down, which was prudent, because a pick-axe was already rattling on them and a crowbar was being inserted into the joints, while some whippersnapper with a penknife was trying to prise open the padlock on the latch.

'The people here are all good patriots,' I told the one with the crowbar, and the answer I received was, 'Since when were Jews patriots?'

I stood there in silence and stared him in the eye. Manny came and stood by me, swinging his staff. The three of them stood observing us sulkily and whispering to each other. They were very similar, like two brothers and the son of one of them. Then they took their leave.

I sighed with relief. I remained standing alone with Manny a moment longer outside Solly's shop. Only now did I notice that the blind was slightly scorched at the bottom and that water was trickling out from under it.

'It's odd', Manny remarked, 'that they should have chosen this particular house. Over there', he said, pointing two doorways back, 'the windows and doors are unprotected. Didn't they notice?'

'That's exactly the point,' I said, because Karpeles had opened my eyes. 'The Czechs fight with the Germans, and both sides take every opportunity to slander the Jews.'

It was no accident that the paving stone had broken Karpeles's window and that they were trying to plunder Solly's shop. I started to fear for him, and I pointed to the courtyard entrance. We could try entering that way. I tried the door handle at the gate. The door was bolted from behind, of course, but I knew a trick of Solly's and was aware that there was a gap in an unlikely place right down near the ground where you could put your finger through and raise the iron bolt. The front hall was next to the kitchen. We went through it and along the narrow passage to the little room at the rear beyond the salon, from which Solly was able to observe his lady clients as they tried his taffetas, chiffons, silks and cheviots against their naked skin.

'Is that you, Addie?'

There wasn't the slightest trace of fear in Solly's voice, as if he wasn't even aware of what was going on outside.

We went into the shop. He was sitting on the counter, evidently drunk. His otherwise pale face was bright red as were the veins in his blue eyes. He held an old-fashioned foil in his hand.

'How did you quench it?' I asked. A bottle of champagne stood on a chair. It was half empty, so I took a swig and passed it to Manny. 'Wherever did you come by it? Or is it one from before the vine plague?'

'My thirst with champagne', Solly laughed, 'and the fire with water. They're idiots. They can't even set fire to a house.'

I recalled that burning duck which had also fortunately failed to set anything alight. I introduced my friend to my relative. 'Solomon Weiss, draper and milliner; Karl Emanuel, Count Arco-Zinneberg, my nobler cousin from the Tyrol.'

'No need to overdo it,' said Manny and shook Solly by the hand.

Solly jumped down from the counter. 'This is very embarrassing. Excuse my attire.' He was wearing nothing but his drawers.

Manny was unperturbed. 'It is an honour for me to make your acquaintance whatever the circumstances and to be well disposed to you.' He bowed, straightened up and added, 'I must apologize, Mr Weiss, for arriving unannounced, but we thought you might be in grave danger from those people outside.'

'An orator,' Solly said out of the corner of his mouth and dressed unperturbed. 'Why isn't he in parliament?' I felt he was needlessly caustic.

'Manny got into hot water back home so he's been exiled to my place,' I said by way of explanation. 'By the way, Solly – do you drink from two glasses?' I pointed my index finger at two goblets standing on the floor in front of the counter.

'You won't be cross, will you?' my friend replied with a guilty expression. At that moment I was convinced that my Gita was in the adjacent dressing-room, and all I could feel was the blood rushing to my face. Then someone peeped from under the curtain. It wasn't Gita Fuksová but Luiza Svátková. It's true that I had briefly kept her as my mistress, but that was many years before. As I tried to recall what she had been like in bed the only picture that came to mind was a fuzzy image of her closed eyes and her mouth emitting fake moans.

'*Servus*, Addie,' Luiza smiled, just as she used to. I calculated that she must be as old as I was. She came out in her birthday suit, and by no means did she look as good as she had that time. She did a naked curtsy, and Manny started to court her. Solly looked a trifle disconcerted, but then he seemed to take it in his stride and went for two more of the precious bottles.

A generosity that was sadly lacking in me.

Not to mention in the government of this country. The next day handbills had been pasted up around the city announcing that a state of emergency had been decreed throughout the royal city of Prague. The last time it had happened was two years earlier, but even then nobody knew how long it would last. The cause might have been the latest disturbances in Prague, but maybe we were carrying the can for the Young Czech deputies who had created an unbelievable and disgraceful rumpus at the last session of the Vienna parliament when they pulled out the wooden desktops from their benches and smashed them against the top desk. This might be an emphatic reprisal by the Austrian government.

I received a telegram from Mama. She enquired how Karl Emanuel was faring in my care, whether blood was really being shed in Prague and whether anything had happened to us. In a postscript she asked when we were intending to visit them at Stránov, and she couldn't resist a PPS telling me not to think up excuses and to bring Manny there as soon as possible.

I went to wake him up and immediately conveyed to him the news. To my surprise he didn't look the least put out. He washed his face in cold water, dried it slowly and with a good-tempered expression on his smooth face went over to the window. Fixing his gaze on the house opposite he delivered loftily the a brief eulogy to the Czech countryside. 'The countryside of my childhood's summer months is what I missed most in the Tyrol, Addie. We can set out straight after breakfast.'

It crossed my mind that he might have taken one of the miraculous pills, and I then took one myself. It was going to be a long day. In view of the declaration of a state of emergency there was no reason to delay our departure.

I had the concierge pack our things, and I sent the valet for a carriage. Then I sent a telephone message from the exchange on the Lesser Square saying that we would arrive that evening. The local factotum would deliver it in under three hours straight to my mother at the castle. I was not entirely at ease with the possibilities of modern communication, that awesome shortening of the distance between relatives and other unpleasant elements of one's existence. At noon I felt like another of the pills, but I resisted the temptation.

VII

Stránov Shadows

Blood Ties

I persuaded Solly to go with us. He would help dispel the unease caused by the family seat and its inhabitants. I hardly knew anyone at Stránov any more apart from my parents, our neighbours and a few of the servants, and yet I always managed to find people I didn't want to meet and would end up bumping into them somewhere unexpected. For instance, I didn't want to meet the teacher who used pay calls on us at one time. He used to sing me the praises of the Czech language and literature and their delights, and then he would steal sugar from the kitchen. I also had no wish to meet the mayor's wife who, when she was about forty and I scarcely had any facial hair, had me take her into the library where I was to choose for her something by Schiller. When we were alone she knelt down in front of me on the floor and crawled around on all fours, sticking out her backside and searching for the book in question on the lowest shelf. Nor did I want to encounter Father Wenig, the parish priest. Every time I went to church he would stare at me as if he knew some secret about me. Whenever I left the confessional he would look disappointed, as if I had hidden something from him, and once he threatened me that I would one day pay for my haughty lack of interest. He used to give me goose-pimples, and I started to avoid the church. Years later I talked about it to Rosina or Luiza, and whichever one it was responded by asking me to supply his address, as she was sure it could turn out to be a goldmine for her.

But my worst memory of Stránov I still carried within me. So to help shorten the journey – and to banish from my memory that unpleasant spectre that regularly surfaced – I imparted it to my companions in the carriage conveying us from the station to the castle via meadows, fields and remnants of forest.

'I can't abide the stench of horses. They make me cough and feel nauseous. I didn't often have to smell it – we were in Stránov from mid-June to the end of September – only my father stayed there longer in order to launch the hunting season and get in plenty of shooting. Then he would join us in Prague at the beginning of November and would have rows with Mama, who made him attend the first balls of the season and would entreat him to guard his tongue when they were in society. His patriotism was important to him, and he didn't conceal his misgivings about the court and the government. As a result some people were afraid to associate with him, and Mama reproached him for it.

'One July when I was approaching my seventeenth birthday, and the summer was unbearably hot, Mama came to my bedroom in the foulest of moods. You know what I mean. She started to chastise me for not behaving as I should for someone of my standing. I spent all my time reading like some schoolgirl from the city – and novels of all things! And what she needed was someone to keep an eye on the servants, and I was to go straight away to the stables make sure the horses were being properly looked after and see to it that no unauthorized persons were hanging around there. After all, servants needed a good talking-to every day. We had to, otherwise things would get out of hand. Do you get the picture? I couldn't stand those moods of hers. I refused because it was nonsensical and went back to my divan.

'In my room the light was dim, and it was cool, unlike outside, and I had started to read *The Monk*. Do you know the novel?'

'Naturally,' Manny said and smacked his lips. Solly commented that he was no novel-reading schoolgirl from the city, so I poked him with my elbow.

'My father had had it sent directly to me from a London bookshop for me to practise my English, and the very next day I couldn't tear myself away from it. I didn't even go down for meals. I just stayed shut up in my room with the book. I was reading the best part, where Ambrosio and Matilda use black magic to overpower the innocent Antonia. Their plan was to violate and murder her –'

'It looks as if I'll have to start reading after all,' Solly butted in.

'Except that Mama', I continued, 'was so furious that I had refused to carry out her order she seized the book from my pillow, slammed it shut, opened the window and threw it out into the moat. Can you imagine? That moat had protected the building in the days when Stránov Castle served a defensive purpose. I started to berate my mother, telling her that she was not to take such liberties with me any more, but at that moment my father appeared in the doorway, and I immediately shut up. Then I went off to the stables.

'Everything there was in perfect order, of course, the horses currycombed, fed and watered. The groom just happened to be leaving, and he told me in the doorway that a milkmaid by the name of Dorota was waiting for me at the back. He said she apparently had permission, and from the look on his face the permission probably didn't come from him. I found it a bit odd because we had recently dismissed some Dorota because she had been up to something. And here she was back again. So I went to see what it was all about.'

'The right decision,' said Solly. 'Was she pretty?'

'No. But don't rush me. She was squatting on a stool, sucking a blade of grass and was in no hurry to be brought to heel by some nobleman's brat. She could have been a year or two older than me, but in those days I wasn't able to judge.'

'What was her hair like?' Solly wanted to know.

'Like a gypsy's, tied with a red fairground ribbon. And her skin was suntanned. She was no beauty. Her thick eyebrows were faintly joined above her nose, and she was heavily built, with rounded shoulders and breasts like two pumpkins. Dreadful.'

'Dreadful,' Manny echoed and wiped the perspiration from his forehead with his handkerchief.

'She had a backside like a Steiermark gelding and tree trunks for legs. Her belted smock only reached her knees, and over it she wore a black apron that had white marks on it as if she had been rubbing against a whitewashed wall. And she also had no shoes, and her feet were filthy.'

Manny sighed. He was hunched opposite us and in fact slightly below us, as he was heavier than the two of us together and was placing the carriage springs under serious strain. He picked up the hat that lay on his lap and started to wave it in front of his face. 'You have all the luck, Addie,' he said, fidgeting on his seat, as if it was even more uncomfortable than before. 'You always had more interesting experiences than me.'

'You've nothing to envy.' I took a swig from the hip flask that Solly proffered me. It was Jamaica rum. 'I asked Dorota what she wanted of me, and she didn't reply. She brazenly pushed past me and led one of the mares out of the stable. The horse was already saddled and bridled, and all I could do was ask her who had given her permission. She simply said, "The person who gives the orders around here." Totally unbecoming, I'm sure you'll agree, and it went from bad to worse. Outside she mounted the horse and rode out of the small gate into the park. Except that no one was allowed to ride in the park or, rather, not in the front part that was specially laid out. Anyone who wanted to ride in the game preserve had to skirt around the park. And that silly goose who didn't even have any right to ride our horses was breaking the rules.'

'So you had to go after her,' Solly laughed. 'A military stratagem.'

'I'm afraid you're right,' I nodded, 'and the rookie didn't see through it. I had them saddle me a horse, a shorter wide-haunched chestnut mare who didn't look as she had any devious intentions. As you know, I've no great love for horses, but I tried to ride at least moderately fast, and the mare obeyed like clockwork. I rode into the park. I saw Dorota a short distance ahead riding among the trees and apparently waiting for me. I called to her to get off our English lawn straight away, but she urged her horse on and rode deeper into the park. I lost patience. I dug my heels into the chestnut and galloped after the girl. I caught up with her by the stream – mostly because her horse was nibbling ash-tree shoots while she stood in the stream washing her grubby apron. Her smock was hitched up and tucked into her belt, so as not to get wet. And as she stood there bent over in the water she asked me whether I didn't want to dip something, too.'

'Which you did, of course,' Solly said with certainty.

I shook my head. 'I had no idea what I should want, even though she offered it so blatantly. I told her off for being so insolent and breaking the rules, and then I ordered her leave the park with her mount. Then I sat down on the bank and waited for her to do as I had asked.'

'But she didn't,' Manny guessed.

'Of course not. The bed of the stream was all stony, but she didn't mind. She waded over to me, grabbed me by the legs and tugged. There was nothing on the bank for me to catch on to apart from moss and grass, so I slipped downwards. She was immensely strong. I fell on my back into the water, and my back hit the bottom. I don't know how I managed to get up, but I do recall how cold the water was. I thought that Dorota would be horrified at what she had done, but I was wrong. She laughed in my face, and I can still picture those big yellow teeth. I was outraged and gave her a slap around the face and then another one so that she started to cry. I expect she would have liked to have hit me back, but she didn't dare go that far, after all. I felt dreadful, but what was I to do? I climbed out of the stream and left her there. I led both horses back to the stables.'

'I thought she would seduce you,' Solly commented disappointedly.

'She should have gone about it different way then,' I retorted. 'That evening my father called me into his study and made me recount the entire incident with Dorota. Then he told me to stay in the room, and he went off to find Mama. I heard a loud cry. The row lasted at least an hour. I read Goethe's *Faust* with my hands over my ears and regretted that I didn't have my English novel with me. Mama came in. She was white as a sheet and her hair was a mess. I was expecting *Faust* to be thrown out the window, like *The Monk* before him, so I immediately handed it to her. She stood there motionless with her hands shaking and said, "Just in case your father decides to give his side of the story, I want you listen first to what I have to say. He used to run after that Dorota, you see. He had engaged her at the castle as a stable maid, and in the spring he even taught her to ride. I got to hear about and told him to end it. He obeyed me and dismissed her, but he had only managed to do without her three weeks before he was secretly back with her in the village again. I saw that there was nothing else I could do, so I summoned her back to the castle and proposed to her to exchange the old one for the young one, and I paid her a lot of money. I didn't think your father would come to his senses when he found out, but I thought he wouldn't vie for the favours of some silly goose with his son who is old enough not to spend his time buried in books, when all's said and done. And you went and spoilt it, like everything else." Nice of her, wasn't it? Then she left the room and banged the door behind her. Since then she and father haven't had much to say to each other. How long is it now? Thirteen years.'

'Oh heavens,' Manny sighed. 'And I was so looking forward to Stránov.'

'Don't worry. Mama will spoil you like one of her own, and you won't even be able to tell that we have a non-speaking home at the castle. It'll be fine.'

I wasn't so sure, though.

'That's mothers for you,' said Solly and looked out the window at a field overgrown with weeds. Dusk was falling. Nobody spoke for the rest of the journey.

It was late evening when we arrived. The castle was dark. Light shone only from the windows in the dining-room, downstairs in the kitchen and the adjacent corridors. I had expected my parents to have lit torches to illuminate the famous Renaissance arcades, which, in addition to the old hexagonal tower, are the most significant monument of our modest seat, but our visit probably wasn't important enough.

We could smell the stench of the animals and the manured fields. I tried to hold my breath but started to cough and was unable to stop.

There was nothing for it. I reached into my pocket and took out the little bottle that my cousin had given me. I swallowed the white pill, and, from memory, as I was still without my watch and slowly coming to accept that it was lost for good, I counted the seconds, minutes and a whole quarter of an hour until it finally started to work and I was finally able to breathe calmly the night air full of its vulgar countryside odours without danger of coughing. Solly woke up and held out his hand, so I tipped out one of the mysterious globules from the bottle. I was curious to see what it would do to him. He washed it down with rum from his hip flask. It was a bold thing to do.

We drove through the main gate, which had been left open for us, and the wheels of the carriage clattered on the stone bridge over the moat. The bridge was hidden in darkness. Such economies were a novelty for me – to penny-pinch when it came to pine torches, which always used to light up the bridge when we were expecting guests . . . I felt a trifle ashamed in front of my friends. But as soon as we entered the courtyard the butler was already waiting to welcome us, together with servants carrying lanterns.

It was an unexpected pleasure to alight from the carriage and stretch my limbs in the night air. Solly jumped down from the step and staggered. Then he raised his head, sniffed and said that his stay in the country was already doing him good. Manny leant on his stick, as if his knees had suddenly lost their strength. He looked around emotionally at the places where we used to play together as children every summer.

We were led into the English hallway, which looked ancient but which was precisely five years old. It was created during the last reconstruction and was paid for out of the money made from the sale of the Prague palace, and it was out of character with the castle's neo-Renaissance appearance. But Mama wanted an English hallway, and now she had it. A few Gothic walls had to be demolished in order to create it. Now there was plenty of space. Manny was enthusiastic about the changes. 'It's a Neuschwanstein in miniature,' he gushed.

As soon as our coats and hats had been taken Mama came out to greet us. It was good of her to wait up for us so late into the night. I embraced her, and then she wanted to embrace Manny, for which he had to bend down to her. She expressed astonishment at how he had grown, and when she saw how much it embarrassed him she turned to Solly. I introduced him as my best friend, the owner of a millinery and drapery shop in Celetná Street, and when she said, 'My son has spoken most highly of you', he kissed her hand. Unfortunately he then kissed the other hand, too, and forgot to release them both until I took them away from him.

I knew she wouldn't have any objections to Solly's origins. The first thing that interested her was property, then social standing and only after that race. Mama is the most modern of countesses in the country. Besides, a landowner by the name of Taufer rented half of the castle from my parents, and a better example of a *nouveau riche* would be hard to find.

Solly bowed lower than a footman to her and promised that he would be her most helpful servant, and he increased his favour with her when he complimented her on her elaborate hairstyle and the reddish hue of her hair. This was odd because my mother's brown and considerably greying hair didn't have any hint of gingerness. I wondered what Solly actually saw. She told him that flattery was wasted on her because she was fifty-four, but she wasn't ashamed of it, she said, and, in fact, she felt much younger, particularly when she went for her morning drive.

I tried to maintain an obliging and cheerful expression.

We sat down informally at one end of the enormous table, Mama opposite Manny who spoke enthusiastically about the castle and assured her that the rebuilding had been to the good and that it was now more beautiful here than before, and he just couldn't recognize it, however much he tried. We were grateful for the marrowbone broth that Mama had prepared with the cook, adding to it her speciality – home-made noodles from Mrs Rettigová's cookbook, which my companions could not praise highly enough. Then came pâté with fresh bread and pickled vegetables, and, not that she needed to, Mama apologized for not knowing what time to expect us as the trains from Prague were often late. My friends stuffed themselves as if they hadn't eaten for a week. 'It's the fresh ozone,' Manny declared and crammed one half-slice of bread after another into his mouth. It made me feel slightly faint, as a result of which I drank more. When the carafe of wine was empty I called the footman, who was usually to be found in the adjacent pantry for the preparation of cold dishes. Mama told us that the other servants, who had waited up for us, had been sent to bed, and there would be plenty of time tomorrow. After all, we must be tired after our journey.

On this occasion my patience snapped. Had it been ten years earlier I would have given in and gone to bed and been glad to have a warming-pan at the bottom of it. Now I refused to be manipulated by my mother, so I pushed back my chair and requested the key from her. She gave me it, and I went to the cellar on my own.

I anticipated a nostalgic pilgrimage to the depths beneath the castle, full of memories of my youth when I used to take advantage of an unlocked door and set off on expeditions to the cellar in search of wine. I was thus thoroughly spoilt, while ignorant of the fact that the vine plague had been raging for years and good wine was worth its weight in gold. Then my father caught me at it and made sure the cellar was kept locked.

The outcome of my descent was far from romantic, however. My trip to the subterranean space hewn out of the marlstone rock at the beginning of the thirteenth century helped clear my head but aggravated my breathing. The cellar wasn't particularly humid, but the centuries of dust, which no one had cleared out of the dark nooks and crannies or from the frame of the wooden staircase, induced coughing more rapidly than Prague when enshrouded in industrial fog. The magical pill lost its power down there all too rapidly, it seemed to me. Miracles in Stránov – out of the question!

I walked among the barrels and racks with a handkerchief over my face and an oil lamp in front of me in my right hand. My eyes were streaming, and the lamp burnt miserably, so I reached out blindly for two bottles and then took another one. That would suffice.

Upstairs I felt better, but when she saw the bottles Mama started to protest, saying she might have known I would go for the best wine.

I couldn't believe my ears, so I pretended not to hear and started to open the bottles one after another.

'It's the sweetest blend of the '93 vintage,' Mama lamented. 'It's not ready for tasting before Advent the year after next – or even the following New Year –'

'Permit me to correct you, Countess,' said Solly, coming to my rescue after studying the faded ink of the label. 'The '93 vintage should have been drunk two years ago because it has no potential. Don't you recall how it rained the entire month of September that year? Not to drink it would be a sin.' It was a masterful piece of bluff. Mama managed only a gesture of resignation and went off to her room.

Perfect. I shook Solly by the hand. Manny looked disconcerted, but then he shook his hand, too. We could drink and chat at our ease. The country was finally smiling on us.

We got on to politics. Solly declared that he quite liked what was happening in Prague, even though he only regarded himself as one-third Czech, and I said I didn't like it in the least, that the whole thing was eyewash and that I was ashamed of what the Czech representatives were up to in parliament; but for their boorish behaviour nothing need have happened in Prague, even though it was probably the result of secret-police provocation and had very little to do with some language law or other.

Manny shook his head, and suddenly there was a look of utter dismay on his face. He said that he didn't believe it of the police because if he did he would feel he was in prison and would have to consider emigrating to America.

'Thousands are leaving,' Solly remarked, and Manny fell silent.

Solly looked at me for a moment, and with a vague smirk he said he had a surprise for me, if I cared to hear it.

'Surprise me then,' I challenged him.

'All right. A certain pharmacist came and asked me about you.'

'So what?'

'Nothing. That's all. He wanted to know what I knew about you and what your attitude was to our government in Vienna.'

'It could hardly have been of interest to him,' Manny commented. 'The nobility aren't involved. What could he care about Addie's views?'

'This one cares a lot,' said Solly, without the trace of a smile now. 'There are rumours going around Prague that he may not be very clever, but he is able to find out a thing or two from people and then he runs off with it to . . . to his contact person, let us say. What he lacks in discretion he makes up for in diligence.'

I was extremely sceptical. 'Come off it! An informer who is quite well known? I know nothing of the sort about him, and I pay no heed to slander. He's my pharmacist, a harmless half-educated oaf with a blinkered outlook on the world who shuffles home, keeping close to the wall, and tots up his profits – rather like a dentist or birth attendant. I wouldn't suspect him of underhandedness.'

Solly scratched the pale-coloured stubble beneath his chin and gave Manny a sidelong glance, as if judging whether to continue the conversation. He apparently decided that he should. 'Forgive me, Addie, but although you have a sufficiently broad outlook on the world you still behave like a donkey with a carrot dangled in front of it, totally oblivious to everything around it. It just keeps on following it, even though it'll never catch up with it. Except that in your case it's not a carrot dangling in front of you but a juicy bit of cunt.'

'Pah! That's rich coming from you,' I snapped.

'How could you know anything about informers?' Solly continued.

'All you do is look down on people with that monocle that you don't even need. You don't express a view on anything, and you don't get involved. It really is a mystery why the poor sod asked about you at all.'

That tone of his didn't put me out. It usually made its appearance when Solly was in his cups.

'I've read the *Bestia triumphans* manifesto,' I objected, 'and I agree with it unreservedly. And now I intend to save that house in Jewry by buying it if I manage to get some cash. Is that so very little? I'm not interested in politics, so I'm doing this, at least.'

'It's preferable to your being interested in politics. The Old Czechs are finished anyway, and you'd hardly sympathize with the opposition.'

'So what's it all about? Who'd be asking questions about me of all people? And why?'

'It's on account of your papa, Addie,' declared Manny, whose presence I had completely forgotten. I was so bowled over by his assertion that I couldn't open my mouth.

'Do you have some information on this, My Lord?' Solly asked.

Manny shrugged. 'Only from my parents. They are not pleased that Addie's father is involved with the pro-Czech cause. They don't understand it and say it's not fitting.'

My head swam, and the wine turned sour in my throat. 'Father supported the Old Czechs, but so what? Nowadays he hasn't the slightest interest in politics as far as I know. He certainly doesn't talk about it.'

'Not with you,' Solly nodded. 'But look here, that pharmacist knows something, albeit from entirely different sources, of course. See what a broad outlook you have?'

I felt sick and had no wish to continue the conversation, but Solly carried on. 'He mentioned some letters bearing Count Arco's seal, and therefore the censor has no access to them. But the police always find a way, don't they? They cunningly opened one of the letters and discovered in it some lines that could land your father in gaol– such as for breaking the law about incitement against the monarchy and his imperial majesty . . . Your papa is in correspondence with radicals, Addie. And when they need to deliver something to him they send their man by train. The post office isn't to be trusted, is it?'

I couldn't cope any more and wanted to get away, but I wasn't in the least tired. 'It's mere fantasy,' I said and reached into my pocket for my watch, which was goodness knows where.

'Possibly. That's your hope, isn't it? For nothing to happen, nothing to change, just so that you can fornicate in peace with your girl, and when you get tired of her you can find another.'

That made me see red. 'And what about you? What do you do apart from sneaking a look at your fine ladies from the back of the shop? Mind you, it could be that you're a spy these days, recruited by the prying ignoramus from the Three Moors pharmacy.'

'It would take more than that to offend me, Addie, and I'm aware that you're cross. But I hope you believe me about that pharmacist. I simply wanted to warn you.'

'I believe you.'

'Thanks. Oughtn't we to go to bed?'

'That's the best idea of all,' Manny agreed and got up from the table.

When I wished him good night he shifted his gaze.

I led my friends to the guests' quarters and then went to my bedroom. My former bedroom. The wardrobe and the chest of drawers remained, but the decorated writing-desk had gone and the four-poster had been replaced by a simple bed with just a headboard. All my old watercolours and gouaches that I painted in the castle park had been taken down from the walls. The cross was still there but not a single novel remained on the cupboard beneath it where my books were once stood in a row. Instead there now sat a smiling porcelain Buddha from my father's collection of chinoiserie.

Before I went to bed I turned the statuette to face the wall. Then I crept under the quilt. The bed was warm from the warming-pan left there by the maid. I covered only the lower half of my body and pushed the pillow on to the floor, lest the down cause me to cough. I finally closed my eyes and waited to see what images would emerge from the darkness.

It was quiet in the castle, a quiet such as Prague had not known for centuries. Somewhere in its depths sat my father, whom I scarcely knew now, writing something important most likely. After all, he didn't even come to say hello.

VIII

Fresh Air

Helena Tauferová

Someone set in motion the pendulum of the grandfather clock in the passage. After allowing me to have a long sleep it struck ten, and even the castle guests had to get up. I leant over the window-sill and spat into the castle moat, then looked to the right where the road gleamed white between the trees. I caught sight of Mama crossing the road in high boots and giving orders to the steward, who made no attempt to discuss them with her but simply wanted her to leave him alone. I drew my head in from the window like a worm into its crevice and started to dress for breakfast.

My father greeted me affably albeit somewhat coolly and pointed me to a chair at the other end of the table. Manny and Solly were already seated on opposite sides of the table and sideways on to us. I had a feeling that my arrival came as a great relief to them – as if at last they could relax and enjoy their food. My father had finished his breakfast a long time before and had come in for a coffee, but it did not occur to him to join in the informal conversation, although it is exactly what he ought to have done. He was inscrutable.

When I had settled in my chair and ordered Ceylon tea I realized that seated among us was a conspirator against the Austro-Hungarian monarchy. His hair was thinning slightly at the temples, but he still had plenty of it, and he combed it forward in the old-fashioned way. His face was more lined than before, particularly his forehead, and the bags under his eyes were like two wineskins. He was sixty-six. Surprisingly he didn't look much older than Mama, I noted with satisfaction.

Solly was clearly feeling better. 'As someone with a great deal of experience, My Lord, how long do you think the state of emergency will last in Prague?'

'Not long, Mr Weiss,' my father replied, evidently pleased. 'A very short time, in fact. These days they can't afford to do the things they used to. Nevertheless, things are building up to a major crisis, in my opinion. And the monarchy will be shaken to such a degree that it won't be easy for it to get over it. Maybe it never will, alas.'

Solly and I exchanged glances and refrained from commenting on my father's words. Manny blushed, and beads of sweat stood out on his forehead. He raised the gilt coffee cup to his lips but didn't drink, as if something had got stuck in his throat and he couldn't swallow.

'Forgive me, Uncle,' he said, clearing his throat and putting down his cup, 'but how can you know that?'

'Sorry, Manny,' my father said, looking at him sharply, 'how can I know what?'

'That the state of siege, I mean state of emergency . . . After all, it's so shameful. And dangerous. What's the point of this rampage? Our countries have lived in harmony and peace for so many years. And what did I see now in Prague? Thugs and rabble-rousers setting fire to Jews' shops and brawling on the square. Thank you very much.'

'You ought to write speeches for statesmen, Manny,' Father said drily. 'But I can understand your annoyance at those disturbances. You welcomed the counter-measures taken by the state, didn't you? Establishing order at the price of curtailed freedom. That's your opinion, and I respect it. A lot of people believe that the disturbances couldn't have been solely due to some language law, that it was a flimsy pretext for a minor bureaucratic revolution. But I explain to those people that language is a major issue. It's not just a means of communication. That's something you should grasp the next time you think seriously about something. Because it is precisely a thinking tool. How is it with you, dear boy? What language do you think in? Czech or German?'

I gazed at my father, and he was a stranger to me. Only now did I start to believe what Solly had told me the previous night.

'I don't know,' Manny replied, taken aback. 'I think in both languages. It depends about what. At present, as I'm here, I expect Czech predominates. Apart from which I want to express myself correctly. But sometimes a word just won't come.'

'You see. The bureaucrats who rioted against giving Czech equal status would have to be familiar with the correct words, in the same way that previously people had to know the right German expressions when they wanted something from an official body. Those who used to be in a position of superiority rejected it by definition. Equality means the loss of some privileges and the acquisition of new ones. You don't have to fear it, nor do those chumps who go out into the street and cause affray. When I say the state of emergency won't last long, what I mean is that the government will give in to the German faction and introduction of the law will go on being delayed *ad absurdam*. Maybe I'm wrong. It's my privilege. Does my answer suffice?'

'Yes, thank you,' Manny whispered with a mortified expression.

I closed my eyes. How could I ever be my father's equal? All I would like to know . . .

I overheard Manny saying, 'I know what you mean. It's just that I regret the constant division into "us" and "them". I hate it. Like our two families that don't talk to each other – I'm really sorry about that. But our ties still exist, don't they? They can't be wiped out!'

'They can be muddied, not wiped out,' my father nodded, then finished his coffee and stood up. 'But mud eventually settles to the bottom, so don't hang your head, lad. You used to be jollier.'

But Manny had no intention of stopping; perhaps he wasn't able to. 'What am I supposed to be jolly about, Uncle? I thought we were a family, so why such coolness of a sudden? I can't reconcile myself to it. Everywhere I'm met with polite coolness and covert enmity.'

I watched with astonishment as tears welled in my cousin's eyes, then, after being held back for a moment by his long boyish eyelashes, they slowly and symmetrically trickled down his fleshy cheeks into the unbecoming bristles that he had forgotten to shave.

'That's the way we Czechs are,' my father declared impatiently and in a slightly acid tone. 'Thank you for reminding me of it, Manny. I'll sit down and write a letter to your father to let him know that you called on us at Stránov and that you are getting on excellently. Do you agree? And tomorrow, when the state of emergency is lifted in Prague, you can go off and have a good time, just like Adam. You can enjoy the whores and other – admittedly tamer but also pleasant – benefits of our provincial metropolis. Or, if you like, you can stay here with the Countess and me and bid adieu to Adam and Mr Weiss, since they are sure to return to Prague as soon as they are able because our local girls don't count for them and won't sleep with them, just so as you know, and by tomorrow the two of them are certain to be bent on some sort of . . . amusement, which they cannot be without for a moment. Correct me if I'm wrong.'

I had never before heard anyone be given their marching orders in such an acerbic fashion. I couldn't understand what my father had against Manny. My cousin seemingly got the message and stood up.

I expect it occurred to my father that he had perhaps let himself get carried away, because he altered his tone and suggested that we make the most of what Stránov had to offer while we were there and said he would have them saddle us some horses. Then he went out.

Solly gave a low whistle. 'So to sum up: we have been informed that we are to sling our hooks tomorrow, and while we remain here we ought to take ourselves off to the woods and break our necks by falling from our mounts. I'm beginning to get a taste for the country.'

I asked them to excuse my father; I couldn't imagine what had ruffled his feathers. To show he wasn't offended Manny declared that a ride was an excellent idea.

We agreed to meet at ten thirty outside the stable and to wear the lightest clothing for a sunny day, seeing that Solly and I had left our riding outfits in Prague. I chose my travelling trousers and shoes, the farmer's-style linen shirt that I always wear when I'm pretending to Mother that I have an interest in running the estate and a short coat. Around my neck I tied a large blue neckerchief that I intended to use to protect my mouth and nose from the stench of horses and the kicked-up dust and dirt. I wondered for a moment whether to take one of Hoffmann's pills but decided not to. I was not going to risk my horse splitting in two beneath my backside, and a state of torpor in the saddle could make me the butt of ridicule.

I took the side staircase down to the courtyard. Manny and Solly were already standing outside the stable, Manny in a riding outfit that was bursting at the seams, Solly in travelling attire. They were inspecting the horses, an angular stallion and a slender mare, and as soon as I whooped at them they mounted their horses as if they couldn't wait and trotted off. It wasn't very polite of them, but then they were not my guests but my parents'. So I didn't complain.

My knees were shaking slightly. I gingerly swung up on to the remaining mare and placed my unsuitable footwear into the stirrups. Suddenly I was inappropriately high up. The old groom held the horse's halter and handed me the reins and my crop encouragingly, but there was a dubious, malevolent glint in his eyes.

'I'll ride with you, sir. We don't want you taking a tumble the first day.'

It would not have been particularly tactful to challenge him to a duel, so I squeezed the creature's flanks and winced when it set off after its companions and mine. I pulled the neckerchief over my nose, and with all the dignity I could muster steered the animal's four legs through the castle gateway. I managed it. As soon as I was beyond the gate I tried to relax in the saddle and persuade the horse to canter. Neither of us was very successful.

My friends were waiting for me in the field below the grove. I could see fuzzily that my cousin was standing in his stirrups like General Laudon observing a battle, and he was pointing at something.

I looked in that direction and realized with bitterness that I was too short-sighted to see that far. I saw a greyish-white cloud passing below the greenish-grey line of the horizon. Nevertheless, I was able to guess what had attracted him because the scene was so captivating and would never disappear from my memory: just beyond the village above the valley the black line of the railway viaduct with a train puffing along it and letting out clouds of steam. Far behind the train the clouds of steam would lose shape and blend in with the bright, indefinably coloured radiance of the sky. When I was a small boy I used to see it several times a day in the summer months.

I rode towards them, determined to come to a faultless halt. I tugged at the reins and the horse stopped obediently, albeit rather too abruptly for my taste. I started to topple forward but managed to stop myself by clinging on to the horse's neck. I sat stiffly upright in the saddle as if I had swallowed a reed. About a hundred larks were singing in the topmost branches of the birches and rowan trees, totally ignoring us, and I just hoped that if one of us were targeted by them it wouldn't be me. The train tooted twice and disappeared, but only then did the noise of its wheels on the high bridge reach our ears. The smoke rose above the meadows and woods and blended into the clouds above our estate.

'Isn't it splendid?' Manny enthused, turning his head from side to side like a pigeon. 'That scent – it's exactly the same as when I was a child. Everything moves on, but some things don't change. It's fantastic.'

I sniffed, too, and, lo and behold, there was no irritant on the breeze and I was able to breathe freely. Some relief at last. We rode out of the shade of the trees and slowly headed along a balk towards the signpost by the forest.

'I read a romantic story in some magazine', Solly said loudly for us to hear and tipped his bowler hat back, 'in which a young, good-looking and unattached nobleman – a count I think it was – was riding along on a clear day like today through a lush landscape such as we see all around us now, when all of a sudden a black horse came riding towards him with a most beautiful young woman seated side-saddle on its back. Similar, if I'm not mistaken' – he shielded his gaze with his hand – 'to the one riding towards us now.'

We stopped at the crossroads. I could make out two smudges on the winding field path somewhere ahead of us. I couldn't guess the distance as my eyes could just about see as far as the ridge, but I had the impression that the blotches were growing bigger, fluttering and jumping about like mirages in shimmering air on a hot day. Then the sound of hoofbeats reached our ears.

A man and woman, in riding attire to be found in the fashion magazines for ladies and gentlemen: hers new and costly; his slightly the worse for wear. We made room for them to pass, but the woman reined in her horse and the man followed suit.

I realized that I knew her from the days when she lived on a farm down in the village. In those days she had been a squat little girl who went about in city girls' clothes which were always grubby. How long ago had that been? Ten years?

The transformation had me gaping. But for the shape of her brown eyes and thin lips I wouldn't have recognized her. Her face, her neck and her entire figure seemed to have been stretched on the rack; there was no trace of corpulence or grubbiness. She seemed to me too thin, which might have been because of the corset that gave her a wasp waist, but she looked rather tall, although it was hard to judge while she was on horseback. I had to admit to myself that she was quite pretty. Beneath her low, flat-crowned hat with its turned-up brim her lively brown eyes roamed about, while her shiny chestnut-brown hair, intricately combed back and gathered above the nape of her neck, formed a majestic canopy around her head which are liable to be cut asunder by the lower branches of the trees in the game reserve if the rider did not watch out.

Pretty, certainly, but not my type. The chin and nose were just a bit sharp, the eyes rather too close together. Beneath the green riding jacket it was hard to detect much by way of curves, bearing in mind that a corset can swell the average-sized bosom. Her complexion was perfect, however. It seems her father ordered her French cosmetics directly from Paris. He could afford it.

I greeted her with polite indifference. I searched my memory in vain for her Christian name, so I introduced her to Manny and Solly as the daughter of our good neighbour and tenant of half of Stránov, farmer Taufer. The girl attempted a sort of curtsy in the saddle, which backfired because she almost fell off the horse, and the blood rushed to her features. We pretended not to notice. Manny and Solly leant far out of their saddles to kiss her hand but did not endanger her stability on the horse's back. At last I remembered her name but was unable to avoid a slight *faux pas*. 'The Taufers' Ellie – Miss Helena Tauferová, I mean,' I corrected myself at the last moment.

She smiled and nodded politely with eyes downcast. She introduced us to her companion, a certain Fridrich Sova from Chuchle near Prague who taught showy horse-riding. He did not impress me in the least. He had a foppish simper, and beneath his nose he wore precisely the same moustache that I had previously sported. And the hat on his head was only a slightly different shade of grey than my own. I stared at this low-born copy of myself, and I didn't like it one bit.

Helena said, 'I was away for a long time, My Lord, in London. Hadn't you heard? And before that in Reims and Regensburg. Papa wants me to speak foreign languages and be well-informed. But, to tell you the truth, I prefer to be here. I feel at home here, and I don't want to travel any more. I'll help Papa with the farm. I know how to keep accounts, even how to do double-entry book-keeping.'

'You certainly have the best qualifications for marrying a loafer,' Solly laughed, 'and no doubt you'll find your way into the right kind of society. As, indeed, you already have,' he said, encompassing us with a sweeping gesture.

'Things are not that bad yet,' Sova commented sourly.

Silence fell. Helena, her face and neck all red, shifted her gaze quickly from one to another while unable to look any of us in the eye.

'I hope we'll see each other again soon,' she said to no one in particular, her gaze fixed on her horse's ears. Then she urged it forward, and soon her green jacket had blended into the mass of hornbeams.

'Gentlemen,' said the fop from Chuchle, raising his had, 'I'd better catch up with the young lady. The branches are very sharp over there, and what use would a one-eyed book-keeper be?'

Solly grinned, but I wasn't sure what to make of his ineptitude, and Manny blushed as red as Helena earlier. If Sova had not dashed off after her a slap in the face might have ensued.

So Manny lashed out at Solly. 'That wasn't called for, was it? She didn't do anything to you. You know nothing about her. Why did you insult her?'

'Because she wants to get married,' Solly snapped back.

'They all want to.'

'But this one is offering herself.'

'But every one of them offers herself at some moment, for Christ's sake!' Manny yelled so vociferously that Solly had to wipe the spittle from his face, and I was obliged to rein in my startled mare. I waited to see which of them would strike the first blow.

Solly said calmly, 'It looks as if she has managed to enchant you, Herr von Zinneberg, instead of Adam. But I'd advise you to leave well alone, for your own good. What she has beneath her skirts is exactly what you'll get in Prague, except that it will cost you a thousand times less and you can change it at any time. Isn't that so, Adam? Tell your cousin.'

But Manny had already composed himself. The purple gradually drained from his face, and his voice became softer. 'She was an amiable and pleasant young lady. She simply wanted to converse. She just said what she was capable of, didn't she? She wouldn't be out of place in high society –'

'Of course,' Solly butted in. 'Her grasping papa is schooling her for it very capably, and he can't wait for her to take over the running of Stránov. Isn't that so, Adam?'

'I expect so,' I had to agree. 'Her father's interests are all too obvious. Sorry.'

Manny looked as if I had driven a dagger up under this ribcage. 'I intend to go back,' he said turning his horse and riding away.

'The countryside and its unexpected intrigues,' Solly commented with a grin, adding that he felt like a more vigorous ride around the forest and asking if I would join him. I didn't feel at all like a fast ride, and, in fact, I had had enough of horses, so we parted company, and I returned slowly to the castle, following the receding figure of my discomfited relative.

Mama and our neighbour were sitting in the courtyard under the arcade in wrought-iron armchairs shaded by a large yellow parasol. They were perusing some papers, a new rent agreement or something of the sort, in which I hadn't the slightest interest. It didn't even occur to me to go over to them. I simply raised my hand, and in my haste I noticed that they looked startled, as if they had seen a ghost. Mama called something out to me, but I didn't catch it and pretended not to hear. Manny was goodness knows where. I went in through the service entrance, ran up the spiral staircase at the rear and when I reached my bedroom I made straight for the little bottle of pills. What appeared through the thickly ribbed glass to be at least three or four tablets turned out to be only fragments, which were damp and sticking to the sides of the bottle. So I treated myself to my last dose of the white miracle, stuck my pipe, tobacco and matches in my pockets and took a peek out of the door. The air was clean, and my breathing was fine. I was calm and at ease with the world and my family. Things were now all right at Stránov.

In the cellar I reached for one of the bottles. It offered itself *sotto voce* when I ran my impatient fingers over it. So I hid it under my coat, went to the kitchen for a cut-crystal goblet and took the iron corkscrew down from its hook.

Thus armed, I went up to the top of the main tower. It was cool beneath the stone casque-like roof. I bolted the trapdoor in the floor and lay down on a divan of mouldering leather, which my father used to have in his study before he exchanged it for a new one. I filled a pipe and lit it. The smoke curled up to the pointed roof and clung to the stone wall. Reading the label I found I couldn't have chosen a better wine: a sweet '87 Sylvaner from Alsace.

That was the year of my twentieth birthday, and I was intending to enter the diplomatic corps of the Austro-Hungarian monarchy. Ten years later, ten years that slipped by so fast that they felt like only one, I was still 'making up my mind', but I had realized long ago that it was too late. My state of health would not permit me undertake major journeys.

I don't know what the time was when someone thumped on the trapdoor from below and wrenched me out of dreamless sleep. I slid back the bolt and raised the trapdoor. Solly was trudging up the tower steps. He looked around him and started to give me a ticking off: they had all spent hours searching for me, and the Countess had declared that her son was behaving in a cool even hostile fashion and had called her husband to account. He had left for Prague, however, without telling anyone anything apart from the coachman who had taken him to the station. He had apparently received some telegram, but no one had seen it.

'And Ellie the book-keeper', Solly added, glancing at the remains of the wine against the narrow window and then drinking it straight out of the bottle, 'was apparently intending to canter to the castle along with us, do you mind. Your Mama and Taufer were totally bowled over when we each returned separately and couldn't comprehend how we had left her in the woods with that dubious individual who is teaching her to ride. She was afraid there had been some contretemps. She wasn't far wrong, was she?'

I had to admit that the assessment he made of Miss Tauferová near the woods had been accurate. She certainly hadn't dreamt up such a romantic encounter on her own, poor thing.

I told Solly to pack as we would be leaving by the evening train in spite of the state of emergency.

But, as usual, he was a step ahead of me. 'I've already done it. And

I've made peace with your cousin, in case you were worried. We can leave for Prague whenever we feel like it. They've lifted the state of emergency – yes sooner than expected, exactly as your father predicted. But we won't take Manny with us.'

'How so?' I said in surprise.

'Do you mind? When I informed the Countess that we wouldn't be staying any longer, she started to persuade him to remain here as long as he liked. You look surprised.'

I nodded. 'That's an understatement.'

When we had settled ourselves in the carriage late that afternoon and I was waving goodbye to Mama I remembered that I had intended to ask for money for the new accommodation, but the state of emergency had intervened, together with Manny, whom she had so much been looking forward to see, not to mention Solly's confidential information about my father, so that I had forgotten my original intention. Now Manny was standing at Mama's side, as a sort of better, bigger and more devoted substitute for me. He was smoking a cigar and turning his head every now and then in the direction of Helena Tauferová, who was standing in the shade beneath the arcade dressed in an intricate costume that was purely city wear, as if she herself were about to set off on a journey. But she obviously wasn't planning to depart but simply waiting to see the back of our carriage. When I raised my arm in greeting she pretended not to see it.

IX

New Times

A Murder in the House

I spent first day after my return with Gita. I could hardly wait for her body, but maybe it was the accumulation of the tension at Stránov that left its mark in the form of red wheals on her bottom and thighs. And I would have happily given her a second helping. How can one distinguish the positive and its negation in lovemaking? A certain doctor by the name of Freud, an academic from Vienna, studies and analyses mental disorders in relation to the sex life, and, according to an advertisement I read, one can make an appointment with him any time. Vienna is a bit too far.

To make things up to Gita I had a three-course dinner sent from Lacronni's, but I didn't hang around. I freshened myself up at the washbasin and noticed in the mirror that I had a healthily ruddy skin tone. Well, well, a short stay in the country and enjoyment between the sheets had managed to perk me up somewhat.

That evening I went fencing. Solly didn't turn up. I expect he was fornicating with one of my former girlfriends. I don't think I'll ever understand his lack of discrimination in such matters. But there were plenty of willing duffers with itching sword hands among the Sokols. I dispatched them one after another with easy hits, and I said to myself that it wasn't fair on them; perhaps I should fence with them left-handed to spare them.

We were noticed by a senior official of the association, a fencing teacher by the name of Poche, whom the youngsters addressed as 'Brother Master', which I found laughable. He cancelled his other symbolic bouts and proposed sword combat with me. Oh-la-la. He looked sure of himself. His magnificent moustache was the picture of virility. So I agreed and sent one of the lads to the armoury. The meritorious Sokol had his weapon with him, and while I was waiting he practised in front of a mirror. I had to admit to that he did not lack a certain agility. He asked me whether we might not fight freestyle – unrestricted by the lines or distance rules that had been established for safety and easier scoring. We were to move freely around the gymnasium, as they used to in the fencing halls of military barracks. Not sport but combat practice. The condition was that we would not attack the opponent's body, only his arms.

Then we began. The skirmisher was literally quivering in his eagerness to avenge his pupils, and so as not to belittle him, I beat a tactical retreat and parried his cuts at the very last moment. Even so it was one of my shortest sword bouts ever. My considerate treatment of Gita backfired. It is not healthy; in my view excessive self-control in bed demands blood – here and now. And so old Brother Poche copped it. When he forced me back to the wall I riposted with an inside cut, and then I made a call and cut from below. He counter-parried out and down, and with a smooth sweep I brought my sword down on his left forearm, which, in his euphoria of superiority, he had totally forgotten to protect.

A cry went up from the group of spectators. The Sokol's split sleeve turned red, and the face behind the soldierly moustache grew pale. I saluted him and offered him my hand. He took it with his right hand, while his left arm hung down like a bit of rag and dripped blood on to the floor. Then they led him away to the first-aid station. The eyes of his students, which moments before had been full of enthusiasm and admiration, now radiated malice mixed with hatred. Nobody had any further interest in fencing, I least of all.

The next morning was windy, and demolition in Jewry was proceeding full speed ahead. Prague had swept all signs of disturbance from the streets and installed an everyday idyll in their place. Resigned to the fact that my old gold watch was lost for good, I made my way to the watchmaker for a new one, fearing somewhat that I would not come by the necessary cash to afford one of distinction that I would not be ashamed to have engraved with my monogram. I had no intention of running into debt

Near the theatre there was a gathering of people making a sedate racket. There were people from the newspapers making notes about something and also lots of curious onlookers – mothers with children and the blue uniforms of the city garrison. The focus of attention was some functionary in a tall top hat and two young men in corduroy sports apparel, with white shirts and shortened neckties and trouser legs gathered above the ankle. One of them was wearing a round yellow cap, the other a yellow one with a label, and they were leaning on a modern type of bicycle: a conveyance having two wheels of the same size, with pneumatic tyres, bent handle-bars, an iron frame and an elongated chain arrangement which I was unable to fathom out at that moment.

They all fell silent when the man in the top hat raised his arm. He was holding a pistol. He shouted 'Go!' and fired into the air. The sportsmen nonchalantly climbed on to their machines, grasped the handlebars, leant on the pedals and set off towards the bridge at a speed that amazed me. The crowd followed after, chanting enthusiastically. There were shouts of 'Slavia!' and 'Na zdar!' and 'Bohemia for ever!', so loud my ears buzzed, but the banner beneath which the youngsters waited under starter's orders a short while before, bore a different message: *Dunlop pneumatic tyres, Belfast*. Aha.

The man in the hat measured the bicyclists' time on a large silver pocket watch that was also a stopwatch showing minutes and seconds. I started to have second thoughts about whether I really wanted a new chronograph at all. But I went to the watchmaker's anyway.

The bell above the shop door tinkled as I entered, and a sleek young fellow rose from the counter and made a stiff low bow, informing me that he was at my service. Marvellous. I handed him my card with instructions to show me his collection of pocket watches but only the new ones; I wasn't interested in second-hand goods.

My card clearly impressed him, which was a good sign. He laid out the instruments on the counter, only the costlier items, not bothering with the cheaper ones. Then he used two keys in a complicated fashion to open a small safe somewhere near his feet, and like a conjuror at a fair he took out a gold Swiss watch with a diamond setting in the middle of the cover. I asked him to put it back on the grounds that it would cost me my entire annual allowance, and he imperturbably replaced it ceremoniously in the safe and locked it conscientiously. His movements were mechanical, like clockwork. When the spring ran down he would stop. Then I would gather up all the pocket watches on display and take them away in my pockets and sell them for a song to the rag-and-bone men and black-marketeers at Madame Golda's. Count Arco, the new phenomenon of the Prague underworld. A career at least.

I weighed the watches in my hand, one after the other, opening them, testing how easy they were to wind up, listening to their velvety tick. The watchmaker tried to persuade me to take one of the biggest gold ones: it need not be diamond-studded – he would let me have a chain for an appreciable reduction, and he willingly give me a year to settle the bill, provided I made a down-payment of at least a third of the price.

He might even have persuaded me had I not noticed in the shop window a curiosity: a miniature watch without a chain and instead a leather strap either side of the silver case that was scarcely bigger than a gulden. On one side the strap had holes and on the other a tiny buckle.

'What is that?' I asked, pointing at the oddity and asking him to show it to me.

'I took a consignment of them,' the watchmaker said apologetically but brought it to me, 'from an English supplier. I wouldn't normally bother Your Lordship with something of this sort, but, on the other hand, this instrument is not without interest'

'One wears it on one's wrist, doesn't one?'

'Yes. I'll put it on you if you'll permit me. The left or the right?'

'I don't know. The left, I suppose . . . I can take a look how the time is going when I'm fencing,' I smiled.

He attached the watch and stepped back. 'There. A bit odd, don't you think? Like . . . I'm embarrassed to say what.'

'Like a suspender. You're right. The watch looks like a suspender. Unlike a pocket watch you always feel you're wearing it. That it's with you. Part of your body.'

'Be so kind as to remove it, My Lord. It doesn't suit you. I personally . . .'

'What?'

'I personally would sooner walk down Ferdinand Avenue in a skirt than with that on my arm, My Lord.'

'Why?' I asked, shaking my head. I examined the watch on my wrist and took a look at it in the mirror. 'You think it looks feminine? Do I look feminine to you?'

'By no means.'

'I beg your pardon?'

'Not in the slightest. I don't know what gave me that impression. The light from the shop window . . . You are such a refined gentleman. Like that watch, if I may make so bold.'

'Hm. You don't have anything sturdier, do you?'

'Not any more. I did have two others with a silver bracelet. They were bought by two members of the American Ladies' Club, for trips to the country, as they explained to me. There is no way to attach pocket watches to ladies' formal or travelling wear unfortunately. It would require a necklace . . .'

He had put me off slightly. 'I don't really look effeminate when I have it on my wrist, do I?'

'Heaven forbid, sir, not in the least. If you like it I'll be delighted to sell it to you, and I shall order a replacement strap for when this one wears out. It suits you very well – splendidly, in fact. And I'd advise you to forget about anything sturdier – we won't be ordering anything of that kind. Your wrist is so slender that it would be far less suitable. Although this one . . .'

'I know. I'll look exotic with this on my arm. But why don't more people wear them? They're practical.'

'It's not too tight, is it? Let me see.'

'Don't touch me.'

'Do excuse me. I simply wanted to show you how to wind it up and set the time.'

'I'll manage.'

'Of course, and if not I am at your service, with a thousand apologies, My Lord. You see, these wristwatches are such a fashion around the world just lately, but I don't like them. And they haven't caught on. The manufacturer is Swiss, but he doesn't have the patent, and I'm sure he's not alone. The watches are worn by women who have to work and need to have their hands free, and their attire doesn't allow them to wear a pocket watch, and for some reason they don't want to wear a chronograph around their necks. But how many women are there like that? Moreover, when one takes into account that the thing is not exactly cheap one arrives at the reason why it has not sold well.'

'Nonsense. It's only a matter of time. I foresee a great future for this instrument. One's hands are freed! *Touché*!'

'Ha-ha, most amusing, My Lord. I did hear that the English troops have used them with success, particularly the officers and the cavalry. It was from England that I received them.'

'You see. Do you know what? I'll take it.'

'An excellent decision, My Lord! It's a great pity that I don't have one with a gold case. I could order one, though.'

'How long would it take?'

'Three or four weeks, six at the most.'

'No. I'll make do with this.'

'As Your Lordship pleases. May I wrap it for you? I have a handy little box.'

'I'll leave it on my wrist. How much do I owe?'

I paid a trifling sum, and while I was waiting for the watchmaker to fetch some change from the decorative-goods shop next door I looked closely at those tiny silver hands in the mother-of-pearl watch face showing eleven thirty-three, precisely the same time as all the other chronometers in the shop. Then I noticed the trademark, *Lord*, written in black in fine minuscule italic letters just below the figure twelve.

Lord. The modern nobleman's watch. So be it.

After lunch I visited Loggia House. The door in the courtyard gate was open, but I found the yard almost empty. The goat, lying on its side under the arch of the vault, turned its penetrating eyes on me and bleated. But no sign of any step-ladders or painted canvases, just a ladder lying alongside the wall and several grey pigeons who observed me with coos of surprise from the baroque gallery. I went upstairs and frightened them off. They flew up crossly to the rooftop. I knocked on the door and windows, all in vain. It crossed my mind to do the rounds of the local taverns, but there are not many of them here on the edge of the Old Town and Jewry; there are just shops, coal and timber yards and potato stores. Goodness knows where the Urzidil brother had got that beer the other time. I sat down on a bench by the wall, lit a pipe and blew the smoke through the balustrade over the grey courtyard. The noise of the city could be heard only faintly. I stayed half an hour. Nobody arrived, and I didn't feel like leaving.

I wandered as far as the synagogues and then turned away from them and headed for St Peter's Quarter and the lagoon, more or less resigned to not coming upon the brothers in that zone of pits and trenches. Apart from the honking of geese from the nearby river it was unusually quiet in the lanes. The mills weren't turning. I arrived at a squat tavern with a thatched roof, which resembled a country cottage. On one side was the entrance, on the other a lean-to shed from which could be heard the bray of a donkey. Four dovecotes made of old barrels with holes drilled through the base perched high above the roof on long poles. They looked like bulbous poppy heads. The perches were crowded with grey birds, and I kept outside the range of their droppings, which created odd little pyramids on the paving stones outside the alehouse. The stench was borne off on the wind upstream in the direction of the Jewish Town and the Lesser Quarter. There was a bleached water wheel on the creosoted inn sign hanging from an iron pole. I went through the door.

I closed the door behind me and immediately sensed the tension aroused by my arrival. Nobody spoke. The light was dim. The three tiny windows that were open admitted only the suggestion of light and were incapable of clearing the thick cloud of tobacco smoke. None of the tables was free. The labourers from the mills were sitting around drinking beer and chewing their pipes and made no attempt to conceal their antipathy towards the customer who scarcely fitted in here. I placed my handkerchief over my nose, and their expressions became even gloomier. It was out of the question to turn and leave. So I headed for the bar to order a glass of kummel and drink it standing up, but then a hand was raised by the window beckoning me to come and sit down. I squeezed my way between sweat-soaked backs and found myself looking into the smiling face of Belisar, the flunkey from Friedmann's brothel. He was sitting on a chair by the window. He jumped up and gestured to it.

'What a pleasure, Your Lordship. I'd more likely expect to see the Chief Rabbi in here than yourself. But take a seat now you're here.'

I sat down on the chair and looked around. The others had ceased taking any notice of me, although the conversation was somewhat subdued. The innkeeper came over to us, and I ordered schnapps for myself and Belisar and soda water for us both. But I received a blank look, and Belisar whispered to me that they were unfamiliar with soda water. They had a liking only for spirits and beer. So we drank spirits. Belisar told me how Friedmann's singular inn had been evicted and stripped of everything that could be taken away, including the window frames, the doors and all the furniture. The only inhabitants now were rats and the ghetto's poorest residents, who had been gathering there ever since handbills started to appear on walls with the inscription 'URBAN IMPROVEMENT'.

'It'll be hard to get them out,' Belisar declared, nodding his head and tapping the side of the glass with his filthy teeth. 'They'll creep out with the rats when the ball on the chain of that demolition machine smashes into the wall.'

We drank a toast to the glorious memory of Friedmann's establishment, and then Belisar guffawed. 'I heard you're going to move your one from Golda's. That's the talk. They say you'll leave her in the lurch and pick up a new one, someone younger. Is it true? They say you've got your eyes on that Jewish beauty.'

I must admit he took me aback. 'Gossip! The beauty possibly took my fancy for a moment, and maybe I did I get a glimpse of her once, but I know nothing about her, and, in fact, I'd forgotten about her.'

'I see.'

'Have you heard anything about her?'

He laughed once more and wiped his nose on his sleeve. 'Not just heard, I've seen her, too, with my own eyes, would you believe? The old fellow wanted to distract attention from her and dreamt up some scheme – she's too beautiful, you see. So, guess what, he dyed her hair with some muck or other. He must have applied at least three layers of it.'

'Ahem. Very odd. Why ever would he do such a thing?'

'A redhead Jewess is enough to put any bloke off, isn't she?'

'Really?'

'A Jewess. And a redhead.'

'That's not my impression.'

'But that's what they say. But who knows? There's a superstition that they're as treacherous as Judas but that they bleed like the man from Nazareth when they pierced his side. It's superstition, I know. But they bring bad luck, I'm sure you agree.'

'I see you're an expert.'

'I'm bound to be, aren't I? I've been in service in posh establishments for thirty years already. And you wouldn't credit it, but a customer has bought me nine times already – the last time was last spring!'

'You're definitely a sought-after commodity.'

'You bet.'

I cleared my throat. 'So that father of hers or granddad or uncle . . . What is he exactly? That man preserved her honour by dying her hair red? Amazing!'

'Exactly so. The authorities would take her off him, you see. He had to borrow lots of shekels from the moneylender to escape the fires of hell by the skin of his teeth. And of course he didn't have the wherewithal to repay them, did he? After all, it was all he could do to find somewhere to live in Jewry for himself and the girl. And so two debt collectors came for the money – one like a golem, the other like a bollard – and they were wanting interest naturally. But the girl opened the door to them, and when they got a sight of that ginger mop they were no longer in any mood to smash the old fellow's fizzog in, particularly when the girl told them that if they didn't leave them alone they would wake up the next morning hanging from a lamp-post, and they'd live just long enough to realize they were hanging there by their own entrails. And so they scarpered, the giant and the midget.'

'How do you know all this?'

'Gossip. You try to hush something up in Prague. They say the girl's a witch. It's not my opinion – the red hair was only dyed – but, ever since that tirade against the debt collectors, people have been giving her and the old man a wide berth. And you ought to beware as well. Just put the little Lilith out of your head or she'll she scratch your eyes out.'

'Except that I bought her some shoes, so she has a reason to be grateful.'

'Or a reason to feel indebted. And that's not good. She'll set the Kleinfleisch on you, and that'll be that.'

'What will she set on me? The Kleinfleisch?'

Belisar suddenly looked as if he was about to throw up. He finished his beer and sat staring into the room with a blank expression.

'Well?' I urged him. 'What is this Kleinfleisch?'

'The Kleinfleisch, of course – the monster. But he wouldn't dare touch you. That's out of the question. You're a goy – and high-born into the bargain. He has no power over you. Forget that I mentioned it.'

I gripped him by the shoulder and squeezed. My fingers were immediately covered with something greasy. 'What's this all about, Belisar? What has some Kleinfleisch to do with that girl, for God's sake?'

Why are you so het up about it?'

'Once, a long time ago . . . I saw it written up on a door not far from here. The word filled me with horror when I was a child.'

'I can't say that words horrify me.'

'But what is it? Who is it supposed to be?' My heart was thumping with terror like a small child, and, as if he had heard, the innkeeper came over of his own accord with two more glasses of kummel.

'It's a kind of bogeyman or something,' Belisar stammered, 'but you mustn't mention its name or it'll come for you. That's the idea behind it. It's used to scare kids, but you wouldn't credit how many grown-ups are scared stiff of it, too.'

'So the Kleinfleisch is some kind of apparition?'

'That's the size of it.'

'What else?'

'That's all.'

I felt like belting him. 'Did you ever see it?'

'Me?' Belisar croaked and a few heads turned in our direction. 'I'd hardly be here if I had,' he added more quietly. 'And I can't tell you any more about it, because that's all I know.'

I was flabbergasted: to come across a bit of one's childhood, an unexplained mystery and one of the most powerful experiences of one's life from the lips of a local in that smoke-filled tap-room.

Belisar could see that something was going on inside me. He blinked his crusty eyes at me and sipped his beer, as if considering escape, but then he slumped on to the window-sill and said, 'It wasn't my intention to cause you offence, My Lord. There's no reason for either of us to reprove the other, is there? Listen here, just to show you I'm no scoundrel and I'm not trying to pull a fast one I'll tell you something to cheer you up. If you're interested in that girl, regardless of whether she's a princess or a witch, look for a little grove of three trees. That's where she lives. That's unless they've dragged her off somewhere else, which I doubt, because I think they're safe where they are. And now I've got to fly. I've got a new job in Chamois Street, and it's nearly opening time. Please make a visit, My Lord.' He snaked his way through the drinkers and slipped out of the door and was gone.

I had another drink and pondered on all the things that the obnoxious gnome had been blathering about, trying to work out what was true and what was of importance for me. I settled on the most significant information: the garden with the three trees, because that gave me something I could work on. I had recently passed a wall that could conceal just such a grove.

It was getting dark outside. I made my way back towards the Old Town to see whether the Urzidil brothers had returned in the meantime. The area around the convent was all holes and trenches surrounded by ropes hung with red-and-white pennants. Cats or rats might risk running across the narrow gaps between the chasms; humans would have difficulty. I had to take a roundabout route and lost my way when night suddenly fell. There used to be a Jewish bathhouse somewhere around here, I said to myself, and my eyes searched the gloom in vain for its onion-shaped roof. Then the night air enfolded me in a lane with a broken streetlamp. There was a cold breeze, and a dog howled behind a wooden barrier. I started to shiver, and I suppressed a fit of coughing. I walked on. The barrier came to an end, and I found myself walking alongside a damp wall and then a length of rope until I eventually reached a solid street corner. Running from it in what I guessed was a southerly direction was a reliably wide road, in which the streetlamp revealed a sharp bend. I set off along it, meeting not a soul. Then, from an open gateway, I heard a shout for help: the pleading voice of a woman. Then there came a scream and a sudden silence.

I entered the courtyard together with people who had hurried here from the surrounding houses. Lamps came on in windows, and dark heads appeared one after another. A small throng of poorly dressed people crowded around a woodshed built on to the wall. They were about eight in number, and they were talking in excited, horrified voices. A short way away by the rainwater butt a girl was lying in a pool of blood. To judge from the position of the body and the unnatural bend of the head, her neck was broken.

They were all looking at her as if spellbound, including a small girl in a blue blouse with a white scarf around her neck. Some young man with a black moustache was telling the rest that she was still alive half an hour ago; he had seen her arrive. A woman in a white wimple was wringing her hands, clearly wanting to say something but unable. Beyond her a swarthy man in a kaftan peeped out from behind a door. The lamp on the wall above the dead girl was not alight, but behind the Jew the orange light from an oil lamp shone through a ground-floor window. I looked upwards – a window directly above her but right up near the roof was wide open.

One of the women leant towards the dead girl at the same time as me. I tried in vain to find a pulse in the limp wrist. She was warm but cooling with a dreadful rapidity. The muscles beneath the skin seemed to want to react to the pressure of my fingers, but blood no longer flowed through the veins beneath them. The girl's face was rigid, the mouth open as if in a cry, the eyes open wide and filled with tears. A trickle of bloody mucous ran from her nose. Blood also ran from the dead girl's ear and from beneath her matted hair.

Someone said they would run for a doctor, and I told them they should send for the police, too.

Then we waited. The women stood by the wall saying something to each other in low voices. They looked at me as if I were responsible for the death. It was understandable, as I was not from around there. I lit my pipe and went inside the house. I climbed the staircase to the last door before the loft, and I pushed at it. As I expected, it was unlocked. The open window opposite responded to a draught; the two halves of the window banged against the frame and then flew open again. I walked across the room, the furnishing of which consisted of a bed, a chair, a small table, a wardrobe, a hanger and a cylinder stove. Everything was worn and shabby. I looked down into the yard. The women's faces were upturned, and when I stuck my head out one of them pointed at me and screeched. I quickly hid myself and looked around the room. I was seeking some clue to what had happened. When I found nothing I went back to the yard.

The women were talking to a man with a lined face and grey hair and wearing an expensive suit. Some young lad, with the look of a bumpkin, all dishevelled as if he had just been dragged out of bed, was writing something in a little notebook. As soon as the women saw me, the one who had pointed up at the window said, 'That's him.'

The men eyed me, and they didn't seemed to be satisfied with what they saw. Maybe they were expecting someone else. The older man, who had pale round eyes and furrows not only on his forehead but all over his face, eventually spoke. 'Deputy Police Councillor Herrmann.' Then he nodded towards the young man. 'Assistant Detective Listopad. Now tell us who you are and what you are doing here.'

I introduced myself, giving my name and title, which did not impress them although it did the women who started to murmur something, and the detective – Listopad – sent them away. I informed them that I had arrived just a short while before when the girl was lying in a pool of blood in the yard and that the women had seen me arrive when it was all over.

'What were you doing inside the house?'

'I went to look for something there.' I cleared my throat.

'What were you looking for?'

'A phantom,' I blurted out without knowing why.

Herrmann looked cross, but Listopad sidled up to him, and he no longer had the appearance of a bumpkin. On the contrary. Narrowing his eyes, he whispered something to his superior, and when the older man expressed an objection he took him one side and started to reason with him. Then he beckoned to me. 'Let's take a look at the deceased.' A doctor was kneeling on one knee by the girl, a bag at his side, but he didn't even bother to open it. He looked up at us. 'Take a look at this, gentlemen.'

He pointed at the girl's face. The facial muscles had relaxed by now, and the eyes were dull, although the look of terror had not yet left them.

'The face bears no indication of a struggle. The nails are short and clean. Both her legs are broken and her pelvis, too, most likely. She therefore fell on the lower part of the body. The impact was too great and flung her to one side. The blow to the head came obliquely and was naturally fatal. The head bounced back in the opposite direction causing the spinal column to fracture, resulting in instant death. Had she fallen less awkwardly and been a bit luckier she might have survived the fall. That is if it was a fall.'

'What is your conclusion?' Herrmann asked. But we already knew the answer.

'I can't say for certain, but most likely she jumped out of the window of her own accord. So it could be suicide.'

'But I heard that scream,' I objected. 'She was terrified of something, you can see it on her face.'

'It could be an indication of acute hysteria,' the doctor responded in a disapproving tone.

'Someone terrified her. A lot,' I insisted. 'Maybe someone intended to do her harm and she jumped out of the window.'

'You were upstairs,' Herrmann said.

'Yes but only afterwards.'

Listopad looked upwards and mumbled something indistinct between his teeth. Then he turned to me. 'Does the word "Kleinfleisch" mean anything to you, by any chance?'

'I've heard of it. You're right that I thought I might find something of the kind in the house, that's if I had any idea what it might be like.'

'And what do you think it is?'

'I don't know. Something terrifying. I might have encountered it a while ago, also in Jewry, not far from here.'

'What did it look like?'

'I don't know. It was dark.'

The police councillor's deputy reflected for a moment and said, 'Detective Listopad will take your address. If a crime has occurred here you will be considered a witness. If it was suicide we won't need you any more. You can go now. Maybe we will still require you to give evidence, so please do not leave Prague.'

I left, and could feel their enquiring gaze on my back. My head ached. There were hundreds of questions buzzing about in it and no answers.

I thought about Belisar, who had mentioned Kleinfleisch, and Listopad, who had uttered the word not long afterwards on the spot where a murder had perhaps taken place.

Most of all I yearned to swallow one of those miracle pills of Manny's – except that I didn't have any left – and then sleep for a very long time.

X

A Jewish Bogeyman

Dr Hoffmann

Next morning I went to see Solly and told him everything. The moment I said 'Kleinfleisch' my friend smiled and nodded. He handed me a cup of coffee and said, 'Kleinfleisch is a figure from Prague's Jewish folk tales. The Prague Golem is familiar to people in other countries, it's nothing new, but Kleinfleisch is an obscure being and is not well known outside the former ghetto. But whereas the Golem sowed terror chiefly among adult goys, while children regarded it at most with immense respect – and indeed lots of people still believe in it – Kleinfleisch was, from the outset, a bogeyman to frighten naughty Jewish children. The story of it dates back to about the middle of the century when the Jewish Town was joined to Prague and the traditional residents were allowed to move out, and those who could afford it did so, because there was no room to breathe – the way it still is, in fact. My parents also moved into the Old Town, and I don't blame them. Well, and then poor folks moved into Josefov, people from beyond the gate, Christians and Jews alike. Suddenly it made no difference. There were empty little houses here with tiny backyards and high roofs. They crept in like rats, and now, fifty years later, only urban improvement will get them out, and I often tell myself that it is high time, otherwise Josefovites will suffocate in their own shit, they'll dissolve in the slurry like in lye, and that filth will beget the plague.'

Coffee dripped from my cup on to my pressed trousers. I rubbed the place with my handkerchief, but the spot remained. 'But you don't believe that. Bürger talked about the plague at that meeting, and Preininger's study warns against it, but if it wasn't for demolition life in Jewry would go on.'

'But people get murdered there. First Rosina and now that girl they heaved out of the window. It's odd that the police asked you about Kleinfleisch. It wasn't out of the blue.'

'I'd leave Rosina out of it. This death is different. Some young servant girl about eighteen years old. It's as if something forced her to hurl herself out of the window into the yard. And then that reference to Kleinfleisch straight afterwards . . . And I most likely met him once. He's dressed all in black and has no face. Or if he has it's disfigured. He was waiting there for someone.'

'Maybe he was waiting for you to take to your heels,' said Solly. 'They used Kleinfleisch to scare us when they were afraid we'd succumb to the goyish world. "If you eat pork or all that ham that the butcher craftily offers you for free Kleinfleisch will come for you and bone you with his knife."'

'Kleinfleisch has a knife? I didn't see anything of the kind that time.'

'You weren't a prospective customer. He could tell, so he scarpered. But when we were small I don't know what we feared most – the bloody face or that long butcher's knife . . . It's odd. Those child-hood fears had gone completely out of my head, and who brought them back to mind? You.'

'And don't forget the chest of drawers and to bolt the door at night.'

'I won't. Ugh. Well, well. I'm almost thirty, and Kleinfleisch is back here again. Maybe I'll start carrying a sword like they used to. At night, at least. But what use would that be against a bogeyman?'

'It wasn't a bogeyman that killed Rosina.'

'I know. And this girl only needed to set eyes on it and she's dead.'

'It's odd, isn't it?' I lit myself one of his cigarettes. It had bluish paper and wasn't particularly fragrant. 'Just when urban improvement is invading the Jewish Town with slogans like hygiene, health, water-mains and electricity, a bogeyman turns up that scares Jewish children to death, and when it feels inclined it cuts their throats. Somehow it doesn't tally with a modern metropolis that is supposed to be the equal of Paris or Vienna.'

Solly demonstrated how the smoke from the cigarette must be inhaled right down into the lungs. I tried it and was rewarded with an insistent rasping cough. I had some drops with me from the doctor, and I dissolved some in a glass of water. They didn't help much. My head swam, and I gasped for breath. When the coughing fit finally started to abate and I was able to breathe shallowly while wheezing I lay down on the divan, and Solly waited patiently for me to grow calm.

He then made a surprising announcement. 'I went and saw your pharmacist yesterday. I waited outside until the shop was empty, and then I dashed in and gave that nasty little snake in the grass a bit of a drubbing.'

I raised myself on to my elbows. 'You should have kept it to yourself, Solly. It's pointless. They'll come for you.'

'You don't think I'm going to put up with the fact they tried to burn down my shop.'

'And what did he have to do with it?'

'Possibly nothing, but a few days before I'd refused to collaborate with him, hadn't I? And the story goes that the disturbances were whipped up by the secret police. And so they most likely decided to kill two birds with one stone, because there was no case of arson anywhere else. Just at my place.'

'And the pharmacist?'

'I told him that if anything of the kind ever happens again it'll be his pharmacy that burns down and with him in it. And then I asked him just by the way, seeing that he was so good at gathering information, whether he didn't happen to know where I could find Dr Hoffmann. And just imagine –'

'He told you.'

'Yes. So go and pay a call on that miracle doctor.' Solly took some money out of the till. 'I can lend you some if you haven't the cash. Try to beat him down so he doesn't cheat you. The apothecary said he is supposed to be leaving soon.'

He handed me a wad of banknotes. 'Buy his whole stock, Addie. You can pay me back in instalments out of your allowance. You'll find him at the sign of the Three Horsemen. You know where it is?'

'On Weighbridge Square.'

'He's renting an apartment there. Off you go then.'

He raised the roller blind and went to open up.

'Business is going to be brisk today and not just for me.'

I did as I was told.

Dr Hoffmann couldn't have been long at that address. They had always rented out rooms and apartments at the sign of the Three Horsemen on a short-term basis. It was even said that for a consideration one could rent a room with a big bed for an hour and bring along up to four other persons regardless of sex. My requirements were more modest. I gave the porter a half-crown, and he conducted me to a green-painted door. I knocked and heard from inside 'Herein.' I entered a spacious room with large but not particularly clean windows. The porter closed the door quietly behind me.

Sat at a writing-desk with his back to me was a slim short-haired man, thinning on top. He wore a white shirt and a shiny waistcoat from a suit. When he stood up and turned around he did so with the gracefulness of a dancer. His legs were clad in carefully pressed trousers with a pin-stripe and polished light shoes that made almost no sound on the floorboards.

He came over to me and waited for me to offer him my hand.

'Count Arco, if I am not mistaken. I am Dr Felix Hoffmann at your service. I was expecting you. Please do me the honour of taking a seat. You are a welcome guest.' He spoke German without any sort of accent that might betray where he came from.

'How could you have been expecting me?'

He sat down in a seat opposite me, formally erect yet relaxed and oddly calm, the picture of a man reconciled with the world. He placed his hands on his knees and from time to time needlessly smoothed the hair above his temple. The necktie beneath his chin was bright blue, a slightly darker shade than his eyes. His small mouth, which was hard to see beneath his moustache, had a permanent smile, perhaps out of politeness.

'It came to my notice that you were looking for me and also that my distinguished friend Count Arco-Zinneberg was just now in Prague but has since gone off somewhere.'

'He won't be away for long. He's in the country staying at my parents.'

'I myself am only staying in Prague until tomorrow. I had to move. I'm rather fussy about my accommodation.'

'You don't like it in Prague?'

'On the contrary. It's simply . . . But it's of no importance. I heard you'd tried a preparation similar to my own.'

'You have admirable sources of information, Doctor. You are right: I received a small bottle from Karl Emanuel with whom you are acquainted. But he didn't say he got it from you.'

'Thank you, I'm glad to hear it. If he offered you something it was a copy, of which more and more are turning up. My own preparation – I've given it the name 'heroic' – is twenty times better. Alas, I am unable to devote the time to advertising it adequately, and I certainly can't afford to have it patented. You must understand that the Bayer chemical company claims patent rights to a similar preparation, with the same chemical composition, and to a certain extent I see the sense of it. They are afraid of forgeries, too. Their lawyer actually went so far as to denounce me in the German press as someone who had stolen their recipe. Improper behaviour, don't you think?'

'I'm sure he had no right to do so.'

'Of course not, even though he rightly argued that I used to work for Bayer in their chemical laboratory. They were only too pleased to engage me at that time. I have been a champion of acetylation from the word go, and I helped invent a medicine against fever – I was just the kind of man they needed at Bayer's, and I was content, too. But then I fell out with my employer about the production process and the degree of risk at the testing stage –'

'Wait a moment, Doctor. I don't understand all this.'

Hoffmann became slightly uneasy. He smoothed down his hair and looked out of the window into the street, as if afraid of something. Then he went on. 'Tests on rats, of course, but if I am to tell you the entire truth I have to admit that we also carried out a series of experiments on human patients, too – cases where nothing else would have helped any longer. They were our volunteers. They had only months of life left to live.'

'And how did the tests turn out?'

'Excellently. We achieved a 70 per cent improvement in patients with chronic coughs, and we also had excellent results with asthma patients. Naturally there were also some people with cancer, and we at least made their remaining days more pleasant. Our medicine turned them into happy individuals reconciled to their fate and to God.'

'Amen.'

'I beg your pardon?'

'Nothing. Then you left Bayer's.'

'I did, because they placed a somewhat different interpretation on the results of my tests, disregarding the positive side and concentrating too much on the preparation's negative aspects, particularly its addictiveness. My phenomenal substitute for the much more dangerous codeine wasn't good enough for them, and they produced a substitute for it. Do you see?'

'I'm afraid I don't.'

'The board decided to reject my proposal for further research into the heroic preparation, and instead they started to manufacture a similar medicine. That is why I left.'

'I assume you a looking for a situation with a competitor.'

'Yes, but it's not easy. Bayer's people have been spreading a rumour around Central Europe that my pills are poisonous while theirs are safe.'

'And yours aren't poisonous?'

'They are to a certain extent – just like theirs. The body becomes accustomed to the drug and copes with the undesirable effects, but it gradually needs more and more of it, and the positive effects are increasingly weakened. And naturally I don't know what will happen when the dose is tripled or quadrupled. I didn't have time to test it.'

He reached into his pocket, took out two small bottles and handed them to me. They were identical, made of ribbed glass and full of light-coloured tablets. One of them had a coloured label bearing the words *Heroin, hydrochlorate* and the round emblem of the Bayer trademark. The second had a white label with the words *Hydrochlorate plus*. I unscrewed each lid in turn and tipped out a single tablet on to my palm. Bayer's was lenticular in shape, perfectly formed and pure white. Hoffmann's fell far short of that standard: the edges were not sharp and were crumbling in places. It also had a yellowish or ochre tinge. The tablets that Manny had given me were much whiter, and the label was blue.

'So colleagues have now turned into competitors,' I said, and resisted the urge to swallow one of the two gems, preferably both at once. 'And other manufactures are treading on their heels.'

'How could I compete with Bayer?' Dr Hoffmann sighed. 'You can see for yourself that my homemade improvised tablet-maker can't match the standards of Bayer's machines. I used to get better results, but don't be put off by the colour. When I left Bayer I took nothing with me, and yet I am obliged to hide from detectives in the pay of the company's lawyer. I took only my own records and the manufacturing process. Just my own things.'

'Except that you were their employee. That's the problem.'

'And their problem is that they forced me out prematurely. It needs two more years' research, if not three.'

'Do you want to sue them?'

'I'd lose my case in court, and they could have me prosecuted. All I want is to find fresh scope for further research.'

'Is that why you came to Prague?'

'Yes. But I realize now that it won't be possible to work here: police everywhere, public and secret, demonstrations and even a state of emergency. It's impossible. I'll go back to Germany and risk major difficulties with Bayer, or else I'll leave for America.'

'Lots of people have chosen a similar solution.'

'But I can't afford the journey, Count Arco.'

'I would happily assist you, but I'm not particularly well off myself at the moment, and I'm about to buy myself a smallish house. A friend has lent me a certain sum to buy as many doses of your medicine as you are willing to sell me. What do you say?'

'How much can you afford?'

I took out my purse, riffled through the bank notes and handed him just over half of them.

Not a single muscle moved on Dr Hoffmann's face. 'That will buy you my entire stock. I need to get rid of it.'

'Don't you want to count it?'

'There is no need. Take a look.' Still holding the money he went over to the wardrobe and took out of it a leather kitbag, the sort that was used for stagecoach travel, as large as a middle-sized suitcase. He opened it. It was full of a yellowy-white glitter.

For a moment I was lost for words. Then I asked stupidly, 'How many people would that save?'

Hoffmann replied in a flash, 'How many people would it kill?'

'I can really take away all of it?'

'You have to. And I must get away. By and large it was worth your while waiting.'

'And yours.'

'I don't deny it.'

'I almost coughed up my lungs. Why don't they sell those little bottles of Bayer's here?'

'That's not my fault. It's the fault of Bayer's people. I expect the market here isn't promising enough – that's very much the way they think. In all events, be careful how you use it. It's an analgesic and also mildly hallucinogenic. In the initial stages it can induce colourful dreams, but the effect wears off in time. The same applies to the anxiety states.'

'How many bottles are there?'

'One hundred and seventy-seven.'

'That will last me more than ten years.'

Dr Hoffmann laughed. 'Congratulations. In the meantime the tablets will have disintegrated or the damp will get to them. But you won't be needing to take them for so long. I'm sure that in a year or two I'll complete the necessary tests and acquire a patent for a medicine that will be far more effective and safer than this one or Bayer's or what Karl Emanuel gave you.'

'So our deal is completed.' We shook hands. I tied the bag with the leather thong attached to the top and headed for the door. 'I sincerely hope we'll meet again,' I said in parting.

'Unless I leave for America.'

The grey-haired inventor gave a bow and was once more the picture of sophistication.

I parted from him in the doorway and carried away ten years of healthiness along the lengthy corridor of the house of the Three Horsemen.

At least I thought so at that moment.

A black-haired woman with peacock's feathers woven into her hat was coming upstairs and heading towards me with swaying hips, her shiny scarlet costume rustling softly. I moved out of her path and inclined my head. She smiled and glanced with interest at the kitbag. I instinctively hid it behind my back. The woman turned down the corners of her mouth and disappeared through the door of the nearest room. I looked around. Dr Hoffmann was still staring after me from the other end of the corridor. It was impossible to make out precisely the expression on his face from that distance, but it struck me that the woman's smile had migrated to that spot.

At the ground floor I swallowed the pill that Hoffmann had just given me for comparison. The other, the one from Bayer, I threw into the gutter.

XI

A Jewish Princess

An Unexpected Visit

I took one that evening and another the next morning as soon as I woke, even though my lungs were not troubling me. Prague started to give off a fragrance. Not in the sense of a Parisian perfume but of calm, happiness, contentment.

Like a Sunday. I was enthralled by the new day that totally forgave my idleness, unlike the other six.

Then doubt started to creep in. Isn't it still Saturday? Or Thursday? Probably Thursday. I glanced at my new watch. It was there, even though I was otherwise naked – clad only in time. Am I speaking? I asked someone out loud, and I heard nothing. I started to laugh.

I examined the chronograph, its mother-of-pearl face and the little hands of fleeting silver. They showed seven minutes past nine. I waited for the big hand to reach the eight. Seven and a half. Seven and three-quarters. I was living so much more slowly. It was beautiful.

I opened the window and caught the sound of someone with a rich operatic voice singing with great relish and enormous resonance 'Where Is My Home?' It was me. A beautiful singer of a beautiful song. Hadn't I read in the newspaper that it was banned? I hadn't, someone is saying at that very moment. That pigeon sitting on the window ledge and observing me through the glass. Someone has shut my window. I fell back on to my bed and slept. *'Wo ist mein Heim? Mein Vaterland? Wo durch Wiesen . . .'*

A gendarme stood in my bedroom stinking of sweat. Paradise was over.

My lord this and my lord that. I wrapped myself in my blanket and gave him a gulden from my purse. He took it, touched the hilt of his curved sabre and wiped his nose on his sleeve. He requested me not to disturb the peace; my singing could be heard from the street apparently. The window was open. Incredible. But I didn't find it amusing.

'Of course,' I said. 'I was having a dream. Can't you hear those machines?'

The gendarme listened. The excavators and diggers couldn't be heard, but to my surprise he nodded, 'Yes, My Lord, but don't do any more singing.' With the money in his pocket he took his leave.

I got dressed and went for a wash. Downstairs in the concierge's lodge I drank a vile cup of chicory and nibbled some fresh bread, and then I strode out into the Prague streets with a light head and heavy legs. I vowed not to take even one more of Hoffmann's pills until the next day. But I was unable to take my mind off that amazing stockpile. All my peace of mind and certainty in a kitbag under my bed. This was the way to walk around Prague. I headed for the ghetto. This would be the day. I knew it.

My sense of direction in the labyrinth of the Jewish Town had not been reduced in the least. On the contrary, I felt that the entire ground plan of Josefov was laid out in my brain like a map in front of my eyes, and I was bound to reach my goal. I walked between the synagogues and found the lane between them. I gave coins to several beggars with outstretched hands and found myself in the little street called the Sheds. I had been here once before but hadn't known what Belisar knew.

The opening was plunged in semi-darkness. A narrow little house like a crooked chimney cast a slanting shadow. It was morning still. Some sort of dark mobile flock fled before my feet. They were rats that had been feasting on a pile of mouldering potato peelings and were now creeping into holes in the walls either side of the gateway.

A little further on, where the low tiled wall began, a striped cat was looking down at me as if I were a hero who had dared to disturb a knot of vipers. I reached the wall and looked over it into the garden. In it stood three slender trees. A triangle was stretched between the mulberry, the pear and the plum trees, a line on which washing was drying. Ladies' underwear of pitiful quality. Since I had no idea what side to enter by and hadn't the slightest desire to retrace my steps and circle the jumble of pathetic little houses and flaking hovels I clambered up on to the wall, swung my legs over and jumped down into the garden. My trousers and overcoat ended up covered in white, brick-red and grey streaks and caught a few cobwebs, and before I had finished dusting it all off as best I could and looked around for a way into some building or other I found myself confronted by the old man I had encountered that time in front of the old clothes shop. He was holding a curved knife of the kind used for cleaning horses' hooves.

There was something of the fencer in his determined stance, which, I thought, did him credit. But as soon as he tried to say something manly he choked and put his hand over his mouth, thereby no longer covering himself.

'Take one of these.' I unscrewed the cap of the little bottle and handed him a yellowish-white pill.

'You're always giving me something,' he growled.

'It's a medicine.'

He took the pill, scrutinized it and put it in his mouth. I heard him crunching it in his old but still fairly sturdy teeth.

'Who asked for your help?' he said with his mouth full of crystalline powder. 'We're not beggars.'

'Are you referring to those old boots? They were for your ward. I would buy her something nicer if the choice were up to me. I'll get her a new pair made by my shoemaker. What do you say?'

'What are you doing here anyway?' he asked by way of reply.

And so I followed suit. 'Do you rent this place?'

'I asked first.'

'I came to see you.'

'Why didn't you come to the door?'

'I would have willingly, but I couldn't tell which was the right one, so I came over the wall.'

'It's there.' He pointed to a door in a low building crouching in the shadow of the taller houses. The garden was part of a larger courtyard, closed in on all sides. In one corner there rose a dunghill alongside a wooden privy.

'But you can't detect it from the street. There are several gateways into the courtyard, but nobody would guess there was a little cottage and garden here.'

'That's true,' he smiled. Then he took a deep breath; there was nothing blocking the air passage any more. 'That was some powerful medicine you gave me. How did you find us here?'

'I lost my way around here once, and I recalled these three trees. Then someone reminded me of them – he said this was where you happened to live. Your name's Karafiát if I'm not mistaken.'

'It was to be expected, that someone would squeal on us.' Karafiát nodded his head and spat on the ground.

'I wouldn't it call it that. It was friendly assistance.'

'So what do you want of me?'

What did I want, indeed? 'To offer help,' I replied, none too convincingly. 'Or something like that.'

The old man narrowed his eyes behind his spectacles. 'And why would you do that? You're a philanthropist?'

'That would be an exaggeration. I am Count Arco.'

'The one who buys poor people boots, eh?'

'Yes, boots, too, when the occasion arises.'

'And brings them pills when they have asthma.'

'I need medical treatment myself. I have understanding for people with illnesses.'

'You're goodness itself. It's been a pleasure. I hope we meet again. You may leave by the way you came in.' He turned around and strode briskly across the garden towards the cottage.

'Wait a moment.' I caught up with him, took him by the elbow and steered him into the shade of the three trees. 'Look here, Karafiát. Save that kind of behaviour for someone else. Any time now you're going to have to move out of here. Everything will be knocked down, the entire ghetto, and where will you go then? But I happen to be buying a house in an area where there will be no demolitions. And the house is quite large. When I move in you can live there with the girl.'

'But meanwhile we're here, and we're fine.'

'Yes, for now. But what about tomorrow? Or in a week's time?'

'It'll sort itself out in a week.'

I might as well have talked to the wall. But then an idea came to me.

'I don't want to scare you, Karafiát, but this quarter isn't safe. Two murders have occurred around here. They both have something to do with a monster called Kleinfleisch . . . Do you want your girl to end up in his claws?'

The wrinkled skin on his throat tightened and lost is reddish tint. I had hit the nail on the head.

'Kleinfleisch, you say?' He was trembling, his impertinence had evaporated. 'I heard about it, but they say she was a streetwalker, one of those part-time ones, of which you have as many in this city as you have respectable women.'

'So what? Do you think Kleinfleisch makes a distinction? He's got a very sharp knife, and he kills on sight.'

'I thought he would spare Jews.'

'Just the opposite. Kleinfleisch is no golem. You never know whether he'll spare you or cut your throat. Think about that girl. See how low that wall is? How easily I got over it? Imagine Kleinfleisch standing on the other side of it. Can't you see him? I can. If he stretches out his arm it'll easily reach this spot between the trees. And that delightful creature . . . What's her name?'

'Berenice.'

'And Berenice happens to hanging out the washing. Just imagine this white laundry spattered with blood.'

Karafiát closed his eyes. I lit my pipe, offered him my tobacco pouch and waited under the mulberry tree for the old man to pull himself together.

'Berenice has no parents,' he said, puffing out smoke from his pipe. 'I represent them. I was the one who named her. I thought up the name Berenice myself,' he added, and his pride lent momentary colour to his drab voice.

'What was her original name?'

'It's of no importance. She doesn't even know.'

'May I see her?'

'I expect you want to see how the boots suit her, eh?' he said in his expressionless voice.

'Yes.'

He led me into the cottage. The girl was seated on a stool by the window so that she might observe our entire conversation in the garden without being seen. She had a book open in front of her. She now rose from it and came to meet us. She bowed, took my hand in hers and kissed it.

This was another Berenice, and yet still the same as she was outside the junk dealer's shop. Her hair was black and glossy, her eyebrows, too, and also the eyelashes around her large brown eyes. She wore a faded girlish dress with a white pinafore, and she had those boots from the junk dealer's on her feet. In that gloomy parlour her face and neck shone and so did her arms.

For a moment I wondered whether she was real. Maybe the old Jew was a creator of ingenious mechanical puppets and was now intending to demonstrate one for me.

I gently pinched her cheek. 'Are you studying?' I pointed at the book she was reading and then reached for it. The title read *Aus dem Leben eines Taugenichts*. 'Well, well, Eichendorff. It came out in Czech not long ago.'

'You see, Your Lordship,' Karafiát intervened, 'Berenice used to go to school, but now she is sixteen, and I could hardly enrol her here in Prague. The authorities would send us back to where we came from.

And I don't want any bother. I don't even want to remain in Prague, but the girl should be here . . . And you, if I've understood you rightly, have an interest.'

He twisted it nicely. I let him present my proposal to her.

She showed no surprise, as I would have expected. They must have already talked to each other about such a possibility. She seemed reconciled to the idea, and her reply was well rehearsed. 'Whatever you wish,' she said obediently. May she repeat it a dozen times more.

'Now run outside, Berenice,' said Karafiát, 'and bring the washing in, so His Lordship isn't obliged to look at it.'

She went out into the garden carrying a wicker basket. I realized that the moment had now arrived. I offered him the remainder of Solly's money. 'That's as much as I have at this moment. I could possibly find some more by next week. Will that cover your travel expenses? So where are you planning to go?'

'I'd rather keep that to myself, if you don't mind,' he said and glanced outside at Berenice. I had the feeling he was doing a mental calculation. 'You told me you would take complete care of her.'

'Of course. You have my word. You can be assured that she will come to no harm with me.'

'Can you take her with you straight away?'

'No. That is to say: yes. You're right. There is no point in delaying it. The officials from the city authorities will arrive on your doorstep a few days from now. In all events they would take Berenice from you, and you would be summonsed for not having officially registered her residence.'

'I know.' He held out his hand, and I put the money in it. 'I take you at your word.'

'You won't find better.' The transaction was sealed.

Berenice came in with the basket in her hand, and as if she had heard our conversation she started to tie it into a bundle along with a few little things. Then she tied about a dozen books with a leather strap, including the Eichendorff. I offered to carry it, but she would not hear of it. She took her leave of Karafiát with a brief embrace. There was no trace of warmth in it. It was a gesture for my benefit.

He led us out of the cottage via some interior passages and into a yard full of wood stacks and clucking hens and then through a dark passageway on to the street. There I sent some lad to find us a cab, and no one said a word while we waited. Passers-by looked at us with interest, and I returned any inquisitive glance in such a way that the person immediately went back to minding their own business, apart from two young men who stood in the arcade of the house opposite smoking long, narrow pipes and whistling at Berenice now and then. I let them be.

A battered cab drove up drawn by two needlessly fat horses. The cabman in a long cape loaded the luggage, and we sat down inside the cab. When I glanced out of the window my gaze met the eyes of old Karafiát. They wore no expression and were devoid of life. He leant stiffly against a wall and made no movement, as if he were dead. Then the cab moved off, and I looked at Berenice. She was curled up in the corner of the seat crying. I took her by the hand. 'Things will turn out well for you at home with me.'

We spoke little on the way to Long Street. Berenice leant half out of the open window, her chin propped on her arm, and let the rushing wind fan her face. Then, when she wanted to draw my attention to a group of black-and-white kittens sitting on the staircase of one of the evacuated houses, she addressed me as 'Sir', and I asked her to call me Addie. She nodded with her eyes fixed on the street and indicated more and more cats in windows, in passageways, on fences and among the resting demolition machines that didn't concern the animals in any way. Berenice said she had never seen so many cats in one spot. I remarked that they were attracted by the rats escaping the demolished houses.

She shook her head. 'That's not it, Mr Addie. The cats are the souls of those murdered houses, and they are terribly confused. When they tear a bird to pieces they will go to hell. If they bite a rat they'll go to heaven.'

I laughed. 'It depends what crosses their path first.'

We drove out of the Jewish Town gate, and soon we were in Long Street. I paid the cabman, took the luggage and showed the girl the way into the house. It was my ill fortune to find the concierge standing in the passage, a broom in one hand and a pipe in the other, as if he were waiting for me. He came straight over to me and was taken aback when he caught sight of Berenice. I told him I had no time for him.

'But, My Lord,' he stuttered at me as I went upstairs, 'I have to warn you . . . I've cooked him –'

'You don't have to!' I barked at him. 'It's no business of yours who will be here with me, and anyway I'm moving out any time now. At least, I hope so.'

That silenced him. He crept back into his cubby-hole like a startled spider. But I had acted rashly, as I immediately discovered. I put my key in the lock, but it was already unlocked. I went into the passage and then into the room with Berenice at my heels. Someone was seated at my table drinking coffee, his travelling cape tossed over a chair. It was my father.

I shall never forget his expression: affable and maybe slightly apologetic at first when he raised his eyes from his cup, which he hugged in both hands as if warming himself from it. And then, as soon as he set eyes on the girl, his face showed amazement, disgust, outrage and antipathy in succession.

He put the cup on the table. 'Your mother', were his quiet opening words, and they were the worst I had ever heard from him, 'is always complaining that you take after me. But as God is my witness you do not. More's the pity.'

'That's what you came to tell me? You needn't have gone to the bother,' I said quietly and asked Berenice to wait in the next room. Not surprisingly she looked startled.

'Perhaps I ought to leave.' My father got up from the table, and I made no move to stop him. Then he sat down again and pressed his hands to his temples. 'I have an awful headache.'

I took off my coat and poured some water into a glass from a jug. I placed it in front of him and one of Hoffmann's pills next to it. 'That will relieve it.'

My father took it and swallowed it with some water, staring silently out of the window. I sat down on the divan and waited.

'Look here,' he said at last, and his tone was bitter, 'you know what things are like at Stránov. Taufer, whose forebears were serfs and subsequently stewards to our ancestors, has the wherewithal to buy us out, including our satin handkerchiefs with their stitched monograms, as soon as half of our castle ceases to be sufficient for him. I won't sell it to him, and I won't let you mother do it. But what about you? I can't rely on you in any matter at all, and, in truth, I'm reconciled to the fact that you will be the end of our line. No, don't interrupt. I thought you had some savings, seeing that you wanted to buy a house here. You get a decent allowance, don't you? No? Well that can't be helped, we can't afford to pay you more. I know it's awkward, but you'll just have to go out to work. The question is what you will do. I might be able to find you a post, but the rest will be up to you. But at this moment I urgently need to borrow some money. It is for the Czech cause.'

He stopped talking in order to catch his breath, and I poured him some claret into the empty glass. 'I didn't know you were involved with the Czech cause.'

He drank thirstily. 'But it's not possible to stand aside, Adam. Just look at the northern border areas. I never minded the Germans, but the way they are throwing their weight around there is scandalous. They are taking over one village after another, even whole towns, and that is really not on because the population there has always been mixed. And, just imagine, those industrious Germans are raising money to take over the leading firms, They have a joint agreement, they act in unity, have shared treasuries and they pay into them. Their investment societies have bought up one brewery after another. They own pharmacies, bakeries and slaughterhouses. They're trying to get their hands on grain silos and concentrating on the hop gardens. They give me the creeps.'

I laughed. 'So it's to do with beer. The most important thing in the life of a Czech and a German.'

'It's no laughing matter!' he snapped. 'The countryside is rife with Germanization, and the moment the two populations clash the victors will drive out the vanquished and thereby saw off the branch they're sitting on.'

That made no sense to me. 'Why? You take too bleak a view of things, Father.' I gazed at him and couldn't recognize him. That refined and learned man, who had always preferred privacy and given precedence to the reading of Goethe and Shakespeare and studying his collections of chinoiserie and erotic prints, was collecting money for some obscure national cause.

'We have selected a dozen communities', he continued, 'where it is vital to invest in Czech schools and associations, even taverns that mustn't fall into German hands. I'm therefore asking you for a loan. I want nothing else from you, seeing that you refuse to get more deeply involved and the only thing you care about are your whores, by the look of it.'

He had insulted me but not enough.

'I'll see what I can do,' I said mildly. 'I'll send you something within the week, and you can build a second National Theatre in northern Bohemia.'

'Are you scoffing at me?' he retorted with a mixture of annoyance and sadness.

'You despise me and yet want to borrow money from me,' I replied calmly.

It looked by now as if he was going to leap up and slap me around the face, but he remained collapsed in his chair. Then he said with a sigh, 'Just in case you didn't know, your mother has been trying to arrange a marriage with Taufer. A marriage between you and Helena.'

I should have burst out laughing, but I couldn't. 'That'll come to nothing. Such a morganatic –'

'That's just what I say, Adam. Moreover, now that that cousin of yours is fawning over Miss Taufer it rather thwarts your mother's plans.'

I have to admit that he had managed to surprise me. 'Manny? Good for him.'

'Not really. His parents will never sanction such a relationship, and he is dutiful, unlike you.'

We drank our wine in silence. Then he got up and looked around for his overcoat. I brought it to him. I offered to get him a cab, but he refused. I promised once more that as soon as I had something I would send him a telegram, and we would agree on how to hand the money over to him. He nodded, lost in thought. He was dressed and ready to leave. Once more we were lost for words.

'I understand you,' I blurted out, and I sounded like a patient in a lunatic asylum. 'That poor girl I brought here. She is no tart. I want to help her.' I was annoyed with myself for my fawning vocabulary. But I had to justify myself somehow. A sort of obedience and submission to my begetter. I wish the ground could have swallowed me up.

'I'm not reproaching you for anything. Do what you see fit. You became an adult a long time ago,' said my father with a cold smile, his gaze fixed to the wall. Then he left.

I closed the door behind him nice and quietly and then went over to the wall to which my father had addressed his closing words. I took a look at the toe of my black patent-leather shoes and then deliberately and with full force kicked the plaster until my shoe was completely white, as well as my trouser leg up to the knee.

When I had pulled myself together, Berenice Karafiátová was standing in the doorway to the next room and shaking like an aspen.

She would have to get used to it.

XII

A Noble Middleman

An Apparition in Little Pinkas Street

With Berenice I was slipping into a situation that I had avoided with Gita. I would never have thought it. When a young woman whose property consisted of only a few basic things moved into my apartment it aroused the attention of the neighbourhood. I had yet to receive a visit from a vigilant policeman or from a representative of the parish, but they both started to appear outside my house more frequently than in the past. A moral gentlemen in civilian clothes and a man of the cloth who was unfamiliar to me as I don't go to church. I wasn't sure what those old dames from the neighbouring balconies or those two fellows saw in Berenice, but the entire neighbourhood was fired with curiosity about the beautiful, orientally arrayed girl. And what would Mama say?

Solly started to pay me more frequent calls than usual, never missing a day, and on Wednesdays he appeared both morning and evening. He made Berenice a gift of four dresses, which he altered on a sewing machine and then wanted her to wear around the apartment and to execute pirouettes. I treated him to schnapps and chided him for gawking at her so transparently, although I myself found it hard to take my eyes off her. She was particularly irresistible in a new dark-coloured costume with lace sleeves and Turkish trousers gathered above the ankle (although she received a completely different outfit for walking outdoors), as well as a lace blouse beneath which her corset showed black and diaphanous sleeves and trouser legs that her olive skin shone through. Her drawers were white, however. Solly swore he had 'searched Prague from top to bottom, but black ladies' underwear is impossible to buy in this provincial dump – it's a crying shame!'

Once, when she was leaning over to pour us tea and her small but rounded breasts almost poured out of her bodice – although not her nipples, of course – Solly declared in quavering tones that he couldn't understand how he could ever have wanted to marry a Catholic.

Outings with Berenice attracted people's gaze, but I was afraid to leave her at home alone. I had a sense that someone might take her from me. She had no objections to living in my home. It was unlikely she had ever known anything better, but so long as she had one room and I the other there were actually two bedrooms. I was afraid that if Manny were to return suddenly from the country, where he was enjoying my mother's hospitality, I would have nowhere to put him.

The girl behaved towards me with disarming trust. I would buy her perfumes, powders and bath oils, which had the same effect on her as it used to have on Gita and the girls before her – glass beads, pearl ear-rings, a fine silver anklet with gems, a bone bracelet with carved roses (I avoid rings on principle). The silliest little trifle elicited gratitude, which Berenice, unlike the others, conveyed in just a look.

Should I have been surprised? One guardian had been replaced by another – richer and younger. I was something like an uncle for her, and I searched within myself for an answer to the question whether I minded or whether, on the contrary, it gave me a new sense of fulfilment far removed from anything physical. In that respect she was innocent, and it was plain for me to see; any ulterior thoughts immediately received a drubbing from my bad conscience. On the other hand, I was conscious of how she won people over, such as how she gradually wrapped the poor concierge around her little finger by her admiring praise – of his well-swept courtyard, his perfectly cleaned windows and his window boxes with their French marigolds and pelargoniums (which I consider the most bourgeois of flowers). He carried up buckets of water for her when she wanted a bath and made sure she had enough wood for the stove lest the young lady's exotically curved nose should risk a cold or that splendidly slender throat be inflamed by insidious catarrh.

I marvelled at what a girl like that was capable of by the mere fact of being. Charming, clean, smelling of soap, in starched and ironed girlish clothes. I had to admit to myself that I had never experienced anything of the sort with any of my previous girls. Possibly with Gita – it had certainly been heading in that direction with her.

It came as a surprise when I started to miss Gita.

Twice I took Berenice with me to visit the Urzidil brothers, and on both occasions they were not at home. The third time I went alone and called in at Madame Golda's to see Gita. I drank Sekt with her in the morning and penetrated her body twice, once on my arrival and the second time when I was leaving, but I shouldn't have done it because she didn't stop crying the whole time, saying she had heard something about that beauty and was terrified that I would abandon her. I assured her that I would continue in future to count on her as my housemaid, laundress and cook, and I would pay her something for it until such a time as she found someone to marry her. That made her even more miserable. I made love to a weeping girl and was it . . . for real?

That day I found the Urzidils in at the Loggia. They gave me an enthusiastic welcome and informed me that it was going to be possible to sell the house. They had bribed some official at the town hall, and he promised them that the property could not in any circumstances be included on the list of buildings destined for urban improvement. That would require the urban plan to be amended. They told me the official had been surprisingly cheap. It struck me that the brothers were slightly tipsy, although I saw no sign of any beer jugs on that occasion.

We agreed that in the coming days we would undertake the next requisite steps to transfer the property. They were expecting the money from me by the end of the next month. They were unexpectedly generous about that.

'The entire sum if possible,' Alois warned me.

'But we don't mind a bit of horse-trading,' Richard added.

'We heard tell you were going around with some abandoned young woman. You were looking for us, weren't you? You were here with her, so our neighbour told us at the tavern.'

'You know how things are,' Alois said in turn. 'I personally wouldn't be seen out with her in the daytime, if you know what I mean, My Lord. You have to wait till it's dark. During the night in Prague you can by yourself a little chimneysweep, sweep his chimney, send him home with sixpence, and his mother will be as happy as Larry. That's how it's done. But flaunting yourself in the daytime with a schoolgirl, it's something people in Prague don't like to see, that's for sure.'

'And should you wish to bring the young miss here when we're home', Richard declared, adopting his brother's tone of voice, 'I'll paint her for you.' I was beginning to find their company irksome.

I promised to obtain the money or the deal would be off. Then I went home and tried to fathom out why I was suddenly bothered by other people's opinions of me. I found it particularly surprising in the case of the two painters.

But there was nothing to be done, except one thing: I equipped myself with a small doctor's bag, filled it with Hoffmann's little bottles and set off around town. The following evenings I played the door-to-door salesman, knocking on the doors of well-to-do burghers and chiefly doing the rounds of the remaining brothels in the Old Town and the former Jewish ghetto. The places were seething with life as if those establishments were writhing in a death spasm.

I walked from one end to the other of Chamois Street, Fish Street, Saaz Street, Josefov Street, Gypsy Street and Rabbi Street and even Stew Lane. I moved on from Madame Golda's to Sojka's, from Sojka's to Kautzky's, from Kautzky's to Goldschmidt's, and I was also at Napoleon's. I offered a quarter of a pill to taste for free, and the success of my sales strategy surprised me. Before I had gone around the Jewish quarter and the Old Town three errand boys caught up with me on the street and were demanding large supplies of my precious goods. Then, when they had worked out my regular route, they started waiting for me at Madame Golda's. Whenever I turned up there and ordered myself a cognac they would produce some cash and buy a few packs. I should have realized earlier that the number of middle men would increase and that the more hands the heroic pill passed through the higher the price would rise – but I changed my tactics in time. In fact, I was rather proud of myself. All the interested parties told me that they had sole authorization to purchase, and they were loath to tell me whether they had been sent by one particular customer or several. In each case I would sell three to five pills – exceptionally a half or even a whole bottle – and would implore all purchasers to use the preparation in moderation and only to spread the good name of Dr Hoffmann among reliable people, lest it came to the ears of the authorities or – God forbid – the police. Nevertheless, I suspected that since my first rounds had aroused such interest it would not be kept secret for even a month. On the other hand, I knew from my parallel life in the brothels that the city's shadowy *demi-monde* was sometimes more capable of protecting its information than Prague officialdom, which basked in the sun of imperial grace.

On the fourth or fifth night I was returning via the lanes of the Jewish Town, exhausted as never before in my life. After all, I was actually doing some work for the first time! It was four fifteen and still dark everywhere, but I started to hear bird-song from the direction of the river, possibly from Letná Park on the opposite bank. Then it fell silent again. My pockets were bursting with bank notes. I reflected blissfully that I had plenty of time to settle up with the Urzidil brothers. What I was carrying in my pocket I would send my father by post. He would marvel at how well his prodigal son was doing, and should he happen to mention it in front of Mama (which was not entirely likely as they spoke together so rarely) he would simply be playing into my hands. I was planning to use part of the money to pay back some of what I owed Solly – a fifth, let's say – and the rest I would spend in the company of Berenice and then Gita, whom I had neglected so much in recent times. Anyway, I would soon earn some more, maybe not as much, but it was highly likely that the heroic pills would continue to be in demand – needed, in fact, and even regarded as indispensable – that our mad Prague would be mad about them.

I swallowed a pill and realized that I could no longer conceive of life without the medicine. And I had no desire to. It was a crutch that I intended to lean on manfully, my new faith that would make me whole.

I walked along Butchers Street enjoying the silence before dawn, but then I got lost in the poorer part of the ghetto. There wasn't a soul about. A damp and slimy mist, reeking of the river and refuse, was stealing into the street, chilling my fingers and nose. My moustache was bedewed as if I had just been drinking beer. Still, it was better than dry air bereft of odours but full of dust. My cough, which used to be a constant presence either manifest or latent, was now an absence. My windpipe was not inflamed, and a coating of phlegm no longer formed as protection but also as a source of suffocation; gone was the need to expel it with such difficulty. The cough had vanished from this world and found refuge in the depths of hell. I took deep breaths of festering air and felt that I loved this city in spite of all.

I stood with eyes closed in the middle of the street and breathed deeply, intoxicatedly. I opened my eyes and caught sight of a small brown dog, quite a pretty mongrel with legs proportionate to its body and a white bib. It sat in front of me on its hind legs, leaning on its forelegs, observing me in the hopes of some titbit. I looked around me and tried to recognize the houses near by. I surmised that it might be Old Maisel Lane, but most of the houses here were still standing. I found myself beneath a two-storeyed building with a bay on corbels. Inserted into the stucco was a large Star of David, and the arched windows grouped above it were reminiscent of the tablets of the law that Moses received on Mount Sinai. Ah, yes. Lesser Pinkas Street.

Now I knew where I was. A bit further on the wall around the Jewish cemetery grinned at me.

I decided to return home and was pleased that I would soon have a new address, that I would live in my own little house with a baroquely curlicued gallery. Then I came again upon the dog that was observing me a little while earlier with such interest. It was sniffing the air like a pedigree pointer; indeed there could have been some pointer blood in its veins. It was on all fours now, with its beagle's ears and dachshund's tail at attention. It was staring into the lane behind me where no streetlamps yet shone, but the gateways were still open and black because of the darkness. Then I heard a voice, resonant although whispering. It struck me that it was how people sometimes speak on stage.

'Don't be frightened. Come here.'

I would have said it was a man's voice, but can one distinguish such from a woman's when whispering?

The hairs on the dog's back bristled.

'Who's there?' I called into the darkness and tried in vain to make out where the whisperer was concealed.

'Don't be frightened. Come here,' it repeated. And then, after a moment of silence, 'I'll do you no harm. I've got something for you.'

My legs grew heavy, and I could not move a step. He was out of sight, but I already knew who it was.

I would have expected the mongrel to take to its heels, but it meekly crept towards the voice and disappeared into the dark passage-way.

Then the whisper laughed, and the animal yelped. It dashed out, flew past me and stopped by the cemetery, spinning around and around and snapping at its rear end. Then the laughter was heard once more and it sped onwards. In the place where, moments ago, it had a tail there was now just a stump. The animal left a dark trail behind it. I felt nauseous.

I inserted my monocle into my eye, my hand shaking as never before in my life, and then I watched as in the darkness of the passageway materialized a figure, as if someone was in the process of cutting it out of paper. First a hat, then shoulders and a long cloak. It came closer, scuffing the soles of it feet on the paving stones. It was real.

It was the nocturnal apparition from those urban improvement pits. The shadow hesitated, stopped and then crept closer. Solly was right: it was folly to go out at night unarmed.

The figure struck a match, which it clenched in its black-gloved fingers and illuminated itself. The black cape reached the top of its neck, just below the head, on which a hat rested. Between the hat and the cloak there was neither neck nor face, just sinewy meat, a countenance of lacerated scarlet flesh in which there yawned three black holes: eyes and a mouth. They were as dark as all the places not reached by the dim light of the match, but from the lower hole something protruded – a slender dog's tail that wriggled like a captured grass snake.

The apparition spat it on to the ground. 'Do you like me?' it moaned and moved a step closer. 'See what I look like. I'm Kleinfleisch.'

Then the match went out, but the shuffling steps could still be heard. When it struck another match the monster was holding a long kosher butcher's knife and juice was trickling from a hole in the meat.

It is but a small step from a bad nobleman to a good coward. I had the feeling that my legs stayed there, that Kleinfleisch had sliced me in two and I was running away from him only from the waist upwards. But I did have them, they were below me, and I had never known them run so fast. I held on to my hat lest it fly away.

Then I was in another street and panting wildly. A cart of churns stood outside a shop. Some housewife was placing a couple of pence into the milkman's hand. They looked up goggle-eyed to see who was dashing past them. I looked back. Kleinfleisch wasn't behind me. His butcher's knife had not pierced my body, only fear.

I reached Long Street, along which a group of women street sweepers was walking. I tapped on the concierge's window and had to wait for him to wake up and let me in. 'A long night out again, sir?' he mumbled as I walked past him. I left him there without an answer and staggered upstairs. Once inside the apartment I peeped into Berenice's room. She was still asleep, completely hidden beneath the coverlet. I closed the door quietly, swallowed a Hoffmann pill and stretched out on the divan with a kitchen knife within reach of my right hand.

XIII

A Black Morning

A Long Day

Zuzana Hrabalová is dead. I learnt this from Deputy Police Councillor Ignacius Herrmann not in some police station but in his spacious office to which I was escorted from home by his colleague, Detective Listopad. Well, at least they didn't send a uniformed officer for me first thing in the morning. I had slept scarcely three hours.

I had been seen during the night in Jewry in a state of extreme agitation, they informed me. They had been told it by a certain Otylie Meyrinková. She said I had been dashing along the street like a maniac, and I had ignored her, even though we were well acquainted. She had been looking for a friend of hers who was ill. She was bringing her some medicine. She had not found her in the brothel where Zuzana worked. So she had gone to check her digs that were two doors away. Her bedroom door was open, an oil lamp was burning on the table and next to it sat a human head. The head had a neck but no shoulders. The rest of the body was under the table. The table top was a sticky pool of blood, as if someone had emptied an inkwell on to it.

'What frightened me most of all was the thought that Zuzana might open her eyes again,' Ota went on to say in her statement and also that she had vomited but not lost consciousness. She had staggered out of the house, and before she managed to find a gendarme she had seen with her own eyes a former client of hers who had maintained her some years ago. He was none other than Karel Adam Count Arco.

I also had to make a clean breast of it. Not the entire truth, of course. I made no mention of Hoffmann's pills. I informed Herrmann that I had spent the night with a prostitute. I gave Gita's name; she is good at backing me up. And I added that they needn't question her any more about it, and I also told them that the expression Kleinfleisch that had been mentioned last time now meant something to me. I recounted my personal encounter with the Jewish phantom, and Listopad took careful notes of what I said. I asked them to let me see Otka, as I would like to have it out with her face to face and in their presence, but Listopad said she was not there.

Then they talked about possible motives, citing about a dozen: money, debts, jealousy, envy, revenge, sexual aberration, ritual murder . . . I can't recall the rest. They wanted to know what I thought about it all. I replied that if they were asking me whether I saw a connection between Zuzana's murder and the deaths of Rosina and that girl who fell (or was pushed) out of that window, then no obvious connection occurred to me. Prague was a dangerous place and the former ghetto even more so.

For some unknown reason Herrmann asked me about my parents, so I told him them they were getting poorer and poorer and that our line would end for good and all when I died.

'The nobility's good old days ended a hundred years ago,' Listopad commented, as if approving the process, and he wanted to know when I would be making my next visit to Stránov.

I replied that I had been there not long ago and expressed surprise that the police were informed about it. Herrmann frowned; all of a sudden there was a tension between them that I did not understand.

'Consider yourself confined to Prague, My Lord,' he said at last and summoned a uniformed lackey to escort me to the exit from the building.

There was no end to surprises that day. When I went out into the corridor I caught sight of Councillor Bürger seated on carved bench.

He was reading a booklet with his head sunk deep in his shoulders, and as I passed him he threw me an angry look. He uttered no word of greeting, nor did I.

Outside, Herrmann's assistant Listopad caught me up and declared that he would accompany me. I walked quickly and he trotted along-side me. It was impossible to fathom him. I found his behaviour repulsive and also confusing. And I had an awful headache.

'You know he was going around the brothels,' Listopad began.

'Who?'

'Councillor Bürger. Not what you'd expect of him, eh?'

'Probably not.'

'Do you know anything about him?'

'Nothing apart from the fact I can't stand the man. But there's a lot of people I can't stand.'

'Precisely. He's not very popular.' Listopad lengthened his stride and swept his long sweat-soaked hair back from his forehead. I kept my face turned away from him so as not to smell his armpits. 'Have you ever met him?'

'I expect so. I recall some kind of rally where he was quoting Preininger's report about the living conditions in Jewry.'

'That's right, hygiene and light against mould and vice,' Listopad sniggered. 'But last night we nabbed him in the red-light district.'

'Do you mean to say he spent the night in police custody?'

'Yes, at the station. The gendarmes brought him to us in the morning. He threatened to make a complaint about us. Let him go ahead.'

'I see. But there's nothing I can tell you about it. I bid you good day.'

'Wait a moment. He didn't go inside, you see. He just spied from behind a window and pasted a piece of paper on the door saying that the house would be demolished by order of the city council.'

'A private initiative by a devoted official.'

'It's odd isn't it? But it's far too soon in the case of those buildings. They're not due for demolition for another year.'

'And your conclusion is that it was just camouflage and in reality it was he that murdered that poor woman.'

'Either he or you in a Kleinfleisch mask. After all, the effects of those pills on the brain haven't been studied, have they?'

I stopped in mid-pace and he with me. His eyes remained fixed on me, but now they shone with childish glee at having caught me out.

That was more than I could take. 'If you are referring to my remedies, I can provide you with a sample, Mr Listopad. But allow me to point out that Zuzana Hrabalová's murderer need not be a half-comical, half-horrifying bogeyman. Things can happen simultaneously, and there need not be any connection between them.'

'Of course,' he nodded eagerly, 'such as your use of the hydro-chlorate – it also needn't have anything to do with its sudden appearance all over Jewry.'

'It's simply a good remedy. A very good remedy. Without it I would be ill, and I would have to leave Prague and go somewhere a lot further away than my parents' country place. I would have to spend the rest of my life in a sanatorium.'

'That would suit me.'

'But not me.'

'You're fortunate then. You can't go anywhere anyway. We intend to keep a close eye on the illegal sale of that substance. We'll catch the person selling it. We'll charge him and hand him over to the court.'

'That's a relief. I was starting to have my doubts about the effectiveness of the police.'

'And the police are starting to have their doubts about you, would you believe?'

'What do you want me to say in response? That I am insulted and surprised?'

He took me by the elbow, and I extricated myself from his grip in a somewhat theatrical manner. He glanced at his hand as if making sure he had not soiled it with something smelly and quickly put it in his pocket. Then he said, 'What if we stopped beating about the bush? I won't concern myself with what you use to "treat yourself" in the privacy of your home and not even whether you sell some of it to rich Jews and whores, not to mention who it is you've moved into your apartment and whether she is even of age. Pshaw – watch, I toss it behind me. And in return, My Lord, you will report to me once a week about your father's anti-Austrian activities. Only to me – we won't involve old Herrmann in this. Let him solve the murders. Agreed? You'll invite your father over and have a nice chat with him – behave like a proper son at last. You've a tendency to neglect your parents, after all. Admit it. Take a leaf out of my book. I'm grown up, and I visit my father whenever I get the chance, and we always talk about life together. Do likewise and then pass it on to me. That's not too much to ask, is it? For your information I'm a zealous sort of an officer, hee-hee, and it looks as if there are more of us all the time.'

I gaped at him in astonishment, dumbfoundedly watching the artful smirk as it broadened. Then I delivered a resounding slap to that grinning visage.

His astonishment matched my own. He shook his head from side to side, raised his hand to his ear and uttered a resentful 'ouch' in the reproachfully self-pitying way of a boy beaten up at the school gate. Then he pulled himself together and started to back away.

But I didn't administer a second slap. I stepped up to him and whispered in the uninjured ear with a boldness supplied by the heroic remedy in my pocket. 'Actually you're lucky you work for the police, otherwise you could have expected a duel, Listopad. Officially I am not allowed to engage in combat with a policeman. But there are other ways of settling scores. Goodbye.'

I left him there and did not look back. As the weather had turned out fine I swallowed a Hoffmann pill and drank two small glasses of schnapps and a bottle of soda water in the Drum tavern, which now stood amidst mountains of stones, sand, earth and gravel that had been piled up there to be used for raising the level of the embankment. The building materials looked as if they were about to bury the tavern any moment, but I did not care. Prague's bells started to ring at the churches in the Lesser Quarter, the New Town and

167

Hradčany marking midday and scaring the gulls that flew hither and thither in flocks above the river. I lit a pipe, and shortly afterwards I felt the tension, migraine, disquiet and restlessness dissolve in a blend of reliable heady essences of tobacco, alcohol and hydrochlorate. The image of a woman's head on a table in some garret grew fuzzier and was no longer so intrusive. Had it been the work of Kleinfleisch? Or of someone who wanted it to look as if it was. On the previous occasion it had been enough to terrify the girl into jumping out of the window of her own accord. If she hadn't, would he have used the knife on her, too? And how was it possible that police investigators, including Ignacius Herrmann himself, had arrived so soon? Had they received a tip-off from someone? They were linking me with it and ordered my 'confinement', but Prague is one enormous detention room. Like me they have no idea whether the death of Rosina Weinerová was linked with those murders. And what was Councillor Bürger up to? Wandering around Jewry at night all on his own, uniformed officials ready to protect him from anyone who might recognize him as the zealous sanitizer of the Jewish Town and reach for a paving stone to settle accounts with him.

I was hungry. I glanced at my watch. It was seven minutes past noon. Previously I used to wake up at this hour and have breakfast but not today. After a night in which I had been threatened by a spectre with a knife I had learnt in the space of two hours that morning about the vile murder of a poor girl, and on top of that a police extortionist had proposed that I inform on my father in return for being left alone by the authorities. It was truly not a morning to write home about.

I told the tavern keeper to send a potboy to the popular place of entertainment known as Golda's – the side door and the staircase running up the side of the wall to the first floor – with a message for Miss Gita to meet me at the Drum tavern and not to take too long about it. Then I ordered luncheon: veal sweetbreads with millet porridge and a jug of wine. I intended to make up for my missed breakfast.

Gita arrived shortly before two o'clock in a green-and-yellow dress with double fastening, a turquoise hat with white ostrich feathers and a pure white parasol carried over her arm. I excused her tardiness, and I couldn't have cared less whether someone saw us together. No doubt the police were dogging my every step. We drank one coffee after another together and then Madeira wine, while I was regaled with the gossip about the latest murder that had already done the rounds of Jewry, even though the newspapers were supposed to wait till the evening or the following day to publish the news.

'So it's definite,' Gita said crossly. 'There's another state of emergency on the way. Zuzana Hrabalová was murdered by a phantom known as Kleinfleisch, which the Czech patriots say has a German-Jewish identity. There'll be ructions again, Addie, you mark my words.'

I pointed out that I had heard Kleinfleisch that night, and he had spoken Czech, but she was adamant. She tossed back a glass of the sweet wine and declared, 'It was a ritual murder, Addie. I heard it from the girls who saw Zuza eating sausages. The Jews couldn't forgive her for that and sent him after her to chop her head off. It doesn't mean a thing that he spoke Czech.' I asked her if she had spoken to Otka, and the tone of her voice changed immediately – surely I wasn't associating with Otka again. She had had her chips and I shouldn't touch her with a bargepole.

I turned my gaze away towards the cathedral, which a commendable association has decided to complete, and took no more notice of Gita's talk. I mused and listened to gulls, hearing with astonishment within their cries a strange regularity until I realized that there were two overlapping sounds, their shrieks and the ticking of my watch. And I revelled in the combined effect of wine and Hoffmann's pills, which was capable of displacing the noise made by the demolition machines; they were at work in Jewry as on any other ordinary day, but they were now miraculously distant, as if they were making their racket not around the next corner but in the hospital gardens or even way outside Prague in somewhere like Libeň.

What aroused me from those pleasant contemplations was, once more, Gita. She had not noticed that I wasn't listening to her, but now she was talking about something else – namely the medicine that had become all the rage in the Old Town, how everyone was using it and how those who know how to were busily trading in it. I started to pay attention. Gita was going on about how Madame Golda had brought some. Some young fellow, some errand boy, had sold it to her, but Madame had known about the remedy ages ago but under a different name. It was apparently not very different from morphine, but this hydrochlorate wasn't so dangerous; it was gentle and a much more modern than morphine and truly medicinal. 'Look, Addie. I've bought some for you. You ought to try it for that cough of yours. But you don't cough any more, do you? That's miraculous, Addie, it must have a remote effect! That's unlikely, though. I expect it's because I've been praying for you to get better.'

I stared at her in amazement. 'You pray for me?'

'Yes,' she nodded, and only when she noticed my surprise did she start to blush.

I didn't know how to respond, and I was relieved that Hoffmann's miracle staved off emotion as well as coughing and also that Gita had no intention of halting her litany. 'And I haven't told you yet what the girls thought up when Madame brought it and gave them a pill each. Just imagine, first they swallowed it and they had a fantastic sensation in their mouths and all around their faces. I found it was great for my eyes, and it helps clear my nose, like when you take a peppermint drop, would you believe? And Madame said it helped her get rid of the wind, and that gave Frankie an even better idea and she scrounged another pill and right in front us she reached under her skirt into her drawers and stuck it in the front hole, and you should have seen her knees buckle under her, and we had to grab her to stop her falling flat on the ground like a frog, and she gasped all the while like girls who put it on – I never put it on for you, Addie, you know that, don't you? – and, look, I've got half a bottle of it from Madame, and I'll show you I can do it the same as Frankie, look, I haven't got anything on under my skirt, I'll put it on a spoon like this and in it goes! Now nobody'll take it off me. What's up, Addie? You've got a face on you like a plaster saint.'

I looked at Gita with pity and maybe even compassion. She had increasingly left me cold in recent months, and she was even starting to disgust me. For a long time already being with her meant not just doing what I liked with her body but listening to her endless prattle and wondering all the time whether I still found her lewdness appealing or not. And I was already tired of it. Almost the only way I could more or less cope with her and achieve unadulterated satisfaction was when she was asleep.

I settled the bill, took her by the elbow and steered her to Golda's, to the cage I had no reason to lock any more. But if I left it open Gita would pay the price, just like the girls I had previously kept.

I called in at home and exchanged a few words with Berenice, promising her that I would enrol her in a school as soon as possible, and I was overjoyed to see the spark that flashed in her eyes; loneliness does not scorn even the company of the gaoler, and she was still unsure what the change of uncles signified. Maybe she was scared to ask, and I was scared to think up some reply. In her plain calico dress with its clover-leaf pattern she looked so pure and vulnerable that I decided to leave again quickly. I stuffed bottles of white pills into my coat pocket and locked the apartment behind me. Downstairs I banged on the concierge's door and repeatedly impressed on him that he was not let anyone upstairs after the young lady, not even a gendarme. Then I reminded him that I would be moving out any time soon. He didn't look as if he intended to bemoan the fact.

Selling in broad daylight was not as easy as in the night-time, but I had no time to waste. The pills' popularity and the hawking of them was spreading like wildfire, and I had to act fast, because as soon as the police got their hands on it and had it analysed by some university laboratory they would be bound to discover that it was an opium derivative and immediately put the kibosh on the heroic escapades.

I visited a few of the better inns. The waiters were curious. They had already got wind of something and were prepared to keep a stock,

171

and I was a generous supplier. In one establishment they took me into the kitchen and offered me claret. In exchange I let them have a few half-tablets to try and then I left them two full bottles for a handsome sum of money. I sold another bottle to some street whores' pimps and then a thin pimply girl came and brought me to a milliner's shop. The milliner could have been in her forties and wanted to buy everything I had. She told me she had consumption, but fortunately she could afford to pay. She didn't look ill. I sold her seven tablets, and when I was on my way out she threatened to denounce me to the police anonymously unless I sold her at least three times as much. I agreed on condition that she pay me four times the amount she had paid for the seven tablets. She called me a thieving Jew but paid up.

In the end I had more money than I had anticipated that afternoon, and it occurred to me to call on my notary and arrange a meeting with the Urzidil brothers, who had, one hoped, by now managed to settle the formalities about selling their house. I walked as far as the Little Market, and in front of the telephone exchange building with its bristling tower, from which dozens of wires led to connectors sprouting from Prague's roofs like mushrooms after rain, I first heard and then set eyes on a noisy mob. Prague folklore. The shouting was in Czech and German.

I realized it was to do with some woman who had been organizing a public collection here for several days if not weeks. I had read about it in the press. Passers-by were exhorted by several tin signs and a band of child assistants to spare just two hellers towards the building of Czech schools in villages on the country's frontiers. The woman had managed to three-quarters fill a glazed cabinet bigger than herself, which was guarded day and night on the pavement outside the telephone exchange by well-built Sokol members. But now it looked as though a group of irate men was preparing to seize the collection by force.

'What's going on?' I asked a stout swell in a shiny top hat and a pin-striped morning coat that was too tight. He was standing in the arcade of a medieval house holding a stein of beer in one hand and smoking a Virginia cigar. It seemed to me that the sight of the quarrelsome crowd gratified him.

He looked me up and down and appeared at a loss what to make of a well-dressed man with a miniature watch on his wrist and a gold-rimmed monocle of about the same size in his eye asking such a naïve question.

'The size of the collection', he replied, although it wasn't what I had asked, 'surprised everyone. My guess is that the hellers in the cabinet would amount to about fifty thousand crowns.'

'And that doesn't suit some people.'

'The patriots are enraptured, sir! But there were others who were not so pleasantly surprised, if you see what I mean: namely our Germans, who have started to organize their own rival collection outside the New German Theatre. Underhand, don't you think? You haven't been to see it? The Germans went the wrong way about it, though: they collected money before a performance and asked for a gulden straight out. The trouble is that they're putting on Wagner's *Meistersingers* – do you know it? And the audiences are small. People in Prague don't understand Wagner.'

'So the collection hasn't been a success,' I deduced.

'Communicating vessels of the economy,' the man in the top-hat gesticulated genially. 'Wherever there is a surplus there has to be poverty at the other extreme. You look like an educated gentleman, sir, upon my word. Have you read Marx's *Capital*? What do you make of it?'

I shook my head and realized that I was unable to make him out either. I offered him a bottle of hydrochlorate at half price, but he brushed it aside and went on orating. I grasped from what he was saying that some group of German students had got drunk that afternoon on Sophie's Island and had now arrived to smash the Czechs' glass cabinet.

'As if the Czechs themselves wouldn't mind smashing the glass cabinet they're forced to live in, eh? Don't you agree?' The man raised his eyebrows knowingly and my flesh started to creep. I nodded in agreement and took my leave, sure in the knowledge that I had managed to choose a paid police informer out of the crowd as my interlocutor. Well, at least he had been too intent on his task to realize that the hydrochlorate was the substance that was being so merrily traded on the black market.

A brawl erupted in the crowd outside the telephone exchange. Some Germans – about fifteen altogether – carrying rolled flags emblazoned with the Austrian eagle started to lunge with them at the people guarding the collection and at the woman organizing it. Sokol members dashed to her aid accompanied by some of the onlookers, chiefly journeymen and young labourers. Someone started shouting that he would protect the collection with his life, while someone else was groaning in pain. Strangest of all, the first gendarme I came upon was around the corner in the Old Town Square. He was eyeing the pigeons on the Marian column suspiciously and seemed oblivious to the racket coming from the Little Market.

The Urzidils were home, along with their goat. The brothers were in high spirits, drinking to some success or other with the help of a jug of beer and a tall, narrow bottle of liqueur. They immediately offered me some, but I declined.

They told me I had come just at the right moment and said I really ought to take a drink because that very day they had bribed two actuaries and their superior – all three extremely cheap apparently – in order to get official confirmation that their house was not for demolition because it was being acquired by an important nobleman. I was heartened to hear it.

Then they asked for the deposit, and I immediately spread it out for them on the table; this gladdened them even more. Alois bellowed some unintelligible shepherd's ditty and performed a pagan-style dance while Richard clapped in time with him. I filled and lit a pipe and listened to their future plans, how they were moving to the New Town where they would open a studio and paint portraits of rich burghers and church dignitaries, as well as some prince of their acquaintance. And my portrait, too, of course; they would give me a discount. I asked for a receipt for the deposit, and while Alois withdrew to the courtyard with razor and washbowl Richard scoured the living room for a clean sheet of paper and an inkwell; at the same time he tried to persuade me to go with them to a brothel where they had some new dusky girls. Had I experienced lovemaking Hungarian style?

I put the signed receipt away in my wallet and promised to pay them the rest of the money at the bank within two weeks, so that it would be paid after the house had been transferred to my use. I shook his hand, and Richard remarked that the word of a nobleman counted for a great deal in his book and that our transaction would be successfully concluded beyond a doubt. I replied that an artist's word was unquestionably as reliable as my own – not that I believed it, but at that moment I had no option but to put my trust in that eccentric pair.

When I was leaving, Alois waved at me in the courtyard with his razor. He was shaving in front of a mirror over the washbowl; one cheek was shaved, while unshaved bristles showed through the white foam still covering the other. A paint brush lay on top of the soap bowl.

XIV

Berenice in the Bath

Manny in Trouble

One gloomy morning on a Wednesday I was sitting at a marble-topped round table in Ulbrich's Café in the Old Town and not looking out through the large window because outside greasy dust hung in the air, not only at the level of the paving stones or high in the air but at mouth, nose, ear and eye level, and all that rolling leaden greasiness blurred your eyesight, slowed your step and stifled your breath, enveloping everything dead and living with its lethal membrane – overcoats, houses, dogs, statues, poultry and lamp-posts. Beneath its weight the pigeons no longer bothered to take to the wing. Demolished houses whirled around their city like ghosts, now in the form of cats, now as poisonous clouds.

I was smoking a pipe, the only thing that helped to combat that loathsome atmosphere when I was obliged to wait for the evening to take another hydrochlorate tablet. But for the fact I had prescribed those intervals between doses and that I had the willpower to abide by them I would have already had at least five of those pills inside me and would have been incapable of any thought or action and would probably have never dragged myself out of bed ever again, except in a coffin maybe.

I was drinking coffee from a red-and-white striped cup. They wrote in the *National Gazette* about the medical success of that Viennese doctor Professor Freud who is increasingly a topic of conversation and who is able to diagnose and often even cure symptoms of serious neurosis in his patients – most of whom were women. I said to myself that it might be an idea to take a trip to Vienna, in spite of the police ban. Perhaps he could sort my head out, too, because when I look out of this café window it seems as if the people outside are taking absolutely no notice of the black dust cloud about to clog their lungs. Maybe I'm exaggerating everything much more now that the effect of Hoffmann's heroic miracle is waning.

I caught sight of a young couple: a ludicrously youthful pasty-faced man in a peaked cap with a blue and red scarf around his neck, undoubtedly a gift from her, a girl who looked slightly older and was so beautiful that one was inclined to be envious. She walked confidently at his side in a black outdoor costume with orange trimmings, swinging a parasol and making sure that her every step caused everything to sway, including her bosom, which respired freely beneath her clothes, without bones or stays or other ingenious means of physical confinement.

They were holding hands, and as they passed the café the young man lifted her pale hand to his bristly chin and gave it a hasty kiss, and she, without blushing, raised his knobbly paw to her pouting lips and paid him back in kind. I had never seen the like. How outrageous . . . and how fantastic . . . I turned away and calmed my trembling knees.

Hm. The things one saw in Prague these days.

I glanced outside once more. They were still standing there, looking inside, directly at me, as if wondering whether they ought to come and join me. All around them cobwebs of smog floated down from the defaced sky, but they themselves were sunlit – like on some romantic illustration. Then suddenly they were gone.

I was instantly beset with the dejection of one who is envious but old enough to know that he is not fated to experience something of the kind. I was old. And old men read newspapers and get hot under the collar about the state of the world. I gave it a try.

They wrote about everything possible. For instance, that the

Prague anarchists had started to publish their own review. I really couldn't have cared less. They also wrote that the Church of John the Baptist on the Balustrade had also been demolished, which I did care about. How is it that it escaped my attention? And would I notice if they demolished St James's . . . or St Gall's. And they wrote that Libeň would be promoted to the status of town . . . goodness, that ghastly little village by the Rokytka? . . . the next thing they'd be asking to be linked to the metropolis on advantageous terms . . . where would the limits of Prague be then? . . . somewhere near Brandýs? . . . Kutná Hora? . . . or Olomouc? . . . would our castle at Stránov become part of the wider centre of the capital city? . . . the Counts of Arco with a seat in Prague once more? And they wrote that the Prague workers were setting up their own trade-union organization . . . whatever next? *Bestia triumphans*! . . . a blow-out is on the way . . . the trough is filling, potato soup is on the menu . . . no borders, no limits anywhere . . . crowd in while we can, we'll cut free from tradition and the devil take the hindmost . . .

It was a fact: I was becoming an angry old man in my thirties. If only I was better at being angry. It all dissipates immediately.

I leafed through the political pages. It was different and much worse. There were demonstrations against Badeni in Vienna; tens of thousands of people in the street and the threat of bloodshed and martial law in all the big cities. The government was expected to resign. The Austrian Germans' hatred of the Czechs was growing stronger. Supporters of independence were under preventive arrest, and everyone was terrified of the unpredictable anarchists. And the twentieth century was only a couple of years away

I felt weak. I folded the *National Gazette* and had no wish to see it any more. I downed a glass of kummel and snapped my fingers at the waiter to bring something else to buck me up. I had not slept the previous night. The previous evening Berenice had prepared a surprise for me, and I wasn't sure how to come to terms with the experience.

I had come home early. It was eleven thirteen. I opened the front door with the concierge's duplicate key and quietly crept upstairs to the apartment. Usually an oil lamp was burning for me but not this time. It was dark everywhere. I took off my overcoat and waistcoat, hung my hat blindly on a hook, slipped out of my shoes, unfastened the suspenders below my knees and removed my socks, which were sweat-sodden after an entire evening engaged in my heroic business dealings. I removed my braces from my shoulders and pulled my shirt out of my trousers, resolved to clean my teeth with the hygienic green powder (I would leave the blue stain remover with the ghastly taste for another time). But while I was still in the passage I thought I heard a sound like a lavatory being flushed. I tiptoed along the cold floor to the bathroom door and discovered to my surprise that it was warmer there and noticeably humid. A feeble yellow light showed under the bottom of the door. I quietly pressed the handle and opened the door.

The girl had her back to me and didn't look back when I came in, although she must have heard me. A candle shone in a niche, and the coloured bottles of perfume, fragrant oils and herbal tinctures glittered in its light, but what shone most of all in the semi-darkness of the bathroom was Berenice's black hair. It hung down her back into the steaming water. There was little to be seen of her naked flesh, just her arms and shoulders. The candle in the niche was in front of her. I became jealous. She was enjoying all her maidenly beauty, while I was going to make myself scarce and pretend not to have seen such a gorgeous sight. But I banged into the door with my elbow.

It was at that moment that I was disabused about Berenice. Instead of curling up in the bath and waiting for me to disappear, she grabbed the sides and slowly stood up. Just as when the moon stands in front of the sun so now Berenice stood before the light from the candle, letting the light creep around the contours of a dark silhouette with a girlish waist and a grown woman's thighs and hips. The water flowed from her skin and her hair. The drops on her fingers shone for a moment and fell into the bath.

'Come here to me, sir,' said Berenice and remained standing there with her gaze fixed on the flame.

'I told you to call me Addie,' I replied in a faint voice.

At that Berenice turned around, but I still saw the same thing, the illusory silhouette of a naked female body, except that there was something more: in the gloom the girl's eyes glittered, and above them, around her forehead, shone a band of gold metal. It looked like gold, but I had never bought her anything of the kind and I had never seen it in her room.

She perceived my surprise and touched the tiara with her wet fingers. 'That's the only thing I own. It's possibly from my mother, but I can't be sure. The only reason he didn't take it was that he was afraid to touch it. But I'll gladly give to you, Mr Addie, should you want it.'

I made the excuse to myself that I didn't really know what I was doing, but I did. I took off my shirt and put in on a chair and let my trousers fall to the floor along with my drawers. Berenice gave me her hand. I took it and let her draw me into the bath.

She made me kneel down by pressing on my shoulders and then, also kneeling, she slowly washed me gently with a flannel. It would have been innocent if my back had been turned. This way I could not help gazing at her, although I had no wish to. And I certainly did not want to appraise her, but how could I do otherwise? It was out of the question.

I therefore tried to be brief if there was no avoiding it. She had firm breasts with small, dark erect nipples. The hair in her crotch was thick, and lots of black hair could be seen in her armpits, too. There was even a fine layer of hair on the back of her forearms and legs and on the inside of her thighs. If she had seemed partly a child only moments before, that impression had now been utterly dispelled. In the candlelight dark thistledown was also evident on her top lip. The eyebrows nearly met above her nose and the eyelashes burgeoned forth from her eyelids like long unruly sedge. I recalled that village concubine of my father's that Mama had once put my way either out of revenge or desperation. Such an inappropriate yet inevitable association . . . I was perplexed by how unlike Dorota Berenice was, and I was in even greater disarray when I realized that in that semi-darkness she resembled her.

I lifted her breasts, and then I gently clenched my hands around her neck. 'Did you do it with him?' I asked. 'You know what I'm talking about?'

What I was talking about was now importunately rubbing itself against her thigh. We looked down at it. It was sticking out of the water like a bridge that the builders hadn't finished.

'I do,' she said quietly. 'He wanted me to do it with my mouth, but I didn't like it, so he forced me. We managed it a couple of times, but after a while he gave up when he saw I didn't want to. Anyway he was old.'

'And how did you talk about it? Just in passing? Like talking about lunch?'

That took her aback. 'Talk about it? We *never* talked about it. There was just one occasion when he told me that he would leave me intact down below.'

'It would be incest. It was anyway.'

'But we're not related, are we? He wanted me to fetch the highest possible price. After all, you knew I was a virgin when you bought me.'

'But I didn't buy you,' I said, and they were the words of an impostor. 'Now continue with your hand.'

She took it in her hand, and she didn't need to jiggle it for long. She turned away with her belly soiled and started to wash herself. For an instant I hoped that it was all a bad dream after taking Hoffmann's pill. She looked over her shoulder and smiled as if asking whether I was satisfied. I climbed out of the bath dirtier than when I got in. I left Berenice in the bathroom and went to bed. Without lighting a lamp I swallowed a pill in total darkness and stuck my head under the pillow.

Now I was turning it over in my mind in Ulbrich's café. When all was said and done I wasn't the first to abuse the girl, and so I hadn't caused her a shock in the matter of intimate human practices. And I had no way of knowing what went on in that head behind the fine golden tiara.

That afternoon I eventually got up from the round table with the marble top and left the café on unsteady legs. I headed for the New Town Sokol gymnasium, and I reached it after thirty-five sweaty minutes.

They brought me a sword and I started to practise in front of the mirror, hoping that Solly would appear. He didn't arrive. There was only 'Brother Master' Poche in the fencing hall with two of his pupils. I proposed a bout with all three at once. They looked at me as if I was a lunatic from the nearby St Catherine's Asylum, and then the older man sent the youngsters away.

'Like last time?' I asked, just to make sure, and he nodded impatiently.

We saluted each other and went on guard. He attacked immediately with a cut from inside and above that I only just parried. He was a teacher who knew how to teach, and he went after me in the same way I had him on the previous occasion. And he was incredibly fast, to the point of impetuousness. I riposted and made a lunge, driving him towards the mirror, at which moment I gazed helplessly at my wounded forearm. The hit had been achieved by a feint from below and a lightning fast cut that amounted to little more than a flick of the wrist. My sword fell to the floor, and I saw over Poche's shoulder the reflection of the look of surprise on my face.

I convinced him that I had no need of professional medical attention, so he bandaged my arm and summoned a cab. His eyes held a look of unconcealed satisfaction. No doubt he couldn't wait to trumpet and celebrate his victory. I didn't begrudge him it.

'I expect I'm lucky', I said as he was knotting the bandage, 'that we were aiming at the manchette not the body.'

'Then there has been an understanding, My Lord. Since we were not keeping to the line it went without saying that we were striking at the body and I went for your side. Your arm got in the way,' he said dryly.

I shook my head. 'But you nodded in agreement when I asked if we'd be fencing like last time.'

'I went for you last time in exactly the same way as today,' he hissed. His red-rimmed eyes flashed like shards of glass. He turned around and marched away.

Well, well. It looks as if greybeards are also prone to bloodthirsty resentment.

I left the changing-room. I now felt worse than in the café. There was nothing for it but to go home and meet Berenice there. I wondered whether I ought not buy her something pretty but dismissed the thought – because then I would be treating her the way I treated Gita.

As I alighted from the cab I heard my name and looked upwards. Berenice was leaning out of a window with an expression of alarm, and she was saying something that I couldn't hear. I tried a natural, reassuring smile and walked in through the passage.

I was met there by the concierge.

'I have His Lordship the second Count sitting in here,' the concierge mumbled. 'I apologized to him, saying you had forbidden it, but he is still cross. He says you'd have been bound to tell him if you were planning to move him out.'

The second Count? So I'm the first? I took him by the arm and squeezed, which was not a good idea as the wound I had suffered at the gymnasium started to smart as if someone had sprinkled salt into it. 'I don't understand. The police are here, are they? They want to take me away?'

He goggled at me. 'Please, it is time you moved out and took the young lady with you. I don't want anything to do with the gendarmes. There are always strange people hanging around outside the house these days.'

I wanted to go upstairs, but he led me into his apartment on the ground floor and pushed me into the kitchen. There, hunched up on a rickety chair, with a glass of beer in his hand sat my Tyrolean cousin Karl Emanuel.

He stood up and was about to embrace me in his good-natured way, but I indicated my bandaged arm just in time.

'A duel?' he blurted out in unfeigned dismay and concern.

'Something like that.' I asked the concierge to pour me a glass, too. He was more than willing, and he started to pour out excuses, too, saying he was only obeying my order that he was not to let anyone go upstairs. I told him I would remember him when I came to write my will. He looked delighted.

I took Manny upstairs and explained that I had another guest whom I couldn't turn down, and for his part he excused himself for not announcing his arrival. He bowed to Berenice, and she curtsied back. Manny declared that he was sincerely gratified to meet her again and asked how the boots suited her. In return she asked him how he had enjoyed his stay in the country and whether he wouldn't mind if she remained in his room for the time being as she had nowhere else to go. Then she went into the next room and closed the door behind her.

Manny was disconcerted. 'Isn't she a bit young for you, Addie?'

I asked him not to ask any questions and simply accept my assurance that I had rescued her from the clutches of an old scoundrel. And I added that she was still a virgin and my relations with her were entirely honourable.

'A likely story.'

'Believe me.'

'Some other time.'

'Please, Manny.'

'Do you love her?'

'No!'

'You love Gita.'

'Not her either.'

'So you've got two of them, and you don't love either.'

'That's about it.'

'I'm not going to judge you,' he shrugged. 'If you can afford to live that way.'

'First I borrowed some money, and I've been earning a bit. Listen . . .' I told him the story of how I had come by the stock of hydrochlorate and how it was gradually earning me enough to buy the Loggia, my own Prague palace, a nice replacement for what my parents had been obliged to sell. Then I offered him a pill from a bottle and told him to keep the whole lot, which I owed him anyway. Manny visibly turned pale, tasted the tablet and rolled the bottle between his palms.

'And Dr Hoffmann has left, you say?'

I nodded. 'Things were hotting up for him here. He was afraid they would nab him and confiscate it all. It was to his advantage to get rid of all the chemicals. He can always make some more anyway if he is engaged by a laboratory.'

'And what's your assessment of him?'

'My assessment? If you're asking for my opinion, I have no reason to doubt him. It looks as if he fell out with the Bayer works and decided to go his own way. The trouble is that, unlike him, they own the licence, have enormous means and no doubt the right connections as well. He's just a scientist.'

Manny held the glass close to his face which bore a resentful and weary expression.

'I can see', he said after a lengthy silence, 'that it was a mistake to remain in the country.' Then he told me what had transpired after my departure. He admitted that he had fallen for Helena Tauferová and invited her for a ride the next day. Mama evidently resented it, and she even came to have a 'serious talk' with him (at this moment I put my head in my hands), and she told him that she had certain plans for Helena (here I howled softly) but naturally she could not forbid her beloved relative anything but merely wanted to urge him to consider any moves very carefully, because the ties between our families were already somewhat strained (here it occurred to me to send Mama a telegram telling her to keep her mind on her horses and poultry and stop scheming), but the old Count came in and started to argue with her, and it didn't bother them that it was in the presence of their guest (typical). Manny said it had been unspeakably embarrassing.

'After that your mama stopped bothering me with it and treated me indulgently. I offered to leave if I was in the way, but they said no, they were only too pleased to have me there. It was your father, in particular, who talked me round, which was quite odd, Addie. He wanted me to stay on longer, but I could tell that he didn't like me and found me annoying in some way. It's just in case it happened to emerge, I mean if they were to tell you that they couldn't stand me or my parents or something of the sort, so that you'd be in the picture. You're not cross with me for bothering you with this?'

I hesitated a moment before replying. 'I'm glad you told me. Can you think of any reason why my father should have an aversion to you and yet keep you at the castle?'

'None at all,' Manny replied, while staring out of the window. He looked desperate: there were tears in his eyes, and his mouth and cheeks sagged resignedly. I emphasized that he had the firmest friend in me and added that I had no intention of excusing my parents and that sometimes I didn't understand them.

It was already dark. I forbade him to go looking for a hotel room and persuaded him to make do with my bed and said I would sleep on the couch. He didn't put up much resistance. When he went to bed he lay gazing at the wall with a blank expression.

I offered him another tablet, but he refused. Then I asked him how far he had got with Helena. He told me drowsily that they had kissed several times, but then Farmer Taufer had forbidden any further romantic rides with the foreign Count.

By candlelight I told him about Kleinfleisch, the murder of the prostitute and the death of that maidservant and how I had run foul of the police. That roused him slightly from his lethargy. He said that Prague had become an extremely vile city and he didn't recognize it any more. Then he added that he had also had an encounter with the police in Stránov, albeit at a distance. That companion of Helena's, the fop from Chuchle who had been courting her and accompanying her everywhere, started to be jealous of him, of course, and even tried to insult him with stories about the degenerate aristocracy. Manny had challenged him to a duel – quite calmly, he claimed – and the fellow had mocked him. But then the following day he disappeared with all his things, even though he had a contract with Taufer to give riding lessons for an entire year and he had already received a down payment. The indignant landowner requested that the police search him out and bring him back along with all the expensive clothing and best-quality English headgear and riding boots that he had bought him. But the Chuchle dandy had failed to show up during the time Manny was still at the castle.

'Maybe', Manny laughed, 'those detectives thought I regarded him as a rival, for Helena's favours, I mean. Then he suddenly disappeared . . . What did they imagine? That I'd killed him in a duel and buried his corpse in the woods?'

Then he turned over on to his side, and a few moments later, when he started breathing regularly, I realized he was asleep. I didn't manage to drop off until just before dawn.

XV

Burger

Meister

The month came to its close. I settled up with the Urzidils, and a new tenant moved into the apartment on Long Street the very Monday I had my goods and chattels conveyed to the Loggia.

The employees of the firm Šesták and Sons loaded all of my things on to a removal van, the most pot-bellied and battered wagon in the whole of Prague. Solly oversaw the proceedings. He had volunteered himself. He went around and around the vehicle, turning every now and then to one of the Šestáks to point out to him that this stool or that mirror would be bound to fall off during the journey. The removal men took little notice of him but piled the furniture up to dizzying heights, and where the structure needed support or propping up they would stuff in a rolled Persian carpet, a trunk or a travel wardrobe. Berenice watched it from the window, returning Solly's cheeky smiles and, leaning out into the street, trying to reach the top of the heap on the removal van with a carpet beater. With ribbons in her hair and wearing a gingham dress she didn't look at all like a Jewish princess but like an overgrown child.

The loading was observed by the entire street, particularly by little boys in patched trousers who offered a helping hand for a few pennies. The van also attracted the interest of dogs, about a dozen of which gathered beneath my windows, where they growled and barked at the formless pagoda, which increasingly resembled a monstrous Hussite war wagon preparing to set out on a expedition through Prague on four enormous wheels with outstretched arms formed by coat racks and wrought-iron curtain rails. A gendarme came to inspect us. He read the permit and his colleague did the same a couple of hours later when he took over the beat. Eventually the pile really did reach the level of the first-storey windows. When the Šestáks covered it all over with a black tarpaulin and roped it down Solly climbed up to the top and made himself an improvised coach box among the covered crates. Then, sitting there like a Bedouin crouched between the humps of a camel, he yelled that we could set off. Far below him a photographer stooped beneath the black cloth of his camera and took a number of photographs. Four powerful dray horses were harnessed to the van, and the monstrosity started to move. The homunculus driving it also greeted the comely young lady in the window by raising his hat and thinking to himself: The Count is saying a final farewell to his former residence, and arm in arm with the young lady he's setting off for his new address.

I thought we would take a cab, but the removal van moved so slowly that Berenice and I followed behind it like two bereaved relatives, and we said to each other with laughter that froze on our lips that the heap looked like a gigantic black coffin, conveyed, for some unknown possibly ritual reason, from one tomb to another, and in an upright position to boot. And within it was a Golem. Or Kleinfleisch.

Whereas our funeral procession was led by the very proprietor of the firm Šesták and Sons, who somewhere far in front was requesting the worthy citizens of Prague to make way and wait in their porches or at least on their doorsteps until the precarious load had passed, the tail of the procession consisted of an odd pair of individuals and an even odder musical ensemble: whistling ragamuffins and barking dogs.

As the van slowly made its way through the narrow lanes it was impossible for us to see beyond it, and when we noticed the first officials in black uniforms and stovepipe hats it was too late. They were each standing in a shop doorway, one on either side of the street like sentries, although they actually looked more like undertakers. These first two did not move, but when the load on stagecoach wheels was passing some houses a few metres further on two more were standing on guard in opposite doorways. I realized we had unwanted company. I put my arm around Berenice's shoulders and looked back.

The boys were gone and instead the fifth and sixth black-uniformed individuals were shooing the dogs away with their walking-sticks. Between them walked a tall rickety man on whose sunken face, in the triangle between sharp cheekbones and a witchlike chin, a smile was just forming.

We raised our hats to each other and stopped. The uniformed orderlies surrounded us while the van rumbled onwards. Berenice hung on to me like grim death.

'Councillor Bürger, if I am not mistaken,' I said and waited to see what would happen.

'Councillor extraordinary in charge of resettlement and urban improvement,' Bürger added and let one of his shoulders drop in what was probably intended as an obeisance. 'At your service, My Lord.'

'I don't require your services.'

'You're sure?'

'I'm sure you are aware that I am moving into a house that will definitely remain standing.'

He put his head on one side as if considering this.

'Shall we go?'

We turned our backs on him and walked on behind the van. Four of Bürger's men who were standing in our path looked beyond us for orders and stepped to one side. The councillor came and walked alongside Berenice, but she backed away from him as if he had the mange, passing behind me and putting her arm through mine on the other side. Six of the stovepipe hats followed us several paces behind.

'Why such an escort today?' I remarked conversationally. 'As far as I know you were on your own the last time you visited Jewry – the night of the murder. How did you fare at the interrogation?'

He rebuffed me with ease. 'All right. But the house you bought was originally designated for demolition. I don't intend to investigate how those two crafty daubers managed to achieve the opposite. We can leave the police out of the case.'

'Yes, I can imagine you've had your fill of them. But as far as I know the transfer was legal, and I am moving into my own property.'

'I wouldn't be too sure of that,' the councillor said between his teeth, 'but our urban improvement has come up against a few snags since the publication of that stupid pamphlet. I won't disguise the fact that we have certain problems, My Lord.'

'You mean *Bestia triumphans*? It's the best thing I've read in a long time.'

'It's a squib against progress.'

'No it isn't. It's a pamphlet against the destruction of the city.' I felt Berenice give me an encouraging squeeze. 'A desperate clarion call in its defence,' I added.

'In defence of putrid decay and corruption? Yes, if you allow it. It is a pamphlet in defence of the biggest medieval hellhole in Europe, and the censor should have banned it.'

'You'll just have to put up with the fact that your fingers aren't long enough, Bürger.'

'I am able to take insults from a nobleman.'

'But it wasn't an insult. There's not much that can be saved of old Prague, but it's worth the effort for the little that remains.'

'So you're actively involved in the defence of vice, disease, primitiveness and reaction. You're on the other side of the barricade, My Lord, and I have to warn you.'

'Against what? Against these stick-wielding oafs?'

'You don't want to understand me. I haven't come here to threaten you, simply to give you a warning –'

'Where do their wages come from? City coffers? And are they working at this moment or just hanging about? Or are they your private bodyguards and you pay them yourself?'

That took the wind out of his sails. He was silent for a moment and then said brusquely, 'After verbal and physical attacks on my person I cannot do without them, at least until my mission is fulfilled.'

'Mission? To raze Prague to the ground and build in its place an apartment building starting in Karlín and ending at the hill fort in Zličín? That won't be Prague, sir, but a termites' nest.'

'I simply wanted to clarify your position, My Lord, and notify you that you are not home and dry.'

'How so?' I stopped and took a couple of documents from my pocket: a certificate of purchase of the baroque Loggia House, the copy of an entry in the land register, an entry in the register of house owners and several others.

'In this country any decision can be overturned by another decision,' Bürger muttered without even looking at them.

I started walking again. 'Then such a decision is perverse, and I don't recognize perverse decisions. But I like the word you used a moment ago – reaction. It strikes me I could set up a sort of club of gentlemen from the titled and intellectual nobility, and they would be a bulwark against the suspicious dealing of the city council and its perverse decisions. It could be called the Reactionaries' Club, say. What do you think? It would protect Old Prague and alert people to the danger of its destruction. We'll draw up petitions and organize demonstrations. The students will support us.'

'Students? Do you imagine that students don't believe in progress? That they are as short-sighted as this young lady here? Some relative of yours?'

'That's none of your business.'

'All right, so long as my nocturnal walks in Jewry are none of yours.'

'Go where you like and when you like, Bürger, but I would advise you to take the gentlemen you brought with you today on your night walks. Have you already heard about Kleinfleisch?'

'I read something in the press. Some buffoon playing at spooks.

Those vile criminal phenomena will disappear of their own accord when the Jewish Town disappears, sir. All those semi-dilapidated hovels, those jerry-built caricatures of houses, those puppet-theatre backdrops. I guarantee you that, sir.'

'The older I get, the more beautiful those houses seem to me.'

'Surely not. Such an awful ghetto, the most neglected corner of Europe cannot be allowed to stand alongside the Prague salon that we are building by the sweat of our brows, and in the light of whose splendour and magnificence the city of a hundred spires will enter the twentieth century. After all, even the Prague suburbs are beginning to look better than this Jewish dung heap. Can't you smell the stench of the locality?'

'I've smelt it since my childhood, and I can't imagine the city without it.'

'But I can! Haussmann's Paris boulevards, Vienna's airy promenades – we'll have all that here, and you won't stop us. Even if the city council allowed you to keep your cowering little house, we'll surround it with buildings and department stores like in London and Paris. We'll erect residential towers like in New York, and your shack will lost in their midst like a molehill in a garden full of trees and flowers. Do you really have need –'

At that moment F.X. Bürger started to cough, and Berenice and I went on walking. After a few steps I looked back over my shoulder. There were two of his minions standing by him, while he himself was holding a handkerchief to his mouth, coughing into it and examining it closely. A few moments later he caught up with us, and I offered him one of Hoffmann's pills. The handkerchief, which he was hurriedly stuffing into his pocket, was flecked with blood.

He thanked me, saying he had medicines of his own. 'The only thing that will help is a radical remedy: demolishing these parts and building a new city on a modern hygienic basis. Dr Preininger knows best how to restore Prague's lost health.'

'There are other doctors –' I commented, but he didn't let me finish.

'If you mean that charlatan, that alchemist who was wandering around Prague before he fled from the police, I assure you that I wouldn't entrust my care to him even on my deathbed.'

'He helped me. The next time you cough up blood come and see me at Loggia House. I might sell you a remedy that will bring you relief, if nothing else. Now if you'll excuse me I would like to have a word with the removal men.'

'I beg your pardon, but I haven't finished.'

We stopped and his black bodyguards again surrounded us. And then someone who had suddenly joined us spoke up. 'Count Arco wishes to be detained no longer.'

It was Solly. In one hand he held a cane and in the other a small carpenter's hatchet that he had picked up goodness knows where. Behind him stood three of the younger Šestáks in a short row, leaning on their crowbars and sticks and observing us with interest. And behind them, like a castle wall, rose the stationary removal van. There was no escape route.

We wouldn't have come off well in the event of a brawl, but who knows? Bürger blinked his dark eyes, looked upwards, as if seeking some kind of advice, and said, 'We'll see each other soon.' Then he turned, nodded to his retinue and walked off down the street we had come up.

I thanked Solly and started to fill my pipe. I was glad that my hands weren't shaking in front of Berenice and the removal men.

'We frightened them off,' Berenice whispered. She looked at me in admiration and I was foolishly gratified.

'I'm afraid not,' Solly said with a shake of the head. 'He just wanted to avoid a fight that would have attracted the attention of the police. For some reason he avoids them as much as we do.'

The house had been cleared out and freshly painted. The Urzidils had offered me a favourable price. They had suggested I get an artistic plasterer in to repair and complete the antique elements of the decoration, such as the fluted cornices, the baroque jambs and even the lasciviously grinning masks, but I refused. After the removal it took about a week before all the furniture stood where I wanted it and all the pictures hung in their previously chosen places. I was assisted by Solly and his shop boy, and a couple of the canvases were hung by my cousin Manny when he called on me. Not that he was particularly handy, but I could see that he wanted to be helpful. On my recommendation he was staying at the Three Horsemen house on Weighbridge Square in the self-same rooms where I had met Dr Hoffmann. He looked weary. He had resolved to pay for a woman's favours only three times a week instead of every night, because in his view that was a healthy frequency for intercourse, but he wasn't able to resist it and broke his resolution all the time. A slight aid to abstinence had been the contents of two bottles of hydrochlorate which I had sold him for the price of one, since he was a friend and relative. In return he had obtained for me from a middleman resident at the Three Horsemen some Samuel Gawith Pressed Full Virginia Flake tobacco, which, when rolled up and lit in the pipe bowl, looked like a burning knot of spiders and smelt rather like it, too. This was something the two women of my household – the youthful Berenice and Gita, some seven years her senior – found hard to bear. On occasions, their aversion to tobacco smoke, verging on disgust, as well as their weakness for Hoffmann's soothing remedy, gave them common cause, otherwise their relations were cool. I assured Gita that Berenice was my ward and that I had no physical relationship with her. That was almost the truth. Since our shared bath we had strenuously avoided all intimate contact, which naturally increased the frequency of my slightly intemperate intercourse with Gita – to her considerable delight. In return I made her promise not be jealous and to teach Berenice to cook. In addition they were to share equally the minor domestic tasks and jointly to take care of my wardrobe. The cleaning and the laundry were entirely her affair, however. In the eyes of the neighbours the one was to be my ward and the other my housekeeper. Both formally declared that they were satisfied with the arrangement, and I waited with slightly bated breath how long it would last them. In the Jewish Town urban improvement was rampant, and something along the same lines was planned for part of the Old Town, while we within our peaceful baroque Loggia House shut ourselves off from the world and its police, its officials and its wrecking excavators; one might even say from time itself, which crept in only through the gaps in the outdoor gates and via its sole medium, my little Lord wristwatch. I was pleasantly surprised to see how much the peace of my own home suited me, together with the constant presence of two undemanding beautiful women vying for my smiles, my compliments and my favour. The ideal life of a urban idler according to Count Arco? More or less.

It lasted five weeks.

We were attending an artistic salon where the painter Švabinsky was exhibiting his latest picture entitled *Round Portrait*. Berenice was entranced by the dress worn by the lady in the portrait, and she returned to the painting repeatedly. When she said of it that it was 'as white as moonlight and had frills like orchid flowers' it was clear that she had fallen in love with it. I took her to a different salon – a dressmaker's, and when she had been measured I sent the head couturier around to the exhibition with instructions to sew a dress for my ward exactly like the one in the *Round Portrait*. We chose the fabric at Solly's, of course: the winner was an atrociously expensive silk. The girl spent ages perusing the samples, and I was bored until Solly, with an avuncular smile, sent her to the rear of the shop to the special dressing-room where she could try the textile on her skin in case she found it itchy. Then we took turns looking through the secret hole in the wall. Although Berenice didn't know we were there, she didn't take all her clothes off. She left her chemise and drawers on. Only the upper part of her bosom was exposed, along with her neck and arms and her legs from the knees down. Even so Solly was enraptured, and he begged me to let him have this beautiful woman when I had had enough of her. I agreed, yet I knew it wouldn't happen.

Back home I told Gita that from now on she would accompany

Berenice to the salon for fittings (and I myself tried to restrain myself from gazing too long at the girl's naked shoulder). That worked fine for a couple of days. From their evening conversations I gathered that several changes had been made at the dressmaker's: in Gita's view the gown had been too tight and proposed it be looser at the waist, and the colour did not suit the new purpose that Berenice had thought up for it. The thing was that we had received an invitation to a new première of maestro Antonín Dvořák's *The Jacobin* from young Lobkowicz who had heard that I had my own 'palace' in Prague and undoubtedly wanted to come and see it. (I could just imagine his sarcastic comments, but I accepted his theatre invitation; after all, there was no need to repay it in any way.) So now the dress had been transformed into an evening gown for the opera, no longer white but emerald green. Both women were thrilled with it, even though Berenice maintained that it was a bit big for her now, and Gita constantly reassured her that that was now the fashion and, moreover, it was necessary to take into account that her growing body would fill out quite a bit in a few years.

Then came the day of the première. We slept late because we had a long night ahead of us. From early morning Gita scrubbed the floors and beat the carpet; for lunch she cooked oxtail bouillon and fried a fresh mushroom omelette. She brought a jug of beer from the tavern, and she was so nervous she broke one of the plates with the Arco crest on them. After lunch Berenice went to wash her hair and create a formal coiffure. While she was in the bathroom there came a knock on the door from an apprentice couturier carrying a tied package, containing the completed green grown. I told him to wait, saying it was necessary to try it on for one last time, but Gita sent him away saying it would be all right. Then she carried the package upstairs to get the gown ready.

I was sitting by the window reading a newspaper in which the Deputy Police Councillor Ignacius Herrmann assured the people of Prague that the political and security situation had calmed down – crime and the radicals were under control, and the Czech metropolis was now a safe place to live in – when down the staircase came a magnificent figure with loosely flowing hair, dressed in a sumptuous glistening green robe. And the hair wasn't black but red, and the body within the dress was not that of a girl but belonged to a robust woman with mature hindquarters. The robe was bursting at the seams around the hips and the arms. The breasts were fighting their way out like rebels under arrest, and the golden jabot looked like a little handkerchief for mopping perspiration from the décolletage.

The male gaze is the woman's strategic weapon. I stared, drawn to the live tableau as if by a chain. Its sensual appeal turned me into an animal activated by the snapping of fingers. I was speechless.

Gita tiptoed across to me, pulled up her skirt, put her bare leg across my trousered legs, undid my buttons, took out what she needed and mounted it.

I don't like that style. On principle, the female should be beneath; she should not move but hold on tight, and the aristocracy rigorously honours, extols and cultivates nature, so why change it? But now I had permitted an exception. Why should I begrudge Gita, after all? Let her have a good ride – at the gallop.

Vanitas vanitarum, thenceforth things would go downhill. Berenice stood on the stairs wrapped in a bath towel. She could see her dress riding on me with Gita inside it, softly groaning, and me beneath Gita, not taking care and releasing into her my entire stupidly fertile load.

Berenice, struck for the first time with an arrow from the bow of the malicious angel of jealousy, found nothing better to do than let out a groan (surprisingly similar to the one Gita had produced moments before) and then dash downstairs, throw open the door and run out into the yard.

And then there came a cry, not of indignation this time but of mortal terror.

I buttoned myself as I ran. I grabbed the coal shovel and moments later was standing beneath the overhang of the gallery. Gita was breathing down my neck, and she held out a poker in front of me as if I had grown a third arm. I must confess that I was touched.

On the spot where the Urzidils' goat used to be tied up stood a stranger in a black Inverness cape wearing a low-brimmed top hat with a dark blue bow on the hat band.

Nothing could surprise his pale-blue eyes and certainly not the three of us. He discreetly ignored the girl in front of me and the woman behind me; his cold gaze was fixed on me and me alone. And when he raised his hat he said, 'Count Arco, I presume? Leopold Meister, Deputy Mayor of Prague. But I expect you know of me. I see you've managed to settle in. You're having a jolly time.'

Alderman Meister, that paradoxical cross between plebeian and patrician who christened new locomotives but most likely stole apples from old ladies' baskets at the market, made a derisive bow while I hastily hid the shovel and poker behind my back.

I sent Gita and Berenice upstairs to change into their own clothes. I pointed at my watch saying that Berenice was to be ready in twenty minutes. In point of fact there was still plenty of time before we were to leave for the opera, but I wanted to indicate to my unwelcome visitor that we had little time to talk. I invited Meister in and offered him a chair.

'They are very charming ladies,' he commented and hesitatingly accept a glass of claret from me. 'Relatives of yours?' He drank cautiously, as if making sure I hadn't offered him something disgusting.

'One is my housemaid, the other my ward,' I said impassively.

'And the ward is a relative?'

'No.'

'I congratulate you. Were you playing tag?'

'Mr Meister – women have never bored me, only men. Apart from the odd exception.'

'Each to his own. So you're pleased with your new home.'

'As you can see.'

'Isn't it a trifle small? After all, the palace that belonged to your father is rather –'

'I am entirely satisfied with it. There are just three of us; Gita also copes with the kitchen.'

'Gita, eh? It seems she used to lived at the brothel known as Golda's.'

'What brings you here, Mr Meister?'

'All right. I'll come straight to the point. It's a proposal. I've come to offer you alternative quarters in place of this house, without the need to sell and buy something else, which would no longer be possible anyway now the new building law has come into force. But an exchange is possible, and it is very advantageous for you. Others aren't so fortunate.'

'In what way advantageous?'

'If you accept the offer you have two alternatives to choose from. Both are equally attractive, and I myself would hesitate which to choose. The former suburbs are now flourishing by comparison with our sad city centre, devastated by the Jewish inhabitants. Within a few years the suburbs will become part of Prague, and nothing could be more advantageous than to move into one of those sunny apartments. Haven't you heard that there will be a tramway to Karlín? And I have an apartment for you in Karlín. Two hundred square metres with all modern hygienic fittings and an American-style kitchen. First-class parquet flooring, an upper storey with a view on to the square, a side-street and also into the courtyard, where the builders have preserved mature trees. The apartment belongs to the city council and will be transferred to your ownership. What do you think?

'Nothing. Please go on.'

'There is one other possibility, and it is also worthy of a nobleman and his privileges. You would remain in the Old Town but would move into one of the new buildings that are currently planned. You can choose your own location. There is no reason why it shouldn't be in Jewry, although it will no longer be called that. However, it will take a few years, and in the meantime we would provide you with temporary accommodation intended for guests from Vienna. It would be for two or at most three years. Then you'll be right in the middle of the city with a hundred and fifty square metres, most likely in the vicinity of Rabbi Street, which will be completed soonest after general hygienization. But you would have to put up with continuing building work, which, in the area of Karlín, is already completed.'

'I can see that you would recommend me to choose the suburb.'

'I don't know. It's up to you.'

'And what about this house? What are your plans for it?'

'There are plans for a stock-exchange building in this locality. They are not definite yet.'

'What stock exchange are you referring to?'

'The new Prague stock exchange – crops, commodities, stocks and shares but, above all, sugar! I'm sure you're informed of the extraordinary success of our little stock exchange – the eyes of the whole of Austria are upon it. And its present building is no longer suitable.'

'This house has stood here for three hundred years. The Loggia is slightly younger, but you won't see anything like it anywhere in Europe.'

'This is one of the ugliest little houses in Prague, My Lord. To be quite frank, I am astonished that you should have chosen somewhere so unworthy to live in.'

I spread my arm in a wide gesture, as if opening a curtain. 'I see around me nothing but beauty.'

Meister shook his head. 'Certainly not, but there's no point in us arguing. I think that on certain matters, we . . .' He raised his eyes, and I looked around. Berenice was just coming downstairs in the new green dress with her hair combed and held in place by a black hat. She carried a shiny black sequinned handbag, and from beneath her gown peeped the toes of patent-leather high-heeled shoes.

Behind Berenice came Gita with lowered eyes. She was wearing one of my white shirts with the shirt tails tied around her waist.

So she had abandoned her resistance to Berenice. She had even arranged her hair in a similar way but without the hat. How childish. And charming.

The alderman stood up. 'I don't expect an answer straight away.

That is not at all necessary. Would a week be enough to reflect on it?'

He walked towards the door, and Gita accompanied him.

'Would you like to ride to the opera in my coach?' he said in my direction. 'There's enough room.'

'We'll take a cab. Good afternoon, Mr Meister.'

'Good afternoon.'

No sooner had the door closed behind him than Berenice rolled her eyes. 'Why couldn't we ride in his coach, Addie? Why don't you have your own? Why always a stinking cab.'

I glanced at Gita, and as she returned the glance her eyes were saying: There you are, you've got what you wanted.

I certainly had. The première wasn't worth a candle, and anyway I couldn't keep my mind on the music. Berenice sat like a whipped cur and didn't speak to me and instead spent the interval smiling enigmatically at a young man in a evening coat lurking near by. I was fed up with her and with Meister's visit, and she felt rightly insulted about the desecration of her new dress. When we reached home after the gruelling opera she took the new gown off in front of me, threw it on the floor by the door and locked herself in her bedroom.

She never wore that dress again.

XVI

Otka

Edification in Jewry

It was getting dark. My watch said it was six forty-seven, and while Berenice was getting dressed I looked in disbelief out of the gallery at how the calm air of the shadowy courtyard, where the day was breaking a moment ago, was becoming denser with a treacly darkness stinking of smoke, as if night was returning. I looked up at the overcast sky and stretched out my arm. The gloom was moist, but there were no raindrops. Then Berenice came out dressed for school. The girls' high school in Vodička Street had enrolled her on the basis of my nobility certificate and half a year's fees paid in advance in cash.

I asked her whether I was starting to go blind or whether she found it very dark as well. She wrinkled her nose and said she could smell rain in the air and that was what it smelt of in Polná just before the pogrom. She adjusted the black cap on her head and settled around her shoulders her new brown coat with its turquoise hems and the same coloured braiding on its flush pockets. Then she brushed a spot of dust from her sleeve – like a lapwing preening its feathers perhaps – an example of innocence and coquettishness in one whimsical paradox. I found her so attractive. If I hadn't known that she was originally an orphaned Jewess from the east I would have assumed her to be a noblewoman. We came out of the house, and I looked up and down the street for a cab, but she was determined to walk. And off she went, as if she didn't care whether I was with her or not. My heart started pounding, and I wanted to yell at her to stop where she was, but instead I caught up with her and took her arm, squeezing her to me until she squealed with pain. We had quarrelled so many times in recent days that I hadn't the strength for any further argument.

We reached the school in a disquieting early morning twilight when the air was electrified like Křižík's lamps and my heart was ready to leap out of my body, and I kissed Berenice on the forehead. She endured it like a brave and dutiful young girl, and when I urged her to hold on to it until Gita came for her in the afternoon she turned on her heel without a word and disappeared inside the building. That's how I'll lose you one day, I thought to myself as I took a last look at the dark doors of the school.

I was pondering at the corner of the street where I might take a good black coffee to wash down Hoffmann's miracle when I caught sight of a narrow closed carriage standing in a side street with a light draught horse and a coachman smoking on the rear box. The window of the coach was open, and someone was sitting by it; that someone had his hat pulled down over his eyes and from beneath the brim was observing me with binoculars held to his eyes with the bony fingers of both hands. That someone was totally engrossed in me and was unaware who was passing his carriage at that very moment – and not alone. I knew all too well, however: it was my cousin Manny, striding along proudly conspiratorial as he was arm in arm with a beautiful young woman in a red-and-green travelling outfit and wearing a charming winged hat on the side of her head, namely Helena Tauferová, the daughter of our nouveau-riche Stránov neighbours, attired in the latest style.

I rejected the possibility of swiftly concealing myself behind a wide poster column, as it was too late, and I waved to them cheerily.

They were taken by surprise and turned back disconcertedly. She curtsied to me, and I kissed her hand, then, with idiotic ceremoniousness, I bowed to Manny instead of slapping him on the back, and he did the same in return.

The person watching us through binoculars from the carriage saw a ceremony of chance encounter. It couldn't have told him much.

'Prague is quite small – sometimes,' I said and stood in such a way that the stranger in the coach should be unable to see me over Manny's broad shoulders.

Manny blushed. 'Helena and I are here incognito, but naturally we have nothing to hide from you. She has just arrived and is hungry, poor thing.'

'Papa couldn't bear to think I might be alone with Emanuel,' Helena said quietly, as if someone might overhear. 'It's impossible to explain it to old people.'

'How is your father?' I said with a smile in her direction intended to conceal my distaste.

'He left yesterday evening for the cattle fair at Boleslav and won't be back until the day after tomorrow. I took a little excursion. I'll go back tomorrow, and he'll be none the wiser. I'm sure you'll understand, My Lord.'

'Naturally.'

'Mama wishes us well. She knows I'm in good hands,' she added, and she slipped her hand inside his sleeve and stroked his hairy wrist.

'I will be pleased if you will pay me a call at my new residence,' I said accommodatingly. 'After all, Manny has already been there. What do you say to a little supper? Gita has learnt to cook venison. I'll tell her to do a roast.'

On hearing the name Gita Helena lowered her gaze and did not look up again. But I noticed how she pressed up against Manny.

'Thank you, Addie,' my cousin stuttered, 'but we have so little time. We are just taking a little walk, and we'll be going back shortly after we've bought bread and some fruit.'

As he spoke those halting words, the two of them turned beetroot, and I decided not to embarrass them further. We said goodbye, and they went their way with obvious relief. I was sure that no one would be asking about the young lady's reputation at the house of the Three Horsemen.

As I walked off, I reflected on what a remarkable person Manny was, and it struck me that I no longer knew anything about him. What I found most astonishing was his physical self-indulgence and his unselfconscious uncouthness in his dealings with girls when he was buying their charms, in contrast to his youthful gaucheness and faltering shyness on the occasions when he was unable to prevent himself being emotionally drawn to a woman. I am incapable of separating things like that.

I glanced once more in their direction and was wondering how that romance would turn out and to what extent the landowner's daughter would manage to string him along when the black carriage pulled up alongside me and a bony finger from the open door indicated to me to get in. I would not have done so had the pale, furrowed face of the Deputy Police Councillor not emerged from beneath the hat.

'Come and sit down, My Lord. Do you know where I'm taking you?'

I raised my hat. 'How should I know?'

'Do get in.'

I obeyed him. The carriage was narrow. I sat down opposite him. By the window hung some open manacles, firmly attached to a ring fixed in the window frame.

'They're for me?'

Herrmann shrugged. 'You don't look as if you're about to run away.'

'And ought I to?'

'If Listopad's opinions counted for anything, then I expect so. But I seldom share them, which is why he is so useful to me, if you see what I mean.'

'I don't.'

Herrmann shrugged and knocked on the ceiling. The carriage moved off. 'Something happened last night, you see, My Lord. Something serious. Listopad thinks you're involved. And so I went take a look outside the school this morning to see for myself the look on your face.'

'And what did it tell you?'

'That you felt like boxing Miss Karafiátová's ears.'

We laughed. 'Well, you were spot on. How did you know I would be here?'

'You're followed from time to time. You must have expected to be.'

'From time to time?'

'We ascertained where you had the young lady enrolled and where you bring her. That's simply logical. By the way, her origins didn't bother them in any way?'

'No. Do they bother you in any way?'

'That's of no consequence. If you intend to take care of her honourably, that is your affair. But it is possible that some of my colleagues might regard it as immoral, at which moment the police might undertake visits of inspection at your residence.'

'And who would come? Surely not that Listopad of yours?'

'I'm afraid so.'

'I can't stand him.'

'I fully understand that. But tell me before we arrive, how are your parents?'

'They are in excellent form. Thank you for asking.'

'The man you were talking to outside the school, it was your cousin Karl Emanuel, if I'm not mistaken. Count Arco-Zinneberg.'

'I see you are fully informed.'

'By no means. Quite clearly you met by chance. Who was the lady?'

'A neighbour of ours from Stránov. But there is nothing to get worked up about, Mr Herrmann. My cousin has a great appeal for the ladies. They think he's rich.'

'And isn't he?'

'All I know is that he receives an allowance of sorts and is able to blow the lot.'

'Did he ever mention anything to you about working for the government or the imperial court?'

The question totally took the wind out of my sails, and for a moment I wasn't able to say anything, and even then I found it very hard to maintain a neutral tone. 'Manny? No, he's never divulged anything of the kind to me.'

'Of course,' Herrmann nodded and glanced outside. 'That makes sense.'

Then he fell silent and left me rummaging through the previous conversation as well as I could recall it. I tried to work out whether Herrmann was trying to give me a hint about something.

'Tell me,' I said after a moment, 'how you, Listopad and the other policemen were able to be on the spot so soon that time when the girl fell out the window and I was among the first there.'

The grey man smiled with his grey lips. 'What's your explanation, My Lord?'

'I don't know. It niggles me. Had you already received a tip-off that some armed lunatic with a lump of meat for a face was roaming the Jewish town?'

'Good thinking, and half correct. But it wasn't quite like that. There had been several deaths. Rosina Weinerová, whom you knew. But then, of course, there were two other prostitutes, with their throats cut in the same way, like piglets. And that evening our informer actually saw Kleinfleisch. We were just a few streets away. It was bad luck. If we'd have been nearer that girl might have lived. Just like the woman I'm taking you to see.'

The carriage stopped in Jewry at an odd spot, at the corner of Joachim and Narrow Street, opposite the house known as the Lime Kiln that formed a right angle with another house, and amazingly another house grew in between them at the crossroads. The buildings opposite had been razed to the ground and the rubble cleared away, and at the place where a new building site would be there stood some forty two-wheeled wooden handcarts on which were drying the pungently smelling urine-tanned skins of cattle, pigs, goats and cats. A pack of dogs was weaving its way through the carts and heading towards the crossroads with its multiple muzzle. There was a sound of whining. All the tails were drooping.

Right in the middle of the crossroads stood a tall green pump with a handle and a curved spout on either side above wide troughs. The horse cabs always gave it wide berth in order to avoid colliding with it. The iron cylinder had a lamp fixed on top. I knew the spot. It was a long way away from the next light at the other end of the street, and maybe that is why the illuminated pump resembled a lighthouse lighting up the Prague night. At eight o'clock in the morning the lamp was already extinguished, even though the sky was so black, but something seemed not quite right about it the moment I stepped down from the carriage and placed my monocle in my right eye. A defensive action on the part of a nobleman who senses danger and trouble.

The crowd of people on the little square gazed at us with a hundred eyes. They weren't all unfamiliar to me. I recognized among them the photographer from Letná in his flat cap; he had his box with its handle which he was turning at that moment. Next to him stood a man in the same grey hat that I wear. It was the riding teacher from Stránov. And there was a third person there, a fellow with tousled hair and a simpleton's expression. He crept out of the crowd like an eel and headed straight for Herrmann. It was Listopad. He ignored me. The two of them said something quietly to each other while I looked around the square. Across the mouths of each of the streets stood a cordon of uniformed policemen. There must have been a score of them. Seven or eight men in plain clothes were standing around the lamp-post, and there was someone lying at their feet, but it was hard to see.

It started to rain. Herrmann took me by the elbow and steered me towards the pump. Listopad followed at my heels. The men in front of us made way, and I saw on the ground a headless woman's body with arms and legs outstretched. Her striped skirt was pulled up, and under it could be seen the white legs of her long drawers. Several dark wounds gaped open in her chest, where the bodice and black blouse were ripped to shreds, and a forensic doctor was examining the injuries with some kind of spatula. In the absence of the head the corpse's white neck looked grotesquely short, and there was no dark drying mush pouring out of it. Several horse droppings lay near by on the earth and gravel. But I knew where to look for the head, the only person there who did, amazingly enough.

I turned up the collar of my coat and regretted that I had not taken an umbrella. The raindrops splashed on to the brim of my hat and were absorbed by the soft felt. When Listopad asked me whether I recognized the body, I raised my shoulders and then let them drop. 'The body no, the head yes.'

Listopad sidled up to me and exclaimed that I really ought not make fun of the public officials of the city and the monarchy, particularly not at this moment, but Herrmann came over to us and raised his hand to stop him. Then he stared at me and waited. The noise of the rain forced me to raise my voice.

'Did nobody notice it? Really? Or are you just testing me?'

Listopad looked confused and turned around twice as if expecting a prompt from somewhere or an anarchist's gunshot. Herrmann's grey stare told me he wasn't playing games. So I raised my finger and pointed upwards.

'Otka Meyrinková,' I said. 'Yes, we were acquainted. It was she who accused me of the last murder. It's as clear as day.'

And Herrmann quickly whispered: 'But the day isn't particularly clear today, is it?' He looked upwards and with him all the plain-clothed detectives.

Water trickled down the dark lamp. It looked as if the half-closed eyes in the pale face were shedding their tears through the filthy glass.

We buried her alongside Rosina, alongside Zuza and the other poor women. The sun shone, and it had miraculously turned warmer. I didn't go to the funeral in manacles, Berenice and Gita had furnished me with a firm alibi for that night and early morning. The detectives ascertained that someone had brought the corpse to the little square between Joachim and Narrow Streets at daybreak, and the head had already been severed and placed inside the lamp just after the flame went out. The police launched a relentless manhunt for a highly dangerous individual known as Kleinfleisch, and the city council issued a reward of five hundred gulden for his apprehension. Old Prague heatedly frisked its moth-eaten body like a dog groping in its coat for a tormenting flea, and in its crooked hovels and twisted lanes and filthy backyards it hunted a ghost. A spectre. A bogeyman.

I started fencing again to overcome my melancholy and get fit, spending hours on end in the gymnasium from Monday to Friday. Solly used to turn up only in the evening, and we sought relaxation from our duels in ludicrously brief bouts with Sokol members who were motivated by their diligent willingness to get some extra lessons for free. Poche watched from a distance. He had no interest in further skirmishes, and I no longer had any intention of paying him back. I would wipe the sweat from my forehead with a handkerchief, and when it was wet I would take a break. I had to leave my watch in the changing-room or the sweat-soaked leather strap would have stunk like a bridle-bit after a brisk ride. After fencing I would take a look at myself in the mirror, but it didn't look as if the fat around my kidneys and stomach was contracting at all. I couldn't understand it. At the age of twenty I was the idlest young man in the Czech lands. I used to pretend I was preparing myself for a diplomatic career, but most of the time I just read novels, gallivanted around the city and drank with a crowd of *nouveaux riches*, and yet I didn't put on any more fat than would fit under a fingernail. Now, at the age of thirty, when every night I shared a bed with Gita (even though I wanted to ditch her), I could fence all hours, drink about the same amount of wine as in those days (when I can get hold of any) and still get fatter and fatter like a porker. Gita used to say to me, 'Be glad you're alive. If you lost weight you'd turn into the bogeyman that hides behind the broom in the kitchen', but Berenice would make fun of me and call me Uncle.

Occasionally Manny would visit the gymnasium, but it took a lot to persuade him. We have lazy blue blood from our common ancestors. He wasn't bad at fencing. The good grounding one gets at an early age lasts for a lifetime, but it was hard to kindle in him a spark of competitiveness. I noticed that he was less talkative and more staid. His joviality had disappeared, and he was withdrawn, lost in goodness knows what thoughts. Armed with a foil he acquitted himself well for someone his size, but as soon as a put down his weapon he would flag, fighting for breath and looking for somewhere to sit down, at which moment he would clap his hands over his heart and complain about the dust kicked up in the fencing hall. He looked ten years older. He used to send out for tankards of beer, which only made him more lethargic, and each time he would reach into his pocket for a pill and quickly swallow it. On one occasion I asked him if it was Hoffmann's hydrochlorate, and first he nodded but then shook his head. He left all of my questions about Helen Tauferová unanswered, and his anguished expression permitted no further enquiries.

Although Solly tended to adopt an attitude of reserve towards my cousin he suggested that we should organize a spectacular birthday celebration at Golda's. I pointed out that Manny didn't have any birthday at that time, but he said it didn't matter. And so I agreed to pay two-thirds of the cost, and he would arrange it all with Madame Golda. I sent Manny an invitation for the following Saturday, saying they had a surprise lined up for him at Golda's. The messenger brought a reply within the hour: he would come, but in his view nothing and no one would surprise him. Well, well, our gay bachelor was starting to feel his age.

We arrived at Golda's at eight. The door opened, and we were greeted by the Madame herself with three girls in tow. They were new – I hadn't seen them before, at least – as if there were no plans to knock the place down. They were all dressed in underskirts and laced into short corsets that pushed up their breasts and ended not above but under the nipples. Charming. They introduced themselves as Eva, Frankie and Venus. They took our hats and scarves, and before taking us into the main room they sat us down on stools and offered us an aperitif. The Madame held a tin bowl into which she poured green absinthe from a bottle, and each of the girls dipped first one and then her other breast in it. Then they thrust their alcoholic comforters into our mouths. I had the good fortune to end up with Venus, who had the biggest and softest breasts; clearly I enjoyed Golda's favour. Solly was visibly jealous and licked Frankie right up to her chin, insisting that 'two titties aren't enough when they're so undersized'. Madame seized him by the ear and dragged him off to the main room, while we followed behind accompanied by the girls. I was slightly ill at ease, and Manny's hands were shaking. He reached into his pocket and pulled out a little bottle of white tablets. I slapped his wrist, and he put them away again.

Along the walls of the salon there were tables with savoury pastries and fruit wine. The empty plank floor in the middle had been cleared for dancing. A swing hung from ropes attached to two hooks in the ceiling.

Behind the bar a girl known as Lay Sister got lazily to her feet. Hanging from her shoulders on leather braces was an accordion, which was attached around her waist by straps; otherwise she was quite naked. She started to play and sing German and Czech songs, flitting around and rubbing her reddish arms, the well-worn accordion and her well-groped dimpled bottom against various parts of us. The three girls with the exposed breasts danced with us in a ring, pressing themselves to us and leading us in a ludicrous imitation of dances: first a waltz, then polkas and then something that most of all resembled a sailor's swaying gait. With each dance they changed partners, and I silently congratulated Madame that none of them was ugly. Then we went and sat down. Manny received a cream cake and a knife. He cut it into a dozen pieces and shared it among us and the girls equally, but Madame received the largest piece. The girls stuffed themselves as if they had not eaten for a week. They squealed enthusiastically about the cake, and they were up to their eyes in cream. I gave my portion to them, and Solly did likewise. They grabbed at the cake and almost fought over it. They were thrilled and grateful, and they were amazed that anyone could willingly forgo something like that. I ordered champagne from Madame. She warned us frankly that it would be very expensive, and she lied that she had several bottles reserved for me and me alone. It looked as if Manny was finally beginning to relax, and I was prepared to spend a fortune on the evening.

We drank. I smoked my English pipe and kept an eye on Manny to make sure he left the hydrochlorate alone. The show that the girls then performed for us was announced as 'a spectacle for patriots'. They dragged a leather mat to the middle of the dance floor, the sort one finds piled up in gymnasiums (no doubt a gift from one of the 'brethren'), and placed it a few paces in front of the swing. The girl who introduced herself as Eva now sat on the swing. She was now wearing a short white skirt and stockings with horizontal black and white stripes and no garters. She started to swing, and since she had the swing beneath her bottom and legs slightly apart we were afforded a furry spectacle. Lay Sister accompanied it with a song about a dreadful crime in the meadows, how the Jews cut the throat of a blue-eyed girl there. Suddenly Frankie rode in from the room next door on a tall penny-farthing bicycle. She, too, was dressed solely in a short skirt and stockings, in her case with vertical yellow and black stripes. She rode around the dance floor three times, sticking out her bottom like a proper devotee of modern sports. We applauded. Frankie placed herself in the path of the swing, and Eva bumped her with her knees, at which Frankie feigned a fall and landed on the mat with her legs in the air, and once more we applauded enthusiastically. Then she went over to the table for a riding crop and started to whip Eva's bottom in time to the swing. Eva started to scream blue murder, but she swung many more times before she jumped off and started to box Frankie's ears. They tumbled on to the mat and the yellow and black Austrian stripes vanquished the red-and-white Czech colours. Frankie stood over Eva and stepped on her neck. At that moment Venus arrived on the scene, and she, too, was in Slavonic colours except that her stockings had a pattern of red-and-white diamonds. She started to throttle Frankie, while Eva tripped her up and all three were rolling on the mat, pulling each other by the hair and simulating ferocious combat. The Czech colours were victorious, Frankie ended up on all fours, being smacked with hand and riding crop. Then we were invited over to the live tableau in order to spank the Austrian bottom. It was surprisingly pleasing. Only Manny was in two minds, but the girls knew how to deal with it: Eva and Venus offered him their bottoms, too, as well as the strictly neutral Lay Sister. Manny was the guest of honour after all, so it was natural they should treat him favourably.

Then things rapidly went downhill. I remember that the stink of smoke, alcohol and sweat started to be so bad that I yelled at Madame to open a window. But it was after ten, and that meant giving Lay Sister a bottle to shut her up and taking away her accordion, otherwise there was the risk of a policeman bursting into the establishment. I was drunk and doing silly things. I declared that I had no intention of breathing such stinking air another single minute, and Madame snapped that I was the one that had created all the smoke with my pipe.

'But he's not breathing,' said Solly and put his pocket mirror to my nose.

'I'll give it a kiss.' said Frankie, grabbing it out of his hand, squatting down and pressing it on to her crotch. It was nicely printed on to the mirror.

'It's a veritable daguerreotype!' Manny marvelled and rummaged through his pockets in search of something suitably shiny. He found no mirror, and to the amazement of all present he broke down and wept.

'Here,' I said, handing him my monocle, 'take this as a present from me.'

This moved him to further tears. Eva took the monocle from me, bent her legs and spread her knees, slipping the lens up under her skirt and quickly taking it out again. But it was only smudged.

Manny put it in his eye socket nevertheless and winked. 'Do I look like a nobleman?' he asked, and we applauded him.

'Otka is only a couple of days under the sod, and here we are acting like pigs,' someone complained as the women were leading us to the door, and then I realized that the speaker was me. I'm only superficially callous, and, worst of all, I'm reconciled to it.

I started to resist, saying I had to pay my respects to Otka, and I would do it upstairs in a bedroom with Venus, but Madame hissed close to my face with her sour breath, 'Gita's waiting for you, My Lord.' And she was right.

Then I was standing in the street, and the night air was cool. Solly was breathing it with me. Manny had remained inside; with all the wine and spirits he had drunk his appetite for bed had increased, and the girls had a celebratory bonus prepared for him

My top hat found itself on top of my fuddled head, my coat around my shoulders and my scarf around my neck. Somewhere in Jewry a door banged. Solly tripped, and something made him laugh.

'Let's hope he won't go swallowing those pills,' I said. 'They don't mix well with alcohol.'

'Don't worry,' Solly replied and waved a little bottle in front of my face. 'I noticed you were worried about him, so I saved him from temptation.'

I could think of no better response than to bow to him, and he did the same to me. I repeated it and he, too, all the while grabbing at our hats as they obstinately toppled off our heads.

I suddenly felt ill. We were staggering home, resting at every street corner. At midnight we found ourselves by the river. There was a faint stench of fish in the air, otherwise it was fresh with no trace of dust, sewage or grease. We were by the lagoon, much further than we were intending to go. The tall pointed roofs of the watermills loomed black in the moonlit night.

'I'm most at home here,' I said to Solly, who wasn't listening. We returned in the direction of the Agnes Convent, failed to find it and emerged in a street I couldn't identify. It could mean that we were back in Jewry, which was confirmed when we raised our heads. The houses were pressed close together. They were leaning to one side like the tower in Pisa, and there were no stairs up to the tallest of them, just iron ladders with wooden extensions tied to them attached to the wall. There was no light in any of the windows. And it was right there that we were brought up short by something odd: a child's whining interrupted by a nasty fit of coughing. The sounds seemed to come from above. At ground level and up the level of the first floor it was total darkness, but above that the clear night was lit up by the light of the moon and stars. We could make out a hole in a crude extension to one of the houses, and the crying seemed to come right from there together with the feeble yellow glow from a candle. The opening looked like a cave, and a long iron ladder for chimney sweeps led up to it from the lane.

'Come home.' Solly tugged at my sleeve. 'Jews can fend for themselves.'

'Maybe they're not Jews.' I groped blindly for the cold iron of the ladder. One rung, then another, then a third. Before I knew it I was high above the ground and climbing higher.

'Do you want kill yourself?' Solly muttered from below, and something trickled into the gutter. 'The Count wants to kill himself. I'll moisten it a bit here for you so you have something soft to fall on to.'

'Go to bed,' I called to him and clambered like a monkey until I reached the hole knocked into the wall, in front of which a ring had been attached to the ladder and a plank wired to it. The rungs continued up to the roof. I knelt on the seat and looked down. The street below me was like a long dark pit, another of the urban improvement trenches. My head swam, and I held on tightly to the plank. Then I turned around and tried thumping with my hand on the stiff sheet that hung in front of the opening. No candles burnt behind it any more. Dust rose from the cloth, and I started to cough.

'Hello!' I coughed through a crack. 'This is the imperial and royal police. Throw down your weapons in the name of the law, and come out with your hands up!' Solly, who was now standing on the ladder just below me, sniggered into the night.

Inside it was as silent as the grave, and I imagined what would happen. Kleinfleisch would sweep aside the curtain and cut my throat with his knife, and his hollow laugh would be the last thing I perceived as I fell out of this world.

Fear grabbed me by the collar and dragged me into the opening. My hat did not go through and sailed down into the street. I banged my head on the crooked wall and crouched there like a prehistoric caveman.

'I'm here,' said Solly behind me, and he struck a match. He was hatless, too. We squatted there like two dwarves and gazed at the smelly candles on the filthy floor which had stopped smoking only moments before. I groped for one of them and touched the wick to the flame. We inspected the cave in the resinous light.

It was six or seven paces long, and a ten-year-old child might stand upright inside it. The ceiling was formed of the crudely hewn beams of the roof, the walls were of masonry, rags, skins and fence palings. Beneath a massive crossbar on the other side an unwashed woman lay curled up with a bundle tied to her belly. She was watching us in terror.

The bundle contained a child with a large head. In the light of the candle it looked grey. It was wheezing terribly, and pus ran from its eyes and nose. Solly covered his mouth and nose with his handkerchief. It stank there like a dunghill. Dirty napkins were piled up by the palings, and a covered pail stood alongside, like in a police cell. Water glistened in a tin bucket near by. It looked clean. A gnawed packet of sea biscuits lay on an improvised shelf on the wall; it couldn't be kept entirely safe from the mice.

'I've not stolen nothing,' the woman said and pressed the child to her scrawny chest. Her voice was coarse, and she had a gypsy accent. She must have been fairly young, but the sharp-cut features, dark eyes and crooked nose reminded me of pictures of fairy-tale witches.

We asked after the child and offered to get hold of a doctor, or, even better, we could take it down and carry it to my own doctor. She replied that she had no money. Solly started to explain to her that there were institutions in Prague that would take care of it, but she started to rattle on at him in the gypsy tongue until he stopped talking.

'The child is scarcely breathing,' I said. 'It'll die here.'

'I'll bury it in the river,' she snapped and held out her hand. 'Give me a crown and buzz off to where you come from. Or I'll push you both down.'

Solly started to laugh. He looked around the tiny chamber and commented, 'You certainly have some strength, gyppo. Did you knock this down yourself?'

'I found it here. They promised me work, then they beat me and gave me a baby,' she replied a bit more calmly, almost resignedly. 'What's it called here?'

'What?'

'The city down there. Are you are halfwit or what?'

'That city's called the Pearl,' Solly whispered. 'Do you like pearls?'

'I do. But there's none in this city. Just wicked people. Like you two.'

I took out my wallet, but then I put it away again. I asked Solly to hand over the little bottle that he had taken out of Manny's pocket.

I held up the bottle in front of her eyes. It glinted briefly in their blackness.

'Look here. These are pearls. They can cure. Give one to the little one, and you'll see.'

She nodded. I unscrewed the top, took out one tablet, broke it in two and then into quarters. I offered her the four white fragments on my palm. 'Medicine. You must give it in separate doses or it will kill the child.'

She took one of the pieces and put it in her mouth. For a moment she sat dumbfounded and then the hint of a smile appeared on her face. Sadly there were regular gaps between her teeth.

She grabbed another piece. Solly said, 'Steady!' but she pulverized it between her tongue and the roof of her mouth and gave it to the child in spittle as a lengthy kiss. I started to count. When I reached fifty the infant became calm and started to breathe normally.

'Don't forget,' I said, raising a finger in warning, 'you have to give it quarters if you want to keep it alive. And you take one pearl a day, no more, or you'll become a slave to it. When you have none left ask for the Loggia and come for some more.' I gave her the bottle, and it disappeared immediately inside the bundle with the sleeping child.

Solly and I groped our way out, and when I was letting down the curtain after us I glanced into the room and asked the gypsy woman, 'What work didn't you get?'

She raised her eyes sleepily, showing again the gaps in her teeth. 'What do you think? You really are a blockhead.'

'Some whores are incredibly fortunate,' Solly philosophized as we climbed down the ladder, 'while others have no luck at all.'

'It depends on who they happen on,' I remarked and anxiously held tight to the iron rungs.

'Precisely. When they happen upon a sucker like you they're in easy street. If they happen on Kleinfleisch it's amen.'

'I've know some who happened on both.'

We had reached the bottom. I jumped down from the ladder and started to look for my hat in the dirty lane. I couldn't find it, nor Solly his. I got home at one thirty. My head felt light and completely clear.

XVII

Events at the Loggia

A File from the Town Hall

There were arrests in Prague. The police had launched a purge of the 'radical elements', as they wrote in the newspapers, and there was not a soul about anywhere. I knocked on the glazed door of the apothecary at the sign of the Moor shortly before opening time.

The pharmacist did not even appear surprised. I locked the door behind me, and I ordered him to sit down behind the counter. I leant on it with my elbows and gazed at him for a moment. I informed him that I knew about his snooping and if he didn't want a thrashing he had better answer a few questions. He agreed unreservedly.

I wanted to know what the new situation in the city meant and whether a state of emergency would be declared once more. As a reliable informer he immediately expatiated at length. 'The secret police have uncovered a plot against the empire. They were actually planning to assassinate the intended heir to the throne, can you imagine – Crown Prince Franz Ferdinand himself and here in Prague of all places. The anarchists infiltrated the country unmolested. No matter, but that fact had to be kept secret at all costs, so that it didn't give others ideas. But it fell through. They're from the south, you understand, and they won't find much support here, and this lot didn't. The Balkans' promised contacts in Prague failed, and someone shopped them.'

'It wasn't you, by any chance?' I asked.

He laughed without moving his jaw. 'Excuse me, but I don't have any contacts with anyone. But what I can tell you, My Lord, is that the champagne corks are popping at the police headquarters as we speak.'

I invited him to tell me how he himself perceived the standing of the Czech lands in the monarchy and whether we ought not at least to enjoy the same status as Hungary.

He blenched visibly. 'We're small fry for something like that and constantly at loggerheads, that's obvious to anyone with a bit of sense – the Czechs have never been capable of ruling themselves.'

So I asked him whether he would like the opportunity to speak Czech as well as German at the office where he paid his taxes.

He replied ingenuously that he couldn't care less about Czech, but since it was his mother tongue he didn't intend to forget it, besides which well over half his customers spoke to him in Czech, and he wasn't going to risk his profits over it.

'But if it's well over half of them', I argued, 'then isn't the situation of official departments similar? The Czech language belongs there the same as German.'

He gripped the counter frantically and shook his head. 'I don't want to know this, My Lord. Don't tell me anything. I don't want to know anything any more.' His eyes were beseeching me to go.

'I am telling you it nevertheless. And if you're interested, my opinion on whether the Czechs deserve their own independent state –'

'No!' The pharmacist put his fingers in his ears and started to back away, but I reached across the counter and grabbed his tie, pulling him back again.

'I'm willing to tell you,' I continued. 'Up to now I couldn't really have cared less. But now I do. If those mastodons in the town hall want to turn Prague into a modern city along the lines of Paris, then I'd sooner it were the metropolis of an independent Czech kingdom.'

The pharmacist started to sob, and I let him go.

'Do you want to kill me?' he said, sitting down on his stool. Then he took out his handkerchief and blew his nose. 'I'm obliged to tell them. Never divulge such things to anyone. Above all, not to them.'

'So don't you tell them either.'

'I can't do that. I'm not capable of it.'

'You suffer from information diarrhoea. Prescribe yourself a cork.'

'Please leave me alone. You can't behave like this. Nobody behaves this way. Go away or I'll go and find a policeman.'

'You're not going anywhere,' I said as calmly as I could. 'You are never going to contact the police again, and if they come after you will inform them that all your sources have dried up and that you are ending your cooperation. Is that clear?'

'They'll close my pharmacy. They'll take away my concession. I know what they are like.'

'I don't think they'd do it, but even if they did – you'll move to the country and run your own business. They won't care about you there. At least you'll save your life.'

'My life?'

'Yes. Realize that I would have you on my conscience – which would be another offence against me. Do you know how Kleinfleisch kills? He perforates you. He'll cut off your head and stick it on top of your shop sign. And I would do something similar to you – and stick a gold piece in your gob. And if they gaol me before I get the chance to do it there'll be others who will do away with you in some elegant manner, quietly and reliably. So think again. And give me a box of tooth-whitening powder and some mouthwash.'

He collapsed on his stool. I had to hand him the goods myself from the shelf and leave the money on the counter. The apothecary was beside himself with terror. There was suddenly a very bad smell, and I decided to leave the door open to clear the air.

So much for that.

In the street dust swirled up from the demolished houses and settled on my coat, my hat and my hands, entering my mouth and nose, as the houses scattered into the atmosphere wanted to linger a little longer in the city where they had spent many centuries – within its very inhabitants. But I didn't keep the houses inside me; I coughed them out along with drops of blue blood. Hoffmann's miracle was gradually ceasing to give relief unless I took at least three doses a day and went to bed with the chickens.

Father and I exchanged regular letters. He invited me to Stránov together with my dubious women. This didn't please Mama, he wrote, in fact she found it unthinkable, but he assured me that I was not to take it into account. I promised him that I would make the journey in the foreseeable future and spend at least three months there. But I didn't tell him that I intended to postpone it if possible. My father had learnt from his sources of information, which I wanted nothing to do with, of the reply I made that time to that ridiculous individual by the name of Listopad. According to his logic, which I don't understand, he deduced that I might take part in his anti-Habsburg conspiracy, which went hand in hand with his Czech nobleman's patriotism. On top of that he was grateful for the money I had sent him. Lo, the lost bond between father and son has been found! The trouble was that I didn't share his feelings so wholeheartedly, except about the city that was disappearing before my very eyes and being transformed into something comfortably uniform – neat housing developments and palatial office buildings.

As I discern anew every day, parents are an infernal nuisance to the very end. Not even pills, tobacco and women's bodies give me a moment's relief from them.

At night I earned money and did a feeble amount of good. As the stock of heroic pills dwindled their price on the Old Prague market soared, and the dealers and well-off users were willing to pay three times as much as I had charged a month before. What I didn't manage to sell in the evening I distributed around Jewry, finding my way into filthy hovels, climbing ladders to rooftop extensions and knocking on doors where the official municipal seal had been broken, and I would offer them to anyone who looked ill or who told me they were. Ill-smelling beggars, the lame on crutches, cripples with hooks in place of hands, the legless who moved around on barrel tops with wheels attached, old grannies reeking of smoke who sold their grandchildren on street corners, the last inhabitants of the Jewish town – they all reinforced my newly acquired conviction that there was something that was still worthwhile: themselves, Gita and Berenice, my friend Solly and also my little baroque Loggia.

It was getting harder and harder to defend the house. One night I came home, and as I came through the gateway I could hear someone singing in the courtyard. It was Berenice. She was standing in the gallery in just a long night-dress and singing something beautiful in Yiddish with her face turned to the sky. Gita was sitting beneath the arch on a stool with a washboard in a tub. She was sobbing into her apron, and when she caught sight of me she ran up and I noticed that she had a knife for peeling potatoes clenched in her hand. I backed away, but she threw her arms around my neck and blurted out something about Kleinfleisch. He had come into the yard where she was washing something. She had forgotten to close the door in the gate. He was suddenly standing by her and silently watching her. She wasn't aware of him until she heard the scrape of his soles on the flagstones, and she looked straight up into the black holes in the raw meat beneath the hat. He drew a knife out from under his coat and waved it about, but Berenice had appeared on the gallery above and started to sing. Kleinfleisch had listened for a moment and then turned around and left.

'I could smell blood, Addie,' Gita muttered, and I prised the kitchen knife out of her fingers. 'I was waiting for flies to swarm around him. It's just as well they are not flying at the moment.'

I stroked her. And I awarded myself an imaginary kick up the backside for not having locked the girls in the house with three padlocks.

'Why didn't you hide afterwards and lock yourselves in?' I asked. My voice was shaking.

'Berenice didn't want me to. Ever since the monster left she's been standing there singing. She's terribly brave, Addie, I was the one who almost broke down. But it's also possible that she's lost her marbles.

Well, at least you're here, Addie. You'll stay with us now, won't you? Don't go anywhere without us any more.'

Berenice kept on singing. I climbed up to the gallery after her and closed her mouth. I took her hand and led her indoors. She was pale and chilled, but her bright eyes were sane. They contained satisfaction and triumph.

In the kitchen I poured them both out a sweet liqueur and asked Berenice to translate the song for me. She recited it in Czech as a clumsy poem, word for word, as the Yiddish words came into her mind:

> 'Beautiful as the moon, fragrant as a spring day
> Fell from the sky a gift into my arms.
> My happy day has come.
> You shine like the sun, you bloom like a rose,
> Your teeth are white pearls.
> Your hair is magical.
> Your eyes are the twinkle of a comet in the sky.'

She said it was a love song from the ghetto. And she stared fixedly at me. Gita leant on the stove and started to cry once more. I sent them both off to bed.

In the depth of night I listened in my bedroom to the rustle of mice in the loft, the sound of cats on the roofs and occasional drunken singing from the street. I couldn't get to sleep, so I lit a pipe. I thought anxiously of Gita, because I had taken her on not only as an official housemaid but I also supported her as my mistress and bore full responsibility for her in the eyes of the public and the law. And yet I knew that as soon as she started to age I would have to replace her with a younger woman, as I had already planned anyway a while before, and the painful certainty of my own weakness distressed me. The best thing, I fantasized, would be to fall in love, like Solly that time with that Catholic girl. My fate would be straightforward. I would become a pariah. My parents would reject me and disinherit me. And I would have what I really wanted, and the feeling made me blissful. But however rounded were the hips of my red-headed beauty and however bountiful were her breasts, her soul was like a plate: flat and clean. It was so easy to dirty a plate. Or even break it. And I didn't want that.

I also thought about Berenice. I saw her as a promise, as the golden chalice of an inscrutable Cabalist, from which I would first learn to drink and which – perhaps – would provide me with refreshment into old age. But how long would it take before I started sleeping with her? And would I manage to hold on to her at all?

That's when it happened. She answered one of my questions herself, as if she had snatched it out of the nocturnal ether.

She knocked on the door, opened it and slipped inside. Before she managed to tell me that she couldn't sleep and could smell my pipe I asked her, 'Did your mother sing it to you. Do you remember her at least that way – through that song?'

'It was the one who brought me up and sold me that sung it to me. I don't remember her at all. Will you give me a tablet?'

I gave her one. Berenice washed it down with the dregs of the wine that remained on the table and came over to my bed. She lay down on her back, spread her legs and bent them at the knees. We made love in the smoke-filled room. I was smeared with blood, and afterwards she told me that there had been almost no pain. I had also felt almost no pain, just a slight abrasion since her insides were not yet accustomed to submit.

'I was thinking about it before you arrived,' I said to the open window. 'Is that why you're here?'

'I've been thinking about it', Berenice replied, 'ever since Klein-fleisch came into the yard and I could think of nothing better to do than sing. I was sure he was going to kill us – me and Gita. And I dread-fully wanted you to be with me.'

I sat on the bed and stroked the hair lying loose on the sheets. 'I'll protect you.'

*

Next morning, when Gita came back from the market with eggs and bacon, she found an official notice stuck to the gate of the Loggia. It stated that the house was in an urban improvement zone and was due for demolition. She tore it off, and suddenly there were two men standing there, one tall, the other short, and they told her that it must not been torn off because it was an official document belonging to the town hall. And they stuck a new notice with the same text and official stamp. Then the short fellow pinched her bottom, and the tall one smeared her face with the paste from his paste pot. 'Kiss the brush, you little scrubber,' he told her. She was about to kick him in the crotch, but he dodged, and the short fellow tripped her up. Then they threatened her that the notice had to remain on the gate come what may or else. She came back sticky, dirty and scarlet with rage. I regretted that I always left my épée and sword at the gymnasium. But I picked up an axe in the yard and thus armed went out into the street. They were already gone. I ripped the paper off the wood, but a few tatters still remained there. Unfortunately it was the part of the notice where it said in black and white: *Urban Improvement Zone*.

I put on a black suit and went straight to the town hall. Some flunkey of a porter stopped me as I entered, asking if I had an appointment. I told him I was going to file a complaint and I couldn't give a damn about any appointment. He fished out a form for me to fill in and told me that I had to submit it to the registry. My complaint would be dealt with within fourteen days and the decision sent to me by post. On the green-painted wall behind him I noticed a box with a telephone apparatus, and I requested him to make a call to executive official Bürger who knew me and who would see me immediately. The flunkey smirked sceptically but turned towards the telephone. Without any further delay I went over to the staircase and searched for the name of F.X. Bürger among the brass plates with the titles and posts of the officials and the numbers of their offices. Then I run up to the second floor and entered the office without knocking.

Bürger was sitting at his desk, on which there were two stacks of paper. In the gap between them, placed so as to be immediately visible, lay a black six-shooter. One of Bürger's hands rested on the desktop next to the gun, the other clenched a handkerchief. The official was shaking all over as he strove to hold back a fit of coughing.

I sat down opposite him. The porter burst into the office apologizing and asking for permission to call the guards. Bürger sent him away, and after a moment's hesitation he put the revolver away in the desk but left the drawer open.

He was waiting for me to start, but I remained silent. And so he started to speak, while coughing all the time.

'A meeting of the Urban Improvement Committee was called, not on my volition but by the town hall administration, at which Dr Preininger presented a new report on the level of hygiene in the Old Town and the former Jewish quarter. He appealed urgently to all of us to speed up the urban improvement programme and the construction of a water-main and sewers. Your house, My Lord, stands in the path of blanket demolition of unsuitable buildings. It stands above the proposed junction of the underground tunnels. When you bought the house you complicated the situation for us, and we tried to find an alternative solution with the building experts – please believe me. And we came up with one. But Dr Preininger informed us that your house would thereby be, in his words, 'a festering boil on the body of a clean and healthy city'. Moreover, avoiding your house would have increased the cost of the programme by an unjustifiable amount, and the achievements of the urban improvement programme would have been undermined. Tuberculosis always returns to a body that has not been totally cured. In view of the state of the bedrock beneath the house it is impossible to bore tunnels through it either for the water-main or for sewers. It requires a very deep trench so that the tunnels can be constructed from above. Preininger alarmed the committee, and all of them, I repeat, all of those present, raised their hands in favour of the building's compulsory purchase.'

'Including you.'

'All of those present.'

'But I won't sell you the house.'

'Mr Meister and I requested the Finance Committee to offer you a revised price, closer to what you paid the previous owners. You have no alternative. I was intending to inform you about it today, but, as you see, I am not well, and you pre-empted me. I arrived in the office half an hour before you.'

'And if I refuse to sell?'

'Although we disagree, I trust won't come to that. But should it happen we'll request an order from Vienna for the building to be confiscated.'

'You won't do it.'

'Look here. It's a standard, and indeed just, procedure. Sometimes the individual must give way to the community. They do it in all countries.'

'Such as?'

'I could mention France – admittedly they have a republic there – but I could also cite monarchist England. The individual must not stand in the way of progress, My Lord. Otherwise progress will sweep him aside.'

'I want to talk to the mayor.'

'He's in Vienna.'

'Then with Meister, at least.'

'Mr Meister is there with him.'

'Really. I assume they are submitting an application to the office of approvals for the confiscation of the Loggia House.'

'No. There's time enough for that . . . although not much. The purchase offer will be delivered . . . any day now. I advise you to accept it. There is nothing else you can do anyway.'

I sat motionless and watched a cough explode from his thin lips and tears from his dark eyes. What had to come out could no longer be confined. Bürger swayed in his chair and flapped his hand at me to leave. I could hear within his tortured hawking the hoarse rattle of demolition machines, but it was only the sound of his mechanical churning out of words. Without doubt he had no wish for me to see him in this humiliating situation, but I remained nailed to the chair.

I was waiting for the blood, and it wasn't long in coming: in a twinkling Bürger's hand was full of it, and the desktop and piles of documents were sprinkled with red. At last I could stand up. I went around the desk and shut his fingers in the desk drawer into which he had reached in panic for his revolver. As he swiftly withdrew his hand with a yell his chair overbalanced and he fell on to his back. I knelt on him, my knee pressing down on his uninjured hand, and I reached into my pocket. He was writhing in spasms and choking on the red foam. And carefully, making sure he didn't bite me, I forced one of Hoffman's heroic pills into his mouth.

Before a minute had elapsed on my wristwatch F.X. Bürger had ceased to cough and spit blood, and he had stopped squirming and resisting. There was confusion and terror in his eyes. It served him right.

I stood up, took the revolver out of the drawer and stuck it in my pocket.

'Send to the Loggia House for a further dose,' I said as I was leaving his office. 'I'll let you have one pill a day. If you leave me in peace you can have them for nothing. If that notice appears on my gate again you won't get any more, not at any price. Don't send that purchase offer. Otherwise I'll make you eat it right in front of me.'

Bürger lay on his back with his eyes closed, panting and saying nothing. As if he couldn't hear. Perhaps he had fallen asleep from exhaustion and the effects of the pill, but most likely he was feigning it to get me to go. I left him there, and downstairs I gave the porter a gulden. He promised to keep quiet about my visit.

I took a cab from the town hall to the gymnasium. I fought seven épée bouts with avid youngsters, ceremoniously took my leave of them and took my weapons home with me. It gave me a salutary sense of safety to walk the streets of Prague with a sabre in one hand and an épée in the other, not to mention the six-shooter in my pocket.

Safety pro tem at least.

XVIII

Manny's First Confession

Scoundrels in the House

The Emperor had sat on the throne for almost fifty years. It was permitted to speak about it in the Czech lands, as we were reminded daily. The celebration would take place the following year; it was to be 'not only a European but also an international spectacle', as the newspapers wrote.

Some things one mustn't talk about, as I knew and confirmed at Karpeles's café the next day where I had been invited to Viennese Sachertorte by Manny. Above a table with newspapers extolling the sovereign I observed that in the year of my birth Mexican republicans had killed the Emperor's brother. And, eight years ago, Manny added sadly, his only son Rudolf had died. We started talking about it. I was interested to know what the nobility at Harnack thought about it, and Manny shrugged. The official line was that Rudolf took his own life because he couldn't cope with his duties. That version was also supported by Manny's parents. But there were many, including himself, who held the view that Rudolf had been disposed of by a group of advisers to the Emperor, who had already stripped him of political power, because – and Manny started to count on his fingers – the crown prince had been a liberal with friends among the educated Jews, a morphine addict and a passionate womanizer infected with syphilis, and its progress in his body was becoming visible.

'I once heard a similar view expressed at Stránov,' I was about to say, but I was interrupted.

Someone, in a café where we were supposed to be sitting on our own, swore out loud. It wasn't Karpeles; he was still standing behind the counter, but at this moment he set off with a napkin over his arm in the direction of a separate booth. He bowed, exchanged a few words with someone, then stuck something in his pocket. In his other hand he now held a spattered cup on a saucer. For a moment nothing happened. Then an inconspicuous man in a thick woollen suit emerged above the edge of the booth. He put on a bowler hat and headed for the door. The Sachertorte turned sour in my mouth. Manny stopped eating, too, and gazed after the man in the hat. When he was outside I went to take a look in the booth. There was a huge dark-brown stain on the tablecloth and a few smaller ones around it. The cloth retained an imprint of some hasty scrawl. It was impossible to tell what the man had written, but he had been in such a hurry he had spilt his coffee.

'I'm going to have it out with him,' I said and was about to dash out, but Manny's tone of voice held me back.

'Wait, Addie. Don't do anything rash. Maybe it was just a coincidence, and even if it wasn't . . . If you thrash one of them he'll set two or three others on to you, and they'll be armed. I know what I'm talking about.'

'And what are you talking about?' I sat down and tossed off a glass of absinthe.

Manny looked nonplussed and old all of a sudden. 'I've had some unpleasant experiences of it, of a political nature,' he said finally.

'Why didn't you tell me before?'

'There was no reason to. But, believe me, if they decide to go after somebody, they'll get him. And family background is no barrier to them.' Manny's cheeks were now red, and droplets of sweat had formed on his top lip.

I did nothing to conceal my surprise. Karpeles sauntered over to us, and I asked who the fellow in the bowler hat was. He naturally replied that he had never seen him here before. I asked him to kindly inform us of his presence next time. He bowed, but his lips were pursed in refusal. It occurred to me that he had also fallen foul of them.

I waved him away, and when he was out of earshot I let fly at Manny. 'Why did you invite me here? And why did precisely that have to happen? I've not been set up, have I?'

'Do you suspect me?' he blurted despairingly, but it looked as if he was still a long way from indignation.

I shook my head and raised my hand. 'Sorry. I'm beginning to read the runes, and I've started seeing spies everywhere.'

He was gazing at me with a perplexed expression, and there was a reproachful glint in one of his eyes, while the other was dark with fear. Only now did I notice how thin he had become. His cheeks were no longer like pink hams but more like half-empty bags of flour; their unhealthy hue was now masked by freshly grown mutton-chop whiskers, similar to those worn by the Emperor but black, of course, with a few grey bristles here and there. His shirt collar projected from his neck, and his expensive scarlet tie adorned with a gold pin bearing the family crest hung loose and crumpled.

'But don't I perhaps have the best cause for dissatisfaction? Eh?' I pressed him and held his gaze for a long time until he let it fall back to his glass. I started to fill my pipe and waited for his response, while the silence thickened and hardened.

Finally he spoke. 'You have cause to a certain extent. I'll tell you, and then you can judge me if you feel like it. Look – something happened at Stránov. I got myself into a real pickle, and I don't know how to get out of it.'

He took a little bottle of the heroic remedy out of his breast pocket, unscrewed the top, tipped a tablet into his hand and swallowed it. At that moment my suspicions started to grow stronger, and somewhere deep in my memory an alarm went off.

'Something to do with the Taufers?'

He nodded wordlessly and waited for the tablet to take effect and calm him down.

And so I asked him another question. 'How did you actually come by those pills? They were so similar to Hoffmann's hydrochlorate . . .'

'Yes,' he nodded. 'It has something to do with what happened afterwards with Helena and me. I'll tell you everything. Bit by bit.'

'Out with it, then.'

'I was a morphinist. Like Prince Rudolf, you might say.'

'Who of us isn't?'

'This was something else. I couldn't do without it any more. And at the castle it was impossible to conceal it from the servants or the relatives who visited us. I stopped taking part in the hunt. I didn't talk to anyone, I just lay in my bedroom and enjoyed the calm that the drug afforded my nerves. But my parents decided that they could no longer put up with it, that it disgraced the family and that I would have to be cured of my dependency.'

'The disgrace bothered them more than the fact you were ruining your health. Naturally.'

'You know it yourself, don't you? I left for a certain Swiss sanatorium to undergo a special course of treatment, but everyone was told that I was displaying early symptoms of tuberculosis, so I had to go to the elevated climes of the Alps. And so I went. The mountain air did me good, but I was dreadfully bored among those pastures. The women there were either old and ill or young and ill –'

'May the good Lord preserve us from such.'

'– and the doctors gave me strange medicines, including strong herbal liqueurs, and soon I was unable to do without them either.'

'And that fire didn't put the other fire out.'

'I thought my parents would be disappointed again if I returned as a former morphinist with a new penchant for hard liquor, but something else happened, because, as you see, I am capable of looking at that absinthe standing in front of me another two hours without needing to take a sip from it. I like spirits, but they're not essential for me, if you see what I mean.'

'So what is essential then?'

'That's the thing. I discovered there a doctor by the name of

Hoffmann, but he wasn't employed there, nor was he undergoing treatment like we unfortunates. One morning he struck up a conversation with me on the terrace, and I blurted out everything to him. I had a great need to make a clean breast of it to someone. He was very understanding and was not prejudiced. He suggested a solution that was not ideal but far less drastic and much slower than morphine or alcohol. He offered me the heroic medicine. The early version that you later tried out yourself.'

'So it was Hoffmann, after all. And I bet he also told you the story about how he used to work at Bayer's factory . . .'

'He really was working there still in those days, Addie. But he felt cheated – like an unacknowledged genius. And you wouldn't believe how closely and with what enthusiasm he watched the improvement in my condition, how I was able live comfortably from day to day without the world filling me with terror and driving me under the coverlet with morphine drops in my belly. All I needed at that time was one heroic tablet a day. In those days it was the ones with the blue label.'

'Did he sell you everything he had?'

'I had them send me some money, and I bought a decent stock. Then I was able to go home. I hadn't written to my parents about it, and I turned up unexpected. I meant it to be a little surprise. I wanted to prove to them that I had strong willpower, that I would get down to work, that I was ready to travel and maybe go into politics even. I was intending to tell them all of that.'

'But the welcome-home party . . .'

'Didn't happen. They were discomfited – as I was, too – as if to say, what are you doing home so soon?

'And so they packed you off to your relatives in Bohemia.'

'Not quite yet . . . or, rather, yes. They sent me here. I had a heroic supply of mental peace and you here. But things would have been different if you still owned your Prague palace. This way it's harder. That's why I spent such a long time at Stránov, and then you moved house. Except that now you've got two women at home.'

'Berenice is still a child.'

'Tell that to the school board.'

'Don't go thinking –'

'I think nothing. But I would only be in the way there. Wherever I go I'm in the way, Addie.'

'Piffle. You don't want your absinthe?'

'No.'

I drank it. 'So what happened with Helena?'

'It went to pan.'

'To pot.'

'To pot. She disappointed me terribly. The time you met us here in Prague . . . it ended shortly after.'

'Her father forbade her to see you.'

'Yes, but that wasn't the main reason. She wouldn't really have noticed him. She's good at manipulating him when she feels like it. The worse thing was that she was up to her neck in some nasty politics with him. And that was like a bullet from a firing squad for me.'

I suspected what I was about to hear, yet I wished that Manny would tell me something else, something totally banal, like something from my own life, a story of infidelity and vengeance or jealousy or envy beyond the grave. Something from a romantic novel for housemaids. But he told me exactly what I had feared.

'Helena behaved like a friend of the family and treated me like a lover, and if you had wanted her, as had been agreed, moreover, she would have used you instead. She informs on your family to her father, who gained your mother's trust a long time ago, as you are aware. But his interest is not simply as a neighbour or a landowner. He also learns about various things and takes great care not to ask directly. And then he passes them on. Your father suspects him and talks even less to your mother now. It's also because he strictly keeps her out of his anti-Habsburg activities, otherwise she would be in the know and would know how to behave with an eavesdropper like him – a spy, in other words. It's a dreadful state of affairs. Your father's in an unenviable situation. But there's nowhere else for him to go, and if I understood correctly he doesn't want to give up his patriotic activity.'

'He told you that himself?'

Manny hesitated before replying. Then he nodded. 'Yes.'

'That's odd, Manny. When we were together at Stránov I had a feeling that something about you bothered him.'

'Really?' He seemed taken aback, but only momentarily. 'Oh, yes, now I understand. I think we upset him at first, Mr Weiss and I, arriving in such numbers. He might have found it disturbing, don't you think? And then, when I stayed on, I got in his way. But when I told him about Helena – that Taufer uses her as a planted informer – I became his confidant.'

'So you told him about Helena.'

'Yes – that she turned out to be a snake in the grass. She probably knew from the outset that your mother's plans were futile. She recognized a long time ago that you wouldn't be interested in her. But she went on playing the well-behaved daughter of the wealthy neighbour for your mother's benefit, a promising acquisition. But during that ride Weiss insulted her in the presence of you and me, and you didn't care. I think she hates you for that. When you and Weiss left she started to make a play for me. And she succeeded. I found her enchanting. Still do, alas.'

'Women.'

'Precisely. I wasn't the first man she slept with. She is very free-thinking in such matters. She's a libertine tart. That suited me, of course, but then I saw through my emotional mistake. I slept with her three times, then here in Prague, the time you met us. And she gave me an assignment, would you believe?'

'Wait. Let me guess. She wanted you to make regular visits to Stránov as a guest . . . and supply her with information about me and about my father. And in return she would sleep with you.'

'Spot on!'

'But you went and told my father about the threat he was under.'

'He was in shock. He couldn't understand why his neighbour was doing it, let alone involving his daughter!'

'It's just possible', I reflected, 'that he wants to use it as a way of getting his hands on the whole castle. Once he's got Father gaoled it'll be quite easy.'

'So now you know. Sorry for causing such a mix-up.'

I held out my hand and he clasped it.

'I must – no, I want to ask you now, Manny, to come and live with me at the Loggia until you're able to return home. My stock of heroic pills isn't so big now, but from now on we'll share it.'

He smiled happily, and his deflated cheeks became rounder.

'It's like an offer I received not long ago. But that one didn't include the pills.' He gave a dry laugh.

'Well, well. And who was the offer from?'

'Your father.'

'For you to return there?'

'Yes.'

'And you accepted it?' I marvelled 'What could there possibly be for you for at Stránov now? You'd die of boredom.'

'Your father and I thought up a plan. A double game, if you know what I mean. I would pass fabricated information on to Helena, such as that your father was setting up an underground organization intending to foment unrest and demonstrations in Prague and the big cities, and I would get from her important information about Taufer's doings and machinations. She had regarded me as her ally, but I would actually be your family's ally. Not bad, eh?'

It didn't know what to say. I gazed into my empty glass and rued the fact I had such unpredictable relatives.

I cleared my throat. 'It doesn't seem safe to me. It'll just provoke the police.'

'But the police will investigate your father and discover it's not true. They won't have any other sources but Helena and Taufer, and they'll stop trusting them. That's how modern intelligence services operate, Addie. The Russians are masters at it, and the Austrians are learning from them.'

'I don't like the sound of it. It'll get us into trouble.'

'I've got it under control.'

'Like that morphine?'

He looked miffed. 'Don't worry. It'll work.'

'I only hope you know what you're doing.'

'Of course. And I've still got some pills, thanks. I'm setting off for Stránov as soon as I can. It'll be best that way.'

'If you think so.'

Manny got up. 'I must go now. I'll let my parents know what I've decided.'

'I'm sure they'll be delighted.'

'I never know what to expect, Addie. But at least I'm doing something that has a reason at last.'

'A purpose.'

'Yes, exactly.'

'May God be with your efforts.'

Manny took my irony seriously. Or at least he looked as if he did. He looked back at me, and he was beaming like a country bumpkin.

I called Karpeles over and ordered another absinthe and a carafe of water to dilute it. I went over in my memory everything I had learnt and tried to guess what Manny had been unable or unwilling to tell me. It looked as if he had found himself substitute parents in his thirties and even how to be of service to them. I found it appalling.

Manny's unexpected confession was not the only evil omen of that day.

As I was returning home I could see from afar that the gates were plastered from top to bottom with notices. They were transcriptions of the now familiar guff from the town hall, and they were stuck on so well that only some of them could be torn off. As I leant on the door in the gateway I discovered that it wasn't locked. Someone had left it slightly ajar, even though I had taken especial care in recent days. Then I noticed that there was something wrong with the lock. It hadn't been prised off or broken into, simply filled with axle grease.

I walked into the yard, but nobody was there. A basket stood there with bleached and mangled bed linen. A few pieces were strewn around the paving stones. The door into the house was closed, but it opened when I pressed down the handle. I examined the lock, and my fingers were soon covered with greasy black smudges. So I had had another unannounced visit, as was soon confirmed when I entered the dining-room.

The chairs and the dining-table had been overturned, there was a crack in the glass of the dresser and the drawers were all open. Silver forks and spoons were strewn over the floor.

'I can't leave this place for a moment,' I sighed, and only then did I notice Gita in the next room. She was lying on the couch. She was naked yet looked as if dressed for a masked ball. Her body was covered in layers of feathers in irregular patches. They came from a quilt that had been ripped open and now lay in shreds on the ottoman; there were even more of them on the floor. The skin on Gita's left cheek had been lacerated, and around it there was a purple bruise reaching up to her temple. I placed my ear on her half-open mouth. She was still breathing, thank God, although in feeble gasps. I placed my hand on her chest. I could feel no heartbeat, but the skin was warm. My fingers were covered with feathers mixed with glue and axle grease that someone had smeared her with from her feet up to her neck. I brought water and washed her all over, including the wound on her face. She was slowly coming around. When she opened her eyes she wriggled and agitated her legs as if to kick me away, and she started to scream. I gently closed her mouth and told her that I would prepare her a bath. She burst into tears.

Later, when she had got rid of the feathers and was washed and dried, she related to me over freshly roasted coffee what had happened. She had accompanied Berenice to her piano lesson then fetched the washing from the laundry and was on her way back to the Loggia to cook dinner. And those two were there again. They were standing by the gate like last time, the tall one and the short one, but instead of just one notice they were covering the surface from top to bottom. She had shouted at them, but the short one suddenly opened the door in the gate, which she had definitely locked on her way out, and the tall one pushed her inside with the basket of washing and clenched her arms behind her back. She resisted, but it was no use. They had dragged her into the house, and he had opened the lock effortlessly with some skeleton key. The short one threatened her with a knife, saying he would slash her face. She asked them what she had done, and the tall one said they were debt collectors, and the little one – he was called Bung – said she owed him something. But all he wanted was to do was sort her out. He spat at her and struck her in the face so hard that she fell over and lost consciousness. It was obvious what had happened next: they had smeared her with axle grease and glue and tried to cover her in feathers, but they were not very successful. Gita added that if I was going to ask whether they took turns at her she could put my mind at rest – she was sure they hadn't. They had left nothing in her down there.

'And even if . . .' I said and kissed her on the forehead. Then I left her sitting in the bath and went to see what the two of them had stolen. They hadn't touched any valuables, which meant they had been well paid for the job, but they had taken away my remaining stock of hydrochlorate, not leaving a single pill behind. And both of my swords had been destroyed. They had broken the sabre but been unable to do the same to the flexible épée, so they had simply twisted it into a ring and wired the tip to the hilt. I guessed that if they had been sent by Bürger they must have also looked for the revolver. But I carried it with me.

I didn't want to go to the police. It would have been hard to report the theft of Hoffmann's miracle. But I could get some redress. That afternoon I ordered some patent locks from the blacksmith, and he came with me to the Loggia to take a look. He told me that the previous locks could have been picked by a child. He recommended me to put bars in all the windows, but I refused. Then I visited a antique shop in Ungelt that specialized in stabbing and cutting weapons. He also sold and restored antique military armour.

I chose a light sword with a flimsy pedigree. Some pseudo-nobleman had had it forged over a hundred years earlier. *František Josef Pachta of Rájov, Baron at Bezno* was engraved on the blade along with the year AD *1785* and a sword-maker's mark in the shape of a target. It oddly suited me, as the village of Bezno and the baronial estate there were not far from Stránov. The hilt was even decorated with gold leaf. It was obvious that the sword had never been used in battle and had been carried simply for show. It was as sharp as a razor. Along with it I took a new épée from the French workshop of La Mouche, and the armourer gave me a discount. No one had ever bought two weapons from him at once.

Then I made my way home. The evening was cold and dry. The wind churned up the dust in the streets, and I had nothing with which to protect myself. My old familiar cough returned with a strength and intensity that I had almost forgotten in recent weeks, as if taking vengeance for all the time it had been kept in check by Hoffmann's hydrochlorate. I didn't have a single pill left. I sent Gita to the Three Horsemen to buy as much as Manny was willing to sell me, but she returned empty-handed: the count had moved out that afternoon, and apparently no one in the house knew where he had gone.

I knew where he was. Manny had rushed back to Stránov with disturbing haste.

XIX

Council Meeting

Visit to F.X.B.

A few days later I went to order a piano for Berenice. She fancied 'a little pianino with green lacquer'. At the firm of Krátky and Son I chose an instrument with the Öser trademark, 'a discontinued model at an attractive price, eminently suitable for beginners', as the proprietor assured me. The lacquer was black, and it most resembled a three-storey tomb with a viewing terrace. We struck a deal that it would be delivered that same day. I happened to be in the Fruit Market when an automobile drove through it, the first Czech-made one, as I discovered later. Decorated with Slavia pennants, it zigzagged through the narrow streets at walking pace, stinking and rumbling, and on the busy marketplace it caused a rumpus among the children, and ladies crossed themselves. It was preceded by an announcer of sorts, who dispersed the Prague townsfolk and poultry and asked directions to Marian Square from all and sundry. The combustion engine clattered and gave off smoke. At the side of the chauffeur in his cloth cap sat a young woman in a broad-brimmed hat, over which she held a pink parasol, as if the sun was beating down mercilessly. The vehicle was pursued by a throng of coughing children.

The evening newspaper later wrote that the chauffeur got lost in Prague like a perfect country cousin, turning into a narrow lane that was recommended to him as a short cut and ending up at the foot of a steep flight of medieval steps. He was thronged by idlers, and when the police dispersed the assembly to allow the automobile to reverse out of the trap it turned out that someone had removed and carried away a shiny brass piston pin. And so they brought two stout dray horses to tow the vehicle back to the country from the Old Town.

It struck me how inspirational it could be for people under threat, for the people of Prague whose ancient settlement was being changed by someone from outside into well-oiled, reliably running hygienic machines for rental and private accommodation. The English Luddites – what did they do when textile machines stole their livelihood at the beginning of our epoch? They went and gave the machines what for. They paid for it, but their actions were manly and understandable, and they were motivated by crystalline logic. The factory owners learnt that their employees would not let them walk all over them.

I called on Solly at his shop and complained about my tribulations with the town hall and the attacks on my house and my women. Solly was deeply saddened, but when I asked him if I should give up, at least on account of Berenice and Gita and their safety, he immediately snarled 'Never', even before I had managed to reply in similar vein. He watched with sympathy how his reaction delighted me and caused me to cough. We had a drink, although alcohol was feeble comfort, but then Solly announced an interesting piece of news: a public session of the city council would be held in the coming days, where Preininger's new report would be commented on, and legitimate residents of Prague, namely, all property owners, would be able to express their views there. Solly added that it would be a heart-rending experience and he would accompany me there. I gratefully accepted his offer.

Inspired by the Prague pilferers I set off for Jewry at dusk, skirting the trenches and cutting across levelled plots where they had not yet started to excavate foundations and approached two black monsters glistening with oil: imported demolition machines, before whose size and might cities ten times the size of Prague had been brought to their knees. I took a look at their controls, which resembled in some way the levers in the cabin of a locomotive, but in other places the levers looked like the equipment in a modern automobile. It seemed to me too rough and primitive for me to be able to damage it in any way. A case of dynamite might do the trick, but I did not have one.

I decided to bide my time. I accompanied Berenice to school and waited for her again in the afternoon. Gita had strict instructions to padlock both the yard door and the house door and to open the door only to people she knew for certain. I called in at the pharmacist. He looked fairly calm and said he was pleased to see me, and in between these polite formalities he let drop that he had said nothing to anyone since my last visit. I congratulated him, and in addition I gave him the news that I had acquired a revolver in honourable combat with someone and that I would not hesitate to use it should anyone stand in my way. He nodded to indicate that he knew, and when I asked where he had received the information he denied everything, adding that he had heard about my difficulties and he thanked heaven that his pharmacy didn't stand in the urban improvement zone. I retorted that that meant nothing, because my own house hadn't stood in it either, but then they had arbitrarily extended the zone, and the moment that Dr Preininger took a closer look into it he could expect to find a white notice from the town hall adorning his glazed door. Then I put five gulden on the counter and asked him for morphine – telling him to obtain it at an extortionate price if necessary and as much as he was able. He put the money in a drawer and promised to order it, saying he knew a doctor who could see to it.

When I arrived home I found there an invitation to an extraordinary public session of the city council, signed by Leopold Meister, the Deputy Mayor of Prague himself.

The following day I presented it at the side entrance to the town hall and was asked by the attendant if I was carrying a weapon. 'Just my gloves,' I said and looked around for a cloakroom. But there was no cloakroom for visitors.

I went upstairs to the gallery which was almost full. Solly was already there, chatting to some girl, whose father, as I learnt later, had gone in search of the toilets and entrusted his daughter for a moment to this well-attired and well-spoken blue-eyed gentleman.

Solly whispered something in the girl's ear, and she laughed. Typical. When he caught sight of me he raised an eyebrow and nodded. The girl looked around, curious to see for whom the was greeting was intended. She was good-looking and possibly beautiful. Solly gently took her by the chin and turned her face to him. It surprised her, but she didn't draw back, and her imminent protest was silenced with a kiss. She jumped up, but Solly was already bowing to her and telling her something, no doubt the address of his shop. Then he waved to me and pointed to the other side of the gallery, and I followed him. A heavily built man of some fifty years was coming up the aisle towards the girl with an angry expression on his face, no doubt her father.

'Her name is Cecilia. She is the daughter of carrier from Fish Street, and she was nineteen last month,' Solly informed me when he sat down. 'And she is of mixed parentage, would you believe?'

'Woah!' I said and put a new monocle in my eye. Solly leant both his elbows on the handle of his stick and smiled. Then he raised his right hand, the one he had held the girl's chin with a few moments ago, and smelt his fingers. 'An expensive powder. I knew she'd be classy.'

'Do you think you'll see her again?' I asked and watched the hall beneath us fill with officials in uniforms or black tailcoats. Lord Mayor Podlipný took his seat at a higher table, along with the Deputy Mayor Meister; next to him the executive official Bürger, two other top dignitaries and a grey-haired man with a goatee who was the only one in the enormous room in light-coloured attire, more suited to a summer walk by the river than a public meeting of the city council. I guessed it was Dr Preininger, the chief physician of the royal city.

'If Cecilia doesn't come some other will,' Solly commented and offered me a peppermint sweet. The carrier threw him suspicious glances from the other side of the gallery, which Solly studiously ignored.

The first to take the floor was a man by the name of Richter, an elegantly dressed councillor with a double chin and brilliantined hair. He announced a piece of news that was not on the agenda of the meeting. It concerned the arts commission of the city of Prague that had been set up shortly after the publication of the *Bestia triumphans* pamphlet and the subsequent written protest by distinguished residents of the city against the blanket urban improvement of the Old Town and Josefov. That commission had just resigned because its members had the feeling – as the councillor put it sarcastically – that the city hall did not respect their demands for restrictions on urban improvement.

'How could we, the elite of patriotic Praguers, the truest of Czechs, allow so-called artists to influence our decisions?' Richter asked and immediately replied, 'We could not, I tell you! Our responsibility to the royal city of Prague and its future European development and economic benefit will not allow it! No disrespect to artists, our architects do commendable work, for instance – the National Theatre, say, and also . . . But not many people know what they are paid for it! Thousands of gulden from the city coffers go to them, but just consider, there's nary a peep from them about it. What they keep for themselves and painters, too. Do you know what one of these painters receives for one miserable portrait? None of us is paid that kind of money. And people such as these now seek to criticize us? Let them go ahead and dissolve their "Arts Commission". We don't have any need of it. After all, we have a mandate to take decisions –'

At that moment Solly whistled, stood up and shouted into the hall, 'We want to hear Preininger! That's what you called us here for, isn't it? Tell that oaf to shut up or I'll spit on his head.'

There was a murmur in the hall. Hisses of indignation came from below, while the gallery laughed. Solly sat down calmly. We looked towards the high table. Podlipný looked as if he had just woken up from a doze, Meister's face bore a granite expression, Preininger looked alarmed and Bürger, who was holding a pair of opera glasses pointed straight at us, now put the instrument down and rose sulkily to his feet. He cleared his throat several times, but he didn't start to hack or choke. I knew very well to what he owed that.

'It would appear', he said, not too loudly but loud enough to restore calm, 'that some less-than-polite riff-raff have managed to find their way into the town hall today. This is intended as no offence to the decent citizens here present. But I must warn spectators that should there be any further disturbance at this council meeting the gallery will be cleared.' He let his words take effect and added, 'And now I would ask the prestigious Dr Preininger to acquaint our esteemed Lord Mayor and honourable councillors, as well as the public here present, with his alarming report about the unfavourable state of urban improvement.'

Preininger stood up and spread some papers out in front of him. He glanced at them from time to time in the course of his speech, but he mostly spoke off the cuff.

'My Lord Mayor, ladies and gentlemen, it is embarrassing for me to be obliged yet again to make a public speech and take up my time and your own, but I have a duty to you, the city and the health of its inhabitants. Urban improvement is not, as some of you may think – and write stupid pamphlets about it – a devilish demolition of the city. It was decided on many years ago, and it is supported in law, and every citizen had an opportunity to express his view on it. Urban improvement is, just to remind you, redevelopment and moderni-zation, together with the elimination of unsuitable and unhygienic buildings. No more, no less, and therefore it is a matter of great regret to me that certain members of the artistic community in particular have demonized it so lamentably. None the less it is now impossible to halt urban improvement. It has now progressed so far that there is no way of turning back. It is necessary to continue with the work in progress. I'll give you an example – the much-criticized rebuilding of the north side of the Old Town Square. Everyone can see how propitiously it started. Two completely new buildings now stand there, the comfort, elegance and hygienic equipment of which fully complies with modern European standards and exceeds them in certain respects. I therefore appeal to the public, and above all the artists who ably imitate its voice, so that one gets the impression that the whole of Prague is conspiring against urban improvement, to abandon their misguided fight in favour of old Prague! Do these rebels really want rats to return to our city, together with typhus, dysentery and, God forbid, the plague? The Jewish town attracted those dangerous rodents for centuries. Its demolition is a purge bringing in new and purer blood.'

'You swine of a goy,' whispered Solly and gripped the handle of his stick so hard that his knuckles were white. I put my arm around him to calm him, while realizing how insulted he must feel by the doctor's oblique anti-Semitism. He who, on principle, did not acknowledge his origins.

Preininger drank some water and ended his speech with the words, 'Yet again the number of diseases had dramatically increased in recent months. And where did this happen? In the oldest quarters! The Jewish town is full of stinking cesspits. If ever that all surfaces along with rats, Prague will face an apocalypse, and we will all be infected with the plague. *Bestia triumphans*! If the author of that defamatory and cruelly unjust pamphlet is sitting among you,' he said, pointing at the gallery, ' then let him kindly visualize how those bestial rats are taking over the government of Prague! Thank you for your attention.'

The doctor bowed, and the councillors applauded him. The gallery remained silent. I began to realize – and those around me also, I'm sure – that the public session was most probably convened on account of Preininger's speech. This was confirmed by F.X. Bürger who now took the floor once more.

'The city council forthwith announces proceedings for the demolition of a further twenty-one houses. The company responsible heretofore for urban improvement has been paid three thousand gulden, and we will continue to remunerate it in the same way. I believe it to be an honourable offer and advantageous for the city. The houses concerned will be appropriated, and their residents will move out within thirty days of notification. At the same time they have first refusal for purchase of the new building plots to be created after the demolition of the buildings. It is astonishing that there has been such sluggish interest in the newly created plots.'

'The plots are dreadfully expensive! Six hundred gulden for two square yards!' someone called from the gallery, but now Podlipný the Lord Mayor stood up and raised his hand for silence.

'They only *seem* expensive,' he said. 'We are asking six hundred gulden for the best corner plots; for the plots along the main streets four hundred and fifty at most and only two hundred and twenty for the cheapest ones. Moreover, every new builder is exempt from land tax for a full twenty years. You must realize that these are the most lucrative plots in the city's land register. We have now been dealing with it in council for seven weeks and have offered plots to large and genuinely solvent banks, and I am delighted to announce to you that thanks to the diligence, self-sacrifice and negotiating skills of Councillor Meister two institutions, the Provincial Bank and the Commercial Bank, have consented to purchase entire blocks of plots after demolition of the old buildings. But this means that it is essential to carry out the urban improvement in a blanket manner, not house by house. The banks are requiring the creation of an entirely new avenue from the Old Town Square to the river. It is a priority of this council to eliminate everything that might stand in its way.'

Podlipný finished speaking, and Bürger looked straight at me. He even gave a faint smile as he supplemented the Mayor's comments. 'And whoever continues to thwart the council's plans will be duly punished, whatever their class or station, whether hard-working entrepreneur or indolent layabout.'

'As soon as the banks are involved it's all over,' whispered Solly.

I smiled back at Bürger – all my bitter hatred I kept to myself. The Loggia stood in the way of that new avenue, I now realized. So no underground water-main or sewer, but instead a straight boulevard paid for by the banks to make big money from in future. I was grateful for the fact that I didn't have the revolver with me, because otherwise I would have discharged all six rounds without hesitation. At this distance it would have been a sad end for some of those seated below, and my anger was directed at specific individuals – those seated at the raised table. I suddenly had a swarm of vampires in my lungs, tearing my flesh with their wings and teeth. The pain was unbearable, but I kept the cough inside me and went on smiling at Bürger.

Then I realized that Solly was no longer seated. He was on his feet, banging the handrail with his stick and yelling at the representatives of the town hall. 'All right! You say you intend to treat everyone the same, but they're just words not based on any facts. You built a new grammar school in the Lesser Quarter on a spot where a building two hundred and twenty years old had stood. The Arts Commission – that was still functioning – stipulated that the new building must have only two floors, not four as planned – because that old building had only had two. That is right and proper. And you complied with it, and you had yourselves photographed shaking the hands of the artists from the commission –"Prague will not be massacred," they subsequently wrote in the press, "the urban improvement will proceed sensitively and with respect for the city's antiquity and charm."'

'And you, sir,' Preininger interrupted, 'really want the artists and the city to be at loggerheads at all costs? After all, the new school is an enormous success for both parties.'

'The grammar school', Solly said, pointing his stick in Preininger's direction, 'was simply a pretext for you. A pretext to build taller and broader buildings.'

'Nonsense,' said Bürger in his husky yet amazingly penetrating voice. 'Each plot is fixed. It cannot be extended either by extra floors or over the footpaths. Charles IV of blessed memory declared that it was a malady of the German cities and it would not be permitted in Prague.'

'Something else is happening,' Solly carried on smoothly. 'The combining of plots that was mentioned earlier. There used to be narrow lanes between the individual houses and also between groups of houses. But now the lanes are disappearing, and where there are no lanes there is no life. How is it possible that rules were respected for a school, that grammar school that you display everywhere, but not for apartment buildings?'

'Wait a moment,' Preininger protested. 'There are certain hygienic requirements –'

But Solly didn't let him speak. 'Hygiene is your religion, Doctor, and I appreciate you cling on to it like a leech. But for me it is just a word. The apartment buildings that you allow to be built on historical plots do not respect what previously stood in their place. They have four storeys, gentlemen, and this is twice too many, and some of them even have habitable lofts. New apartment buildings with attics! How many of them are there in Prague? Seven? And more are on their way? Yes, in spite of the fact that nothing was ever built here in such a bombastic fashion. A palace was a palace and a house was a house. Nowadays there is just one bloated apartment building in place of the other two. I've no idea who is going to live in it, although I'm sure that someone will be able to afford the rent in the end. I would merely like to point out that the builder of those magnificent dwellings for everyone, who himself is not exactly penniless, is sitting directly below me. His name is Štoll, and between you and me it truly is a well-known company.'

One of the councillors in tailcoats got to his feet. He was purple with rage. 'You'll pay for that!' he roared into the astounded silence. 'I will sue you for defamation of character. I'll see you serve time for it, sir, because nobody's going to wipe their dirty boots on me.'

At that, a gaunt man with a pasty face stood up in the first row of the gallery. His thinning hair was tousled, and his whiskers were closely trimmed. He looked like a consumptive. He adjusted his pince-nez in order to get a better view of Councillor Štoll, and with as subdued a voice as Bürger's he spoke to the builder and the town hall administration. 'My name is Mrštík, and I am author of the *Bestia triumphans* which some of you here may be familiar with. All I want to say I have already written, but it is confirmed for me every time I encounter executive power. You councillors hate us. That wouldn't worry us too much. Worse than that, however, you hate our city, those houses that we seek to preserve. I am unable to understand your hatred, but I sense it as the vilest stench imaginable. This is not the stench of the Old Town, or Josefov, or the Lesser Quarter, let alone ancient Hradčany. It is a stench that is yours and yours alone. You emit that stench, and you spread it around you any time people fervently speak out in favour of something that does not generate profit.'

That is how the man spoke, and then he sat down. But now Solly stood up and, pointing at him, said, 'A round of applause for the new mayor.' I started to clap, and the entire gallery joined me. There was uproar downstairs. The councillors were showered with invitations, pencils and dirty handkerchiefs. Those affected stood up and demanded protection, and it arrived forthwith on a signal from Meister. Armed guards burst into the gallery and started to force their way towards us in the first row. Solly and I held each other's hands until we were forcibly separated by burly fellows in uniform. The occupants of the gallery were forced towards the exit. Solly and several other men were handcuffed. I remained free. I followed Solly, close on his heels, although jostled by the crowd.

The men in uniform were standing below the staircase and overseeing the exodus through the side entrance. As soon as the guards handed over someone in handcuffs the police led him away to a police van with barred windows. When I lost sight of Solly and the corridor was empty I turned around and went back in but not upstairs. Instead, I headed for the main doors to the meeting room. There was nobody guarding it now that the troublemakers had been expelled and taken away.

I listened in. The person speaking at that moment was Leopold Meister. I managed to catch fragments of what he was saying. 'The Arts Commission betrayed our trust . . . the urban improvement plan is the voice of the people of Prague . . . We must fulfil what we planned . . . A handful of self-important intellectuals, who . . . But we will maintain a rational standpoint and a sceptical attitude to primitive fanaticism . . .'

The nearest of the councillors noticed that someone was walking through the aisle between the benches, and they turned their heads towards me. The rest went on listening to Meister's speech. There was a roaring in my ears. I took my invitation out of my pocket and brandished it, as if I were a messenger bringing an urgent message to the high table. I registered a few curious glances, and I returned encouraging smiles. I came upon a steward further down the aisle carrying a tray with a jug of water and glasses. He stood to one side to let me pass and even bowed to me. So I kept going and did not even stop at the rostrum on which the high table stood. I had to leap up on to it as the steps were on the other side.

I found myself face to face with Dr Preininger. I dropped the invitation, took a glove out of my pocket and struck his refined features with it. My aim was bad, and I caught his eye-socket. Preininger's hand went up to his eye, and he sobbed like a child.

Podlipný blurted out, 'How dare . . .' and rapidly backed away along with his chair. He did the right thing. The most important thing now was to maintain my speed and balance. I made my way carefully along the edge of the rostrum until I reached Bürger at the other end of the table.

He, too, pushed back his chair and quickly stood up, no doubt having learnt a lesson from our previous confrontation. 'He's got a revolver,' he wheezed at Meister, but the latter remained in his seat, fixing me with a cold gaze and declared without emotion, 'Well, well, Count Arco. Do you intend to go on causing us harm?'

'You, certainly,' I replied, and I slapped his face with full force, first from the left, then from the right.

Up to that moment my improvised performance had been conceivably effective. Except that Meister withstood the blows without moving. The skin where I had struck him started to turn purple. We waited for the inevitable. There was a sudden hue and cry in the hall, and I felt someone below the podium grab me by the leg and pull me down. Before I was dragged down by numerous hands I lost control of my lungs and bronchial tubes, and I spurted forth a stream of coughing. It was red in colour. I spattered Meister's head and white shirt front, as I choked on phlegm and was gradually dragged down into the cauldron of incensed councillors. Then I was lying on the floor far below the podium, feeling blows rain down on my face and body, some of them feeble, others as hard as stone.

High above me I could see in the thicket of forearms the pale face of Leopold Meister, who had come around the table, jumped off the podium and leant over me. Into the tumult that raged all around me he pronounced eight very clear words. 'We will settle it once and for all.' He said it with a smile on his face. The blood that had gushed out of me trickled down his face and drops of it had soaked into his clothing.

The last thing I remember of those turbulent minutes was the face of Councillor Štoll. A violet-blue Chinese lantern, that's what the builder resembled. Ready to burst. With an exhausting effort I drew my leg up to my stomach and kicked upwards as sharply as I could. The soles of my shoes struck the lantern and tore it. Then I lost consciousness.

I was not lying in a hospital bed or on a prison pallet but in my own bed. I felt no pain. At the table sat a young bald-headed man writing something. It was Dr Kubin. I sat up and stretched my arms, wiggling my fingers. Nothing broken anywhere. I felt my head. It was bandaged, but my face seemed to be in one piece. The doctor looked over at me and then came and sat down on the side of the bed.

'They didn't kill me?' I said, in an attempt at a jaunty tone. 'How do the bruises suit me, Doctor?'

He shook his head. 'They gave you a beating but nothing serious. My colleague Preininger and Councillor Meister stopped them. They told them who you were, and it worried them.'

'It still works sometimes then. What about Bürger?'

'I wasn't there. But there's talk of the incident all over Prague.'

'What's the time?'

'Five thirty.'

'Who drove me here?'

'I've no idea. That ward of yours came to fetch me, and your housemaid took care of you. Very nice – I mean, capable. You've got a cut on your forehead, not very deep but not to be sneezed at either. I've put a dressing on it and bandaged it. I'll have to take a look at it later and apply a tincture to it. I have to admit that she took good care of you. A veritable field nurse.'

I found it odd that my head didn't ache at all. The doctor read my thoughts and pointed to a row of little bottles on the table. They contained a clear liquid. 'That', Kubin said, 'was brought here by your pharmacist in person. He was delighted to see you were in pain. Do you know what he said? That the substance will help you get over the worst and you'll stop hating him. Odd that. Have you got something against him?'

He asked the question in such a way that I wasn't obliged to reply. So I replied indirectly. 'Some people are best held in check, as far as is possible.'

He grinned knowingly. 'If you think so. In all events that morphine came in handy. It must have been heaven-sent, as I could never have prescribed such a quantity.'

'You said my injuries aren't serious.'

'Altogether trifling, My Lord. You have a very hard skull. But you had a paroxysm of coughing, and there was blood on your clothes. Your lungs are in a bad state. I gave you an injection and noted immediate alleviation. I venture to estimate that this medicine will prevent further coughing and vomiting of blood for the next ten or even twenty days. It all depends on the dosage and the progress of the illness, of course. I do recommend, however, that you leave immediately for some pulmonary sanatorium while some sort of treatment is still feasible. And now I must take my leave.'

Dr Kubin left. I stayed in bed, as he advised. I felt like sleeping.

It was he who woke me the next morning when he came to give me my next morphine injection and ordered continued bed rest. I requested a half-dose because the narcotic effect of the morphine bothered me: I slept too deeply and I had dreadful dreams before I woke up. Gita told me I groaned, but I was now unable to recall what I had actually dreamt about. Wretched morphine couldn't compare with Dr Hoffmann's fantastic hydrochlorate. I didn't know what day it was, nor the hour; all I could feel was how heavy my eyes were once more, when at that moment Berenice and Gita came into my bedroom. I couldn't see their faces; their heads were bandaged, and they were both wrapped in some filthy rags. Both of them laughed beneath that vile attire. I persuaded the doctor, who was there once again, to give them an injection, because they were both ill and needed it very badly, but Dr Kubin, whose bald head had got suspiciously bigger, smiled spikily and warned me against wanting the bandage removed because it would kill them instantly – that is unless I wanted them killed, and he started to snigger like them. Berenice and Gita then danced, and while they danced they started to take off their clothes and the doctor joined them; his head got bigger and bigger and when they three of them were exposed he started to prod the women with his swollen sex, which aroused further malicious laughter and unbridled hilarity. Someone's knocking, I told them, but they turned around and around two hands above the ground, like on a fairground roundabout. Both Gita and Berenice had outstretched legs, and Dr Kubin had thrust his fingers between their legs, calling to me not to be jealous, for heaven's sake, because he was simply examining them, and then beneath their bandages the women's mouths opened wide, and they groaned and hooted with laughter. Someone's trying to break the door down, I called to them and then got up out of the bed and went to open the door, but there was no one in the passage or on the staircase. I went downstairs, the staircase was incredibly long and must have gone right below ground. I found myself in the courtyard beneath an enormous gallery, so big that the sky couldn't be seen above it. Someone was standing by a pillar. Black hat, black coat and a raw, red lump in place of a face. A hole opened in it. I made out the words: 'Look what I've got.' The figure tossed down a sack that it was carrying over its shoulder and untied it. It contained a dozen women's heads, and hidden among them in the dark blood were the heads of Gita and Berenice. 'How much? How much will you pay for them?' Kleinfleisch asked me, and the heads in the sack sniggered.

'Wake up,' said Dr Kubin with urgency, and he actually slapped my face. 'I thought you had fainted. You've had a very bad reaction to it, My Lord. I'm afraid it's not going to work.'

'I don't want any more of it,' I gasped from beneath my eiderdown. Sweat streamed down my face.

'I must ascertain the precise composition,' said Kubin and started to put the little bottles into his doctor's bag one by one.

'Be so kind and inject my girls with it. It will do them good. Look at the state they are in.'

Gita and Berenice were leaning against the wall by the door, their faces as pale as the surrounding plaster. It was obvious that they desperately needed a tablet. They were moaning like Holy Marys. But there were no pills to be had.

'I cannot risk it, My Lord, and you know that as well as I. They are not ill. They will have to put up with being without morphine or tablets, just as you will, even though you are much worse off than they.'

The doctor promised he would come the following day and ordered me to stay in bed. When he had gone I told Gita to help me get dressed. She started to protest, saying she would not lift a finger, but Berenice put some clean underwear on the bed.

'I'm going to get my property back,' I informed them as I squeezed into my trousers. Once I had my chronograph on my wrist, my hat on my head and my coat over my shoulders I felt a little more confident. 'If I don't return by morning', I declared resolutely, 'go and find the Deputy Police Councillor. His name is Herrmann. Give him answers to everything he asks you.'

Berenice nodded, but Gita crossed her hands over her chest and turned towards the window.

I stuck a fencing sword in my belt and concealed it beneath my coat. The loaded revolver weighed down my pocket. I knew where I had to go, remembering what Richard Urzidil had told me when I visited the Loggia House. F.X.B. lives in the Lesser Quarter, in the building of some savings bank built recently. I would find it.

My had swam, and I staggered. Berenice supported me unselfishly. 'Follow her example,' I told Gita, who sent me to the depths of hell, which was precisely where I was headed. They both helped me out of the house and hailed a cab for me in the street. I kissed them both goodbye and got in.

On the way to the Lesser Quarter across the bridge I pondered on how I would go about it at Bürger's. Would I let myself be announced? And what if he wasn't in? I had to get in there somehow, that was obvious to me. I hoped I wouldn't end up using the revolver, because this time the police would definitely lose patience with me.

The tall angular building stood in a location where I remembered the old-fashioned houses typical of the Lesser Quarter. Dusk had recently fallen, and the savings bank was closed, although there was a light on the top floor. The building had two entrances, both partly glazed. One was ostentatiously ornamental and equipped with steel bars. Behind it were offices. The other was less pretentious and led to a side staircase. I tried the handle, but the door was locked. I made up my mind. The street was almost empty. Then I did what every thief knows how to do. I waited for a carriage to appear, and very soon two of them passed by. I used the butt of Bürger's pistol to smash a triangular hole in the glass of the door long enough to get my forearm in. I reached the key and turned it. The door didn't budge. It was also bolted. I slid back the bolt, and my way was free.

It was dark on the staircase, and I didn't come across a living soul, not until I was almost at the top landing, when a shadow rose out of the gloom. I stopped and waited, and so did it. When my eyes had adjusted themselves to the darkness I could see that the man was oddly diminutive, stockily built but with legs as short as a child's and a large bushy head. He stood tensely, his hands gripping his chair as if intending to pick it up and hurl it down.

'What do you want here?' he burst out. There was annoyance but no fear in his voice.

'You're the one called Bung, aren't you? I'm Count Arco. Bürger is expecting me. You may announce me, Bung.'

'I don't think so,' he retorted. 'Hop it, mate, or you'll be sorry.'

'I fear not,' I said and came slowly up the stairs one by one. I found it odd that he did not put on the light. Perhaps he meant to take advantage of the gloom. There were now just seven steps between us. The dwarf reached into his pocket and took out an object that resembled a large pea pod. He flicked his wrist and a blade sprouted from the pod with a loud click.

'One step more and you'll get it in your guts. No one beats me at this game.'

'And no on beats me at this.' I drew my sword from my belt, gripped the handrail and made a fencing thrust, stepping upwards on my right foot and lunging with my weapon straight up and forward. The point of the sword touched his throat. 'Put the knife down while I count to three. Otherwise I'll strike. One, two . . .'

The knife hit the edge of the step, ricocheted and bounced down the steps towards me. I would have achieved as much by aiming my revolver, but with a sword in one's hand death is always closer.

'And now, Bung,' I said without removing the sword point from the dwarf's neck, 'take me to Bürger.'

He obeyed but not to the letter. When he knocked on the door and opened it someone else was seated in a leather armchair when I entered.

Listopad hesitated for a moment as to whether to remain seated but then decided to rise to his feet. He swayed over to us, took the dwarf one side, whispered something to him and sent him away. He offered me his hand to shake, but he did not expect me to offer mine in return. I walked past him and inspected the apartment. It was comfortably furnished, even discerningly, as if from a catalogue. The dark-blue hangings at the window were drawn, and the oriental carpets smelt new. Everything was pristine, without a speck of dust. As if nobody lived here. I sat down on a bentwood chair and laid my sword on the polished dining-table.

'Where's Bürger?'

Listopad favoured me with one of his insolently ingratiating smiles. 'Threats from evicted people who didn't want to move out, you know the sort of thing. It could no longer be taken lightly. The councillor has moved to a safe apartment for the time being. He'll come back here when it all calms down.'

It was important not give anything away. I resisted the urge to smash a glass case containing crystal glasses. 'He stole something of mine,' I said calmly.

'And you of his.'

'You mean the weapon? He was intending to use it against me.'

'You assailed him in his office.' Still with the same smile.

'I had been cheated. He and Meister added my house to the urban improvement list although it did not belong there.'

'And so you've come to chop him up?' He pointed to the sword on the table. 'You'll get an opportunity to, you know.'

'I don't understand.'

'I can't talk about it now, but call in on my superior tomorrow. He's got a sort of surprise for you.'

I was taken aback and hesitated. Then I picked up the sword from the table. 'I was intending to visit him. That suits me fine.'

'On account of your old chum Weiss? We've got him slammed up, and he'll rot in gaol.'

'I think not.'

I headed for the door, but Listopad walked around me and barred my way. 'You just can't imagine', he said, his smile now gone, 'how lucky you are not to have been shoved in clink with that Jew friend of yours. For what you got up to in the council chamber you could have been sent down for two years' hard labour. I would be curious to know if you're aware who you've to thank for your freedom.'

'Of course.' I pointed upwards. 'And you?'

He laughed, but his eyes were full of vindictiveness and rage. 'Oh no, My Lord, the person who spoke up for you was Alderman Meister.'

'Really?' I said, feigning indifference. But it came as a surprise. 'Why would he do that?'

'I think you'll get the message soon. By tomorrow, I reckon. Definitely. So long, then, My Lord. Have a good sleep before tomorrow, and don't set foot in here again.'

I walked slowly downstairs. I crossed the bridge and set off in the direction of Golda's to see whether she didn't have something similar to Hoffman's miracle, or even if she had anything left of what I myself had recently sold her for a good price.

I couldn't find the renowned establishment. Where the tavern once stood there now yawned a pit with rope stretched around it. An iron demolition machine rested near by. The windows of the houses still standing in the vicinity were black, and the glass had been smashed.

I had promised myself much more from my visit to F.X.B. But it gave me hope that it would soon be sorted out once and for all.

As if something of the sort were possible.

XX

Challenge Accepted

Kleinfleisch for the Last Time

I observed his withered hands that spanned the furrows of his face like a bridge. Ignacius Herrmann's notorious calm had abandoned him, but he retained his composure. A sort of dry, desperate glow seemed to emanate from behind the veins of his greying blue eyes, but his mouth was at a loss what to say. I waited in the chair opposite him. I prepared myself for all possible eventualities, even the worst, such as that Solly had caught pneumonia in prison and died, but what Herrmann finally told me flabbergasted me just as much. I ought to have allowed for this possibility, too, because alongside the coffee that the Deputy Police Councillor had ordered for me stood a leather doctor's bag. Without trembling, the policeman's hand opened it and brought out into the light a little bottle full of the heroic tablets. And there were at least twenty of the bottles altogether. Without hesitating I unscrewed the top, tossed a grey-tinged white tablet into my mouth and burnt my tongue, the roof of my mouth and my throat as I washed it down with hot coffee.

Hermann gave a faint smile and said, 'I said to myself you'd be missing that muck. It's medicine, I know. And I don't care in the least, My Lord, what you choose to poison yourself with. No, don't interrupt me now. This time, as I expect you realize, it's not about Kleinfleisch nor about a scoundrel and murderer who calls himself that. Nor is it about your friend who is in one of our cells. It's about you – you and the people you insulted.

'I can see that have an inkling of the mess I want to deal with now. What you did at the city council meeting was outrageous, but, all things considered, it is not out of keeping with our chaotic times. I can understand that as an aristocrat you feel the land is slipping away from you – and the land was your domain for centuries. But nowadays the Czech population don't care about you – and do forgive me for saying so. You don't fit into any category. No one takes you into account, and but for your father we would have more understanding and even sympathy for you. Have you read Darwin? According to that learned gentleman you are a species destined for extinction. You're not dangerous, you're rich – although, according to my information, even that doesn't apply to your family. I'm fully aware that your financial difficulties are none of my business. And I truly could not care less how many prostitutes or Jewish foundlings you share your home with. You're so harmless that the imperial and royal police could benevolently turn a blind eye to you.

'Or, rather, you *were*. I didn't believe you'd share your father's patriotic fervour. You're too much of a loafer and hedonist for that – no offence intended. Even so, something has changed just recently, and I am getting information from my people that you're beginning to behave more and more like a radical. I would have ignored the fact. From all of those reports one would judge he already knew you well. And then you came to the town hall and behaved so stupidly. What made you do it, for heaven's sake? You slapped the faces of officials who are only doing their duty, and you'd have lost your house anyway, come what may. After all, you were offered generous compensation. And then you do that. Like a child throwing a tantrum. All right. These things happen. But it would never, ever have occurred to me – and I mean this absolutely seriously – that a vindictive child would also be found on the other side. And that your challenge would be accepted with relish.'

'I beg your pardon?' His last words had confused me, but they contained the promise of something reassuring. Heroic blood now flowed through my veins, my lungs were working without a murmur and I was seized by the glorious feeling that the world was finally functioning as it ought – according to ancient albeit unwritten laws.

Herrmann went on speaking. 'It is difficult for me to deal with, let alone come to terms with, so don't make it even harder for me, because I am now obliged to forget what I am and what I've been for my entire active life – someone defending the laws of this country. You could disagree on the grounds that the Austro-Hungarian empire is led by the Emperor, and you'd be right, but you know as well as I do that the real power is not wielded by the court but by the elected government. And that applies to the royal city of Prague, too, My Lord. Insults, violence, rabble-rousing, these are all things that should be dealt with by the courts. I myself would like to see that – yourself in front of a judge – ha-ha. But things are going to take a different turn, alas.

'So listen to me carefully, you avenger of Prague cottage-dwellers. F.X. Bürger wanted to issue a summons against you for rabble-rousing and for the verbal and physical assault of public officials, even though, as far as I know, you failed to touch them with those gloves. Dr Preininger and Mr Podlipný, the Lord Mayor, were going to do the same. But someone else talked them out of it. Yes – Deputy Mayor Meister. That highly placed individual, whose contacts include members of the government, has decided to regard that public insult as a challenge – and returns it with a challenge to a duel. Not even his superior could talk him out of it. Not bad, eh?

'Now you're in a fit state to fight, if my eyes don't deceive me. I therefore repeat, Karl Adam, Count Arco, that you mortally insulted Mr Leopold Meister by striking him with a glove. If you accept the conditions the duel will be secret, of course. In other words it will take place with my knowledge but not with the knowledge of the police. And it will take place tomorrow morning at six thirty in Letná Park. So, I've said what I had to say, and it certainly gives me no pleasure. Now, your questions, please.'

Calm, peace, drowsy joy. How paradoxical. I felt myself to be high above Herrmann and didn't really have any more need to speak to him. Not at that moment, at least. I was floating in the smoke of my pipe, just below the ceiling. I drew on my pipe, and it whistled. The bowl heated my palm like a tiny flying stove. I laughed and fell back into my chair.

Herrmann observed me with raised eyebrows and was probably wondering whether the person opposite him wasn't a lunatic. I tried to concentrate and then surprised myself by asking, 'Where did you get these pills? They are mine, aren't they?'

'Yes. They were stolen from you by two tramps,' he replied, and questions started to line up neatly in my head.

'I thought it was Bürger.'

He said nothing in reply but simply turned up the corners of his mouth. Police facial expressions.

So I tried a different tack. 'If you really want me to agree to this tomfoolery – a duel with that disgruntled old cove – then tell me the truth.'

Herrmann was not so easily coerced. 'I knew you'd want to bargain, but I thought you'd suggest a different deal.'

'Namely?'

'That you'd want to get Solomon Weiss released.'

'That goes without saying. It was the reason I came here anyway. Thinking you'd want something from me in exchange. And again I want to hear the truth. Those two scoundrels, the big oaf and Bung – they're Bürger's men?'

Herrmann hesitated for a moment and nodded. 'He hires them. They guard his new apartment and stick bills.'

'And also harass, collect debts and beat up people up here and there.'

'Just so.'

'And the police tolerate it?'

'They tolerated you for a long time.'

'Do you know who Kleinfleisch is?'

'No. He's disappeared since the murder of Otka Meyrinková.'

'That's not my impression.'

'Then you know more than I do.'

'I don't know. Who is Listopad?'

'Detective Listopad? But you know who he is.'

'Why do you keep him on? If he's supposed to be investigating murders, how is it that he is mixed up in political matters?'

'I expect you're referring to the activities of Count Arco senior.'

'Yes, my father has decided to nail his patriotic colours to the mast. Quite frankly I don't understand it but am able to respect it. Police interest in him is impertinent. My father does no damage to Austria.'

'I'm not so sure of that, but that's something for others to deal with – such as Listopad.'

'Why don't you get rid of him?'

Herrmann smiled only with his eyes; his lips were pursed and he replied caustically, 'It's a childish question. There's no way I can get rid of him, can I? It's time the penny dropped at last. He's planted on us to report to Vienna about the administration of the Prague police. He is here to keep an eye on the way the Prague police operate, to keep an eye on the police board – and on me, too, of course.'

'An informer informing on the police.'

'And an extremely active one. He has no private life, no wife or fiancée, no easily perceptible vices, such as girls or absinthe or opium. After all, you know what he looks like – like a bumpkin.'

'And yet he's a policeman's through and through.'

'He hasn't got anything else. People like that are a great asset to the system.'

'I never want to see him again.'

'You will if you accept Meister's conditions. He wants to observe the duel.'

'Surely not. Can't you forbid it?'

'The powers that be in Vienna are behind him, which means the ones here, too.'

'Listopad has ties with the town hall? With people in its administration?'

Herrmann sat up. 'Ties?'

'Property. Money. Services. Does he do something for them?'

He laughed. 'He doesn't have to.'

'So he's got something on them then? Is that it? And when needs be he obtains information from them about other people.'

'Possibly.' He scratched his nose, which I took to mean agreement. And so I tried to speculate.

'So Listopad most likely knows the identity of Kleinfleisch.'

At last I had managed to unsettle him. He fidgeted nervously and leant forward in his chair. 'What leads you to deduce that, My Lord?'

But by now I was no longer in any doubt. 'It's starting to make sense to me. If Listopad is an informer with contacts in the city administration he is bound to know the identity of Kleinfleisch. The murders of the prostitutes are not a matter of indifference to him. On the contrary, they suit his purpose very well. Because the ones behind the murders are the people who want to see the blanket demolition of the Old Town and Josefov.'

Herrmann leant towards me with unfeigned interest in his eyes. 'Now I see what you mean. You believe Kleinfleisch is a bogeyman to scare the residents who don't want to move?'

'Precisely. An ancient Jewish bogeyman. And it makes no difference how many Jews remain in Josefov. A homicidal monster will make an impression on everyone.'

'A good hypothesis. Kleinfleisch needn't be a single blackguard beneath a mask. It's not a ghost or a perverted lunatic, nor even a fanatical moralist with a grudge against prostitutes. It's a hired killer sowing terror in Prague.'

'And who kills in the service of the town hall.'

'I admit that it must suit the town hall.'

'And Listopad knows about it.'

'That's why the investigation didn't get off the ground. Well, this will be an end to it now.'

'I'm sorry, Mr Herrmann, but I wouldn't be so sure. Everything will come to an end when the urban improvement is over, and as long as Listopad has his instructions and his influence he won't allow you to close the case . . . What's the matter?'

Herrmann suddenly became ashen and went stiff. His eyes didn't blink, and no muscle moved in his face. I thought he had had a stroke. I leapt out of my chair and went to help him, but he stopped me with a gesture of his hand. I poured him some water from a carafe and offered him a heroic pill. He refused it and opened a window. Dusty air blew into the office, bringing with it the distant din of demolition machines.

Then he spoke with great effort. 'I'll hand my written resignation into the police board this very day.'

'Don't do that. I accept Meister's conditions, whatever they are. God willing some matters will be solved once and for all.'

The old man nodded, came around the desk and shook my hand. 'All right. I know what you'll reply, but I am obliged to ask. Do you already know the name of your second? Am I wrong in assuming that you will choose Count Arco-Zinneberg?'

'It will be Solomon Weiss,' I replied and watched Herrmann trying in vain to conceal his surprise. 'May I hope,' I said, looking at my watch, 'that he'll be a free man as of noon today?'

'You may,' he nodded and accompanied me to the door. 'And for my part, My Lord,' he said in parting, 'I sincerely hope that we are not seeing each other for the last time.'

I waited for Solly outside the city gaol. When he came out he was dishevelled and had circles under his eyes. He told me he had hardly eaten anything, but someone in there had had some cards, so he managed to run up a debt. I took him to lunch and told him all about what I had heard from Herrmann and what awaited me, and Solly's brave expression became grave. He wanted to wait for Meister's second with me at the Loggia and talk him out of it. When Gita caught sight of us in the yard of the house she took charge of Solly in a maternal fashion and went to prepare him a bath. He was visibly thinner. There were dark circular bruises on his rib cage with torn flesh in the centre. They looked like animals' eyes that grown attached to his body in prison. He was reluctant to talk about it. Gita came to wash his back, and he pinched her thighs. She poured hot water on his head. I left them there and went to see Berenice.

She was seated at her new piano. The music sounded faultless, but she kept on returning to one particular motif. When she had played it for the fifth time I asked her what she was playing. She hadn't realized I was there, and I made her jump. 'A Liszt nocturne,' she snapped with irritation, leaning on the keyboard so that it thundered but immediately put her hands in her lap. With her gaze fixed on the black lacquer, which palely reflected her olive-brown face, she said into the silence, 'It's called *Liebesträume*.'

I leant towards her and put my arms around her from behind. There was nothing under her blouse but her small smooth breasts, so I undid four of the buttons and slipped my hands under the fabric. When I touched her warm chest I discovered I had given her gooseflesh. She squeezed my hands and raised her head. We kissed. Then she slipped out of my embrace and went over to the door, telling me to wait, that she would lock the door. But I stopped her and sat her on my lap, leaning my head on her shoulder and hesitating over whether to tell her, but in the end I had to give her the news: that by tomorrow I could be dead or crippled or confined to bed for a long time, that I wouldn't have time to transfer to her and Gita the money I had received from the city for the house, but I would write to my father asking him to take care of them both, in other words, that they would take Gita into service at the castle and Berenice would be provided with a family environment, upbringing and education. She burst into tears, and I was unable to console her. Then I showed her the doctor's bag with the remaining bottles. In case I didn't return home tomorrow she and Gita were to sell the pills, and she mustn't ever think of taking any more of them. She promised not to touch them. I wasn't sure whether I could trust her. At least I could rely on Gita.

Solly and I fenced for an hour and a half in the courtyard, he with Pachta of Rájov and I with the La Mouche épée. We managed very well, even though a sword should not cross with an épée. Solly praised my state of fitness and assured me that the old blighter wouldn't be able to beat me.

Then I realized that someone was watching us from the entrance way and was undoubtedly listening in to us. F.X. Bürger emerged smiling from the gloom by the half-closed door in the front gate wearing a hat and a black coat. He carried a small case of some kind. He looked like a doctor who had abandoned medicine and was coming here to perform an illicit abortion for a bribe.

He said he was pleased to see us again. He ignored Solly, so I introduced him as my second. Now he had to take notice of him, because he himself had elected to render Meister the same service. I invited him in and even offered him refreshment. He refused the offer and asked for his revolver. I told him I would return it to him the day after tomorrow.

'In that case, gentlemen, take a look at the weapons, please.' He opened his case on the table, although I already knew what to expect: two weapons arranged on a base of black velvet, one opposite the other. *Pistolas de duelo*, was inscribed on a silver label. Bürger gave a laugh. 'Had swords been chosen as the weapons Mr Meister would have been at a disadvantage, as I'm sure you'll recognize, and so he proposes this option. I presume you have shot a pistol before?'

'Naturally.' I weighed the gun in my hand. It was a single-shooter, fairly heavy and as long as a forearm. Identical twins. 'This is child's play to use.'

'So please let me have them back,' Bürger said out of the corner of his mouth, as if afraid I would deprive him of yet another firearm.

I put them back in the case. 'I think they will prove adequate to my task.'

'Alderman Meister will offer you first choice tomorrow. He will take the remaining one.'

'So that will be all for today,' Solly remarked, and Bürger turned to him as if he had completely forgotten he was there and that he should have been dealing not only with me but with him.

'Almost. With your permission we will be accompanied by one witness and a doctor. The identity of the witness is of no importance. The doctor will be Dr Preininger. Do you agree?'

Solly shrugged. 'Except that we don't need any witness.'

'That is entirely up to you.' Bürger bowed curtly. 'Six thirty behind the gazebo in Letná Park. I warn you in advance that the funicular will not be in operation so early in the morning.'

'It's still pitch dark at half past six in the morning,' Solly commented. 'Can't it be put back at least half an hour?'

'Darkness, my dear sir,' Bürger replied caustically, 'can prove a blessing in a duel. The point is that the duel should take place. There is no need to spill blood senselessly.'

'I intend to aim for the body,' I said.

He turned his elongated face towards me. He gave me the darkest of looks. 'Alderman Meister also. You may count on that,' he said, and he departed with his case in his hand.

'If you win, they'll arrest us. I don't trust the police,' Solly said, raising his glass of schnapps to the light.

'I don't think so,' I said, shaking my head, and clinked glasses with him. Then I saw him to the gate. We synchronized our watches. I gave Bürger's revolver into his care. He got the message and nodded. We agreed that he would call for me at six on the dot.

I went back in. Scarcely a word was spoken in the house until evening. Berenice and Gita said no more than was strictly necessary while they prepared together a most splendid dinner of duck roasted with potatoes, ginger and plums. They brought from the cellar the 1872 Château Latour that Mama had given me for my twenty-fifth birthday with instructions that it be drunk on my wedding day.

I opened the bottle and let it stand. I didn't touch any wine during dinner. The girls sat at table with me. I shared the meat with them and declared that I had never tasted anything better in my life, which wasn't true – the skin wasn't crisp, the meat tasted of juniper and it needed more salt – but they both looked as if they believed me. Then they poured the wine into a tall glass and waited to see what I thought about the wine. I was able to permit myself the gift of sincerity: I had not tasted anything better in my life. Then I told Gita to bring me two more glasses, but she didn't want to obey, saying it was mine, after all, and she wasn't capable of appreciating it, so I turned to Berenice, whose eager eyes didn't need much persuading. She brought glasses, and I shared the wine. Berenice drank hers too quickly, and she apologized red-faced. Gita sipped hers gracefully, until I realized she was copying me – holding the stem between her thumb and two fingers, sticking her nose into the glass like me, then pursing her lips and emitting ludicrous noises. Then she carefully placed the glass on the table, toppled off her chair and said, 'It was divine. Now I can happily kick the bucket.' They both laughed, and I was delighted with them.

We drank another bottle, but the wine couldn't help but be inferior. I impressed on the girls that I needed to get a good night's sleep, but ever since dinner it was obvious how things would turn out. I took a pill for heroic dreams, and the girls wailed that they were dreadfully nervous and wanted some, too, so I gave them each half a pill, and I went to bed – and they with me. I didn't need to undress; they did it for me. And when I was standing naked in the cold bedroom they laid me on the bed and warmed me up from either side. Gita from the left and Berenice from the right.

An idea struck me. I took the crucifix down from the wall and handed it to Berenice for her to bless me with it. She didn't know the proper way but had a go: she rotated the crucifix like stirring with a spoon, and I kissed Gita beneath that benediction. Then I handed her the crucifix to try a benediction and kissed Berenice at great length.

Then we slept. I woke up in the middle of the night. I was calm and excited at one and the same time. The girls were puffing either side of me, and I didn't know which of them to take first. But at that moment a sound came from downstairs like someone bumping into a chair.

I lay motionless and then slipped out of bed and squinted at my watch by the window. It was two thirty. The sound of a chair being moved came from the kitchen once more, and I knew I had to go down.

I pulled on my drawers, armed myself with Pachta of Rájov and crept downstairs barefoot as silently as I could. None of the stairs creaked.

It was even darker in the middle of the kitchen than in the nooks and crannies and under the stairs. The darkness told me who it was. He stood stock still like a statue. He had a broad hat that was perched a head higher than it is normally worn and a black cape that looked like a massive pedestal that merged with a statue. The door to the courtyard was open half-an-arm's length, and fresh air swept into the room through the opening.

Kleinfleisch said nothing. I could not see the piece of meat in place of a face, but I had a feeling that I could smell it: the sourish smell of freshly sliced tissue drained of blood.

He was aware of me as I was of him. I wanted to go by him, so that I could see him against the doorway where the darkness was not so intense. But the rustle of the cape stopped me. He must have grasped my intent and stepped to one side, because the trapezoid of gloom in the doorway remained empty.

We stood facing each other a long time. My legs started to become stiff, and they were numb with cold from the stone floor. I was anticipating the glint of the knife, at which moment I would aim my sword at it, and if I did not strike the arm I would at least parry his stab. If the waiting went on much longer my legs would have gone completely stiff, and then, I feared, I would have on my conscience the two human lives upstairs. I couldn't permit that to happen

'Which of them have you come to kill?' I said to him.

The darkness hesitated. I seemed to see it lean its head to one side. Then that sour smell wafted towards me once more. Perhaps he was shaking his head. In any case he spoke.

'Neither of them.'

It was said in a whisper. The voice colour was grey, and yet the tone of voice caused needle points to dance on the back of my neck and one to penetrate my very heart.

'So you've come for me,' I said incomprehensibly, and I had to repeat it because my tongue stuck to the roof of my mouth. I breathed through my mouth and tried to calm my shivering. I knew this was the moment of the attack. It would be a black lightning strike.

'Defend yourself, please,' whispered Kleinfleisch, and my surprise at the more resonant tone of voice distracted me. Something struck me hard on the shoulder and my right cheek. It was a chair snatched out of the darkness and hurled wildly at me. The aim could have been worse – and better. I withstood the blow and was back in the on-guard position when the chair hit the dresser.

I fell down on to my left leg and reached out with my left arm for the chair but couldn't find it. I ran my tongue over the teeth on the right side of my mouth, and fortunately they were still there and so was my right eye, which hurt; perhaps I would see again, although at this moment all I could see was blackness, and my nose was not broken. Then came the next attack. I curled up and felt a dark mass sweep over me, headed by a brightly glistening blade. I cut with my sword directly from below but only sliced through the night. To judge from the gust of air my assailant had turned around, and his cape swirled behind him. The knife disappeared once more, which could only mean that it was pointing directly at me. I chopped blindly once and then again and the second time encountered the heavy cloth of the cloak and I only just managed to keep hold of my sword. Then Kleinfleisch attacked again but clumsily. His shoulder bumped into me, and I fell on the floor. Immediately afterwards the knife blade scraped on the paving stones and slid along them straight towards my neck, and I slipped out of its way. I gripped the edge of the table and jumped to my feet, assuming the on-guard position, my sword raised obliquely at forehead level. Facing me was the shadowy trapezoid of the doorway – it looked like the outline of a coffin standing on its end. And that outline was at last obscured by the darkness rising from the floor. The hat was perched crookedly, and heavy, sour panting came from the meat beneath it. I turned my wrist in readiness for a thrust from above, took two short steps and lunged at the middle of the body. The point entered, and I immediately withdrew my sword and returned to my position.

Kleinfleisch uttered a sigh, and his knife flashed again before disappearing once more within the folds of his cloak. The hat swayed, the shadow filled the doorway and then opened the door wide. It obscured the night outside before disappearing into it.

I could have chased after him and finished him off, but I was prevented by the memory of the voice that had spoken to me.

I lit a lamp and carried it outside. The blood on my sword blade looked black. I inspected the lock on the door and went out into the courtyard. It was empty and so was the house. The lock on the door in the gate was undamaged, just like the one on the house door.

Bürger's henchmen, those debt collectors, had opened the doors last time using a skeleton key. The bigger of the two might have been hefty enough to play Kleinfleisch, but the whispered 'Defend yourself, please' still rang in my ears and disproved that conjecture.

I locked up but didn't bother to barricade the door in any way. It was unlikely that Kleinfleisch would return. He was fatally wounded, I had no doubt about that: the sword had gone at least two hand-breadths into the body.

I cleaned the weapon carefully and placed it with the épée ready for the morning. It was a duel with firearms, but I now considered it necessary to have cold steel in reserve.

It was absolutely clear in that dark pre-duel night: there would have been no duel if the impudent and presumptuous individual who had slapped those top officials with his glove had been perfidiously murdered before the confrontation.

I sat in the kitchen until dawn, drinking milk laced with spirits. The two girls, who had been aroused from their sleep and filled with terror by the racket in the kitchen, now stayed awake with me by the light of candles and to the accompaniment of the fire crackling in the stove.

XXI

A Duel in Prague

Manny's Second Confession

I had watched history race by me. I had let it pass me by. What else could I do? But the opportunity to do something had presented itself. To intervene in it. In the compressed time of recent months I had managed to twice. I had done more than in my entire life up till then. I was prepared to bring everything to an honourable conclusion – and even have the feeling of a job well done.

A cab pulled up outside the Loggia at six o'clock precisely. I was standing in the entrance way smoking a pipe, the sword and épée wrapped in a shawl and hidden beneath an old frock-coat. Solly also hadn't had enough sleep. When I sat down opposite him and the cab set off he told me I looked as if I had spent the night engaged in English boxing. I told him about Kleinfleisch, and he gave a low whistle. He expressed the view that the Jewish bogeyman would kick the bucket discreetly somewhere on the bank of the Vltava and would never be heard of again.

We drove across the bridge, dawn was still no more than a promise, the sky was overcast and a cold mist above the river presaged rain. I felt cold. My coat gave me little warmth, and I wore no waistcoat beneath it, just a grey woollen shirt that would show nothing if blood was spilt and which was also very absorbent. My head and face ached, the right side of my face below my eye was bruised and my nose was swollen. I hated cold vinegar compresses that thickened the mucous in my sinuses and formed a hard, impenetrable mass that prevented me breathing, But I had kissed Gita's hands for putting them on me. I had ended up taking another one of Hoffmann's pills, and now what I wanted to do most of all was sleep.

Three swans landed on the surface of the river. I was surprised that one of them was black, but Solly retorted that I was imagining it. I let down the window to see better, but we were already over the bridge. We turned along the hillside and soon stopped by the funicular. The Jewish Town and part of St Peter's Quarter were a black silhouette on the other bank, smoke rose from chimneys above the roofs and in sloping columns merged with a cloud moving slowly through the low sky. Fishermen on the river lit lamps to see their breakfast. Someone's backside gleamed in the half-light from one of the punts. I turned back and looked up at the hillside, above which lay Letná Park.

'We could have driven around it,' said Solly, but I was already rushing up the path, as if I could speed up the clock. My watch told me that we had ten minutes left. We hurried uphill as if in a race to be the first to reach Letná. But when we reached the top – my watch showed six twenty-three – there were more shadows to be seen by the funicular near the gazebo than we would have liked.

One of them peeled away from the group and floated towards us, followed by another. Shapes started to emerge more clearly from the darkness. I tried to assess the situation and panted softly, while Solly huffed and puffed fit to burst. The ascent had well and truly warmed us.

Bürger greeted me and asked Solly whether everything was as we had agreed and whether we had not changed our minds about anything. We assured him that we were ready to carry out what we had agreed. With a faint smile Bürger said he thought it was for the best. Justus Preininger emerged from behind with a tragic expression on his face as if we were preparing for a funeral and not a duel. He shook hands with us, saying he had nothing against me and that he fully understood that people of a sentimental disposition might regard the urban improvement in Prague as an attack on their domain. He added that he had long ago forgiven me the slap from my glove. I wasn't sure how to respond, and to be on the safe side Solly raised his hat and thanked him. The Chief Municipal Physician looked slightly relieved. He offered us water and slivovitz from two flasks and metal cups. We drank to his health, while he drank to a bloodless duel. Solly did not return the flask with slivovitz to him.

I repeated to Bürger that I did not intend to fire into the air. He replied that Mr Meister had no such intention either. Then he checked his gold pocket-watch and I my little wristwatch. It was a minute to half past six.

'Shall we proceed to the matter?' Bürger asked, and Solly invited him to lead us to the place of the duel. We followed him, first Solly, then I and finally Preininger. I removed my hat and long coat as we went and passed both to Solly, in such a way that it was not evident what it concealed. We walked along the gravel path to the silent figures between the gazebo and the station of the funicular.

I stopped in front of Meister and nodded, and he did the same. His face was expressionless. The man whom he had been standing and conversing with heretofore was Detective Listopad. He made an attempt at a kind of double bow of head and trunk – 'My lord . . .' – and the result was ludicrous. Then he straightened up and looked straight at my coat in Solly's arms. 'I am not here in my capacity as a policeman,' he said. 'There is no need for my presence to worry you.'

'And what about him?' I said, pointing at a big oaf standing by the bushes. It was one of the debt collectors, the bill sticker who had assaulted my Gita. His face was in shadow, but I could tell who it was by his bear-like figure and his bulbous bald head like a circus strong man's. He was smoking a little porcelain pipe that didn't suit him at all. Nor for that matter did the mask of Kleinfleisch that I had hesitatingly attributed to him. He would hardly be standing there after the wound I had inflicted during the night.

'Should it be necessary to transport someone to hospital, as I'm sure you'll appreciate . . .' Preininger hastened to explain and pointed to a long covered wagon with two thin horses. 'I myself can only perform first aid.'

'Let's begin,' I said, and Meister immediately lost his composure.

'Yes,' he agreed very quietly and almost with distaste. 'Let's get it over with.'

'Then as a physician and a humanist I can only appeal to both of you', Dr Preininger spoke up, 'to show generosity of spirit, and for the last time –'

'Silence!' Bürger shouted. 'They do not seek reconciliation. They intend to fight. So let us proceed to the matter in hand.'

'Then I would beg a moment's indulgence. I apologize, but I have an urgent need . . .'

He ran off into the bushes and we waited patiently, with our faces to the city. 'Don't you feel cold, My Lord?' Listopad asked, sidling up to me. 'You removed your coat somewhat prematurely.'

'I'm accustomed to fighting in my shirt sleeves.' This was not true.

'But this isn't going to be silly fencing. We'll be shooting, didn't they tell you?' Meister let fly at me with pointless irritation. Then he pulled off his hat and coat as if burning with impatience.

Preininger returned and cleared his throat.

'That's enough,' Bürger snarled. 'The conditions have been agreed since yesterday, of course.' He leant down to pick up the little case standing on the gazebo steps and opened it.

'Get on with it, Arco.' Meister pointed at the pistols. 'Choose your weapon. And have no fear, young man – they are exactly the same.'

I had the impression that he was addressing me like one of his subordinates from the town hall, and for a brief second I had an urge to insult him again, this time with my bare hand.

Listopad read my thoughts. He of all people. 'Do it to me instead, My Lord,' he smiled through clenched teeth, 'I'll gladly put up with a second one.'

Maybe that's why he's here, it occurred to me. If Meister shoots me it will also represent satisfaction for him, for the slap I gave him that time outside police headquarters.

Solly checked that the weapons were loaded and properly cleaned. Then he nodded. I reached for the one that was nearer to me and with its butt in my direction. Meister did the same with the other pistol.

'Stand opposite me at a distance of fifteen paces,' Bürger indicated to Solly, which was odd.

'Aren't the seconds supposed to stand next to each other?' I remarked. 'For the sake of convention.'

But Solly put his arm around my shoulder, counted out the prescribed distance and turned around.

'Now . . .' Bürger addressed me and Meister, 'now stand back to back with your pistols raised to the level of your faces. Like this.' We did as instructed. 'Stay the way you are, please, and I, too, will walk back fifteen paces and face the other second.' We waited while he paced it out. Our backs were supposed to be in contact, but I found the idea of it repulsive – and so did Meister, I expect.

I felt him breathing and perspiring.

I had to smile at my behaviour. Here I was waiting for a fateful shot with a pistol in my hand and pretending that I didn't know who killed Prague prostitutes with a mask of meat on his face and who had been a threat to me and those I loved.

I knew who it was from earlier. I just had no idea how he could have done it.

I kissed my raised weapon and looked at my watch. A quarter to seven. At that split second I prayed that I would take the secret with me to the grave. I tried to put my monocle in my eye, but the swelling prevented it. I had to laugh at that misfortune.

'And now, gentlemen,' Bürger bawled from the safe distance of the second, 'when I begin to count you will each walk forward fifteen paces, then turn around, aim and fire in your own time. Well then . . . Start walking, please – right now! One . . .'

I took my first pace –

'Two' – I took the second, and the cold air of dawn chilled my back. 'Three.' I imagined what I looked like from above, and I realized that the seconds were standing in the same position as the duellers. Four in the same sign of the cross. 'Five.' A chilling feeling again. 'Seven.' I was sad all of a sudden. I prayed that I was mistaken, that it had been an honourable business after all. 'Eleven.' And, bad nobleman that I was, I sent my prayer – 'Thirteen' – to God.

'Fourteen.'

Just so long as Solly doesn't carry the can.

'Fifteen!'

I took my fifteenth pace and turned around. Meister was faster and had already turned and was taking aim. In a second I checked where the others were. Listopad stood furthest away, right next to the wagon, and he was stroking his beard as if deep in thought. The bald oaf was standing a few metres behind Solly. That was bad. Bürger had remained at the same spot, stiff and slightly bent forward, as if tenaciously withstanding an invisible snowstorm. Yet no twig moved. My right cheek ached, along with my entire head, the right side of my neck and my shoulder. Everything was slightly out of focus.

The universe was absorbed by the shiny dark gun barrel. It was about to end and begin in one single shot.

'I actually enjoy life,' I said to myself and slowly squeezed the trigger with my index finger. It was good to know. I was my own man – and I was content.

A shot was heard.

I wasn't dead. I still had the pain, in my head, familiar and dull. But it wasn't Meister who fired. Nor I. My opponent was aiming a loaded weapon at me and I at him. I lowered my pistol and reached into my right pocket with my left hand to take out my monocle and thrust it into my resisting eye socket that pulsed with pain.

Suddenly the scene was horribly clear. Solly staggered and fell. Bürger had just dropped his extended arm, blue smoke rising from it. Opposite me, with one eye closed, Meister laughed and pressed the trigger. But it was the sort of shot that might be expected from a shivering syphilitic in the final stage of the disease – he was too worked up. There was a rustling in the branches of the tree behind me, and a shower of leaves dropped on to the grass. The duel was over, even though it was my turn to fire. Because it was not Meister I had to aim at now but Bürger. He realized it almost in time.

We turned towards each other like two clockwork figures. He raised his weapon, but mine was already trained on him and the hammer was finally released. The impact spun Bürger around, yanking him like a marionette on a string and then tossing him sideways. As he fell, he, too, fired, but the shot went somewhere over the edge of the hill and did no more damage than a gobbet of spit.

I dashed over towards Solly, who lay on the grass with a gunshot wound, trying to do something with my coat. I kept an eye on Bürger, who was writhing on the grass and crying like a child, but he was probably harmless by now. But someone suddenly interposed himself between me and my friend: the dwarf had leapt off the roof of the gazebo and, just like a monkey that knows precisely what to do to be given a peanut, had rushed at Solly with an outstretched Spanish switchblade that not even Kleinfleisch would have been ashamed of.

I knew I wouldn't catch up with him, but I tried none the less. Luckily Solly was alive and in possession of his faculties; he pulled Bürger's revolver from his pocket, and from where he lay, with one hand around the butt and his index finger on the trigger, he pulled back the hammer with the other hand and fired three shots in quick succession, hitting the target each time. Bung fell at his feet, his face and knife blade buried in the dirt.

I leapt over him and knelt down by Solly, who was bleeding from the right side of his chest. In a panic-stricken voice such as I had never heard from him he said, 'There are so many of them, Addie. We bungled it.'

He handed me my coat, and I fished the Mouche and the Pachta of Rájov out of it. The épée in my left hand, the sword in my right. I left Solly Bürger's revolver, the one with which he had shot Bung.

Our opponents truly outnumbered us, but in terms of firearms and cold steel we were evenly matched, although everything else was bad for us.

Meister was leaning over the moaning Bürger. The bald oaf was slowly moving towards Solly from the shadow of the bushes, carrying a pocket knife in his hand, when someone pressed the cold muzzle of a pistol to my temple.

I stabbed behind me at where I supposed the heart to be beating wildly, but I speared a fat hip instead. Dr Preininger dropped his twin-barrelled lady's pistol and squealed like a badly stuck piglet. I cut at him with my sword and cleft his shoulder in two. He let out a falsetto screech that resounded through Letná and took to his heels. I let him go and advanced on Baldy, who was so preoccupied with his easy prey, Solly, who was unaware of him, that he was blind to anything else. I ran at him from the side and skewered his neck with the épée until the point emerged the other side. Then I twisted the weapon sharply around the vertical axis until I snapped his spine and the épée at the same time. The metal remained inside him.

I did a calculation: three of the blackguards had died too quickly, before I had had a chance to tell them that I wouldn't let anyone get their hands on my women or my house.

I looked around me. Meister was striding towards me with his arm extended and holding the firearm he had taken from his minion. It was obvious that it had been child's play for Bürger to obtain another revolver. He was now quietly breathing his last a short distance away, but his master had me in his sights, and my sword was too short to reach him. He stopped five paces away from me, and his face glowed with victory. I glanced towards Solly. He lay there lifelessly, with a red stain on his waistcoat.

I looked towards where Listopad had previously been standing. And then I caught sight of him. He was crouched behind a tree trunk, watching this particular story play itself out. His eyes displayed total unconcern – about life, the world – everything except himself and his paymasters who assigned him his tasks.

There was a bang, and I was surprised I had lived long enough to look my executioner in the eye.

He only had one left. The other had escaped, rolled upwards. The nose and mouth had gone, leaving only the chin, forehead and ears, or what remained of them, what hadn't disappeared into the hand-sized hole in the middle of his face.

Meister tumbled to the ground, his corpse gripping the revolver. Out of the shrubbery stepped an elegant young man in a light-coloured suit and with a hunter's rifle resting on his arm. He dusted himself down and raised his hat, which was identical to the one I wear. The young swell wore it slightly tilted, impudently and with a smile.

'It was an honour, My Lord,' he said cheerily, and then looked obliquely beyond me to where Listopad was standing. He raised his index and little fingers at him and went his way contentedly. 'Give my regards to your father,' he said over his shoulder and disappeared beyond the funicular station.

I recognized him, although we had only met once. It was the riding teacher from Chuchle, the young fop who was always hanging around Helena Tauferová and then disappeared into thin air when Manny started to court her.

I didn't call after him. And I didn't even thank him. Nothing made any sense to me – and I didn't want to understand it.

Bürger was wheezing as if from an asthma attack. The bullet had torn through his lungs. He was as white as a ghost – a last-minute rehearsal. He paid me no heed; he paid no heed to anything any more, except to a night that would never turn to dawn.

The worst things happen in solitude. As once before, I placed a heroic pill in his half-open mouth and closed his jaw forcibly. Then I stood up, took my sword in the other hand and transfixed his treacherous heart.

I returned to Solly. His wound was not fatal – not yet, at least. He was bleeding a lot. The bullet remained somewhere beneath his ribs or in his armpit, but with his left arm he had no problem in raising Preininger's hip flask to his lips for a swig. I helped him stand and steered him towards the four-wheeled vehicle.

'That was supposed to be a duel? I'd sooner top myself,' he repeated over and over again, and we were both weak at the knees.

Then he was unable to walk any further, so I carried him in my arms and sat him down on the edge of the wagon before drawing the awning aside.

Someone was already lying inside. Solly noticed the expression on my face and looked in, too – and then he gave vent to a long and profuse Yiddish curse.

But this was no time for anything – least of all recriminations or explanations – but the hospital. I laid one wounded man down along-side the other, got up on to the box and drove off down the winding route that would take us to the bridge and the other bank to find the Samaritans of St Francis's Hospital.

I looked back before the first bend. Listopad was standing amidst the corpses and writing something in his notebook, the whiteness of which did not yet blend into the dawn by a long chalk.

The covered wagon stood in the middle of the hospital yard, giving the impression that gypsies had arrived at the convent hospital. Solly was now in the care of doctors and the Brothers of Mercy, the other victim had refused treatment and remained lying in the wagon under the awning. I returned with a pot of Arabic coffee and two small cups. I climbed aboard and asked him if I should let down the flaps.

Manny shook his head – he wanted the feel of fresh air before he died.

I handed him a steaming cup with the comment that a short while ago I was much closer to death than he was now. He said he had been incapable of watching that carnage.

'I'm glad you killed them, Addie,' he said with pain in his voice, and he drank the coffee cautiously. The stab wound in his stomach was clearly taking its toll on him, but it was not fatal to all appearances.

'I didn't kill all of them by any means, only Bürger, in fact and the bigger of the debt collectors. Solly took care of the little one, Bung. Preininger ran away, Listopad looked on and Meister, would you believe, was shot by that riding teacher that we met near Stránov Forest . . .'

'Fridrich Sova from Chuchle, he of all people? I remember him acutely well. Would you give me some more coffee?'

I poured him some and with my gazed fixed on the coffee pot I asked him about his wound and how he came by it.

He shrugged. 'Also a duel of sorts, Addie. I deserved it. I had behaved disgracefully.'

'Tell me about it.' I sat down facing him. In the dim light it was almost impossible to see how pale and haggard he was.

'That's not important. But if you like, I could explain to you how that Sova got mixed up in it.'

'I thought so . . . that you knew something about it.'

'Of course.' He nodded with a smile and clenched his teeth. For a moment he just panted but then he tried to grin again, but his gaze was vacant, fixed on quite different horizons than the open end of the wagon.

'Sova', Manny said at last, 'was your father's ally and protector, albeit unbeknown to the old Count. In order to establish himself at Stránov he started courting Helena, and then I turned up, an Austrian simpleton, and spoilt things. But there was no other way. I wasn't good at following orders. Unlike him.'

'What were your orders?'

'To get as close as I could to your father. You weren't aware of it, but he had contacted the young radicals – he, an old man from an old family.'

'Sova is one of those radicals?'

'Yes, and I flushed him out. I realized it much later. Did I tell you about Taufer? Last time? The neighbour, Mr Taufer, was just waiting for the castle to fall into his lap provided he remained loyal to Austria. No matter, but I call it a paradox. I mean, when you consider that your father is a radical compared with him. How could things have got that muddled?' He shook his head and wiped the sweat from his neck before continuing with a bitter grimace. 'And the nice daughter was only too willing to help her papa. Naturally. Did you know that the Taufers have now bought plots of land here in Prague? Where the new Příkopy will be. The latter-day nobility is not blue-blooded, as you know yourself. But it is building winter residences in Prague. It's supposed to be a veritable palace that Taufer is planning to create. A department store with plate-glass display windows and electric lighting – and our Helena will have an enormous apartment at the top of it.'

I didn't know what to say to that or even whether I wanted to hear anything else. 'And what about you, Manny?' I finally managed to say. 'How loyal are you to the Austrian cause?'

'Me?' He held his stomach, and tears trickled from his eyes with the pain. 'The Austrian police . . . Can you imagine? They needed their man here, they chose one, and he had to go. Even though it was the lastest thing he wanted to do.'

'The last.'

'The last thing. What I told you last time . . . Well, when it comes down to it most of it was true, wasn't it? But not the whole truth. Look here – a few years ago I got a woman in the family way, you see. That wasn't unusual in our family, but the girl was from the next village, and she was too beautiful and dreadfully proud. No little skivvy but the daughter of a farmer with a lot of acres. I sent a message to her to come over to our place and we'd agree on a lump sum compensation to settle it once and for all. But she had a different idea.'

'She didn't turn up?'

'There's a rock in the forest a short distance from Harnack. How would you call it – puny? Not very tall, I mean. There is a path that leads to it alongside the stream. Our road-menders look after it, but it's always very muddy. Well, the rock stands above that path, and on it there is a crucifix that is visible from afar, even from the provincial highway if you look hard, but it would be easier with a telescope. A silly little rock. She left her clothes there, Addie, she stripped naked and left her shoes and then jumped off, with that baby inside her, on to our path. And so they found her there.'

Manny fell silent, and I said, for want of anything better, 'I think I'm beginning to understand.'

'That's good,' Manny nodded abstractedly after a very long pause, 'I knew you you'd understand me in the end. In her clothes they found a letter that I had sent her, and the gendarmes confiscated it. I don't think it was her intention – it wasn't revenge. But that's how it turned out.'

'The secret police got involved,' I surmised.

'Exactly. The police never turn a blind eye. I was taking morphine and also those new heroic pills. They had that on me, but it wasn't enough, you see. They couldn't blackmail me on the grounds that Arco-Zinneberg was livening his life up with some chemicals or other. But now they had a clear suicide because of a pregnancy that I had caused and the proof found at the scene of the deed – or just above it. And that did for me.'

'They most likely told you that they'd destroy your family if you didn't cooperate with them.'

'Of course. And I couldn't allow my parents to suffer such a disgrace. So I signed a paper agreeing to collaborate with the secret police. They sent me to Prague, where the city authorities were having problems with the riff-raff in the Jewish quarter. I was to sort it out with the assistance of their man in the Prague police corps. They trust him completely.'

'His name's Listopad,' I said, and Manny shrugged.

'Nice name, loathsome individual. He was the one who thought up the bogeyman. He insisted on terror – only terror would work with the masses and force the paupers out. That's how they do it in Russia, he said. He was also planning to set fire to the old houses. That hasn't happened yet, thank goodness. And I won't be helping him any more.'

'Helping . . .'

'Do you really want me to tell you everything?' Manny asked me with a look of such anguish that my hair stood on end with dread.

They had an absolute hold over Manny. He was ordered to play the role of a fairground bogeyman who would shed real blood.

Suicide and blackmail begat murder. A whole series of murders, far from his home, in provincial Prague – provincial but strategic for Austria.

'That time I met you from the station . . .' I said, trying to rekindle his confession.

Manny sipped the coffee and asked me to pour him some more. 'Of course that wasn't my first visit, far from it. It only looked that way for the play-acting. For your benefit. The task they gave me was shameful, but I'd been in contact with Hoffmann, and those pills of his make everything easier. You stop taking the world so terribly seriously.'

'I know. And you introduced me to the pills on police instructions, too?'

'It was useful,' Manny said dully. 'I was in league with the devil, and so I combined one useful thing with another. You needed help, and at the same time you could be made a dependent object of interest. That's the sort of combination they like – but you know them by now.'

'They have it well thought out.'

'Yes,' Manny agreed, 'and they're improving it all the time. That Listopad will get promotion out of it. What he's managed in Prague couldn't be managed even by Russian spies and diplomats. Listopad has the officials in the town hall over a barrel. People like Bürger and Meister or Preininger lined their pockets from urban improvement to such a degree that it couldn't be concealed any longer, so they had to start sharing with the rest and call the banks in to fill in the excavated hole that Prague had become. Just think what splendid material that was for Listopad – the very elite of Prague and so easy to blackmail. And on top of that he had Kleinfleisch to hand as an instrument of terror to cleanse the Jewish Town. And the police that keep on failing to discover anything . . . And then it suddenly stops. One abortive faked duel – and that's that. Ha-ha! I can't wait for that blackguard Listopad to get what's coming to him, Addie. Bürger and Meister are frying in hell, and Kleinfleisch . . . will soon join them.'

Manny shuddered, bent his legs and curled up. I offered to run for a doctor and have him brought into the hospital, but he shook his head violently. 'Hear me out,' he said from beneath the blanket, in a voice weak with exhaustion. 'A little longer.'

I gazed at that amorphous hunched-up figure and asked myself whether I hated him. If he had harmed Gita or Berenice I would have had to answer yes. But he did harm to other innocent people, so how was it that what I felt for him was compassion most of all?

'And Fridrich Sova?' I asked. 'How did he come to be at Letná this morning?'

Manny freed himself from the blanket. 'Your father wanted him to keep an eye on you. But Sova is a terribly unreliable sort. Where was Sova when Kleinfleisch managed to enter your house so easily, not once, but twice? He's a reckless adventurer, that's what I think. And I'd really love to have challenged him to a duel.'

That surprised me. But maybe it was to do with Helena, some sort of jealousy. 'Come to think of it, those debt collectors took a short cut through my courtyard, too . . .'

'He couldn't be relied on, that's true. But maybe he let things take their course, and he wasn't particularly concerned about your girls. We underestimated him. I had no inkling that he would turn up at the duel today and do what he did. But now I'm really so glad that the stinker did it, you have to believe me.'

He wiped his perspiring face with his handkerchief, then suddenly pressed his hand to his side with a groan.

'I'll fetch a doctor.'

'No. The coffee wasn't good for me.'

'Will you let me see the wound?'

'No.'

'It must be excruciatingly painful.'

'It is.'

'Did you speak to him at least? Fridrich Sova?'

'Yes. He was waiting behind the wagon with that gun, and he actually came over to me. He was grinning at something. I would happily have knocked the grin of his face. But I didn't have the strength. He asked me if I needed help, medical attention, and I told him I was his enemy, so he had better beware of me. I even asked him to go ahead and shoot me or I'd kill him.'

'Gracious. And what did he say?'

'He told me it would be a waste of a bullet, and then the firing started. He disappeared and shot Meister. The fellow insulted me well and truly. But he saved your life, and that's good, Addie, really good. It's the best good in the world.'

'How could you kill innocent women, Manny?' It was a hard question and it hurt me to ask it, but it had to be faced. 'Were you intending to kill mine, too?'

Manny turned away. 'Whenever I asked myself that question', he said after a moment, 'I'd take morphine or Hoffmann's miracle. And I would obey Listopad's orders.' He panted heavily for a long time and wiped the blood from his mouth. 'But I'll tell you. I came to terrify them not kill them. I knew it wouldn't work on you but maybe on them. But that young one stood on the gallery and started to sing something. She's sadder than you think. And I didn't know what to do. That song, it spoke straight to my heart, if you understand me. The fearless heart that I had lost. And so I let them be and decided to undertake a different mission. To kill you, as they wanted me to. The night before the duel, so that Leopold Meister's life and reputation wouldn't be put at risk.'

I gripped his wrist. I wanted to tell him what I didn't feel – that I forgave him. But he guessed and quickly freed his arm.

'There's no saving me now, Addie. I've done too much harm and let myself be misused in the interests of others. It's too late, this is now the end for ever and ever. Thank you,' he whispered. 'You can go now.' He reached behind him and pulled out Bürger's revolver from a fold in the blanket. 'A present from your friend Solly when he was lying next to me. He understood who I was. Farewell, Addie. And tell your father that I would greatly appreciate his forgiveness.'

I realized that I mustn't stay any longer. I jumped off the wagon and went into the hospital to see how things were with Solly. The dawn was grey-blue. Two brothers of the order were standing at the corner of the hospital yard discussing something. Yellow stucco was falling from the wall of the building.

I turned towards the wagon, and at that moment came the sound of the shot. The awning buckled and the startled brothers looked in turn at the wagon and then at me. I told them an incurable patient had taken his own life and that his wish was to be cremated. They started to raise some kind of objection, but I left them there to do what they would with the corpse.

The dreadful suspicion that I had spared Manny burnt inside me like a stab wound. And I will never know for sure.

A dead girl beneath a rock with a cross. And her pregnancy. If it really was. And if she really did kill herself. Might not the secret police have been stringing this emotionally unstable young man along from the outset? The son of an influential old family.

I turned my steps towards the river and walked along the embankment past the urban improvement pits and demolition machines as far as the Chain Bridge. The wind was pleasantly cool. I met a photographer carrying over his shoulder his stand and the apparatus with the barrel-organ handle sticking out the side. As he passed me he flicked the peak of his cap with his finger. The fishermen were busying themselves in their boats as on any other day. The waves from a passing steamer made the little round bodies of the ducks bob up and down. I avoided turning my gaze to Letná Park, but I noticed out of the corner of my eye that that there was an unusual level of activity around the funicular station.

I walked on to the bridge and went halfway along it. Then I stopped and looked down. I saw the dirty water flow onwards, making way for more dirty water. Mud like that never settles, and the bottom can never be cleaned.

Epilogue

Stránov. Taking an interest in the farm's yield, supervising the farmhands, doing the accounts, arguing with the carter – that was all pretence. But I did find something here: our English park. I ride there on a placid old nag who would not break into a run, even though they tried to coax her with a riding crop, because her right hind leg is an inch shorter than the other. They have saddled her every day for me in the recent period. Mama accused me of escaping my responsibilities, but Father doesn't mind at all that his young son takes rides in the English park. Gita was surprised that I did not want to take her with me, and Berenice took offence – didn't I want to spend my whole day with her? I explained to them that wild boar break into it from the forest through a ruined wall and they are dangerous beasts that are ferocious when protecting their young. That convinced them. So it is my habit to spend entire days there on my own. I take notes, and I mark on a map the places that need improving. I will have to hire labourers from the village for the work. I myself cleared away the ugly shrubs around the oldest oaks, using an axe and an East Indian machete, and, even though the work was by no means reminiscent of fencing and left me with bleeding callouses on my palms, I found it satisfying. The trees could breathe again at last. The toil did me good until I found another task. In the middle of the park, alongside a muddy pond and in sight of a decrepit gloriette that was once white, there stood a stone fountain. Nothing had gushed from it for years, and the marble basin in the shape of a shell was full of decayed leaves, dead insects, blackened acorns and broken twigs. The pond stank, so I brought buckets of water from the stream, and I gradually cleaned the entire fountain. I took me two weeks, but I was in no hurry to go anywhere. When I was a child the fountain used to be surrounded by benches. Only one remained, its seat broken. But it was possible to sit on the arm rest. So I would perch there for hours, smoking a pipe and drinking blackcurrant juice, of which there was an inexhaustible supply in the castle cellars.

The idyll didn't last as long as I would have liked. One afternoon I returned to the park, and a coach was just leaving through the castle gate. I found my mother in the courtyard sitting with the girls in the shade of the arcades. She was pale and held a glass of red Madeira in her trembling hand. She informed me that three gentlemen from the police had just come for my father. He would be held in Pankrác Prison and would stand trial for subversion of the monarchy. She said he would write and tell us when we could visit him. She was of the opinion that my father would not survive it.

In fact, we were expecting it. It was odd that they didn't take me away with him.

I went downstairs to Father's study and chose one of his walking-sticks, the stoutest of the lot. Thus armed, I pounded on the door of our esteemed neighbour Taufer, that large landowner. A servant answered the door and told me that her master was not in. He would not return for another week, and God alone knew when Miss Tauferová would be back. Then she slammed the door in my face.

The next day Fridrich Sova arrived at the castle. He no longer had the looks of a fop. He greeted my mother and took a coffee with her, and he spent a few minutes explaining to her that this time he had come to see me. He asked to speak to me in private, in a place where we could be sure no one would overhear us – including her ladyship, the Countess. So I took him up to the tower.

We conversed. He had come to offer me his services. He said he was setting up an underground organization that would work to overthrow the monarchy and establish an independent Czech republic. By means of a revolution, as in France. I stared at him as if he had gone off his head. He looked serious. I asked him how such a republic would deal with the nobility. He replied that it would depend on which side the nobility had been before the revolution. I told him that I was on nobody's side, that the radicals struck me as ludicrously one-dimensional while those in favour of the old order seemed boringly pusillanimous. He remarked that my father held very radical views, too, and asked me whether I considered him ludicrous. I said nothing, and he added that the people who hated Austria had enormous respect for my father, and maybe I should start to hate it myself at last. There was nothing to say to that either, so he went on talking until he finally got to the main point of his visit, namely, that I had no option anyway because in a few days' time, when my father's health would have deteriorated and we would be beside ourselves with worry, Listopad would come to see me and repeat the offer for which I had slapped him that time. Because a live Count Arco was worth more to them than if he was mouldering in one of their prisons, and I would be there helpfully providing Listopad with information. Is that what I really wanted?

I conceded that I had no option.

A fortnight went by, and a vile murder took place in a wood beyond the railway station. Listopad made the mistake of travelling to see me alone. It was never discovered who drove him from the station. The corpse was lying in ditch, and the head was missing. That was eventually found the following day, in Prague, in the erstwhile Jewish Town, high on the white façade of a new apartment house richly decorated with stucco. As they wrote in the newspapers, the murderers must have had the use of a very long ladder. And the nail that pinned it to the wall through its mouth and cranium was the length of an arm from the elbow to the tips of the fingers.

I made a trip to take a look at the house. The head and the nail were gone, but a dark stain still shone through where the wall had been painted over. Solly told me that the building belonged to Dr Preininger. Preininger had apparently been standing for the post of Deputy Mayor but had now had second thoughts and left for Vienna. He wasn't planning to return to Prague.

We went to Solly's to celebrate and opened a bottle of champagne. He wanted to invite some girls, but I didn't feel like it. I actually told him that I was glad to have a rest from women for a bit. The company of Gita and Berenice could prove tiring. Then I asked for his help – I only had one little bottle of Hoffmann's pills left. When I had finished them my cough and feelings of hopelessness would return. He promised to find something, and then we got drunk.

I got up while it was still dark. My watch said five fifty-five. My head was swimming, and I was shivering with a fever. Sleep was no longer possible. Dishevelled, I went out into the street where some of the households were already returning to life and people could be seen having breakfast through the windows – the Emperor had taught his subjects to rise early. A milk cart rattled over the cobbles, and the smell of hot rolls wafted from a bakery.

I searched for the Loggia, which I had been forced to abandon some time before. I suspected that in the place it used to stand I would find just a roped-off pit or neatly swept plot of land.

I found nothing, neither my street nor the neighbourhood that I was familiar with and where I used to walk and hawk my white merchandise. The building work was proceeding at an incredible pace. Dust had not yet settled from the demolition, and new buildings were already rising from their foundations on the other side of palings knocked together from planks; a Forum Praganum that would disappear when the building work was completed. The shape and arrangement of the enclosures enabled one to guess the lay-out of the new Josefov: wide streets that only occasionally replicated the old ones, buildings combined into enormous blocks with angular courtyards, small squares that are actually glorified intersections and one monstrous boulevard – here was where Red Street crossed it, and this is where Butcher's Street was, and you used to have to pass by the garden with three trees to reach Rabbi Street.

I walked across Josefov to the part that was still standing. It was still before daybreak, and I felt like breakfast. I entered a narrow lane where I thought I could smell a baker's shop. There came the weary clip-clop of horses' hooves, and from the opposite direction there arrived a huge wagon covered with a painted awning supported by hoops. I entered the nearest doorway to make way for the exhausted horses with blinkers on their eyes and waited for the colossus to rumble past.

Then the lane was clear, but I remained where I was. Behind the wagon strode a giant in a black cape and with a wide-brimmed hat on his head. Wild eyes and dazzling teeth gleamed from a face that was hard to discern. He was heading straight for me, and I had no weapon.

He stopped and raised his hat and then replaced it on his head. It was no Kleinfleisch but a black man, the biggest African I had ever seen and known from picture books. He leant towards me and said something. It was in English, but I had difficulty understanding his heavy throaty accent. '*I beg for your time and pardon, sir.*' That I understood. So he wasn't going to kill me. He handed me something, smiling from ear to ear with his white teeth. I took from him a small cardboard box with a white inscription and the picture of a white-haired smiling man in a broad-brimmed hat. I raised my eyes in astonishment – the awning of the departing vehicle bore the same inscription, and the same face smiled out from it: *Quaker Oats. Ohio.*

Then I understood what that American was saying. '*Quaker Oats are healthy and wholesome, good for you, sir. Oh yes, even for you, sir. Try them.*' He raised his hand in greeting and ran after the wagon, taking out of it a number of boxes that he hastily handed out among the housewives who were coming out curiously on to their thresholds and eagerly reaching for this free gift.

I started to cough. I took a Hoffmann pill and returned to Stránov by the next train.

As I carried back from Prague a souvenir of the new world and new times I started to miss Kleinfleisch. I tore off the corner of the box and poured into my palm some of what it contained. It looked like half-crushed grain, either dried or roasted. I tasted some. It was an odd food, good and no doubt wholesome but tasteless.

Porridge oats.

Also published by Peter Owen

THE SEVEN CHURCHES
Miloš Urban

PB 978-0-7206-1355-1 • 304pp • £8.99 / EPUB 978-0-7206-1379-7
KINDLE 978-0-7206-1378-0 / PDF 978-0-7206-1377-3

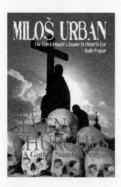

Written in the style of a literary thriller, but with an intriguing historical, even supernatural, mystery at its core, *The Seven Churches* is set in the medieval New Town of Prague, a quarter of the city with a number of Gothic churches. Here K, a misfit policeman subject to extraordinary visions, witnesses a bizarre incident followed by a series of strange murders. Obsessed with the Middle Ages and repelled by modern society, K finds himself increasingly drawn into the shadowy world of others who seem to be trying to reconstruct the 'golden age' of Prague during the reign of Charles IV in the modern-day city. As he digs deeper, evidence emerges to suggest that the murders are being committed by an assassin whose motives are rooted deep in the city's past . . .

Translated into thirteen languages and a runaway bestseller in Spain as well as the Czech Republic, *The Seven Churches* – by 'the dark knight of Czech literature', Miloš Urban – is a bloody, atmospheric modern classic of crime literature and one of the most haunting thrillers to come out of Europe in years.

www.peterowen.com

SOME AUTHORS WE HAVE PUBLISHED

James Agee • Bella Akhmadulina • Tariq Ali • Kenneth Allsop • Alfred Andersch
Guillaume Apollinaire • Machado de Assis • Miguel Angel Asturias • Duke of Bedford
Oliver Bernard • Thomas Blackburn • Jane Bowles • Paul Bowles • Richard Bradford
Ilse, Countess von Bredow • Lenny Bruce • Finn Carling • Blaise Cendrars • Marc Chagall
Giorgio de Chirico • Uno Chiyo • Hugo Claus • Jean Cocteau • Albert Cohen
Colette • Ithell Colquhoun • Richard Corson • Benedetto Croce • Margaret Crosland
e.e. cummings • Stig Dalager • Salvador Dalí • Osamu Dazai • Anita Desai
Charles Dickens • Bernard Diederich • Fabián Dobles • William Donaldson
Autran Dourado • Yuri Druzhnikov • Lawrence Durrell • Isabelle Eberhardt
Sergei Eisenstein • Shusaku Endo • Erté • Knut Faldbakken • Ida Fink
Wolfgang George Fischer • Nicholas Freeling • Philip Freund • Carlo Emilio Gadda
Rhea Galanaki • Salvador Garmendia • Michel Gauquelin • André Gide
Natalia Ginzburg • Jean Giono • Geoffrey Gorer • William Goyen • Julien Gracq
Sue Grafton • Robert Graves • Angela Green • Julien Green • George Grosz
Barbara Hardy • H.D. • Rayner Heppenstall • David Herbert • Gustaw Herling
Hermann Hesse • Shere Hite • Stewart Home • Abdullah Hussein • King Hussein of Jordan
Ruth Inglis • Grace Ingoldby • Yasushi Inoue • Hans Henny Jahnn • Karl Jaspers
Takeshi Kaiko • Jaan Kaplinski • Anna Kavan • Yasunuri Kawabata • Nikos Kazantzakis
Orhan Kemal • Christer Kihlman • James Kirkup • Paul Klee • James Laughlin
Patricia Laurent • Violette Leduc • Lee Seung-U • Vernon Lee • József Lengyel
Robert Liddell • Francisco García Lorca • Moura Lympany • Dacia Maraini
Marcel Marceau • André Maurois • Henri Michaux • Henry Miller • Miranda Miller
Marga Minco • Yukio Mishima • Quim Monzó • Margaret Morris • Angus Wolfe Murray
Atle Næss • Gérard de Nerval • Anaïs Nin • Yoko Ono • Uri Orlev • Wendy Owen
Arto Paasilinna • Marco Pallis • Oscar Parland • Boris Pasternak • Cesare Pavese
Milorad Pavic • Octavio Paz • Mervyn Peake • Carlos Pedretti • Dame Margery Perham
Graciliano Ramos • Jeremy Reed • Rodrigo Rey Rosa • Joseph Roth • Ken Russell
Marquis de Sade • Cora Sandel • George Santayana • May Sarton • Jean-Paul Sartre
Ferdinand de Saussure • Gerald Scarfe • Albert Schweitzer • George Bernard Shaw
Isaac Bashevis Singer • Patwant Singh • Edith Sitwell • Suzanne St Albans • Stevie Smith
C.P. Snow • Bengt Söderbergh • Vladimir Soloukhin • Natsume Soseki • Muriel Spark
Gertrude Stein • Bram Stoker • August Strindberg • Rabindranath Tagore
Tambimuttu • Elisabeth Russell Taylor • Emma Tennant • Anne Tibble • Roland Topor
Miloš Urban • Anne Valery • Peter Vansittart • José J. Veiga • Tarjei Vesaas
Noel Virtue • Max Weber • Edith Wharton • William Carlos Williams • Phyllis Willmott
G. Peter Winnington • Monique Wittig • A.B. Yehoshua • Marguerite Young
Fakhar Zaman • Alexander Zinoviev • Emile Zola